So Many Maybe's

Fond Memories of Imaginary Things

A Novel By Jerome Winslow

Includes the full text of the stage play

Rilke's Dracula

by

Wolf Rilke

BOOK ONE: So Many Maybe's

© 2018 by Jerome Winslow

Contact Email: so.many.maybes@gmail.com

The photo used on the cover was originally called *Nickels Arcade After Dark* by Jim Kuhn and is licensed under the Creative Commons Attribution 2.0 Generic License.

It was downloaded from Wikipedia Commons on 29 June 2018 by Jerome Winslow.

The Maybe's sign was added to reflect the fictional time and place of novel.

Contents

Map of Ann Arbor

1.	Bunny	1
2.	Growing Up	15
3.	Graftons	53
4.	Bonnie	63
5.	Getting Bent	75
6.	Clarkson	85
7.	Brett	93
8.	Camille	103
9.	Out With Friends	113
10.	Open Mic Night	129
11.	Poltergeist	161
12.	Shopping	175
13	The Pool Party	185
14.	GaGa Land	197
15.	Bunny's Story	217
16.	Wolf's Vampire	227
17.	Lois and Amanda	267
18.	Bonnie's Movie	287
19.	Take Care of My Cat	315
20.	Jenny	319
21.	The Art Fair	347
22.	The Holes	381
23.	The Commie Putz	403
24.	Smiles of a Snowy Night	435
	Rilke's Dracula	

"Sometimes, if you repeat a lie often enough,
it becomes true."
"There's no harm in innocent lies. They make
life more fun."
"That's what fiction is."

So Many Maybe's, Page 95.

"Lord, we know what we are,

but know not what we may be."

Hamlet, Act 4, Scene 5 by William Shakespeare

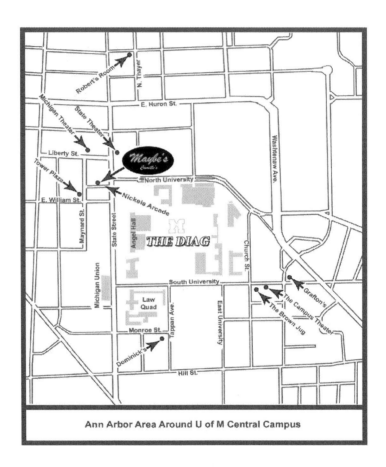

Chapter 1
Bunny

In the early spring of 1971, Robert Bain was sitting by himself at a table in the back of The Brown Jug. The Jug was a small bar and restaurant in Ann Arbor Michigan. It was located on South University Ave. next to the University of Michigan campus and a couple of blocks from where Robert worked. Robert appeared to be staring out the window, but he was lost in one of his frequent daydreams. Barely conscious of the outside world, he was imagining that he was sitting in the Select Café in Paris, France during the 1920s. The Select was frequently mentioned in two books by Ernest Hemingway: *A Moveable Feast* and Robert's favorite novel *The Sun Also Rises*.

Robert was a writer and he went to the Jug every night after work hoping to meet other writers. He was looking for a modern-day version of that 1920s café culture where writers of the so-called, "Lost Generation," like Hemingway and F. Scott Fitzgerald hung out together and talked about writing and art. Unfortunately, The Brown Jug was mostly a college student hang out, better suited to watching the U of M football games on TV than discussing literary topics with a group of fellow writers. So he decided that it was time to give up on the Jug and venture out and seek a new literary promised land, at least in Ann Arbor.

He asked his friends at work if they had any suggestions. One of them, Wolf Rilke, had lived in Ann Arbor for over twenty years and he suggested a place called Many Maybe's. Wolf said Maybe's sounded exactly like the place that Robert was searching for.

That evening, right after work, Robert walked across the U of M college green called The Diag and entered the Beaux-Arts style Nickels Arcade where Wolf had told him Maybe's was located. The Arcade was a short and narrow glass roofed atrium alleyway that was lined on both sides by small specialty shops. Part of the way down the Arcade he found the small café that Wolf had mentioned. He was surprised to see it there. The Arcade was one of Robert's favorite places in Ann Arbor and he walked through it whenever he could, even if it meant going out of his way. Yet he'd never noticed Many Maybe's.

He looked in the window. Maybe's was much deeper than it was wide. A dark oak bar ran along most of the right-hand wall and further down the same wall, there was a small stage with a covered piano shoved back into the corner. The café was simply furnished. Around the outside walls were about ten large, wooden booths and several small tables were crowded in front of the stage.

Robert walked in and looked around. Hanging on the walls over the booths were dozens of photographs. Surprisingly, Robert recognized several of the people in the photos. They were of Ernest Hemingway and his friends in Paris. And Robert immediately realized why Wolf had recommended Maybe's to him. The owners of Maybe's were obviously familiar

So Many Maybes · 2

with Hemingway and the literary café culture of the 1920s. He sat down in a booth that was in the back-left hand corner of the café.

A very attractive middle-aged woman dressed entirely in black came over to his table and sat down and asked him what he wanted to drink and eat.

"I'd like a cheeseburger with everything and a rum and coke."

"How would you like the burger cooked?"

Robert looked at her carefully and took a chance.

"I like it hot on the outside and pink on the inside."

"Smart ass."

"Oh, I'm sorry. I was just…"

She interrupted him. "Don't be. I like smart asses."

Robert felt great. Maybe's was the place he'd been looking for since he moved to Ann Arbor. He removed his *Journal* from his book bag and leaned back and started to write. At some point, he intended to polish up his *Journal,* and turn it into a book that was interesting enough for others to read, and maybe even get it published. But he would have written whether there was a chance his work would be published or not, because he just liked doing it.

Robert's *Journal* included different kinds of entries. His writing was spontaneous and improvisational; he wrote whatever occurred to him when he was writing. Since he was a compulsive daydreamer, it was sometimes difficult to tell whether his journal entries were descriptions of actual events or chronicles of one of his imaginary adventures. And like

So Many Maybes · 3

many young men, Robert was obsessed with sex, so these visits to literary fantasy land were frequently about sex.

*

THE JOURNAL OF ROBERT BAIN

My waitress was exceptionally appealing. She looked to be in her early forties, but she could have been any age. Her demeanor implied the experience of years of living, but her skin was smooth and clear without a single wrinkle even when she smiled. Her otherwise slim body was topped with full, heavy, breasts that sat low on her chest. She was older woman sex appeal personified.

Over at the bar, another beautiful woman was sitting with some of her friends. I was positive that she was a dancer. She looked to be in her late twenties and more perfect than I ever imagined a woman could be. She was the real-life embodiment of the world's most beautiful imaginary ballerina. She had a lovely light complexion and her lips were soft and lightly pink. Her blond hair was up in a dancer's bun and she was dressed in black dancer's stretch leotards that fit tightly over her firm body.

She was sitting at the bar with three other women who also looked like dancers. Along with her astonishing looks there was something else about her that was wonderful. She was completely relaxed without an ounce of tension in her face or body. I hesitate to say it, but she appeared to be in a state of grace.

Despite her great beauty, her confident and relaxed manner made her appear to be approachable, so I found it easy to walk up to the bar and sit down next to her. She looked at me and frowned.

"Who are you?" she brusquely asked with a heavy Russian accent.

"Hi, I'm Robert Bain."

"Why are you here Bain?"

"What do you mean?"

"You want to interview me, yes?"

"Interview?"

"I do not want to give interview now. You should call director before to arrange interview. I cannot promise I have time. I am very busy. Now leave. I am with friends."

She started to turn away from me and I hurriedly said, "Wait, please, I don't want to interview you."

She appeared baffled and asked, "Why not? I am Aglaya Stenova. I am greatest ballerina in world. Everyone wants to interview me."

"Oh. I'm sorry. I don't know anything about ballet."

She appeared baffled again. "If you are big barbarian to not know about ballet, why do you sit here?"

"Because I thought you were a beautiful woman and I wanted to meet you."

She said, "Yes, it is true. I am beautiful woman. You want to fuck me yes?"

"Uhhh....?"

"Okay you can fuck me, but you must do it now. I must sleep soon."

"Uhhh....?"

So Many Maybes · 5

Aglaya stood up off her stool and leaned to one of her friends and said something in Russian. Aglaya's friend listened, looked at me and made an unpleasant face, then she nodded and resumed talking with the rest of her friends.

Aglaya grabbed my forearm and roughly pulled me out the door. I assumed that she was taking me to her hotel, but instead she dragged me down the Arcade and across State Street and out into The Diag and stopped in a patch of grass behind a bush.

She pointed to the ground and said, "We fuck here."

"Uhhh....?"

She sat down on the grass and began removing her dancer's tights. Completely disarmed by her boldness, I stood still like an idiot.

When she had her tights off, she looked up at me and said, "Why you not take off pants? You want blowjob first?"

"Uhhh....?"

I was so confused by what was happening that I couldn't respond to her question. Instead, I quickly leaned against a tree and removed my pants and started to get down on the ground next to her. Before I could, she got up and stood in front of me and looked at me intently. I reached for her. She stopped me and stepped backward. She rose up on her toes and began performing a series of spins in circles around me. Like a naked nymph, she went around me and around and around and around, over and over.

So Many Maybes · 6

I spun like a top, so I could catch every beautiful movement of the astonishing Aglaya Stenova, the greatest ballerina in the world.

She stopped about thirty feet away then ran toward me. I knew that this was my time to shine. She was giving herself to me and I stood firm, waiting for her to jump into my arms. When she was about ten feet away, she leapt high into the air and did the splits at the peak of her leap and firmly drove her pointed ballerina's toe directly into my solar plexus and sent me scrambling...

*

...Robert tripped over his own feet and went flying fifteen-feet across the café and crashed right into the group of four dancers and ended up face down on the floor next to the magnificent blond that he had been admiring.

She turned her head and looked at him and said, "Who are you and why are you lying on the floor next to me?"

Robert turned his head and looked at her and said, "Hi, my name is Robert, a.k.a., The World's Clumsiest Bastard."

She said, "Really? That's a stupid name."

"It was a joke."

"Oh. I didn't get it. Why is it funny?"

As he stood up and offered his hand to help her to her feet he said, "Never mind. It's not important. What's your name?"

"I'm Bunny."

"That's an interesting name."

"Of course it is. My real name was Eva, but Eva is a bad name for a stripper. Besides the name Little Eva was already taken by some singer."

"You're a stripper?"

"Not any more. My boobs are too small."

"I think your boobs are just fine."

"Well Acka you seem like a nice guy but you're not very bright. You're only saying that you like my boobs so you can fuck me. I can spot a guy like you from a mile away, so you'll have to take a taxi before you can bang me."

"What did you just call me?"

"Acka, but if you're going to be sensitive about it I'll just call you Robert."

"Robert is fine. You were saying that you were a stripper."

"Of course I was. Why do you think my name is Bunny?"

Robert had to pause to absorb that little exchange.

Bunny picked up a napkin and handed it to him and asked, "Acka will you do me a favor?"

"Robert."

"Sorry, Robert. Would you do me a favor?"

"Okay. What do you want me to do?"

"When you knocked me down, I sat in something. Would you take this napkin and wipe off my ass?"

"I'd be happy to."

"Don't get too happy now. Let's leave that for later."

Robert carefully wiped off her ass and began to get excited when he felt how firm it was.

He asked her, "What are you doing now?"

"What a stupid question. You know full well that I'm standing next to you while you wipe my ass."

So Many Maybes · 8

"Oh yeah, I know that. I meant, why are you in Ann Arbor?"

"I'm a student at U of M."

"What are you studying?"

"Dance. Why do you think I'm wearing these stupid tights with the wet ass?"

"Lots of women wear tights."

"Yes, but do they have the wet ass?"

Robert paused again. He felt like he was in the middle of a TV comedy routine.

He said, "You must have made a lot of money as a stripper. Michigan is an expensive school."

"I didn't make that much money as a stripper, but I got a lot of financial aid."

"That's terrific."

"I know. I'm really lucky and it was so easy to get too."

"Easy?"

"All I had to do was go into the Financial Aid Office and talk to a counselor for a minute and he gave me everything I wanted."

"Why, were you needy?"

"No, but I think he was."

Robert paused again. He enjoyed being the straight man.

He said, "You're probably right."

"You know what Acka?"

"What Bunny?"

"You can stop wiping my ass now."

Robert stopped immediately and said, "I was only making sure I got all of it."

So Many Maybes · 9

"I can tell. It seems like no man today is satisfied with just a piece of ass."

Robert had to pause again to gather his thoughts. He was getting dizzy.

Bunny said, "Acka, tell me about you. What do you do? I know you're not a stripper because your boobs are too small like mine."

"Do male strippers have boobs?"

"Of course not. Men don't have boobs. So if you're not a stripper what do you do for a living?"

"I'm a writer."

"Oh. That's interesting. What do you write?"

Robert was much too eager to tell Bunny everything about himself. He babbled on and on about his background and how he had ended up in a bar in Ann Arbor. His story bored Bunny shitless and she struggled to stay awake. She leaned one elbow on the bar to support herself and her eyes glazed over. Robert droned on until Bunny fell asleep and her bar stool toppled and she crashed to the floor. Horrified, Robert bent down to help her. She woke up suddenly and tried to sit up. They banged foreheads and she pulled him down on top of her.

For a moment she didn't move or make a sound, then she looked into his eyes and smiled,

She said, "Acka, your story was boring as fuck, but I like having you on top of me so stay here for a minute and talk to me because I have some questions."

"Okay, what are your questions?"

"Acka is a really odd name. Did your mother give it to you?"

So Many Maybes · 10

"No. You gave it to me."

"Why would I do that? I'm not your mother."

Robert paused again. The other customers in Maybe's seemed oblivious to the fact that Bunny and Robert were lying on the floor, but Bunny's friends pulled up chairs and listened to the prostrate couple's conversation as did the waitress who had brought him his burger. They knew Bunny well enough to be sure that her dialog with Robert would be amusing.

"I don't know why you gave me that name, Bunny. Maybe giving comes naturally for you."

"You're right, Acka. Baja says I give it away too easy."

"Give what away."

"Don't be coy with me, Acka. You know exactly what I mean."

"I have to say I do."

"Ohhh…no, no, no. Don't do that because I won't."

"Won't what?"

"Marry you."

"I don't want to marry you Bunny."

"Why not? Is it because my boobs are too small?"

"I think your boobs are just fine."

"You told me that before. I didn't believe you then, but I don't not believe you now."

"What does that mean?"

"It means I believe you now."

"Why do you believe me now?"

"Because I can feel your boner."

Robert paused the dialog again. He did have an erection.

So Many Maybes · 11

But he had no control. After all, he was lying on top of a gorgeous woman. Embarrassed, he started to get up.

She put her arms around his hips and pulled him back flat on top of her.

She said, "I'm disappointed in you Acka."

"Why's that Bunny?"

"I would never have believed that you'd be so rude."

"I'm so sorry Bunny. I couldn't help it."

"Acka, I'm your best friend. You can ask me for help any time."

"Really, Bunny?"

"Of course…Say Acka?"

"Yes Bunny."

"Since you're so God damned impatient to get up, you can fuck me right here."

"It's very kind of you to offer Bunny, but I can't."

"Why not? Is it because my boobs are too small?"

"No Bunny."

"Why then?"

"Because we're lying on the floor in Many Maybe's."

"That's not a good enough excuse."

"Why's that Bunny?"

"Because maybe means yes and Many Maybe's means, YES…YES…YES! and OHHHH FUCKING YES!"

He said, "I'm sorry Bunny. I misspoke. I'll fuck you wherever you want."

"I doubt it."

"Why's that Bunny?"

So Many Maybes · 12

"You don't impress me as a yes man."

Robert was mind bruised and exhausted. He decided that it was now time for him to stop this nonsense and make his move. He leaned his mouth next to her ear and whispered.

Now Bunny was the one who was confused.

She loudly said, "That's a really weird thing for you to say, Acka. No one has a boner as hard as spring steel."

Everyone around them started laughing and Robert turned red. He knew it was really a limp-dicked move.

Bunny said, "Well Acka. I don't think we should fuck here after all."

"No?"

"The people here were rude to us and laughed. I don't want to give them the time of day they don't deserve by watching us fuck. You'll have to come over to my place."

"Okay."

"You know Acka, I like having you on top of me, you know that, but your boner is pressing on my bladder and my bladder is about to explode and I don't think the bartender would like cleaning up a blown-up bladder, so we have to get up now."

Robert smiled and got off Bunny slowly and helped her to her feet.

She said, "Wait for me," and she ran into the Ladies Room.

Robert stared at the clock while he waited. She took forever, and his mind started to drift. He couldn't imagine what she was doing in there.

After twenty minutes, she came out of the Restroom and walked up to him and put her arms around him.

So Many Maybes · 13

She said, "I'm sorry I took so long Acka, after I pissed I decided to take a shit."

"Thank you for telling me that, Bunny."

"You're welcome Acka…Say Acka?

"Bunny."

"I want you to grab your spring-steel boner and come over to my place tomorrow night and we'll fuck like corn dogs?"

Robert started to ask her what she meant by "fuck like corn dogs" but he thought better of it. He'd be an idiot if he said anything that might screw up what appeared to be a sincere invitation to go over to her place and make love to her.

He said, "Okay Bunny. I'll see you tomorrow night."

Bunny said, "Good."

She firmly wrapped her arms around Robert's neck, then pulled herself up off the floor and wrapped her legs around his hips and French kissed him hard on the lips.

Then she said, "See you tomorrow."

She dropped down and pulled away from him and walked out of the café with her friends.

He wistfully watched her walk out and returned to his barstool. She was like a human tornado and she had him so twisted in knots that it took him twenty minutes to realize that he didn't get her address or phone number.

Chapter 2
Growing Up

Robert grew up in Grand Rapids, Michigan in a neighborhood called Vandenwood. His family moved there when he was four years old. Vandenwood was a newly constructed suburban housing development that was rudely slashed into the outer edge of an old hardwood forest called Oakwood that was once part of a private estate. The horseshoe shaped neighborhood was built around a one-block long, dead-end dirt road and consisted of thirty wood frame houses that were cheaply constructed and laughably small. Every house was the same and every identical lawn had an identical two-inch diameter seven-foot-tall newly planted "suburb tree" located precisely in the center of the front yard.

Without exception, Vandenwood's families were white and undereducated. All the women were housewives and mothers, and all the men except for Robert's dad worked for minimum wage in small factories that produced parts for the automotive industry. It was sad, mind-numbing, production-line labor, performed mostly in miserable and unsafe working conditions. They hated their jobs but were afraid to quit. They knew they weren't qualified to do much else.

Robert's dad, "BadBob" Bain, was fortunate enough to escape the production line nightmare by drawing on his Navy experience to land a job as a fork lift operator at Borsht Crate. Borsht Crate built the wooden crates that the surrounding auto parts manufacturers utilized to send their products to the big auto plants around Michigan and Ohio.

When the homes in Vandenwood first went up for sale, the developers placed a twenty-foot-tall, arch-shaped sign that said, "HOMES FOR SALE," across Vandenwood road at the entrance to the neighborhood's horseshoe. Like the houses, the sign was cheaply constructed with inferior materials and it wobbled dangerously during high winds. All the Vandenwood residents agreed that the sign was an eyesore and made their treasured new houses look like abandoned foreclosures, but they tolerated its presence because they assumed the sign was only temporary. But when all the houses were sold, the developers left town without bothering to tear the sign down, and from then on it was known as The Vandenwood Gate. The Vandenwood Gate was like The Brandenburg Gate in Berlin. It marked the dividing line between two different ways of life. Outside of the Gate, were the old affluent multi-acre private estates. Inside the Gate, were the cheap and shoddy tract homes occupied by Vandenwood's unfortunate minimum-wage blue-collar workers.

Like their identical ethnic backgrounds and their identical homes and their identical jobs, Vandenwood residents were identically religious. Except for Robert's family who didn't go to church, everyone on the block were Protestants and attended the Vandenwood Uniform Church that was located immediately outside Vandenwood Gate. The Church's members

So Many Maybes · 16

referred to themselves simply as "Uniforms." However, the perpetually unpleasant BadBob seized upon the "VUC" initials and rudely called them "Vuckers" right to their face.

Robert's house was at the far end of the block, furthest away from Vandenwood Gate. BadBob had deliberately chosen the location so he could live as far away from the Vucker church as possible.

Life inside the Bob Bain residence was mostly hell. BadBob was impossible to get along with. He was continuously pissed off about something and he loudly made his anger known to everyone around him. Robert once heard their neighbor call Bob Bain the most unpleasant man he'd ever met. In the evening, when BadBob got home from work, he sat at their tiny dining room table and stared at the TV that was in the adjoining living room. He didn't care what was on TV. He stared at it blankly as if it was a porthole to a better time when he was in the Navy helping to win the war against the Japs in the Pacific. In those years, he felt like he a had a purpose and an important one too. Now he merely went to work to collect a paycheck so he could feed four people. And he hated it. Overweight and round faced with his jaws moving up and down slightly as he munched on salted peanuts, he drank one can of Pabst beer after another. The more he drank, the more unpleasant he was.

When BadBob Bain was in the house, the other three family members did their best to avoid him. Sadly, Robert's mom had nowhere to go to get away from her miserable husband. Nancy Bain was only 15 when she got pregnant with Robert's

So Many Maybes · 17

sister Dana. After Dana was born, Nancy quit school to raise her daughter and never learned to drive a car. Unless BadBob took her somewhere, she was trapped in their house.

Unlike their mother, Robert and Dana found it easy to avoid their dad. They each had their own small bedroom and a full basement to play in. Since Dana was ten years older than Robert and already in high school when the Bain family moved to Vandenwood, she and Robert were never regular playmates. But they were still extremely close.

BadBob usually slept late on Saturdays, so Dana and Robert had the family's TV to themselves and they got up early to watch cartoons together. Robert's favorites were *Ruff and Reddy* and *Scooby Doo* because they always went on adventures. Dana, being older, preferred the sarcastic wit of *Rocky and Bullwinkle*. When the cartoons were over, they normally turned off the TV and went somewhere else to avoid the inevitable BadBob shitstorm. If it appeared that his dad was going to sleep longer, Robert continued watching the TV to catch a glimpse of the Johnny Weissmuller Tarzan and Jungle Jim Movies that were commonly shown on Saturday afternoons. Robert knew it was risky, so he closely monitored the noises coming out of his parent's bedroom and he stayed ready to bolt for his own room as soon as BadBob ran into the bathroom and sat down on the toilet to blast the world's loudest farts.

During the summer, Oakwood provided infinite possibilities for Robert to play explorer. Although he got along fine with the other kids in his neighborhood, he didn't have anything in common with them. Fueled by war stories told by their dads

So Many Maybes · 18

and a perpetual string of Black and White TV documentaries and movies about wars, Vandenwood kids spent most of their time playing soldier. Robert occasionally took part but he mostly played alone. He was more interested in different kinds of adventure. He imagined himself as Tarzan swinging through the trees or as Jungle Jim swimming through crocodile infested water. Of course Oakwood wasn't really an African jungle, so playing Tarzan and Jungle Jim did present a few practical difficulties. It was full of big trees, so it was relatively easy to turn a rope into a suitable vine for the Tarzan game, but even though he searched carefully through Oakwood and one time did find a very nice swamp, Robert never ran across any crocodiles. The appeal of the Tarzan adventure rapidly ended on the day that Robert fell from a big tree behind their house and broke his arm. It was a serious lesson for Robert. He not only discovered that he wasn't as strong as Johnny Weissmuller, but he was also incredibly clumsy, a condition that would haunt him for the rest of his life. When the notoriously changeable Michigan weather was too hostile for Robert to go outside and play in the woods, he and Dana played endless games of Monopoly in Dana's bedroom.

If TV provided inspiration and Oakwood provided location, then elementary school provided time to plan his imaginary adventures. He was bright enough to get through school without studying which gave him plenty of time to enter his imaginary world and figure out what to do next. He became a compulsive daydreamer, another trait that followed him into adulthood, and he often frustrated his teachers because

So Many Maybes · 19

he seldom paid attention to what they were saying or trying to teach.

On one occasion when he was in the third grade at Whiteview Elementary, Robert's class went on a field trip to the Natural History Museum. After they reached the top of the steps that led to the museum entrance, Mrs. Torque, his teacher stopped the class to explain the rules of behavior during their visit. When she noticed that Robert was in a hypnotic trance and wasn't paying attention, she reached out and gently shook his arm to wake him up. The tiny shake threw Robert off his normally poor balance and he tumbled and bounced down six steps to the next stairwell. His classmates found his nose dive humorous, but Robert wasn't laughing when he hit the bottom and slid across the floor and slammed his head against the wall. Fortunately, he was more humiliated than physically injured and he had a good time at the museum. It provided scores of outdoor playing ideas.

Mrs. Torque was horrified by what had happened and she arranged for Robert to be sent to counseling. Robert's counseling ended after a few sessions when his counselor, Dr. Nescience, couldn't find anything seriously wrong with Robert. Nescience concluded that, while it was true that Robert liked to daydream, he was doing fine in school and got along with the other children and he would most likely grow out of his daydreaming phase and become a normal kid. However, Dr. Nescience did send a letter to Robert's parents stating that Robert shouldn't drive or operate heavy machinery, an odd warning for a third grader who lived in the suburbs.

So Many Maybes · 20

Contrary to what Mrs. Torque might have thought, Robert was never a maladjusted kid. He was just an innocent loser in the lottery of childhood. His dreadful father moved him to a dreadfully boring place with dreadfully boring people and he adjusted by using daydreaming to escape from BadBob and Vandenwood's black hole of perpetual ho hum. As he got older, he discovered that reading offered him almost all of the same benefits as pure daydreaming and it was his reading that made him decide several years later to be a writer.

Robert was never close to his mother. To survive around BadBob, Nancy Bain seldom said anything to anyone and occupied herself with domestic housekeeping duties or making needle point doilies. She cared about her kids, but mostly left them to their own devices.

Robert's sister Dana was already fourteen-years-old when the Bain family moved to Vandenwood, and she was Robert's real mother figure when he was growing up. Dana was a warm and gentle and graceful young woman and she raised Robert well. When Dana was in the ninth grade she decided to become a veterinarian. She went to veterinary school at Michigan State and graduated with her DVM in 1964, then she went on to work in a clinic north of Ann Arbor in Brighton.

Entering high school was liberation for Robert. In terms of distance, Ferment High School was less than five miles away from Whiteview Elementary, but philosophically it was in another universe because it offered advanced classes in interesting subjects like Writing and Literature and Music and Art.

So Many Maybes · 21

Ferment High was also leagues different from Vandenwood and Whiteview Elementary because the girls smelled really nice. Meeting nice smelling women was no small deal for Robert. For the first time in his life, he encountered women that might be willing sexual partners. The girls that lived in his neighborhood and went to his elementary school were Uniforms who were taught to avoid sex at all costs. Consequently, things like provocative clothing and perfume were forbidden.

The Uniform Church was absurdly conservative and preached a strict code of moral behavior that was carefully explained in a hopelessly thick book called *The Uniform Code*. Although the book contained hundreds of specific rules, they could be summarized by a single statement: "Suffering and guilt was good, so it must follow that guiltless pleasure was bad." Like in most churches, if you didn't follow the rules you were a sinner and damned to burn in hell.

Guaranteed damnation is a heavy and unpleasant burden to carry, so most Church members tried to follow the rules. But a life without pleasure isn't worth living, so to keep from blowing their brains out, Uniforms got through the day by convincing themselves that their suffering made them stronger, and this masochistic "no pain, no gain" approach to life became The Uniform Church's singularly approved lifestyle.

Sex was a special case. It was possible for sex to be pleasurable, and if it was, it was bad. But except for adoption, sex was necessary to have children to perpetuate the religion. Therefore *The Uniform Code* permitted Church members to have intercourse for procreation only, but never for pleasure alone and they were required to introduce an acceptable amount of masochistic pain into the process by doing everything in their power to make having sex a miserable experience.

Centuries of successful pornographic literature and art has proven that even the mere mention of sex can cause pleasure, so sex was a prohibited topic of conversation in Uniform households. To keep ignorant young Uniform males with screaming hormones from trying to fuck the neighbor's dog, there was one significant exception to this silence.

If they could find the courage to even broach the subject of sex with their kids, *The Uniform Code* permitted parents to give their children a single rudimentary sex education lesson when the kids were around age twelve. It was codenamed "The Talk." *The Uniform Code* severely regulated the contents of the lesson. In fact, it wasn't really a talk at all. The Church published a pamphlet entitled "The Uniform Manual of The Talk" which was to be read verbatim to the children. The first part of "The Talk" was a simple listing of prohibited sexual activities which included things like incest, sex out of wedlock, masturbation and what the church considered sexual perversion like anal sex and the aforementioned screwing of animals. The second part of "The Talk" was a description of the basic mechanics of sexual intercourse. There was no mention of physical pleasure. For all practical purposes, the church approved version of "The Talk" went something like, "The man sticks his penis into the woman's vagina, then he bounces up and down on her until he ejaculates sperm into her. Then they both go to their separate

So Many Maybes · 23

beds and nine months later the woman pushes out another mouth for their destitute family to feed."

Unfortunately, the terms penis, vagina, ejaculates and sperm were never explained. And books that defined them were either banned from the school library or the offending pages were removed. Tragically, many parents didn't teach their children anything at all, and the neighborhood dogs were in constant jeopardy.

Even though Robert didn't encounter willing women until he entered high school, he learned about sex from his sister Dana. Robert couldn't have hoped for a better teacher. Dana was smart and well educated and sex wasn't new to her.

She planned to give Robert a series of formal lectures on the basics of sex and sexual health and the mutual responsibilities of contraception. But her plan didn't work well because Robert had the same problem with listening to Dana's lectures as he had in school, he drifted off into his fantasy world. So Dana tried another tactic. She knew how much Robert liked to read so she bought him the book, *Everything You Always Wanted To Know About Sex*, by Dr. David Reuben. This plan didn't work well either. Robert was a dreamer, and he found reading Rueben's book about as much fun as reading the dictionary. It was interesting for a few minutes but ultimately deadly boring, so he only read enough of the book to learn the basics.

Although Dana thought that only knowing the basics was better than nothing, she certainly didn't want Robert to think that sex was boring. But time was getting short. Robert's hormones were beginning to scream, and it was only a matter of time before he desired a woman. As a last resort, Dana took what most people might think was the most radical and potentially dangerous path possible. She sent away and bought as many pornographic books as she could find and selected a few for Robert to read. Predictably, Robert devoured the books. Dana's plan had worked well, but it had one unforeseen consequence. It re-enforced his already strong adolescent interest in sex and turned it into an obsession that would stay with him for the rest of his life.

After reading the books, Robert had tons of questions for his sister. Dana answered them as honestly and explicitly as she could, and she was careful to point out where the books ventured into areas of fantasy that he shouldn't take literally. She also explained every vulgar word in the books. To develop his vocabulary, they played word games. He learned the meaning of the socially correct words, like intercourse and having sex and breasts and vagina and clitoris and penis and erection and anus and ejaculate and semen and orgasm and masturbate. He also learned their "dirty" counterparts, like fuck and tits and boobs and cunts and cocks and pricks and dicks and dongs and wangs and hard-ons and bung holes and cum and pound off and beat your meat and even choke your chicken. He liked choke your chicken best because he thought it was funny.

One time, Robert commented to Dana, "Sis, there sure are a lot of words that describe sex."

"Yes there are, Robert. You have to be careful though. Using the dirty words can get you in trouble, particularly at school."

Robert nodded and said, "I understand."

So Many Maybes · 25

Of course he messed up frequently. He once asked Mr. Hammer, his gym teacher, if he could be excused for a few minutes because he had to take a shit. Hammer, who was a stern Uniform, got angry and told Robert to give him fifty, which meant that Robert was to do fifty push ups as punishment for swearing. When Robert, who was never athletic, collapsed after twelve push ups, Hammer sent him to see the school Principal, Miss Furie. Seeing Miss F was never a pleasant experience. She was an angry old woman who didn't like kids. She made Robert stand at attention while she walked around him and raged at him and threatened to call his parents. Robert survived her rage without much effort because a chewing out from Miss F was nothing like weathering a BadBob Bain shitstorm. Besides, Robert knew that her threats were meaningless. Miss F didn't want to make waves with any of the parents or the school board. She hated her job and was only hanging around until she could collect her pension.

Although he didn't consider the trips to see Miss F that terrible, Robert did try his best to stop swearing around school and fortunately some of his teachers even cut him some slack. Many of them were young and weren't bothered by obscenities. The most understanding of them all was Miss Pullit, his Writing and Literature teacher.

*

THE JOURNAL OF ROBERT BAIN
Miss Pullit was the coolest teacher that I ever had. The blueprint for building Miss Pullit's body must have been inspired by a thirteen-year-old's wet dream. She was

beautiful with dark brown shoulder length hair and hazel eyes. Her breasts were absurdly big, and her waist was abnormally thin, and her hips were barely wide enough to balance her huge breasts and form a body shape that looked to me to be ideal for sex. Unlike most teachers who dressed conservatively, Miss Pullit wore tight and thin sweaters that showed every minute contour of her breasts. My favorite was a white one that was shear enough for me to see her bra. I always sat in the front row and she leaned forward on the front of my desk when she was talking to the class. This put her breasts at my eye level and I stared at them and daydreamed that she was naked in bed next to me.

Miss Pullit treated me like an equal, so I sometimes said things I shouldn't have.

One day after class, I went up to her when she was sitting at her desk grading papers and I said, "Miss Pullit, have you ever been married?"

She looked up from her work and said, "No Robert, why do you ask?"

Then without even thinking, I stupidly said, "Oh nothing important I guess. I was just staring at your tits and trying to guess how many men you've fucked."

As soon as I said it, I knew I'd stupidly stepped over the line, even with Miss Pullit. Then in my nervousness I went on to get myself into even more trouble.

I said, "Oh mother fucking shit! I'm so sorry Miss Pullit."

So Many Maybes · 27

I cringed and mentally prepared myself for the verbal violence that I was sure was about to come. Surprisingly, it didn't.

She calmly leaned back in her chair and put her hands behind her head and pushed her mesmerizing chest out directly toward me.

I was trembling with adolescent desire when she said, "Well Robert, that's a hard question to answer. I've never kept count. If I had to guess, I'd say between 150 and 200."

I was surprised that she answered my rude question so calmly, and I didn't even know how to process the incredibly high numbers she gave me. It was something I'd have to ask my sister about.

With a calm face and a calm voice, she asked me, "Is there anything else, Robert?"

I smiled nervously and said, "No Miss Pullit. Goodnight. I'll see you tomorrow."

Miss Pullit said, "Good night, Robert," and returned her attention to grading papers.

I walked out of the classroom as fast as I could. I felt like I had just side stepped a colossal puddle of puke. If I'd sworn like that in front of any other teacher, Miss F would have shoved her ruler up my ass. Miss Pullit was definitely cool.

*

It was during Miss Pullit's class that Robert discovered another of his unfortunate physical talents. But unlike his clumsiness, this trait was the obvious result of genetic inheritance from BadBob. That fateful day began like any other. Miss Pullit was leaning forward against the front of Robert's desk while she lectured, and Robert was staring at her tits and daydreaming about sleeping with her. As the class ended, Miss Pullit gave the reading assignment for the next class and Robert reached for his pencil to write down the assignment in his notebook. He accidentally knocked his pencil on the floor. When he bent to his side to pick up the pencil, he farted. It was a great, mature, manly fart that sounded like a balloon full of air being released to fly around the room, and it was loud enough to be heard in the back row. Although Robert's dad never paid any attention to Robert, and he never taught his son how to do anything, BadBob had generously passed down to Robert the natural ability to fart like a master.

Of course the class thought it was hilarious, but Robert was mortified. He tried to maintain his dignity by laughing with them. Only Miss Pullit saw the pain in his face.

She said, "That's enough. Class is dismissed."

It didn't take long for Robert to connect with his first woman. He met her in his Music Appreciation class where their teacher Mr. Klozzett assigned them seats next to each other because both of their last names started with a "B." MaryJane Babcock was a year older than Robert. She was cute, tall and thin and had straight shoulder length blonde hair.

Robert and MaryJane's relationship developed fast. They went through the classical beginning mating ritual in a week. He immediately started sitting next to her in the high school cafeteria at lunch, and in between classes MaryJane pressed

So Many Maybes · 29

her body against his while they leaned against their lockers. It was then that Robert discovered another of his natural physical talents that would stay with him forever. He got instantaneous uncontrollable erections that shot up faster than Super Man's proverbial speeding bullet. To keep everyone in the hallway from seeing the tent in his pants, he had to hold his books in front of his crotch until he could go into a Men's Room stall and wait until he lost his hard-on. This was often a slow process, especially if he kept thinking about MaryJane or Miss Pullit, and the wait threatened to make him late for his next class. Eventually he found that looking at pictures of BadBob made him go limp fast. Other times, someone came into the Men's Room and sat down in the stall next to him and dropped their pants on the floor and make sounds that often began with grunting noises that were followed by several horribly loud splashes. By the time his stall neighbor reached the splash finale, Robert was struggling not to laugh out loud and he had lost his erection.

MaryJane and Robert's sexual relationship blew past the norm for early 1960s thirteen-year-olds at the first Friday night football game. There, MaryJane was freed from the rather conservative public high school dress code, so she could dress more provocatively. She wore a tight V-neck cardigan sweater without a blouse and unbuttoned the top of the sweater all the way down to the top of her bra, so Robert could see her perky breasts.

Fortunately, MaryJane had the foresight to bring a blanket that they could put across their laps. Although the September

So Many Maybes · 30

night was warm enough to make a blanket unnecessary, it covered Robert's stiff member. While the young couple sat next to each other in the grandstand, neither of them was satisfied with old-fashioned hand holding. So Robert turned and kissed her. It was a crude kiss because he'd never kissed a girl before, but he kept at it and his skill improved. A hung-up parent, probably a Uniform, sitting behind them found their behavior offensive and shook Robert's shoulder and told them to stop kissing and watch the game like they should.

MaryJane gave the woman a dirty look and said, "C'mon Robert let's go get hot dogs."

Robert said, "Okay," and they stood up and left the grandstand and walked hand-in-hand toward the concession stand.

On their way there, MaryJane stopped him.

She said, "I don't want a hot dog Robert. Do you?"

He said, "Not really. What do you want to do?"

MaryJane kissed Robert hard and said, "Robert, I wanna' do it."

"Do it?"

"You know, do it."

"I don't understand."

"God dammit Robert! Do I have to say the magic word?"

"I guess."

She grabbed him by the shoulders and shook him and shouted, "God dammit! The magic word is fuck. FUCK! FUCK! FUCK! FUCK! I want you to fuck me."

Robert had learned a lot of words from Dana. If MaryJane

So Many Maybes · 31

had said fuck from the beginning or tons of other words like intercourse or have sex or sleep with each other or bang or bonk or screw or bone or ball or hump or hammer or plow or diddle or do the nasty or the horizontal mambo, he would have understood but "do it" had never come up.

He gulped and said, "Oh. Yeah...sure. Are you serious?"

"Oh for Christ's sake Robert, DO YOU WANNA' FUCK ME OR NOT!?"

Some smart ass over by the concession shouted, "If you won't, I will."

Embarrassed, Robert turned his back to the concession stand and said, "You don't have to shout MaryJane. Of course I do, but where, I mean we can't just lay down on someone's lawn?"

"I know a place. C'mon."

"Before we go, MaryJane, I want you to know something."

"What?"

"This is my first time. I've never had sex before."

MaryJane said, "Don't worry. We'll figure it out. My mother gave me a book about it."

"My sister gave me books too and we even talked about it a lot."

"Oh fantastic, Robert! This is gonna' be great."

*

THE JOURNAL OF ROBERT BAIN

MaryJane led me out of the football stadium to the baseball field. As we approached the diamond's infield, we heard people's voices coming from somewhere near the backstop. We didn't want anyone to see us, so we ducked behind one of the dugouts. We stopped when we realized that it wasn't normal talking.

A man was screaming, "Oh. Unhhh! Oh! God all mighty!!!" Then he started whimpering, "Oh please, please, I can't take it anymore."

MaryJane looked at me in horror. She was afraid some-one was being hurt over there. We ran out from behind the dugout and the man shouted again and we rushed over to help. We stopped after running less than fifteen-feet because we could see that no one was being hurt, quite the contrary.

The man shouted in rapid fire grunts, "EEEH YA... YO...YO...MA!"

It was our Music Appreciation teacher, Mr. Klozzett. He was leaning back against the backstop with his pants down to his ankles and Miss Pullit was on her knees in front of him maniacally giving him a blowjob. The shout-ing that we heard was Mr. Klozzett having an orgasm he'd never forget.

When she finished, Miss Pullit looked up and saw me and MaryJane standing on the ball field.

Miss Pullit calmly said, "Is that you Robert?"

"Yes, Miss Pullit. I'm sorry we interrupted you. We heard the screaming and thought someone needed help."

MaryJane kept silent. She couldn't believe how casually Miss Pullit and I were talking to each other.

Horrified because we were his students, Mr. Klozzett

So Many Maybes · 33

bent down and tried to pull up his pants. He was too flustered to do it, so his pants stayed down around his ankles and gave us a clear view of his bright white shining ass as he waddled slowly away and faded into the darkness.

Miss Pullit stood up and watched Mr. Klozzett shuffle away.

She said, "Don't worry about it, Robert. He wasn't any fun anyway. He finished way too fast."

She leaned down and picked up her blouse and began putting it on and said, "What are you two doing out here tonight?"

MaryJane nervously blurted out, "We're just out for a walk."

With her huge breasts blatantly visible, Miss Pullit said, "I think that's a great idea. It's a nice night out, don't you think?"

MaryJane nervously said, "Yes, it is."

"Where are you walking to?"

"Over to the golf course next to school."

Miss Pullit said, "Well, I'll leave you to it. I have to get back. I'm working at the concession stand tonight."

Miss Pullit finished buttoning her blouse and walked toward the football field. On her way, she turned her head and looked back at us and said, "Robert, make sure you use birth control."

"Yes, Miss Pullit."

MaryJane gasped.

"Who was that!?"

So Many Maybes · 34

"My Writing and Lit teacher."

"Jesus Christ Robert! Isn't it illegal or something to watch your teacher give another teacher a blowjob?"

"Probably. I don't know."

*

Instead of taking him to the golf course, MaryJane guided Robert across the outfield and into the bullpen and spread the blanket out on the grass and began to take off her clothes.

She said, "We'll fuck here."

Robert started taking off his clothes too. When she was naked, MaryJane grabbed Robert's erection and leaned back to sit down on the grass.

He stopped her and said, "Wait a minute MaryJane, what about birth control?"

"Don't worry. I'm on the pill."

"Oh good."

MaryJane grabbed hold of Robert's hips and leaned back quickly and sat down and pulled him toward her. Robert took one awkward step forward and tripped on his own feet, which he so often did, and clumsily fell on top of her and inadvertently plunged his erect dong into her appropriate target for sexual intercourse. With a dull *Dahwub*, his not so mighty member hit the tight elastic barrier that blocked her willing but unprepared vagina. His boner bent almost in half, then was deflected off to the side like a soft link sausage and he smashed his testicles on her hip bone.

He gasped, "Unhhh!" and ironically given his natural propensity to get erections whenever MaryJane touched him,

So Many Maybes · 35

he lost his hard-on immediately.

MaryJane grimaced and said, "Holy shit Robert! For Christ's sake!"

Robert moaned loudly in testicular pain.

MaryJane said, "God Dammit! Don't try to pound me like you're driving a well pipe into the ground."

Robert frowned and said, "I'm sorry, MaryJane." It was an accident."

He didn't add what he was thinking, *"That you made happen."*

She said, "My vagina's tight. Your cock was too big when you rammed it in."

When she said that, Robert momentarily fantasized that he had a huge manly-man cock.

He said, "Do you mean my cock is too big for you?"

MaryJane rolled her eyes and said, "Oh Jesus! Don't be ridiculous. I'll loosen up. I once put the big end of a baseball bat inside me. We just have to start slow that's all."

Robert's big-cock fantasy became as flaccid as his dick, and he didn't know exactly how to react to that statement about the baseball bat. He guessed that MaryJane liked to experiment.

MaryJane began to give him a series of detailed instructions.

"Robert listen to me. Don't get ahead of things and for God's sake don't try to put that thing inside me until I tell you to."

"Okay."

After his embarrassment, Robert couldn't put his thing inside her anyway. He was so soft that her vagina would spit him out like a wad of wet Jello. She grabbed his hand and put

So Many Maybes · 36

it on her vagina and told him what to do to open her up.

While he did this, MaryJane took hold of him and helped him get his erection back.

She said, "Now put it in slowly, a little at a time."

He did and after a few awkward motions, they were off to the adolescent fucking races.

She shouted, "Robert, now you've got it! Now you've got it. Keep going. Keep going. Keep going."

Robert tried with all his might to keep going. But his entire groin region was burning, and he moaned to himself, *"Oh noh…ohhh...nohhh…"* and he lost control and had an ugly and weak, discharge free, mini-orgasm and voiced a series of crude grunts.

"Unhhh…Unhhh…Unh...ahhh!"

Then he went limp again and popped out of her sounding like a dead fish being stepped on, *Poit.*

She looked at him and said, "Oh Robert, I was almost there. I wish you could have held off."

Robert was embarrassed and said, "I'm sorry MaryJane. I didn't want to come. It just happened. I think I was too nervous."

She kissed him tenderly then said, "That's okay Robert, I know you'll do better next time."

"I promise I will."

Then she rolled over on her back and rubbed the inside and outside of her vagina rapidly and she started to breathe heavily and began moaning.

Her moans got louder and louder until she shouted,

So Many Maybes · 37

"OHHHHHHHH, SHITTTTTTTT!!!"

Robert put his arm around her neck and kissed her hard to keep her from shouting so loud. He was afraid that someone would hear her, and they'd get in trouble. Then MaryJane's whole body tensed hard and she came like a lightning bolt blowing up the neighborhood high-voltage transformer. Her body bucked up and down and she rolled her head back and forth so fast that he couldn't keep kissing her and she screamed like a little girl on a roller coaster.

When she finished masturbating but still was trying to catch her breath, she said, "Ho... oh... ly... shit! Robert. That was a good one."

After MaryJane calmed, she looked over at Robert's shriveled little boy ding-a-ling again.

"You'll do better next time. I know you will."

He did get better over time and MaryJane and Robert had a good sex life for three years until MaryJane graduated and went off to Michigan State. Robert was broken hearted when MaryJane left. They tried to keep a long-distance relationship going but he didn't have a car, so they drifted apart. Robert didn't get laid for the rest of his time in high school. He couldn't get interested in anyone else. He missed MaryJane and foolishly believed that they'd get back together.

During his senior year of high school, Robert announced that he loved books and wanted to be a writer. His sister Dana thought it was a great idea, but his mother worried about Robert's desire because she assumed that writers didn't make any money. Robert didn't care about money. He wanted to

So Many Maybes · 38

write, low income or not. BadBob didn't care what Robert did so long as he left home and got a job after he got out of high school.

Dana threw a graduation reception for Robert because she knew that BadBob would never give him a party. She rented a meeting room at the Pantlind Hotel in downtown Grand Rapids. The Pantlind was within walking distance from the Civic Auditorium where Ferment was holding its graduation ceremony. Robert invited Miss Pullit and some people he knew from his classes. He told his mother too, but he didn't really expect her to be there. She couldn't drive a car and he knew that BadBob wouldn't take her.

On graduation night, none of Robert's classmates showed up. He was bummed until Dana walked in with his mother. It was special for him to see her on his big night. MaryJane even showed up. At first, he was very pleased to see MaryJane and he hoped that it might mean they could get together again. His joy morphed into heartbreak when he saw that she came in with another man. Robert didn't like the guy from the beginning. He was an *INTRUDER!!!* and an intruder had no place being at his graduation party.

Dana felt terrible for Robert when she saw MaryJane and the intruder walk in.

She hugged her brother and said, "I'm so sorry Robert. I invited MaryJane because I thought you'd like to see her again. I had no idea that she'd show up with a man."

"I know Sis. I know you'd never do anything to hurt me."

At almost that exact moment, MaryJane caught sight of

So Many Maybes · 39

Robert and she and the intruder approached him. MaryJane hugged Robert.

Robert weakly said, "Hi MaryJane."

"Oh, Robert, it's so nice to see you. This is my fiancé, Yvon."

FIANCÉ!!! Robert's emotions overtook his brain and he blurted out, "Yvonne is a woman's name. Are you a cross dresser or something?"

MaryJane reacted in horror, "Oh my God Robert!"

Evidently the intruder didn't like what Robert said either, because he hit Robert and knocked him backward.

Never known for his physical grace, Robert spun around and fell onto the buffet table and landed face down into a huge pan of lasagna. With his face and new white shirt covered with tomato sauce, Robert started to get up and go at Yvon. But he didn't have to, because a woman slammed the pointed toe of her high heeled shoe into the intruder's balls. The intruder screamed and bent over forward and grabbed his crotch and fell on the floor and rolled around in pain.

Robert looked up and saw that the kicker was Miss Pullit. She had on an elegant white dress with a plunging neckline that revealed her startling cleavage. Her huge tits were still slowly wobbling back and forth from the vibrations of her foot's collision with the intruder's groin.

MaryJane kneeled next to the writhing Yvon and sobbed.

Robert felt awful. He stood up and went over to MaryJane.

He said, "I'm so sorry, MaryJane. I just couldn't bear to see you with someone else. Not here. Not tonight."

He tried to console her by putting his hand on her shoulder.

So Many Maybes · 40

MaryJane forcefully swept his hand away and stood up and shouted at him with red faced rage, "FUCK YOU, ROBERT!!!"

She bent down and helped the white faced Yvon off the floor and they left.

As Robert watched them leave, Miss Pullit walked up to him and picked up several napkins and tenderly wiped the tomato sauce off his face and she even tried to wipe off his new white shirt.

As always, she calmly spoke to him and said, "Hello, Robert."

"Hello, Miss Pullit."

"You shouldn't feel bad Robert. She was wrong to bring that limp-dicked mother fucker to your reception."

Robert was both surprised and pleased at Miss Pullit's language. He had never heard her swear before.

He said, "Miss Pullit?"

"Yes Robert?"

"I like it when you talk dirty."

"Thank you, Robert...Are you happy that you're graduating?"

"Yes, Miss Pullit."

"What are you going to do now?"

"I'm moving to Ann Arbor to be a writer, Miss Pullit."

"Are you going to U of M?"

"No Miss Pullit. Michigan is an expensive school and I don't have any money. I'm only moving to Ann Arbor because my sister told me that it was a good place to live and be a writer, but I'm going to enroll in the community college there, so I can avoid being drafted into the Army and sent to Viet Nam."

"What were your graduation presents, Robert?"

So Many Maybes · 41

"My sister got me a nice bookcase and an electric typewriter to type my manuscripts with, and a work bench that I can use as a writing table."

"Didn't your parents get you anything?"

"No, Miss Pullit. My father doesn't give a shit whether I'm graduating or not and my mother doesn't have any money of her own."

"I see…I met your mother. She seems nice."

"My mother is a nice, kind woman, Miss Pullit, but her life is shit."

"Why is that, Robert?"

"Because my dad, BadBob Bain, is shit and he treats my mother like shit. She never graduated from high school and she never even learned to drive. All she does is cook and clean house and make needlepoint doilies."

"Is that why you call him BadBob, Robert?"

"Yes, Miss Pullit. Among other things. He's an awful alcoholic that makes everyone around him miserable. Dana is really my mother. She always has been."

"Dana is your sister?"

"Yes, Miss Pullit. You should meet her."

Robert took Miss Pullit to meet Dana.

Miss Pullit said, "It's nice to finally meet you Dana. I'm Lana Pullit."

When she said that, Robert realized that he'd never asked Miss Pullit what her first name was. It didn't matter. She'd always be Miss Pullit to him.

Dana smiled warmly and reached out her hand and said,

So Many Maybes · 42

"Hello Lana, Robert is very fond of you. You're his favorite teacher."

Miss Pullit shook Dana's hand and asked if it was okay if she gave Robert a graduation present.

Dana smiled and said, "Of course it's okay."

Miss Pullit said, "Unfortunately, I don't have it with me. Would you mind if he and I leave and go get it?"

"No not at all. I'll take care of things here."

Miss Pullit said, "Robert, why don't you go into the Men's Room and clean yourself up the best you can. I'll talk to your sister for a few minutes, then I'll stop by the Restroom to pick you up and we'll go and get your present?"

"Okay Miss Pullit."

Robert assumed that when Miss Pullit picked him up at the Men's Room, she would stick her head in the door and call for him. Instead, she walked right in.

She loudly said, "Okay Robert, I'm ready. Let's go get your present."

When a guy standing at a urinal saw Miss Pullit's huge boobs come through the door, he turned and sprayed the wall with piss and said, "Holy Shit!"

Miss Pullit dodged the pee stream and said, "Oh, put that micro-mini ding dong away, dickwad."

She took Robert's hand and pulled him toward the door. PissingGuy stared at her as they went by and urine was still dribbling from his dick.

As they hopped over the puddle on the floor, Miss Pullit glared at PissingGuy and said, "You're disgusting!"

So Many Maybes · 43

She guided Robert down the hall and they entered an elevator. The old hotel's elevator was very slow and their trip to the fourth floor gave him ample time to study Miss Pullit's cleavage in detail. Her white dress was utterly revealing and gave Robert a nice long look at the side of one of her breasts. Robert had seen her boobs before when he and MaryJane caught Miss Pullit giving Mr. Klozzett a blowjob behind the backstop on the baseball field. But that was at night and even though her headlights were huge, he wasn't close enough to her to see her well. Now, standing in the elevator next to her, Robert's view was well lit and unobstructed. He thought it was a pleasant elevator ride.

After they got out of the elevator, they walked down the hall and stopped at a hotel room.

Miss Pullit said, "I put your present in here." She unlocked the door and they went in.

*

THE JOURNAL OF ROBERT BAIN

When we entered the hotel room, Miss Pullit let her dress fall to the floor and said, "Take off your clothes Robert."

I was too excited to move. Fucking Miss Pullit had been my greatest fantasy since I was thirteen.

She walked over and stood by the bed and said, "Please take off your clothes, Robert. I want to give you your graduation present."

I nervously said, "Yes, Miss Pullit."

She faced me and said, "Come over here and stand

So Many Maybes · 44

next to me, Robert."

As I walked over to her she asked me, "How long have we known each other, Robert?"

"Four years, Miss Pullit. Since I was a Freshman." She took a firm hold of my hand and asked, "And Robert, in those four years have you ever wanted to fuck me?"

"Every day, Miss Pullit."

"Okay Robert, it's time."

"Time for what, Miss Pullit?"

Suddenly, she dove face first onto the bed and forcefully pulled me with her.

"Time to FUCK YOUR TEACHER!!!"

"Yes, Miss Pullit."

She laid on her back and spread her legs wide and shouted, "FUCK ME, TARZAN…FUCK ME WITH YOUR MIGHTY KING OF THE JUNGLE KING KONG DONG!!!"

I got up on the bed and kneeled between her legs and pounded my chest and shouted the famous Tarzan yell.

"Aaheeh-ah-eeh-aaaaaah-eeh-ah-eeh-aaaah!"

Then I leapt high into the air like I was swinging from a jungle vine and aimed my human gorilla dick toward the entrance to Miss Pullit's dark and steamy primeval jungle and hit my head on the bed post and almost passed out…

*

…Robert bonked his head hard on the door jamb when he tried to follow Miss Pullit into the room. She turned around

So Many Maybes · 45

when she heard the dull *dwumt!* of his head's collision with the dark-oak moulding.

When she saw Robert rubbing his forehead, she asked, "Are you okay, Robert?"

"I'm okay, Miss Pullit. I just wasn't paying attention."

She led him into the room.

It was decorated with party streamers and a big banner stretched across the wall behind the bed that said, "Congratulations Robert." And there was a table with a couple of bottles of champagne on ice and on the chairs around the table were several wrapped gifts.

She said, "Sit down on the bed and unwrap your presents. I'll hand them to you."

Robert sat down and she stood in front of him and handed him the gifts one at a time. Every box was full of hard-back books including the complete works of Ernest Hemingway and John Steinbeck and F. Scott Fitzgerald, along with Herman Melville's *Moby Dick*, Tolstoy's *War and Peace*, Kerouac's *On the Road*, and Jean Shepard's *In God We Trust: All others Pay Cash*, which was one of Robert's favorites.

Robert was overwhelmed. Miss Pullit came to his graduation reception and no one else's and she wore an incredible dress that she knew he would love and probably make him as hard as a concrete bunker. Then she gave him a very generous graduation present. Hard-back books aren't cheap, and she had bought them on a relatively small teacher's salary. And judging from the champagne on ice on the table, she wasn't finished. He almost cried because he realized that he was special to her

So Many Maybes · 46

and probably, except for Dana, Miss Pullit was his first real friend. Robert stood up and gave her a big hug.

She stepped back and said, "Robert why don't you pour the champagne while I go and change into something more comfortable?"

*

THE JOURNAL OF ROBERT BAIN

I had seen enough movies to know what her words implied. "Changing into something more comfortable" meant she was going to change into a sexy negligée in preparation for making love. I started to get an erection and my tiny novella grew into a major novel destined to win the Nobel Prize. Excited, I pulled my shirt out of my pants and cleared the books off the bed. I had just taken off my shoes when she emerged wearing a Ferment High School sweat shirt and jeans. She really had changed into something more comfortable. Thank God I hadn't taken off my pants!

When she saw me, she said, "Robert?"

"Yes, Miss Pullit?"

"Why are your shoes off?"

I felt like an idiot and answered as smoothly as I could,

I said, "I thought I'd get more comfortable too, Miss Pullit."

*

So Many Maybes · 47

Immediately after Lana Pullit had emerged from the bathroom, Robert's sister Dana knocked at the door. When she entered the room, Dana put a couple of grocery bags down on the table and said, "I'm sorry I took so long. I had to take Mom home first. I tried to convince her to come up here with us, but she was terrified that BadBob would throw a shitstorm if she didn't get right home after Robert's reception."

Miss Pullit said, "I'm so sorry to hear that. It must be awful for her to live in fear of her husband."

"Well at least she got to go to the ceremony and come to Robert's reception."

Robert was baffled by their conversation.

He said, "Wait a minute. Would someone tell me what's going on. I gather you two knew each other before tonight."

Dana said, "What gave you that idea Robert?"

"Oh, I don't know. Maybe it's the way you were talking about Mom and we're all here having this little private party."

Dana smiled and said, "Actually we didn't meet each other until you introduced us. We talked for a minute when you were in the Men's Room and Lana invited Mom and me up to watch you unwrap your presents."

Lana said, "Robert show your sister the presents that I gave you."

Dana said, "Let's get drunk at the same time."

Lana said, "Good idea. Robert has already poured the champagne."

Dana said, "That hotel champagne is awful. I brought the good stuff."

So Many Maybes · 48

*

THE JOURNAL OF ROBERT BAIN

As I showed Dana Miss Pullit's generous gifts, Dana reached into one of the paper bags and took out a bottle of Tequila and three shot glasses and poured three shots. I had never drank before. In fact, I had resolved not to ever drink at all, because I had experienced how BadBob's alcoholism had affected me and Dana and my mother. Since Dana had also grown up under BadBob's alcoholic wing, I assumed that she felt the same way about drinking as I did. Obviously, I was wrong and I had no choice but to drink with her and Miss Pullit. It would be inconsiderate not to.

Dana lifted her glass in a toast and said, "Here's to the future."

Miss Pullit followed and touched her glass to Dana's.

When I didn't, Miss Pullit said, "Touch your glass to ours Robert, it's what you do when you toast."

"Yes, Miss Pullit."

I lifted my glass and we all said, "To the future," and drank our shots.

We drank a couple more shots of tequila and I began to feel warm and good all over and I laid down on the bed. Dana and Miss Pullit assumed that I had passed out and was asleep, but I was still awake. I was lost in drunken philosophical musing.

I was thinking about the evening's events. Although none of my classmates had shown up for my party, the

So Many Maybes · 49

four people that I held most dear had; and they were all women. I had no male friends and I hated my father.

I thought about my mother. Although she had given birth to me, I have no memory of us ever being close. But I had lived in the same house with her for my entire life and I knew her well. I thought of her as a kind, generous, and caring woman. I also felt sorry for her. My dreadful father and the social conventions of the time had stolen her life. And she was convinced that she had no choice but to stay with him.

I thought about my sad reunion with MaryJane. I was ashamed of my poor behavior. MaryJane was my first girlfriend and the first woman that I had sex with, and it would have been nice if we had parted on a friendly basis. Instead, I let my foolish hopes and dreams for a new beginning with her get the best of me, and I acted like an ass. Despite her lack of consideration for me, I should have hidden my pain and acted more gracefully. Perhaps one day, I'll have a chance to make it up to her.

I looked at the two women who were drinking with me and thought about the roles they had played in my life. My sister had always been with me. She was my caretaker and my teacher and my friend, and I knew she always would be. But the situation with Miss Pullit was different. I didn't meet her until I was thirteen and a student under the influence of screaming male adolescent hormones.

Although she was teaching me something about writing and literature, two subjects I really liked, Miss Pullit was mostly the object of my sexual desire, the woman I fantasized about. But protocol, and even law, kept us from getting too close. Certainly, her astonishing body will interest me forever. But that night, on my Graduation Day, that invisible wall between teacher and student had dissolved, and Miss Pullit became something else. She became my friend. Someone I could get drunk with and confide in. It was a wonderful feeling that was only enhanced by the thought of my imminent move out of the BadBob Bain house.

I had finally grown up.

*

Chapter 3
Grafton's

Robert was curled up asleep on the couch when Dana arrived
to drive him to Brighton. The two days after his graduation
reception were exhausting. He had almost franticly packed his
things so he could leave the living Hell of the BadBob Bain
house as soon as possible. And he was overjoyed to feel his
sister's hug before they got in the car.

A few days later, Dana and Robert went down to Ann Arbor
together and they explored the area around the U of M Central
Campus and looked for a place for Robert to live. They found a
small room in a house on North Thayer on the northern edge
of the campus. It suited Robert's needs well. It was cheap, small
enough to keep clean easily and, at the same time, had enough
space for his precious collection of books and his writing work
bench and the other gifts that Miss Pullit and Dana had given
him as graduation presents. It had no kitchen, so he bought a
hot plate and a toaster oven and rented a small refrigerator. But
he had to make do with the bathroom that was down the hall.

He found a job at a bookstore named Grafton's. Initially,
he wanted to work for a small privately-owned establishment
where browsing customers could find used inexpensive
treasures. There were several of those shops around town
but none of them were hiring. Instead, Grafton's was a chain

store located a few blocks down South University from the U of M campus. It wasn't what Robert had hoped for, but he ultimately loved working at Grafton's because the job paid well, and the people were great. Grafton's specialized in selling printing remainders, titles that publishers had overestimated the demand for and printed more than they could sell at regular prices. Grafton's bought up these books and sold them at a discount. They also sold some classics along with current best sellers and magazines.

His boss was a wonderful Italian woman named Teresa Bernini. Robert couldn't have hoped for anyone better. With a perpetual warm smile, Terri made sure that everyone was happy at their jobs. She listened to their complaints and suggestions seriously and patiently, and she made sure they all had the opportunity to earn enough money to pay their rent. Robert adored Terri for her warmth and kindness and cheerfully called her, "Mother Teresa."

Physically, Terri was about the same height as Robert. She was dark complected and had magnificent long black hair and beautiful brown eyes. Her womanly full-breasted, hour-glass shaped figure was soft and inviting and accepting and huggable, and whenever Robert was near her he wanted to open his arms wide and shower her with kisses.

Robert worked in the store's stockroom alongside a young college-aged girl named Jenny Woodward. The stockroom resembled a library with rows of tall metal bookshelves where the store kept extra books until there was room for them in the front of the store. It was Robert's and Jenny's job to sort,

So Many Maybes · 54

price mark and keep the stored books organized.

Although Jenny was not a classical beauty, she was absolutely adorable; the kind of Midwest farmer's daughter that the Beach Boys said really make you feel alright in their song *California Girls*. She was small, only about 5 feet 1 inch tall, with a sensuous well-shaped body and perfectly shaped breasts. She had a perpetual disarming smile and striking tropical-sky blue eyes. Her facial features were warm, and her pink skin was clear and nearly translucent. Her wavy chest-length blond hair laid gracefully over the front of her shoulders.

Robert had conflicted feelings about Jenny. On the one hand, she was a delight to be with. She was cute beyond belief and she could turn the most mundane things into childlike fun. On the other hand, when he was around her, he felt like his genitals went to war with his brain. His balls made his ape-man dork start to wag frenetically in his pants and he wanted to drag her by the hair over to the Michigan Theater where he would bang her brains out in the balcony during a retrospective showing of Tarzan. But there was a problem. Jenny was barely seventeen-years-old, and Robert's brain made him feel like the neighborhood pervert who wanted to fuck the little girl next door.

And Jenny didn't help matters. She was a shameless flirt and so playful and uninhibited and comfortable around Robert, that she felt she could say or do anything. She frequently mooned him or flashed her incredible tits at him. Of course Robert loved it. And he couldn't help but act like a kid himself and make a show of trying to slap her on the ass or rip off her

So Many Maybes · 55

blouse. He was, however, careful not to ever touch her.

Jenny had moved to Ann Arbor to study painting and she was talented enough to be awarded a full scholarship to the U of M Art School. Painting was both her passion and her salvation because Jenny was a man magnet. From the time she was twelve, she was followed everywhere by one or more drooling boys and even sleazy older men with their hormones soaking the front of their pants. Sometimes she enjoyed the attention like any young girl would, but she got too much of it and often found it exhausting. When she was painting, Jenny entered her fantasy land of beautiful colors and shapes and she felt calm and warm and the constant masculine onslaught momentarily faded away.

Jenny lived with Jack, her boyfriend since high school. He worked as a cook in a local restaurant called *BRAAACK'S!* *BRAAACK'S!* was the worst restaurant in the Ann Arbor area. Their menu contained at least three hundred horrible items, most of which were either deep fried in dirty days-old oil or cooked on the grill in a puddle of sizzling, bubbling and smoking shortening. Robert joked that the owners of *BRAAACK'S!* must have named it after the sound of the belch their customers made as they left the restaurant, *BRAAACK!*

No one at Grafton's knew anything about Jack because he never came into the store or went anywhere with Jenny. She seldom talked about him, but when she did she gave them the impression that he didn't treat her well. This worried everyone in the store. They all resolved that if Jack ever hurt Jenny, they would join forces and ram a Magnum of cheap champagne up

So Many Maybes · 56

his ass and pop the cork.

Terri's eccentric brother Norton also worked at Grafton's. Everyone but Terri called Norton, "Nort." Nort was the store's maintenance man. He performed every odd job that could be imagined. He mounted new bookshelves and repaired old ones. He mended torn carpet, repainted walls, replaced ceiling tiles and light fixtures and bulbs. He fixed faulty wiring, cleared plugged toilets and replaced plumbing fixtures. In fact, he'd fearlessly tackle any job conceivable.

It was hard to believe that Terri and Nort were brother and sister. They didn't act alike and they didn't look alike. Nort was two inches shorter than she was and he had a slight paunch. According to Terri, Nort developed male pattern baldness at age nine. In contrast to Terri who was a scorching hot Italian bombshell that every man alive would probably love to fuck, Nort was sexless. He never appeared interested in women unless one of his projects involved building some kind of kitchen appliance. Robert suspected that Nort had no dick.

Nort always dressed the same, in a crisply pressed, dark blue, Bookstore Maintenance Man's uniform and perfectly shined black work shoes with thick rubber soles. Over his left shirt pocket, red embroidered lettering announced to everyone that he was indeed named "Norton."

Although he was a kind and gentle man, Nort seldom talked to anyone. He usually sat quietly at his desk at work, or his recliner at home, and thought about one of his projects. When he had a clear mental picture of the procedures he was going to follow, he stood up and began the task at hand. If something

So Many Maybes · 57

had to be fabricated or repaired that he couldn't handle at the store, he went home to his workshop and parts warehouse to do the work. Terri and Nort lived on an old farm outside of town by the Ipsi-Ann Drive-In Theater. His workshop was inside a metal pole barn behind their house. It was better equipped than a Ferrari Formula One Repair Shop and included a collection of meticulously labeled and cataloged parts that were stored in twenty rows of military grade warehouse storage shelves. In the remainder of the barn, back behind the organized shelves, was a strange place that Terri called, "The Wilderness." It was a vast open concrete floor covered with a maze of piles of what most people would call junk. The stuff was grouped and sorted in some pattern that Nort remembered but seemed completely random to everyone else. Out in The Wilderness were hundreds of odd contraptions such as a foot-powered pottery wheel, a canoe, three outboard motors, six bicycles in various states of repair, an old refrigerator, a '57 Chevy V-8 engine, a pontoon boat, sixteen military green army cots, at least one hundred first aid kits, two hundred cases of military food rations, forty five military Jerry Cans, approximately a billion miles of rubber hose and copper tubing, a couple of street light fixtures, an old anti-aircraft search light, a full-sized propane tank, a go-kart, a ship's mooring post, a ski-lift chair, and a myriad of other things including a couple of carefully covered old cars.

When he wasn't fixing or building things, Nort combed through scrap yards looking for stuff that might be of use. He frequently annoyed Terri by cruising by people's trash piles

So Many Maybes · 58

in his pick-up truck to rescue some old cast away mechanical device that he was sure had great potential.

Robert's best friend, Will, worked the front desk and dealt directly with the store's customers. He was born in San Francisco, but his parents moved to Detroit when he was fifteen. He didn't like living in Detroit, so he applied to U of M and moved to Ann Arbor and studied film. He was smart and a dedicated student of movies as an art form. Will had seen and carefully analyzed hundreds of films ranging from the first primitive cinematic experiments to the latest block busters. He knew almost everything there was to know about the technical aspects of movie and live theater production and special effects.

Although Will came from a vastly different background than Robert, they were almost carbon copies of one another. Both were good natured and pleasant, loved rock music, hated the government and war, and didn't give a damn about money. They were both tall and skinny with blue eyes and brown hair that was so fine and straight that it wouldn't hold any shape. They only wore T-shirts or blue work shirts and jeans and sneakers. They owned no other clothing except for their winter jackets. Will had a rough looking black wool overcoat that he bought at Goodwill, and Robert had a dark blue Navy Surplus P-Coat. When Will started working at Grafton's, Terri had to buy him a decent shirt to work in. Dana bought one for Robert.

Robert and Will were both obsessed with women, but in a different way. Robert was obsessed with sex. His writing was full of sexual fantasy. He couldn't look at a woman without

So Many Maybes · 59

imagining what they looked like naked and what it would be like to sleep with them. In contrast, Will was a filmmaker/poet in the romantic tradition who imagined making pure love to the angelic woman of his dreams. His films usually told the story of a nice guy being betrayed by a heartless bitch, then in the end he meets the perfect woman and they live in bliss forever after. Unfortunately, Will wasn't happy with his movies. He thought they were too romantic and even a bit silly, and it bugged him. But no matter what he tried, the same story always emerged because romance was in his soul.

Wolf Rilke worked at the store's front counter with Will and provided customer service. He was perfectly suited to working with the public because he was naturally outgoing and loved people. He greeted everyone with robust open arms and a warm smile. Wolf loved life. He particularly liked beautiful women, and he was exceptionally adept at shamelessly flirting with them without making them bolt from his presence. He was short, around 5 feet 7 inches tall, and nicely rotund. He had thick salt and pepper hair, and a full, three-inch beard. Wolf was brought up in Brooklyn in a show business family. His mother was an actress and his father was a writer and theater producer. Wolf moved to Ann Arbor to study writing and drama at U of M like his father had, but he only stayed in school long enough to meet people in the Ann Arbor theater scene. Then he dropped out to be a playwright and start his own theater company. He remained in Ann Arbor because he liked the town and he felt the community was a good place for him to write and where audiences would accept and attend

So Many Maybes · 60

his off-the-wall theater productions. He never attempted to get them produced anywhere else because he knew that his plays were so peculiar and outrageous that no sane legitimate theater producer would ever stage them without substantial alteration. But to all of Wolf's friends and his audiences in Ann Arbor, Wolf's plays were wonderful and great fun.

Chapter 4
Bonnie

Will had a complicated relationship with a woman named Bonnie Haines.

Although Bonnie grew up wealthy, her life began poorly. Her parents, Daisy and Tony Haines, were the proverbial jet setters. They and their friends were always on the move. Pickled by barrels of expensive champagne, and flying on massive quantities of cocaine, they followed a non-stop international party. They were married in Las Vegas after a twelve-day drinking and snorting binge that made stops in London, Milan, and Rome and somewhere in Latin America that they only vaguely remembered. Bonnie was born nine months later; an unexpected and unwanted child. In fact, if her grandparents on both sides hadn't stepped in and prevented Bonnie's mother from getting an abortion, Bonnie would have entered this world as medical waste.

Bonnie never met her real parents. Instead, she was raised by her grandparents, Frederick and Vanessa Upton of Huntington, New York. Huntington was located along the Gold Coast of Long Island that was made famous by F. Scott Fitzgerald in his novel *The Great Gatsby*. The Uptons were erudite and wealthy. One hundred years earlier, Frederick Upton's family had made their fortune by investing in several lumber companies that provided wood to rebuild Chicago after it's Great Fire in 1871. He met and married Vanessa in 1922 when he was at Harvard getting his MBA and she was a young professor in Art History.

Every so often, Bonnie would also visit her father's dad whom she called Uncle Judd. Judd Haines was a wonderfully charming, self-made marketing genius that built a Madison-Avenue-based advertising empire from what was once a small, marginally seedy, firm in Brooklyn. Through a combination of aggressive and sometimes annoying persistence, Judd Haines could sell anything from next-to-useless XXXL condoms converted into wilderness water containers, to diapers custom designed to be worn by long-hall truckers who were behind schedule and didn't want to stop to take a leak. But his three biggest clients were Lord Jordon Jones Clothing, Passing Wind Cosmetics and a combination feminine hygiene deodorant/oral laxative named Vagimint. Despite the English Royal sounding name, Jordon Jones was a Korean based company that made knock-off designer clothing, and Passing Wind was an international conglomerate that produced cheap perfumes and cosmetics that were sold under the French name of Sueur de Cheval. When worldly and well-educated Bonnie told her Uncle Judd that *Sueur de Cheval* meant horse sweat in French, Judd Haines almost collapsed laughing. He thought it was a wonderful joke that so many people actually bought it.

As part of his business, Judd Haines' firm would put on lavish parties where he hoped to connect potential clients with magazine and newspaper publishers and television networks. When she was in Manhattan, Bonnie went to Uncle Judd's

So Many Maybes · 64

parties where she often met top models and even a few movie stars.

At one of these get-togethers, the editor of *Extreme Teen Magazine* was taken by Bonnie's exquisite facial beauty and her rare combination of long red hair and almost startling blue eyes. Despite Bonnie's initial objections, the editor convinced her to become their cover girl when she was only fifteen years old. After her magazine appearance, clothing companies offered her big money to pose in their designs for young women. But Bonnie had never wanted to be a model and she didn't need the money, so when modeling became more work than fun, she quit.

While Bonnie's grandfather Upton spent his time running the Upton Lumber empire, her grandmother Vanessa introduced Bonnie to art. Vanessa Upton was an avid art collector and the Upton's multi-million-dollar Huntington mansion was full of paintings by famous artists. Vanessa frequently traveled around the world in search of new paintings to add to her collection, and she took Bonnie along. During her travels with her grandmother, Bonnie visited all of the top museums and galleries in the United States and Australia and Europe and she saw the western world's most famous paintings.

It was during one of their visits to an exclusive gallery in Manhattan that Bonnie met and ultimately fell in love with a painter and art teacher named Jack McSurly. Jack McSurly was cool. The coolest. The penultimate cool artist. When Bonnie met him, McSurly had been around the New York art scene since the 1950s. He was forty-six-years old, dark, handsome,

So Many Maybes · 65

and outgoing and he carefully cultivated his artist's image. His thick shoulder-length dark brown hair was permed and colored to make him resemble Jim Morrison of The Doors. He wore sandals and an untucked, oversized paint-spattered white shirt over his similarly spattered jeans wherever he went. When it was cold in the winter, McSurly wore a long overcoat draped over his shoulders like a cape. Over the years, Jack McSurly had known and exchanged ideas with many famous and successful artists, but he himself was only a mediocre painter. He was known more for his ability to teach than for the works of art he produced. McSurly was a great storyteller and he could enthrall and inspire his students at the Art Students League with anecdotes about his encounters with the big names like Pollock, de Kooning and Picasso. McSurly's charisma and flamboyant manner made him irresistible to young women, and he was notorious for sleeping with his teenage art students. Since Bonnie was gorgeous, McSurly took to her immediately. But the relationship was unfair from the beginning. To McSurly, Bonnie was just another one of his conquests; a beautiful teenage woman that he could frequently bang and be seen with in public. In contrast, Bonnie was seriously in love with McSurly and she naively assumed that she would spend the rest of her life as his exclusive lover. So when he accepted a guest teaching position at U of M she followed him and even paid McSurly's living expenses.

While they were living in Ann Arbor, Bonnie became interested in filmmaking. She and McSurly frequently attended showings of underground films around the U of M campus and they went to the Ann Arbor film festival. During the festival, Bonnie talked with a woman filmmaker named Alexa Frankenheimer. Frankenheimer was impressed by Bonnie's interest in cinema and art history and she suggested that Bonnie should try filmmaking herself.

Bonnie was reticent at first because she was intimidated by the technical complexities of film production. But when Alexa explained that everything Bonnie needed to know could be learned from books, Bonnie decided to give it a shot. She read the books and bought thousands of dollars in equipment, but she didn't make a film because she was stumped. She had no ideas.

Unfortunately Bonnie and McSurly's relationship ended predictably while they were living in Ann Arbor. Hoping to find a suitable subject for a movie, Bonnie was wandering around the U of M campus carrying her camera when she decided to drop in on McSurly at the Art School. On her way down the hallway toward McSurly's office, Bonnie saw him walk hand-in-hand into the Men's Restroom with a blonde, small-breasted, pixie-haired art student named Anna.

Sick to her stomach with emotional pain, Bonnie slowly opened the Restroom door just enough to see inside. PixieAnna was leaning forward against the wall opposite the door and McSurly was madly banging her from behind. In addition to being hurt, Bonnie became enraged. Feeling both betrayed and foolish for getting involved with a famous philanderer like McSurly, Bonnie resolved to make the old bastard pay. She was going to get her vengeance by publicly humiliating him. She

So Many Maybes · 67

knew the Art School wouldn't approve of McSurly fucking one of his students, so she pointed her camera through the crack in the door and shot some Black and White footage of the two in the act. Then she quietly backed out and took her film footage into Detroit and had it processed.

When McSurly entered her apartment that evening, he was confronted by Bonnie standing next to a projector showing the film of him and PixieAnna humping. Bonnie told McSurly to move the hell out of her apartment and to leave Ann Arbor or she was going to enter the film in the Ann Arbor Film Festival where she was sure it would cause quite a scandal, particularly with the University Art School. McSurly moved out and left town the next day and returned to New York. He never even told the University he was quitting.

After she threw McSurly out, Bonnie debated whether to return to New York. Ann Arbor was a nice enough place, but she was separated from her grandparents and there were no famous museums or galleries. On the other hand, Ann Arbor's art scene was active and the people in general were cool. And Ann Arbor didn't have the hassles of big city life either, so it might be a good quiet place to rest while she tried to figure things out.

Bonnie had fallen into a serious depression because her first real love had betrayed her. Like so many writers before her, the emotional pain of depression helped her to discover that she had a natural talent for writing poetry and she began filling notebooks with poems about almost anything that occurred to her. But it didn't take long for her to discover that her poems

So Many Maybes · 68

weren't the beautiful love sonnets she wanted them to be. They were painful journeys to places that she and most other people didn't want to go; deep into the human created Devil's Lair of perversion and physical and emotional abuse.

It greatly disturbed her at first, but she ultimately convinced herself to continue. She thought that since she had recognized her tendency to go down the dark road to ugliness, perhaps she could redirect her creations to be more positive.

Even though she had resolved to devote her time to writing poetry, she was still interested in filmmaking, and she thought it might be fruitful to make a film that incorporated her poems. It was within this context that Bonnie saw the footage that she'd shot of McSurly and PixieAnna in a new light. It was no longer just a tool for seeking vengeance. It was potential raw material for a movie. Perhaps she could combine the McSurly footage with her unpleasant poetry to make something that at least had some moral and intellectual value. A movie called *Holding My Load* was the disturbing result.

HOLDING MY LOAD

A man is having anal sex with a little boy who is leaning against the wall in a public restroom.
A man with a grisly gravelly voice recites a poem:

"Squeeze! Squeeze! Squeeze!
Feel that wretched squeeze!
I Squeezed my juice and held on to it…

So Many Maybes · 69

Long Pause…while the sex continues.

But my action was smooth,
and my pistol was wet.
And such an abounding, affectionate
Friendly, loving feeling, did this beget,
that more wretched squeezing, I would regret.

Long Pause…while the sex continues.

Then I screamed… I'm not alone here.
Others have overcome these same ol' fears.
So come my dear fellows, one and all
let us forget their sad, pathetic tears,
let us throw open our swollen, aching balls,
and unload in their, sweet little rears."

THE END

Unfortunately, although it appeared as if her experiment was a success, the visual imagery combined with the poem to produce a film that was an even more miserable experience than her poetry was by itself.

At that point, she promised herself to finally give up filmmaking altogether. If she didn't, there was a danger that Ann Arbor's suicide rate would go up.

Will and Robert first met Bonnie at the Fifth Forum Theater when she screened *Holding My Load* as part of a Surrealist and Shock Art Film Festival. Since she didn't like the film, she initially refused to show it, but the organizer of the festival convinced her to change her mind when he told her that her movie would be shown along with films by famous artists like Luis Bunuel and Man Ray.

After they watched *Holding My Load*, Will and Robert sat silent and looked at each other.

Then Will facetiously said, "That was pleasant."

Robert said, "About as much as having a tooth pulled."

Neither of them liked watching her film. Still, they were both convinced that Bonnie Haines was talented. Although the images appeared to be solely a graphic depiction of anal sex, their juxtaposition with the horrific poem transformed her film from child pornography into a powerful abstract vision of rape and moral disgust.

As soon as Bonnie walked out on the stage to take questions from the audience, Will was transfixed. He got up from his seat and hurried toward the stage to get a better look at her. Bringing up the rear, famously clumsy Robert tripped on a theater seat, stumbled forward five steps, and fell into an annoyed woman's lap with his hand in a place she didn't appreciate. Will didn't notice. He was staring at Bonnie. She was the most beautiful woman he'd ever seen, with long silky-smooth red hair and unforgettable blue eyes. She was wearing blue jeans and a blue work shirt which was typical of radical artists in Ann Arbor during the 1960s, but Bonnie's revealing neckline and her high heeled boots hinted at an urbane background and the perfect fit of her clothes suggested wealth. Will didn't catch those hints.

So Many Maybes · 71

Instead, he was looking at the female poet of his dreams; a woman whose brain resided in a dark and foreign world. To Will, Bonnie Haines was truly, "Far Out!"

Will and Robert lingered outside the theater and waited for Bonnie to come out the door. Strangely, she was alone. This surprised Will and he asked himself, *"How could such an extraordinary woman be at a showing of her film without having some dreadfully-handsome and ultra-cool guy at her side?"*

Without any apparent inhibition, Will walked up to her and introduced himself.

He said, "Hi, I'm Will and I really admired your film."

Bonnie didn't smile. Instead, she coldly said, "I'm glad you liked it," and tried to sidestep him.

"Oh I didn't say I liked it, I said that I admired it."

Somewhat intrigued, Bonnie stopped and asked, "What does that mean?"

"It means that the film is exactly what you intended it to be, horrible and disgusting, and that means that you're an excellent filmmaker."

Now Bonnie smiled and took his arm and said, "Come on, I want to talk some more."

They walked away leaving Robert standing in the lobby marveling at how easily Will had just picked up a gorgeous woman.

Bonnie took Will back to her apartment and they banged each other's brains out. For Will it was a dream come true. Bonnie was the coolest woman he'd ever met, and he thought that her decision to sleep with him could mean that she was

So Many Maybes · 72

interested in beginning something that he wanted most in his life; a serious, loving relationship.

It was different for Bonnie. Although she wanted a serious and stable relationship as much as Will did, she wasn't sure it was with him. Still jaded by her failed love affair with McSurly, she wanted to be careful. She was afraid that Will was just a guy that she'd impulsively slept with before she knew him well enough to care about him, or to be sure that he really cared about her.

Will also thought that since they got along so well, it might be possible for them to collaborate on a few films. Her approach to cinema was the antithesis of his. He habitually made romantic films which he was dissatisfied with, and Bonnie produced movies that powerfully depicted the darker side of human nature. Perhaps if they worked together, she could help him break his habit and make movies that weren't so romantic and predictable.

A few days after they met, Will proposed the idea of future collaborations to her. Initially, she was reluctant. She liked Will well enough, but they'd only just met. On the other hand, a collaboration might work to her advantage too. She had been struggling with her natural tendency to produce such dark and depressing and miserable work, and she wanted to try and redirect her talent toward creating more pleasant art. So she decided to collaborate with Will under the stipulation that they didn't sleep with each other again. She was afraid that further sexual involvement would give Will the wrong idea about her intentions before she had a chance to get to know him. As an

So Many Maybes · 73

excuse, she told Will that it would be easier to work together if there was no sexual involvement between them. If they were lovers, personal problems might interfere with their artistic enterprises, and in the worst case, lead to failed projects. Will reluctantly agreed to Bonnie's conditions because he wanted her help, but he wasn't happy with the arrangement.

When Will told Robert what they were planning, Robert thought it was an interesting idea. It wasn't a love relationship. It was a merger between Will the movie fanatic and technical wizard, and Bonnie the high powered and exotic art poet with a murderously painful vision of the cosmos. Robert thought that it might be a good combination. However, there was a risk that Will's technical prowess would provide Bonnie the tools she needed to create an even more horrific and miserable audience experience.

Chapter 5
Getting Bent

Since Robert had grown up in the shadow of the conservative and restrictive Vandenwood Uniform Church, he despised religion and it was predictable that he wouldn't get along well with one of his coworkers, Diligence Overkeen. Dilli O was a member of a cult-like fanatic church called, "The Children of The Inquisition," that condemned human pleasure as the work of the Devil and advocated strong measures to rid the world of evil lust and eroticism. To hide whatever sex appeal she might have, Dilli O dressed in heavy wool, floor-length black skirts, and shapeless long-sleeved black blouses buttoned all the way up to her neck. She persistently tried to push her religion on Robert and badgered him to join and be "saved." For someone like Robert who hated religion and continuously fantasized about sex, Dilli O's presence at work was anathema.

Except for BadBob Bain, Dilli O was the most unlikeable person that Robert had ever met. She was arrogantly critical of everything and everyone. With Dilli O, things had to be precisely neat and orderly and organized in her own obsessive way. Robert had once seen her using a ruler to make sure that a book was exactly centered on the bookshelf. When she wasn't looking, he moved the book about two inches just to mess with her.

As he walked to work on the morning after he had first met Bunny, Robert was only partially aware of his surroundings. He was staring at the ground thinking about how great Bunny was and he was angry with himself because he had forgotten to get her phone number. However, he woke up quickly when he walked through Grafton's front door. Dilli O was over by the right-hand wall of the store dressed like a pyramidal-shaped black-clad witch-burning mob member and she saw Robert come in. When he saw Dilli O look directly at him, Robert panicked, and he ran to the back of the store and into the stockroom. Just as he went through the stockroom door, he tripped on a box of newly arrived books and he stumbled forward.

He shouted, "Ohhh... shit!" as he made a desperate attempt to grab one of the book shelves.

He failed, and he went into a half-spin then stumbled backward toward the far wall of the stock room where he collided with Terri. Terri fell back on her rump and Robert ended up sitting in her lap.

Terri said, "Good morning Robert. It's nice to see you, but we can't go on meeting like this."

In front of them, Jenny and Will were leaning against a bookshelf next to several unopened boxes.

Jenny said, "What do you think Will, a 9.4 or maybe a 9.5?"

Will said, "More like a 9.7 because he really stuck the landing."

Jenny said, "You're right, and such a nice soft landing it was."

"I agree, and I think we should probably give him an extra

So Many Maybes · 76

tenth for knocking his boss on her ass."

Robert said, "Very funny. Just once, I wish you guys would give me a 10.0."

Jenny said, "We really can't Robert. Perfection is impossible. The only reason so many perfect tens are being thrown around in Olympic Gymnastics these days, is that the judges are fucking the thirteen-year-old gymnasts."

Robert chuckled and crawled out of Terri's lap and stood up, then offered his hand to help her to her feet and said, "I'm sorry, Terri."

Terri grabbed hold of one of the bookshelves along with Robert's hand and stood up.

She said, "Thank you, Robert…Why the rush?"

"Dilli's on the prowl and I was afraid she'd catch me and set me on fire."

Terri shook her head and said, "Oh for Christ's sake. Don't worry Robert. I'll have Norton install a fire hose out by the front desk."

Terri walked out of the stockroom and Robert tucked in his shirt.

Will picked up a pile of the newly arrived books and carried them out to the front of the store and Robert and Jenny resumed opening the boxes.

Jenny said, "That was quite a stunt, but if you ask me it was a pretty pathetic way to get into Terri's crotch."

Robert laughed and said, "Don't even talk that way, Jenny. Terri is like our mother and, even though she's hot as hell, no one wants to fuck their mother."

So Many Maybes · 77

"I don't know Robert. I know for a fact that there are some real motherfuckers out there."

Jenny picked up a stack of books and walked out of the stockroom to the front of the store and Robert followed her. Will and Wolf were standing next to the counter and trying to calm down an idiot customer who was enraged that one of the pages in a book he'd purchased had a bent corner.

As Robert and Jenny watched Wolf try to pacify the asshole bent-page-complaining customer, Dilli O walked up and stood next to Robert. With a smug look on her face, she seemed to be saying to herself, "*See I told you. I was right. Bent corners are unacceptable.*"

When Robert noticed her, he quickly moved to the other end of one of the discount-book tables.

To get rid of the complainer, Wolf smiled and gave the asshole a new copy of the book and apologized to him.

Wolf shook his head and said, "You're quite right my good sir, I'm so sorry this has happened to you. We diligently labor to catch these unfortunate anomalies in book binding quality. As soon as we unpack books from the box we inspect them to make sure that no pages are bent. But after we put them on the shelf, deviant criminals enter the store behind our backs and secretly deface one or more masterpieces of the printer's art. From the book's point of view, experiencing these surreptitious attacks is called 'getting bent.' Just last week we discovered that a rare and valuable copy of the book entitled *The Farmers Guide to Chicken Choking* got bent. Again, my dear sir, here is your new copy. If we can be of any further service to you, please

So Many Maybes · 78

don't hesitate to ask."

The bent-page dickhead took the new book from Wolf and checked it carefully to make sure that it had no bent pages. Meanwhile Wolf made a big show of flipping the offending bent-page book over his shoulder without looking. It went in a perfect arc, up and over the counter, and landed right in the center of the waste basket. Once the man was satisfied, he turned and left. Amazingly, he never detected Wolf's outrageous sarcasm.

With the bent-page confrontation over, Dilli O walked away from the counter and went to the far corner of the store to resume placing the new books precisely in the center of each shelf. Will kept a careful eye on Dilli while he took the offending book out of the trash and hid it under the counter. He knew that if Dilli noticed that he'd rescued it, she'd take it and throw it away again.

Will shook his head and said, "I swear Wolf, how do you get away with talking to someone like that and not have them strangle you?"

"Will my friend, it is generally a matter of applying a broad vocabulary combined with stylish presentation. But in this case, the man was simply an idiot."

Robert leaned against the counter and watched Dilli O work.

He said, "Wolf, what kind of body do you think Dilli has under those horrible clothes?"

Wolf said, "Sadly Robert, I'm not sure the unfortunate and remarkably unpleasant woman has a body. Indeed, I've

So Many Maybes · 79

never noticed any indication of it. And since I am the world's greatest admirer of the female anatomy, if anyone would notice her body, it would be me. With that triangular shaped heavy blouse-skirt combination she's a five-foot, ten-inch pyramid as precisely shaped as those in the Valley of the Kings in Egypt."

Still studying Dilli O, Robert said, "You might be right Wolf, but if you look real close you can see that her chest juts out."

Will said, "Robert, I can't see her well enough from so far away. Maybe you should go over there and try to measure her bust line."

"Fuck you, Will."

Jenny studied Dilli O and then moved a couple of steps away from the counter to get a clearer view. She held her hands against her face and pretended she was looking at Dilli through a pair of binoculars.

She said, "You're absolutely right, Robert. With my carefully trained painter's eye, I can see that Dilli's chest severely alters her otherwise perfect pyramidal shape and her nipples are visible through those armor-plated clothes...so she must have really big tits."

To his horror, Robert's tail wiggled a little and he said, "Oh shit! I'm getting interested."

He looked down and put his hands over his eyes and shook his head and said, "I'm looking at Dilli O as if she was a woman and not a religious artifact. Oh God, I must be going crazy. What's happening to me?"

Jenny moved her make-believe binoculars and looked at Robert's crotch and said, "Robert, I think you're getting a

So Many Maybes · 80

hard-on looking at Dilli O."

"Kiss my ass, Jenny. I'm going in back."

Jenny said, "I'm right Bee-Hind you Robert."

They walked back to the stockroom. When they got there, Jenny turned her back to Robert and pretended to sort books while he leaned against the door jam and looked out at the front counter.

He said, "You know Jenny I have a good life. I have great friends like you and Will and Terri and Wolf and Nort and I would still love a book whether some of the corners of the pages were bent or not. Life is too precious to worry about stupid shit like that."

Meanwhile Jenny had surreptitiously unbuttoned her blouse and she suddenly turned around and flashed her tits at Robert and shouted, "How about it. Mine or Dilli O's!?"

For a moment Robert stood stunned. Then he laughed and made a move toward her and she quickly ran into the back of the stockroom.

Robert ran after her and said, "Come here, you fucking tease."

Jenny stayed a few steps in front of him and loudly said, "Stay away from me numb nuts."

Terri walked by the stockroom and heard them and went in to see what was going on. With her blouse wide open, Jenny ran right by Terri. Robert, however ended up face-to-face with her. Terri looked at him sternly and made him feel stupid.

She said, "Robert, I'm disappointed in you. Jenny can't help it, she's just a kid, but I thought you were more responsible."

So Many Maybes · 81

Barely able to contain his laughter, Robert said, "Uhhh...I'm sorry Terri."

Terri said, "If you two are going to fuck, I expect to be invited. After all, I am your boss. And we'll go do it in my station wagon like sex starved teenagers. We can't do it in here. Norton might see us and have a heart attack."

Terri walked out of the stockroom saying, "Jenny, button your blouse. You've got fabulous tits, but Robert has work to do."

After she left, Robert quickly headed into the back of the stockroom and went around the end of the shelves until he was out of Jenny's sight. He stood in the corner and faced the wall to do penance like he was a ten-year-old who was caught playing pocket pool during class. He had to remain there for some time because he was as hard as Dilli O's armor-plated clothes. Although he had developed better control over his wagging tail since those early days when MaryJane's slightest touch gave him a zipper bursting hard-on, there was only so much he could take. And the sight of Jenny's amazing tits made his guilty appendage go stiff every time.

After a suitable period of self-inflicted mental punishment, during which time he lost his erection, he walked back to the stockroom door and looked out at Dilli. He shook his head because she really did appear to have big tits.

While Jenny buttoned her blouse, she walked up behind Robert and said, "It's your turn, Big Boy. Show me your cock?"

She reached around him and tried to grab his crotch and Robert repeatedly slapped her hand away.

So Many Maybes · 82

Up at the front counter, Wolf and Will heard him shout, "God dammit Jenny!"

Chapter 6
Clarkson

Sometimes Will and Wolf needed super-human patience. As anyone who has ever dealt with the public knows, people who work in customer service must satisfy a wide variety of people ranging from kind and well behaved to the most wretched, horrifying individuals that legally walk the streets. But Will and Wolf were good at their job and nothing seemed to phase them. Occasionally though, something truly extraordinary would happen. Probably the most outrageous incident occurred when an obviously frustrated woman put in an order for a book entitled *Peace at Last, Secrets for Making Your Newborn Baby Sleep Through the Night* by someone named Dr. B.D. Nakamura.

The special orders were kept in the stockroom and Will went to get it for her. When he saw the title of the book and saw the woman's face he felt bad for her.

He said, "I gather your baby cries at night?"

The woman took the book from Will with trembling hands and opened it to the first page and said, "Yes, my baby cries."

Still being sympathetic, Will said, "My parents say I cried a lot when I was a baby."

The woman grasped the book tight in both hands and her face turned red and she started to shake with rage and glared at him and shouted, "YOU!!!"

Her sudden fierceness startled Will, but he kept his composure.

He said, "Please Miss, I didn't mean to. I was just a bab…"

Will didn't finish because the woman had transformed into a screaming lunatic and hit him in the face with the heavy hardback book.

She shouted, "It's in Japanese! FUCKING JAPANESE!"

Will stumbled backward and held up his arm to protect himself from her repeated bibliographic blows.

He said, "But Miss, I thought you knew that it was in Japanese when you..."

He stopped speaking when she hit him in the face with a hard, right-left-right combination book smacking, and gave him a bloody nose.

The enraged mother kept swinging at him and shouting, "YOU FUCKING IDIOT! MY BABY'S A DEVIL'S DEMON AND YOU GIVE ME A JAPANESE BOOK! FUCKING JAPANESE!!!"

Everyone in the store heard the woman's tantrum and the customers stood around and watched as if it was some form of street theater.

When Wolf and Robert and Terri and Jenny and Nort heard the noise, they rushed to see what was happening.

By the time they arrived, Will was on his back and the woman was sitting on his chest and repeatedly hitting him on the forehead with the book and shouting, "JAPANESE! JAPANESE! YOU MORON!"

So Many Maybes · 86

As gently as he could while still keeping control of her, Robert grabbed the maniacal woman around the shoulders and pulled her backward off Will. The woman struggled violently to break loose.

She shouted. "Get your hands off my tits you pervert!"

She tried to slip down and out of his arms, so Robert tightened his grip and pulled her up and closer to him. Unfortunately, he pulled her right over his own feet and he fell backward on a bookshelf full of magazines which in turn fell on top of the two of them and covered them like a shutting trap door. Underneath the shelves, the woman kept squirming and shouting obscenities and elbowing the defenseless Robert.

He kept calmly saying, "It's alright miss. They'll get these shelves off in a moment."

After an eternity, Robert felt the shelves move. Nort and Wolf lifted the shelves and moved them to the side revealing a prostrate Robert firmly hugging the madly elbowing and kicking sleep-deprived mother.

She started shouting, "Let me go you creep! You're raping me! You're dry humping me you pervert. This is rape!"

A police officer took hold of her and subdued and cuffed her and relieved a *Good Housekeeping Magazines* covered Robert from his battle with the over-the-edge, Japanese-hating, young mother from hell.

Blinded by the bright overhead store lights, Robert blinked his eyes and saw that a police officer the size of Batman was standing over him. The officer reached out his hand and helped Robert get up. When Robert got to his feet, he saw that the

So Many Maybes · 87

officer was a woman, a giant of a woman.

With a strong, deep, almost masculine voice she asked, "Are you alright sir?"

Robert ran his hands through his hair and started to tuck in his shirt.

He said, "Yes, I'm okay. Man, that woman was nuts!"

"I'm Sergeant Jordan Clarkson of the AAPD. What's your name sir?"

"Robert Bain, Officer."

Sgt. Clarkson was huge; nearly seven-feet tall with broad shoulders. She was so big that she towered over Robert like an NFL linebacker giving an autograph to an eight-year-old.

"Mr. Bain, could you tell me why you were under those shelves with that woman. It didn't appear to me that you were raping her like she said, but you did have your hands on her breasts."

Robert shook his head and started to stutter out an answer.

Terri stepped in and said, "Officer, Robert wasn't doing anything wrong. He was only trying to keep that woman from beating Will to death with her book."

"And you are?"

"I'm Theresa Bernini. I manage this store."

Sgt. Clarkson asked, "And who is this Will?"

Still holding a tissue up to his bleeding nose, Will said, "I am, Officer."

"What is your full name, Will?"

Will hesitated then said, "Please Officer, do you really need my full name?"

So Many Maybes · 88

"Yes I do sir. I wouldn't ask for it if I didn't need it. Why are you reluctant to give it to me? Are you a fugitive?"

"No mam, nothing like that."

"Don't call me mam. Call me Sergeant. Let me ask again. Why are you reluctant to give your full name to me?"

"It's an embarrassing name, Sergeant"

"I still need it, embarrassing or not."

Will said, "Okay…my full name is Will B. Free," and he braced himself for the inevitable laughter and smart-ass ridicule he'd endured since he was a kid.

Ridicule didn't come, but Sgt. Clarkson stopped writing and slowly looked up and barely stifled a grin and asked, "Will B. Free?"

"Yes Mam."

She brusquely corrected him, "Sergeant."

"Sorry. Sergeant."

"You wouldn't be joking with me would you Mr. Will?"

Terri interjected, "He's telling the truth officer. I know. I prepare his tax forms. He comes from San Francisco."

Sgt. Clarkson nodded as if the fact that coming from San Francisco clearly explained such an odd name.

Clarkson continued, "Now Mr. B Free, can you tell me exactly what transpired here? Why did this woman start hitting you with the book? Did you sexually assault her?"

Will jumped back in surprise and said, "Oh hell…ahhh… no."

He then related the ridiculous story of how the poor sleep-deprived young mother of a constantly crying "Infant Demon

So Many Maybes · 89

From Hell" went ballistic and how she started hitting him with a hardback book written in Japanese. And how Robert had saved him by stopping her.

*

THE JOURNAL OF ROBERT BAIN
Sgt. Clarkson was in her late thirties and wasn't wearing make-up and her hair was short. Judging from her well-muscled body, she was a strong macho woman who spent ample time in the gym lifting weights and pounding the heavy bag with rib crushing body blows. I have no doubt that she was tough enough to beat the shit out of most men and wouldn't take crap from anyone. But as I looked closer I noticed that besides being big and pro-wrestler strong, she was an attractive woman, a college town Amazon in uniform.

*

As the police took the angry crazy woman away, Sgt. Clarkson looked at Robert.

She said, "Mr. Bain, you should be commended for your actions. You showed bravery and proper restraint while subduing a potentially dangerous perpetrator. Have you thought about becoming a Police Officer?"

"What? Me a cop? I can't even do twenty pushups and I'm so clumsy I can hardly cross the street without tripping on my own feet."

For the first time since she'd entered the store, she smiled and said, "Some proper training can easily solve those problems, Mr. Bain. Here's my card. Contact me if you'd like to pursue an

So Many Maybes · 90

exciting career in law enforcement or even if you only want to just visit the station. The force could use a good man like you."

As Sgt. Clarkson left the store, Jenny said, "She was fun. What do you think that business about visiting the police station meant? You hardly look like the cop type."

Robert said, "I don't know. It was weird."

Jenny said, "You know what I think, Big Boy?"

Robert grinned and fed Jenny the straight line she obviously wanted, "What's that Hot Stuff?"

"I think she saw your big night stick and she wants it inside her special police unit."

Nort looked up suddenly and Wolf and Will nearly collapsed in laughter.

Robert gave Jenny a crooked smile and said, "Oh kiss my ass Hot Stuff."

"Okay Big Boy. Drop your pants."

Terri laughed too but said, "Shush you too. There are customers in the store."

Robert hurried to the back of the store and Jenny followed him.

After they disappeared into the stockroom and when Grafton's was dead silent, everyone heard Robert shout, "God dammit, Jenny!"

And browsing customers looked up to see where the noise was coming from.

So Many Maybes · 91

Chapter 7
Brett

Every evening after work, Robert went to Maybe's and waited
for Bunny to return to the café. He sat in his booth at the
back and tried to write in his journal. But he never did much
writing. Instead, he sat glum faced, drank rum and cokes, and
stared at the door, hoping she'd walk in.

*

THE JOURNAL OF ROBERT BAIN

*I knew that my obsession with Bunny had gone on long
enough. I wasn't doing anything but sit, wait, and drink.
Worst of all, I wasn't writing. But still, each evening, I
returned to Maybe's and continued waiting for her to walk
through the door. Sometimes I thought about why she
captivated me so powerfully. At first the question seemed
easy to answer. She was beautiful, she was fun to be with,
and she openly stated her desire to have sex with me. But
why was she so much fun to be with? For me, a writer,
I think it was her unique style of conversation. Virtually
everything she said came as a surprise, either in content
or style and sometimes both. Even though I felt like I was
an actor in a comedic play without knowing my lines, I
knew I could relax because I was confident that she could
carry the show by herself.*

One night, the waitress in black sat down in Robert's booth and leaned back and said, "So you're a Hemingway fan?"

"How would you know that?"

"I saw you looking at his pictures on our wall."

"You're right, I am a fan."

"So am I…I'm Brett. I own this place."

Robert grinned and said, "Sure you are. And my name is Jake Barnes."

Brett was the name of the principle female character in *The Sun Also Rises* and Jake Barnes was Brett's lover and the narrator in the novel.

She said, "So you've read the book?"

"Seen the movie too, but the book was better"

"Aren't they always?"

"What's your real name Lady Brett?"

"It's really Brett. My mother was obsessed with Hemingway. She claimed he banged her once on a pontoon boat on Walloon Lake."

"Good story."

Brett said, "I doubt it's true."

"Whether it's true or not, it's a good story. Every family needs its legends."

She said, "I've seen you here several times. Why do you always sit back here in the corner?"

"I've been lost in my own head lately."

Brett said, "Since you're a Hemingway fan let me point out a couple of pictures you might have missed."

So Many Maybes · 94

She stood up and led Robert to various points along the wall behind the booths.

"These photos came from stuff that my mother collected. There's too many but I don't have the heart to throw any of them out."

Robert moved closer to get a better look.

He said, "I recognize the ones of Hemingway and Kerouac. They were on the jacket covers of *The Old Man and the Sea* and *On the Road*. My high school teacher gave them both to me as graduation presents."

"Thoughtful teacher."

"She was, I mean is. I still hear from her. She's good friends with my sister."

Brett said, "My mother met both Kerouac and Hemingway, and, like I said, she claimed that she slept with Hemingway."

"Sometimes, if you repeat a lie often enough, it becomes true."

Brett nodded and said, "There's no harm in innocent lies. They make life more fun."

Robert said, "That's what fiction is."

Robert noticed that one Hemingway photo was autographed. He bent down to read the inscription.

It said, "I fucked Maybe Winters."

Robert looked up and said, "Subtle."

"My mother was never subtle."

"This place is named after your mother?"

Brett nodded and said, "She bought it after my dad died and we ran it together until she passed away two years ago.

I've run it since...Here is a photo of Ava Gardner and Tyrone Power who played Brett Ashley and Jake Barnes in the movie."

Robert removed the picture from the wall and held it up beside her and compared the real-life Brett to the movie-star Brett.

He said, "You're much better looking than Ava Gardner and your tits blow hers away."

She smiled and said, "Subtle."

The phone behind the bar rang. Mike, the bartender, answered it and signaled to Brett.

She said, "Excuse me, Jake," and walked over to Mike who handed her the phone.

Robert returned to his booth.

*

THE JOURNAL OF ROBERT BAIN

I watched Brett while she talked on the phone and thought that she was as enjoyable to talk to as she was to look at. Brett was probably about the same age as my mother, but she seemed to come from another generation. My mother was trapped in 1950's housewife slavery: undereducated, unconfident, and unappreciated. Brett was modern: well read, strong and probably loved by everyone she met.

She handed the phone back to Mike and returned to my booth and sat down again.

She said, "What's your real name Jake"

"Robert."

She slowly shook her head and said, "Too bad."

So Many Maybes · 96

"Why?"

"Robert Cohn in Hemingway's book wasn't a likable character."

"Luckily my last name is Bain, not Cohn."

"I think Jake suits you better. So tell me what's bugging you? You always look like a guy with a painful hernia caused by the weight of his own balls."

I raised his eyebrows and grinned at her clever and colorful comment.

I said, "A few weeks ago, I met a beautiful and exotic woman here, and when she left I screwed up and I didn't get her phone number. I've been coming back here every night since, hoping to run into her again."

Brett frowned and asked, "You don't mean that little blond that you fell into over by the bar?"

"So you remember her."

"Bunny is impossible to forget. She's completely crazy."

"That's my problem. I can't forget her either."

Brett shook her head and moved around the booth and sat close to me and put her hand in my lap.

She said, "You met that weird ditz once and lost your mind, but you see me here every night and don't even say hi?"

She appeared to be flirting with me, but I wasn't sure. If a joke was coming, I couldn't see it, so I decided to play along with her.

I attempted to keep a straight face and said, "I know Brett but, to be honest, you scare me."

So Many Maybes · 97

"Why?'

"Because you're so hot that I'm afraid you'll engulf me and melt my cock and balls into yellow weenie dribble."

She leaned toward me and said, "I know I'm hot, Jake, but don't worry, I won't engulf you. But I am willing to drag you into my office and give you a two-hour blowjob to the musical accompaniment of three tubas playing Mussorgsky's 'Night on Bald Mountain' from 'Fantasia.'"

"Uhhh..."

"It's a good offer. Think about it."

"Uhhh...."

She said, "I can feel that you like the idea and it'll be easy for me. Your hammer is nothing compared to my husband's."

My heart sank, and my dick shriveled, and I asked, "How would you know that?"

"Because he's six-feet, ten inches tall and he's hung like an Amish stallion. His hammer hangs down to his knees."

"Must be hard to walk."

She said, "Walking's no problem, but when he turns around fast, the swinging hammer head flies at me like a bowling ball on a rope and can knock me on my ass."

"Does sound like a problem. Maybe you should cut it off. Might be useful as a wrecking ball."

"The next time he's in town, I'll talk to him about it."

"Why isn't he in town?"

"He travels for his work."

"What kind of work?"

So Many Maybes · 98

"He's a hockey player."

I asked, "Hockey player?"

She nodded.

"What position does he play?"

"He's an Enforcer?"

"Enforcer?"

She answered, "He specializes in beating the shit out of the other team's players."

"Sounds like a nice guy."

"He's not."

"Why did you marry him?"

"I already told you"

"Tell me again."

"He's hung like an Amish stallion. But he's insanely jealous of any man I talk to."

I felt nauseous and gulped hard and almost shit my pants.

She must have noticed and decided to give me a break because she said, "Jake, I'm not really married. I am involved with someone though."

I was incredibly relieved and said, "I'm not surprised. Like I said, you're really hot."

"That's what my girlfriend always says."

"So you're gay."

"No. I just said that to get a rise out of you."

"You already did. You felt it."

"I did feel it and I'd like to feel it again. How about Sunday night...You're not religious are you?"

So Many Maybes · 99

"Hardly."

Then the fucking phone rang again, and Mike motioned to her. She got up and returned to the bar.

Although amusing, our tongue and cheek exchange confused me. I wasn't sure whether she was seriously interested in me or not, but I had to find out. I decided to go sit next to her and continue our conversation.

As Robert stood up to leave his booth, he knocked his pencil off the table and it rolled away. He tried to catch up with it, but he stumbled and stepped on the pencil and fell backward, feet to the sky, like a silent film comedian.

He landed flat on his back with a loud, "*UNH!*"

Brett slowly sauntered over to where Robert was lying on the floor. He was groaning and hardly moving.

She looked down at him and calmly said, "Thank you for that pratfall Jake. It was reminiscent of Buster Keaton or Charlie Chaplin and was very amusing."

Robert could hardly breathe but he slowly got to his feet.

Brett smiled and said, "You'll have to excuse me now. I have work to do."

Robert nodded and watched her disappear into the back room of the café and he returned to his booth.

*

THE JOURNAL OF ROBERT BAIN

After talking to Brett, I realized that there were other women in the world that were as great as Bunny, and it was foolish for me to obsess over her.

So Many Maybes · 100

It was time for me to get on with my life.

*

Chapter 8
Camille

Robert continued going into Maybe's every evening after work, but he no longer obsessed over Bunny. He went in to write and talk to Brett and he hoped to finally start meeting other writers which was his purpose for going into Maybe's in the first place. On one of those evenings, he walked into the café and saw Camille standing behind the bar. It appeared to be her first day of work because Brett was showing her around. Camille was so beautiful that Robert lost track of where he was and tripped on a chair leg and crushed his nuts by slamming his groin into the corner of a table.

Everyone in the restaurant looked up when they heard him shout, "Unhhh...Fuck!"

Red faced and obviously in pain, he limped to his booth in the back and sat down and tried to catch his breath. Fortunately for Robert's pride, Camille hadn't noticed him making a fool of himself.

While he sat in the back and waited for his genitals to quit screaming, he watched Camille go about her work.

*

THE JOURNAL OF ROBERT BAIN
She was about 19 years old, only slightly older than Jenny but the difference between them was obvious and

profound. Jenny was still a teenager; a cute as hell tomboy, full of play and the prettiest girl in school that all young men wanted for their girlfriend. Camille was a worldly woman with the confidence and grace that could only have come from experience. She wasn't just beautiful to see, she was an event to witness. Even if I never see her again, I will remember her face for the rest of my life. Neither Bunny nor Bonnie could compare. Camille was tall, about 5 feet 11 inches, with thin arms and long thin legs. Her breasts were nicely prominent but not huge and swayed from side to side with every step she took. Her soft elbow-length chocolate-brown hair flowed around her neck and over her left shoulder until it spread thinly over the middle of her left breast. Her face was a long oval with high cheek bones and her lips were thin and narrow and delicate. She wasn't wearing much make-up that I could see except for what appeared to be a trace of pink blush over her cheeks and some mascara and eye liner to add some drama to her smooth lightly tanned face. Her lipstick was a faint red.

Because of her height, Camille's body looked deceptively slim, but it was tight and firm and curvaceous enough to be at home on the high fashion runways in Paris, New York, or London. In fact, after watching the way she moved, I was dead certain that she was a model recently and could return to modeling whenever she wanted.

Watching her made me ask the question, "What is it about fashion models that make them so attractive?" I think it's more than the fact that runway models are

So Many Maybes · 104

beautiful. I think it's the apparent self-confidence, almost arrogance, that they project with their movements and lack of facial expression. It's as if they are announcing to the world, "I'm better looking than you or anyone you've ever known. Look at me and eat your heart out." But they're also offering us a challenge. "I know you want me, because all men do, so if you've got the balls, go ahead and make a move on me. But beware. I am like a beautiful leopard. Try to approach me and you are taking a risk. On the one hand, I might find you interesting enough to speak with you. And if I think you're worthy of my company, I might let you come close and be seen with me. And if you're really special, maybe I'll even sleep with you. But if I don't like the way you look or act, my reaction would be as unpredictable as that of any other wild animal. I might be kind and simply walk away or I might coldly attack you and humiliate you and chew up your ego and spit it into my toilet and make it swim along with my gorgeous shit that doesn't stink."

*

Even though Robert suspected that he had punctured his ball sac on the corner of the bar table, and even though he definitely didn't think he was "special," he couldn't help but put his ego on the line and accept Camille's challenge. No reward was possible if he didn't try. After he finally regained his normal speaking voice, he moved up to the bar and ordered his routine rum and coke.

So Many Maybes · 105

*

THE JOURNAL OF ROBERT BAIN

When I got nearer to her, I could see the model-beautiful challenge clearly presented in her eyes. They were large and round, haunting, freakishly dark brown eyes. They weren't normal human eyes. They were almost black, impenetrable, wild animal eyes. They taunted me, challenged me to take a risk and begin a perilous voyage to an unknown destination that was too far over the horizon for me to see before I set sail. A journey to a place that could yield me unimaginable treasure, or just as likely, great suffering and misery.

However, I was reasonably sure that, if I did become ship wrecked, I was a good enough swimmer to remain afloat in a commode long enough for my friends to find and rescue me. But unfortunately, after I moved up to the bar, Camille's beauty intimidated me more than I thought it would. I felt like a peasant in the presence of the Queen and I was too chicken to say anything to her. For the rest of the evening, I watched her as she worked. I also tried to listen in on her conversations with other customers, but she seldom talked.

Most female bartenders that I've encountered are outgoing with customers and flirt with the men to get bigger tips. Camille was different. She left people to themselves unless they asked her for a drink. When they did, she said little and gave them what they wanted. Otherwise she quietly and efficiently went about her

So Many Maybes · 106

duties. She never smiled but the shape of her combined facial features created the illusion that she was. Although she didn't come off as arrogant, she oozed that model-beautiful confidence. She knew she was gorgeous and she was comfortable with people like me staring at her. And I suspect that she was tipped well, whether she flirted or not. We live in a world where a woman is often rewarded simply because she is beautiful.

*

It took several days before Robert found the courage to speak to Camille. Coincidentally, on the very day that he had resolved to finally act, he witnessed her give a man that dreaded model shutdown. Robert had just arrived at Maybe's and sat down at the bar when the man asked her out.

Even though the man was only slightly rude, Camille soundly humiliated him. She faced him coldly and stared into his eyes and skewered him by loudly saying, "Look in the mirror behind me. Do you honestly think that an ugly man like you has a chance with a woman who looks like me?"

The man must have felt like he'd been kicked in the stomach. He appeared to stop breathing and his jaw dropped. Then he shook his head, paid up and left.

Watching Camille hammer a guy with so much force did nothing to inspire confidence in Robert. Rather, it convinced him that if he was going to put a move on her, he'd better be careful. If he wasn't and said the wrong thing, wholesale mother fucking rejection was almost a sure thing. Unfortunately, it was impossible to know what the wrong thing or even the right

So Many Maybes · 107

thing was to say, so he sat at the bar and drank too much. After about two hours of staring at her and at least 152 rum and cokes, Robert finally found the courage to introduce himself. Although he was thoroughly drunk, he managed to stay clear headed enough to proceed cautiously. He surely didn't want to irritate her in any way and be invited to look at himself in the bar mirror.

"Hi. My name is Robert."

Without expression, Camille coldly looked at him and said, "I'm Camille."

"Where are you from Camille?"

She studied him for so long that Robert had almost shit his pants in anticipation of inevitable humiliation when she finally answered.

She said, "Nowhere. What about you?"

Robert thought, *"Okayyy...this is going to be rough."*

He said, "I'm from Grand Rapids."

She only nodded and waited for him to say more.

He asked, "What brought you to Ann Arbor?"

She answered succinctly, "School at U of M," and didn't volunteer anything else.

"Where did you live before you lived here?"

"In England."

"Where in England?"

"London."

Robert thought to himself, *"London. I might be right. Maybe she was a model."*

He said, "Did you like it there?"

"Yes. Very much."

After that, she silently stood in front of him with her seductive, confident gaze and hypnotized him with her darkest of dark creepy eyes.

"Why did you leave?"

"My job ended."

The next question to ask her would have been obvious to him if he was sober, but Robert was too drunk to go on without giving the matter some thought. Since he also felt the call of nature, he got off his barstool and drunkenly staggered into the Men's Room and went into a toilet stall where he planned to sit and mentally map out his strategy. As soon as he sat down, the weight of his butt pressing on the toilet seat caused his famous gas main to explode and he let loose with a spectacular rumble of bowel thunder that was as loud as the finale of a Fourth of July fireworks display. It generated a massive sonic boom that raced through the heating ducts and out into the café where it made the walls and window's shake and caused everyone at the bar to go silent. There were even rumors that it was heard out in the Arcade but that was never confirmed.

If Robert could have seen Camille when he was back in the Men's Room blasting his toilet seat to bits, he would have witnessed her completely lose it and reveal that although she was model-perfect and as cold as a mountain glacier, she wasn't super-human. She had a sense of humor.

As it turned out, it was that earthquake of a fart that put a crack in Camille's frozen armor. When Robert sat down at the bar the next day, there was something different about her.

So Many Maybes · 109

She looked at him and said, "Hello Robert."

It was an exciting and unexpected moment for him because she had remembered his name. Then she astonished him.

Expressionless as usual, she said, "I have a gift for you."

Robert couldn't believe his ears. She had hardly spoken to him, but now she had a gift for him. With great anticipation, he said, "A gift?"

"Yes Robert, a gift for you."

She turned her back toward him and let a magnificent, loud, and screamingly feminine, high pitched fart that was perfectly controlled and seemed to go on for minutes. Then she turned around with a gleam in her eye and gave him the slightest of grins. She was obviously pleased with herself.

Robert was impressed. He knew he was in the presence of a fellow master. He laughed hard and applauded.

"Bravo. Bravo. Thank you for that kind gift Camille. We should get together and exchange gifts sometime."

With her grin still firmly in place, and with an exaggerated British accent she said, "Yes, my handsome Sir Robert, I'd love to."

Robert almost trembled at her apparent positive response and he continued, "After that, we should go out to eat and loudly discuss bodily functions."

This time with a perfect Irish accent she said, "Yes, Robert, as sure as the Sun rises over the Irish Sea we should. But we must do so with care. Because I am Irish, and it is certain that after our discussion we will be banished from polite society and be forced to wander the ends of the earth until we can finally find a place in Boston where we can settle down and take a decent shit."

Robert laughed. She was finally shedding her runway-model armor.

He leaned back and crossed his arms and said, "That sounds like an historically significant event to me. A culturally significant holiday should be declared to commemorate it."

"I agree. What should we call it?"

Robert said, "How about Thursday night?"

"That's a perfect name for such an important holiday."

Robert asked, "What time do you get off work?"

"Five thirty."

"Pick you up here at six?"

"Make it six thirty."

Robert smiled and said, "Then it is agreed. The newly declared holiday, now officially known as Thursday night, will begin at six thirty. Now, we must choose the appropriate way to celebrate."

Camille paused with a serious contemplative face, then slowly and cautiously said, "That is a matter that should be given much thought…but may I suggest that we enlist the University of Michigan Band to play *The Stars and Stripes Forever* while you fuck me in the ass out in the Arcade?"

Robert laughed so hard he fell backward off his barstool.

And so it was, that a romance between one of the most beautiful women in the world and a regular guy from Grand Rapids began, kindled by a fart.

So Many Maybes · 111

Chapter 9
Out With Friends

Robert wanted to make a good impression on his first date with Camille, and for the first time in his life he cared about how he dressed. Except for the shirt that Dana had bought him for work, his wardrobe was cheap crap. But he never felt the need to buy some nicer clothes. His wardrobe had never been an issue because cheap crap clothes were common and acceptable in Ann Arbor during the early 1970s, and he got along fine. But now he had a problem. He had to figure out what was appropriate attire for a date with a staggeringly beautiful woman who had probably walked down the fashion show runways in London, Paris, and New York, then he had to put together an outfit he could afford.

Robert had never seen Camille in anything but her work clothes, so he couldn't guess how she was going to dress. Of course, he could have just asked her, but he didn't want to do that. Perhaps rightly, he felt like he should have learned the proper way to dress by the time he was his age. But he hadn't, and he felt like a rube. He wasn't being completely fair to himself. No one had ever offered him that education. Having been brought up in a poor family in a poor neighborhood, he never had access to high quality, stylish clothes and neither did any of his friends. So he hadn't developed any fashion sense at all.

Although he didn't want to reveal his feelings of inadequacy to Camille, he wasn't afraid to ask Bonnie. And Bonnie was the best source of advice anyone could ask for. Bonnie was born in New York, she was rich, and she knew how to dress. The next evening, immediately after work, he sat down next to Bonnie at the theater where she was watching Wolf and Will and Baja, the set designer, discuss the staging for Wolf's new play, an adaptation of Dracula, that was opening later in the summer.

Bonnie said, "Right off the top of my head, if it was an ideal world, I'd say don't worry about it. She likes you, not your clothes."

"I wish that was true Bonnie, but women always care about how people dress whether they say so or not."

Bonnie smiled and said, "Unfortunately you're right. Let's go shopping and see what we can do."

"Right now?"

"No better time."

On their way to the thrift store, Bonnie gave him a great piece of advice.

"Robert the important thing is not to make a big deal about the way you dress. This is Ann Arbor and I know you're not going to something formal like a dinner party or a wedding or a funeral."

"Hardly."

"So relax and quit worrying about what's proper and concentrate on style. Style is what will impress Camille."

They went to several thrift stores and Bonnie attacked Robert's wardrobe problem with her normal fierceness. She would not give up. She went through every pile in every store. She searched all the racks, and checked every shoe, and by the end of the day, Bonnie had created Robert an outfit that was affordable and suited his personality well. Robert thought of himself as an artist, and all of his friends were artists. So Bonnie decided to build on that concept. As much as it irritated her, she used McSurly as a model. Although she hated McSurly, she could never deny that he was cool. McSurly had the cool artist look down to a science. Robert's outfit developed easily from there: a nice oversized white shirt and an almost new pair of brown sandals added to a decent pair of jeans. At the end of the day, he looked like a man worthy of the cover of a new magazine called *Second Hand Robert's Cool Artist Men's Quarterly.*

As they walked out of the last store, Bonnie said, "Robert your outfit is good enough. All you need now is a decent fucking haircut."

"That's hard. I'm like Will. My hair won't hold any shape."

"Just have a barber put it in order but don't let him cut it too short. If you got a short haircut, you'd look like a little boy."

On Thursday after getting his haircut, Robert got dressed and went over to Maybe's to pick up Camille.

When he walked in, Brett and Camille were standing together behind the bar.

Brett said, "Jake, you didn't need to get dressed up, Camille's just going to tear your clothes off later anyway."

Camille said, "Jake. That reminds me. I have to tell you something before we go out."

So Many Maybes · 115

Her serious tone concerned Robert, but he also suspected that she was setting him up for another deadpanned joke.

He braced himself and cautiously said, "What's that?"

"Although I joked about fucking in the Arcade, I never sleep with a man on our first date."

Despite his suspicions, Camille's apparent sincerity disarmed Robert.

"Why's that?"

"I've been hurt too many times."

Robert nodded and said, "I understand."

She smiled warmly and said, "I want to get to know you first. So far, you seem smart and kind, but I want to be sure."

"I understand."

"So tonight, I want to take it slow…real slow... while you jump me like a bull moose and pump my cunt until my clit explodes."

She caught Robert so off guard that a genuine thunderbolt went from his ears through his now paralyzed brain and his eyes crossed and he went momentarily blind and fire shot out of his wagging flame thrower. Then his entire body convulsed, and he fell backwards off his bar stool again.

Brett almost fell over backward too, but it was from laughing. She was still laughing when she went into her office.

Robert weakly got to his feet and leaned against the bar. Funny or not, falling off his bar stool was getting old.

After he caught his breath he said, "Camille…we need to figure out what we're going to do tonight."

Although Robert had tried repeatedly to get Camille to talk

So Many Maybes · 116

about herself, he'd gotten nowhere. And he still had no idea what kind of things would interest her. Every time he asked her about it, she dodged the question and asked him what he wanted to do. He finally quit asking and let her go about her work.

He walked down to the end of the bar and found a copy of *The Michigan Daily* newspaper. *The Michigan Daily* was the student newspaper of the University of Michigan. Although it was labeled as "student," the *Daily* was more than a student newspaper. It was a respected journal that included features on sports and editorials and commentary on University affairs and domestic and even international politics. It was also the place to find out what events were going on around Ann Arbor. Everyone that Robert knew read the *Daily*.

He sat back down at the bar directly in front of Camille while she cleaned the beer cooler.

He said, "Don't you have anything special you want to do tonight? After all, it's our first date."

"I already gave you my suggestion."

"I know, but I called the Michigan Marching Band director and I can't afford to hire them. Their standard fee for providing accompaniment for someone having anal sex in the Arcade is $100 and a crackerjack toy per band member. I might be able to handle the toys, but the forty grand is beyond my reach."

Camille said, "I understand. That is probably too expensive. I'd have to sell a lot of paintings to cover that. I didn't know it was such a large band."

"Four-hundred members."

So Many Maybes · 117

It took a moment for it to sink in, but when it did Robert looked up from his paper quickly.

He asked, "You're a painter?"

She said, "I am."

"Why didn't you tell me?"

"I'm a woman. I expect you to read my mind."

"You're right. I should have read your mind, but I was distracted."

"By what."

"By trying to imagine how great you looked when you walked down the fashion show runways."

Now it was Camille's turn to be surprised.

"How did you guess I was a model?"

"It was obvious. You look, move and have the facial expressions of a model."

"What does that mean?"

Robert stood up and faced her. He smiled then waved his hand over his face and pretended to wipe the smile off. Then he straightened his shoulders and dropped his arms to his sides and paraded back and forth along the bar. He made sure to put one foot directly in front of the other as he walked, and he exaggerated his hip and shoulder sway.

With probably the biggest smile on her face that Robert had ever seen, Camille said, "You look more like an effeminate designer looking for his boyfriend."

Robert gave her an ugly smirk and got back on his bar stool and asked, "Why did you stop modeling?"

"That's a long story. Let's wait and I'll tell you about it

So Many Maybes · 118

tonight at dinner."

"Okay. At least we have that settled."

"What?"

"If nothing else, were going to dinner and talk about your modeling."

Camille bent forward and put her hands in the sink to wash some glasses and Robert returned to looking through the newspaper for things to do on their date.

There were several possibilities. It was Open Mic Night at Maybe's where anyone who wanted to could get up on the stage and perform. Although that kind of thing can be fun, Robert immediately ruled it out because he assumed that Camille wouldn't want to spend her evening at the same place that she worked. At the music school, two famous Spanish guitarists were giving a free concert. He ruled that out too because it sounded boring as hell.

Going to a movie and dinner afterward seemed like it might be a good idea if he could find out what kind of movies she liked.

He lifted his eyes from the paper and looked at her and forgot what he was going to say because she was bent over washing the dishes, and he could see the upper half of her naked tits and nipples through the open top of her blouse. His tail wagged in surprise and he thought, *"Ohhhh...Flubba... Dubba!"*

After about ten minutes of similar mental stammering and paralysis, he took a deep breath, and suddenly blurted out, "Camille do you like boobies?"

So Many Maybes · 119

Even though by this time Robert felt relatively comfortable around Camille, he almost filled his pants with excess amounts of brown embarrassment and his brain screamed, *"Fuck!!!"*

With a straight face, Camille straightened up and without hesitation said, "Of course. Who doesn't? What about you? Do you like the great big ones that bounce like basketballs when a woman runs, or do you like the smaller but more shapely ones that move gracefully like mine?"

Robert laughed at himself hard and it took him a second to regain consciousness.

"I meant movies Camille."

"I know…I'm not a big movie fan but I like to go once and awhile."

He asked, "What kind of movies do you like?"

"I liked *Ryan's Daughter* a lot."

"What's that about?"

"It's a love story that takes place in Ireland. The photography is beautiful."

Then she quit talking and went back to her work washing glasses. She hadn't helped him much.

He asked her, "There's a bunch of movies showing around here but I don't know anything about them."

She dried off her hands and said, "Let me look at the paper."

She studied it for longer than Robert liked, and he was getting nervous. By the time she spoke, he was sure that he saw two flamboyantly dressed flamingo guitarists hanging in a thought bubble over her head.

She said, "I'd like to go see that Kung Fu movie called

So Many Maybes · 120

Wah-zoo, The Feminine Karate Master From Hell, that's playing over at the Fifth Forum. I read a review about it that said it was horribly violent and disgusting and I like that sort of thing."

"You do?"

"No. I was kidding. Kung Fu movies make me throw up."

Robert said, "I've never seen one."

"Don't. You'll probably throw up too."

Robert said, "That still leaves us with a problem."

"Let's stay here for Open Mic Night."

"You don't mind staying here?"

"Why would I mind?"

"You work here."

"That's right. I do work here."

"I assumed you'd want to get away."

"No problem for me. All my friends are here. Besides Brett said that she thinks that tonight is going to be more fun than usual."

Robert said, "Sounds good to me…Until then I'll go back to my booth and do some writing. When you're done with work, we can have dinner before the festivities start."

"Okay, but I've been working all day. I want to go to my apartment first and take a shower and change my clothes."

Robert said, "Why don't I go with you. We can come back here when you're done?"

She said, "If we did that, I'd jump you and we wouldn't go anywhere…Besides, I live right upstairs."

Robert said, "Say Camille, I have a question."

"What's that?"

So Many Maybes · 121

"Why are you calling me Jake. I know why Brett is, but not you."

"Brett told me, and I agree with her. Jake is a better name. From now on, I might call you Jake. Think of it as a sign of endearment."

Robert nodded. "I guess I'll have to come up with a name for you then."

"Make it a good one."

He said, "I'm considering Fanny."

Brett came out of her office and took over the bar until Mike was due to arrive and Camille ran around the bar and gave Robert a quick kiss on the cheek.

She said, "Fanny won't work. I don't have one. Ask Brett for some suggestions."

Camille went out the door to go up to her apartment and Robert asked, "Brett, this is the second time since I came in here that women have changed my name. First Bunny and now you two."

Brett said, "Bunny changes everyone's name."

Robert said, "She does?"

Brett said, "She calls me Bust."

"Fitting."

"Jake, you're not as subtle as Robert."

Robert asked, "Is that good or bad?"

Brett answered, "Good."

When Camille came down from her apartment, she was dressed surprisingly like Robert. She had on an oversized

So Many Maybes · 122

grey silk shirt that she wore over black tights and conservative leather wrap sandals. She had unbuttoned the top four buttons of her shirt and gathered it around her waist with a gold chain with an onyx stone fastener and wore long dangling onyx ear rings.

When Robert saw her, a wave of pleasure rushed up his spine to his brain like a shot of heroin. She looked sensational and he knew he had dressed perfectly for their date. Of course, he didn't know that Camille had deliberately dressed to give him that feeling. She was an expert with clothes and she had been with enough men to know exactly what to do. She wanted him to feel good about himself when he was with her.

Later at dinner, Camille studied the menu that she knew by heart and suggested, "Why don't we share a pizza?"

"Okay. Anything special you want on it?"

Camille said, "Just the normal things. You know, pepperoni, hamburger, maybe some tomatoes. What do you want?"

"I get the same thing every time…I like it made in layers. First a heavy layer of Swiss cheese, then marinara sauce, then a layer of hamburger, more marinara sauce, then a heavy layer of baked beans, pepperoni, onion, more baked beans."

Camille sat silent and stared at him.

He said, "What can I say? I like beans."

She said, "I gathered. Are you trying to turn me on? Beans are famous for causing farts and you know how much I love it when you fart. You're so good at it."

He said, "So are you. How old were you when you started?"

She said, "I blossomed early. I started at age three."

So Many Maybes · 123

Robert said, "That is early. Where did you study?"

"At the local theater during kid's movies on Saturday mornings. If it was too crowded, one of my special butt yodels would clear twenty seats and make Flash Gordon leave the universe."

He laughed and said, "Did you use loud ones or the silent but deadly ones?"

"As loud as possible. Loud ones were more fun. Besides I was a kid so I could get away with it."

Robert shook his head. "What a success story. From Super Butt Yodeler to Super Model."

Camille said, "Robert, all you've told me about yourself is that you're from Grand Rapids. What do you do for a living."

It suddenly dawned on Robert that he'd been so intent on learning things about her that he hadn't talked about himself. But then again, she'd never asked him either.

"I work in a bookstore, but I think of myself as a writer."

She said, "I can understand that. I work in a bar, but I think of myself as a painter. I've seen you writing in your notebook. What are you writing now?"

"It's my *Journal*. When I meet people or I'm somewhere or doing something that I think is interesting, I record the events and write down my thoughts about them."

She asked, "Do you plan to turn those thoughts and events and people you write about in your diary into a book?"

"Maybe. Right now, I just think of it as my writing that I'll do something with when the time seems right."

She said, "I do the same thing with my painting. When I

So Many Maybes · 124

see something I like, I make sketches and write notes on them. Then, I paint from my sketches and notes."

"What kind of paintings do you do?"

"Landscapes mostly. I'm not good at drawing people. I like to paint the ocean, especially in wild dramatic weather."

"Can I see your paintings?"

"Only if you'll let me read your journal."

Robert swallowed hard. He felt trapped. He sincerely wanted to see her paintings, but he was afraid to let her read his writing. He'd never let anyone read his writing because he was terrified they wouldn't like it. But if he refused to let her read his *Journal*, she could interpret it as a sign that he wasn't interested in her art, so he had no choice but to say yes and accept the consequences.

He said, "Of course."

She said, "What bookstore do you work in?"

"Grafton's. It's right down the street from The Brown Jug. When I first moved here, I wanted to work in one of the smaller used bookstores, but now I'm glad I ended up at Grafton's. I've made several really good friends there and I'm content."

"I'm content here too. I adore Brett. I love my apartment and I like my work."

An oversized and ominous bearded figure dressed in a black suit with an outrageous yellow and red paisley vest somehow appeared next to their table.

He said, "Although my ugliness is legendary, and I am as obnoxious as Andy Warhol, you have no choice but to let us join you."

So Many Maybes · 125

It was Wolf accompanied by Bonnie and Will and the blazingly hot exotic woman Robert had seen in the theater with them when he went to ask for Bonnie's help with his wardrobe.

Robert moved over to his left and said, "Wolf, I'm on a date with Camille, the most beautiful woman in the world, and she has rendered your astonishing ugliness powerless."

Wolf said, "Hello my dear Camille. I'm Wolf Rilke and I'm Robert's friend and coworker whether he wants me to be or not. These are my other reluctant friends Bonnie and Will and Baja."

Camille said, "Nice to meet you."

Robert barely heard Wolf introduce Baja. He was hypnotized. She was as tall and thin as Camille and had jet-black shoulder-length hair. Her facial features were irresistibly exotic, and she had incredible luminescent green eyes. She was dressed in a black silky-smooth closely-tailored outfit that showed off every detail of her body. Unlike Camille who captivated Robert with her mesmerizing perfect model face and movement, Baja made him vibrate like a giant sex toy and he wanted to leap across the table and fuck her insanely until his balls exploded.

He nervously said, "Baja...It's nice to meet you."

Baja nodded politely, "Wolf has mentioned you frequently."

"That's a scary thought."

Wolf said, "Baja has designed the sets and costumes for my new opus and she also has a prominent acting role, or should I say prominent body."

With only the slightest of smiles, Baja said, "Only prominent?"

So Many Maybes · 126

Wolf said, "I'm sorry my dear. The most prominent."

Will said, "Second only to Wolf's."

Robert said, "You're acting in this one Wolf?"

Bonnie said, "Not acting…just making his prominent presence known."

Wolf said, "Bonnie, my gorgeous friend, I'll have you know that I've been asked to pose for the centerfold of *Playboy*. The first man ever to do so."

Robert said, "Remind me to keep that issue off the shelf at the store…Camille, Wolf is a playwright and Will is a filmmaker and all around technical wiz. He's doing the sound and lights."

Camille said, "How about you Bonnie? Are you working on Wolf's play too?"

"Yes, I've got a prominent role too. Wolf insisted that I act. I'm considering moving before the play opens."

Will said, "I'm going with her. We're moving to France to study arrogant behavior."

Bonnie said, "But I also have the most important function. I read his plays and make sure they're weird enough."

Will said, "Bonnie is a filmmaker."

Robert added, "And a poet."

Bonnie said, "More poet than filmmaker."

Camille said, "Wolf, what's your new play about?"

Baja said, "It a satirical adaptation of *Dracula*."

Bonnie said, "More cosmic than satirical. Like everything that Wolf does, it comes from another planet."

Baja said, "Wolf and I get along well because my roommate is an extraterrestrial."

So Many Maybes · 127

Camille said, "Baja is an interesting name?"

Wolf and Bonnie answered in unison, "She's from San Francisco."

Camille answered, "Ahhh…"

Robert said, "Camille is a painter but before she moved here, she was a model."

Camille nodded and said, "For four years."

Bonnie asked, "What kind of work did you do?"

"I was a runway model."

Chapter 10
Open Mic Night

Brett walked up onto the stage to start the evening's festivities.

She said, "Good evening. For those of you who don't know me, I'm Brett Winters and I own Maybe's and I'd like to welcome you to our Open Mic Night where, I'm proud to say, just about anything can happen. Tonight we're going to present a program that is different from what we normally do because every one of the performers are cast members of Wolf Rilke's new play, an original adaptation of *Dracula*, that is opening later this summer. I'm afraid that Wolf is here with us tonight, hiding in the back. If you've ever seen one of Wolf's plays, you'd know what a genius he is, and you'll also know why he's hiding in the back."

Some of the audience laughed and everyone at Robert and Camille's table laughed even harder.

Robert said, "Wolf, I didn't know you knew Brett."

Wolf puffed up his chest and proudly said, "Robert my good friend, if I discover a place that serves good spirits and is frequented by beautiful women, you can be sure that every single woman there has been annoyed by me at least once. Besides it's impossible to come here without at least gawking at her."

Everyone at their table laughed again.

Brett said, "Bear with us for a moment. The first skit takes some preparation," then she walked back off the stage.

Will said, "Would you guys excuse me for a minute. I'm taking part in this one."

He walked up on the stage and joined a couple of other young men who were carrying a framework and a black cloth to fashion a curtain across the back of the stage. Then Will went across the room and stood up on a chair and took control of a small spotlight.

Brett walked back up on the stage and looked down toward the audience.

She said, "Wolf…is everyone ready?"

Wolf stood up and shouted, "Yes, my stunning well-constructed Brett, the mighty cast of my play stands at the ready to fully humiliate themselves in public. And as everyone knows, public humiliation is only another way of saying acting."

Brett called to the bartender, "Okay Mike."

Mike turned off the lights and there was a rustling up in front and on the stage. Music started. It was an orchestra playing *The William Tell Overture*. Then Will turned on the spotlight and pointed it at the edge of the curtain. Four women dressed in duck suits with big feathered tails and wearing Lone Ranger masks came out from behind the curtain riding on the shoulders of men who were dressed up as horses. Will followed them with the light as they pranced through the audience.

When the fourth duck reached Robert, she got off her horse and reached down and pulled him out of his chair. Then she climbed up on his back and leaned over and spoke into his ear.

So Many Maybes · 130

She said, "Take me for a long ride Big Boy…then show me your cock."

Robert turned his head quickly and said, "Jenny!?"

She slapped him on the ass and Robert took the cue and followed the other horses around the audience.

After they went behind the curtain, everyone in the café could hear Robert shout, "God dammit Jenny!"

The ducks and horses and Robert walked out on stage and took their bows grand thespian style. Brett walked back up on the stage and picked up the microphone.

She said, "Thank you everyone for that…uhhh…wonderful imitation of an old television classic. I'm sure that none of us will ever forget it."

She looked at the four frog clad women and said, "Where the hell did you get that idea?"

They all looked at each other and shouted together, "WOLF WROTE IT!"

Wolf stood up and took several formal bows and everyone clapped again.

Then a young man walked up onto the stage and sat down on a stool.

Brett said, "Now to my right is Michael Brown. Tonight, Michael is going to read a short story that I recently wrote while I was sitting behind the bar and ignoring some guy who was trying to explain to me why baseball is America's pastime. I've asked Michael to read it, because the story is narrated by a man and I'm often told that I don't look like a man."

Michael began by saying, "No doubt we've all watched a

So Many Maybes · 131

scene in the movies or on television where a traffic cop offers to ignore a woman's traffic offense if she will have sex with him. Brett thought it might be fun to reverse those roles and tell a story where it's a woman cop and a man who was speeding… The story is named *Captain Commander Invades Night Twat's Hidden Lair…*"

One afternoon, I was pulled over for speeding. I was extremely surprised because I was sure that I was going well under the speed limit, but I was taught to never argue with a traffic cop. The only prudent thing to ever do was to be polite, admit to the offense, apologize, and accept the inevitable ticket. So, as the officer walked up from behind me, I took a deep breath and mentally rehearsed what I was going to say. But when she stood next to me, I couldn't say a word. I only stared at her. She was a monster; at least seven-feet tall and probably over 275 lbs. of solid muscle.

She looked down at me and pulled up her utility belt.

With a surprising southern accent, she said, "Boy…I need to see your license and proof of insurance please."

"Excuse me?"

"Your license and proof of insurance please."

I answered as politely as I could.

"I'm sorry Officer, I don't have either. I wasn't aware that I needed them."

She looked at me sternly and nodded and wrote

So Many Maybes · 132

in her notebook.

She said, "Boy...Do you know why I pulled you over?"

I nervously looked up at her name tag and said, "No Officer Mount."

She said, "Boy...I clocked you going sixty-five in a twenty-five zone."

Although I knew better than to argue with her, I was positive that I wasn't going anywhere near that speed.

"But Officer Mount that's not possible. I'm..."

She pointed her palm at me and firmly said, "Stop!!!"

Then she paused and lifted her utility belt again and looked to the side and took a deep breath as if she was trying to get control of her temper.

She said, "Boy...Never argue with a police officer. Get off your bicycle and lean forward against that light pole and keep your hands where I can see them."

At that point, my annoyance was slowly growing into terror. She was a huge Amazon and she was obviously crazy. Only an insane person would give me a speeding ticket for going sixty-five mph on a bicycle. Unfortunately, I had no choice but to do as she asked and hope for the best.

Officer Mount walked up behind me and used her foot to kick my feet wide apart. Then she walked a full circle around me and nodded in approval as she went.

She stopped directly behind me and said, "Boy... Has anyone ever told you that you've got a nice ass?"

So Many Maybes · 133

I stood up and turned around and looked at her.

"No Officer. But thank you for saying so."

"You're welcome, Mr. Brown. Since you do have such a nice ass, I'm willing to give you a second chance if you'll have sex with me. Otherwise, I'll give you a ticket for driving without a license and proof of insurance and reckless driving. Should only add up to about $1000 in fines if you're nice to the judge."

I didn't have $100 let alone a thousand so I had no choice but to accept her offer.

I felt like a gigolo when I knocked at Officer Mount's apartment door that evening. When she let me in, I immediately wondered what the hell I was doing there. She was huge. Her shoulders were as wide as the door and I was fearful that my entire body would get lost inside the mammoth cave that was her vagina.

Still in uniform, she grabbed my arm with a strong grip and commanded, "Come with me."

I thought it was a nicely provocative order, but Officer Mount meant it literally and dragged me into her bedroom.

She said, "Mr. Brown, you and I are going to play a little game and change our names. Do you understand me?"

"Yes Officer Mount."

"For this game, my name is SuperCop and your name is Captain Commander. Got it?"

I nodded.

So Many Maybes · 134

She said, "Now let's give it a try. Who am I?"

"You're Off...ahh...?

She shook her head and said, "Try again."

I nodded sheepishly and said, "You're SuperCop."

"That's better. Now who are you?"

I felt ridiculous, but I kept a straight face and answered, "I'm Captain Commander."

She said, "Good."

She reached into her closet and handed me a weird uniform: a blue spandex nipple length half shirt with a huge policeman's badge painted on the front, a pair of tall black German jack boots with straps around the tops that looked as if they belonged on a NAZI storm trooper, and a white motorcycle cop's helmet with the letters CAPTAIN painted on it. Then she topped off the outfit with a pair of dark aviator sunglasses. She gave me no pants or underwear.

She said, "Take off all of your clothes, put these on and come back into the living room. Don't fuck around. I don't feel like waiting."

There was a full-length mirror on the closet door. I felt ridiculous when I saw myself. The outfit made me look like a poorly hung nude model on a police woman's locker room calendar. When I walked into the living room, SuperCop was standing in front of the couch still wearing her uniform. She told me to sit down and watch her undress. I wasn't sure what she had in mind, but if she expected me to get turned on, I was afraid

So Many Maybes · 135

that I was going to disappoint her because I still felt idiotic dressed as a bachelorette party stripper.

She didn't simply undress. Instead she put on a kind of theatrical performance. She stood about eight feet away and faced me. Then she took off her shirt. She was wearing two bras that were stretched to their maximum indicating that her breasts were much bigger than they normally appeared when she was in uniform. She paused for a moment then grabbed the bottom of the bras with both hands and forcefully and rapidly pulled them over her head. Her huge boobs launched away from her chest more powerfully than nuclear torpedoes. They pushed out more than ten inches from her body and were as firm as a body builder's pecks.

Then she pushed off her shoes and undid her belt. The combined weight of her police pistol and radio and handcuffs attached to her utility belt made her pants slam onto the floor faster than a blacksmiths hammer hitting an anvil. She wasn't wearing any underwear, so I was looking at a lightly hairy, municipal pubic playground. I was turned-on now.

She told me to take down a description of her and write it in my police officer's notebook. Unsure of what to write, I asked her how she would describe herself.

She said that she was a firmly muscled, seven-feet tall, 275-pound Caucasian female with short brown hair and humongous tits.

So Many Maybes · 136

I told her that I thought that was an accurate description.

She nodded once firmly in acknowledgment and said, "Understood."

Then she stood in front of me with her hands on her hips and grinned proudly. She looked like the huge-boobed feminine super hero that was typically on the cover of the kind of soft-core pornographic magazine that is commonly known as a kid's comic book. Then, I swear to God, there was a loud rumble of thunder and the lights in the room started to blink. Sgt. Mount's body turned a deep red, then a violent blast of heat lightning shot toward me and hit my erect grounding rod and knocked me over the back of the couch.

She walked over to me and bent down and grabbed me by my now rigid manhandle and yanked me up off the floor and pulled me to her. She looked down at me and gruffly asked me, "Now, do you remember who I am?"

"You're SuperCop."

"That's right and even though I'm a woman, I'm tough enough to really fuck you up."

I was even more worried then. She was strong enough to break me in half and I was dressed up in this stupid costume and she was telling me how tough she was. I sincerely hoped that she wasn't into the rough sadistic sex stuff. A terrifying image of me handcuffed to a bed with the barrel of a police revolver rammed up

So Many Maybes · 137

my ass flew through my head. Thankfully, that didn't happen.

She bent down so I didn't have to look up into her nostrils and she said, "Wait here."

Needless to say, I waited. When she returned she was wearing a pair of black tights with her head covered by a hood.

She said, "How do I look"

Now, I've been around women long enough to know that there's only one safe answer to that question.

I said, "You look beautiful."

She glared at me and shook her head.

"Don't give me that bullshit. I'm not beautiful. In fact, I'm fucking ugly. My face is as flat as an ape, my jaw is as square as Dick Tracy and my arms and legs look like Tarzan. Don't you agree?"

Now, to quote Elvis, I was "caught in a trap." There was no safe response to that question, so I dodged it completely.

I said, "SuperCop, ugly or not, you've got the greatest tits in Ann Arbor."

She firmly answered, "I agree Captain, but I'm not SuperCop anymore. I changed my name."

I cautiously asked, "Okay...Who are you now?"

She answered, "Who do I look like?"

That was another impossible question to answer. If I got it wrong, there was no telling what she would do so I answered as generically as I could.

So Many Maybes · 138

I said, "I think you look like a sexy cat burglar."

She said, "Very good answer Captain."

I sighed in relief.

She said, "You are correct. I am a cat burglar and my name is Night Twat."

I could barely hold back my laughter at that name. Unfortunately, during all this talking I lost my erection. She saw what had happened, so she forcefully ripped the entire crotch right out of her tights. Then she reached around my nice ass and pulled my groin to hers so hard that our bodies whacked together louder than the crack of a bat. She held me there, then grabbed my flaccid night stick with her other hand and rubbed its tip all over her wide open feline twat. I got hard instantly.

She said, "Here's the sitrep. You're the rough, tough, Captain Commander and I'm the stealthy, almost invisible, cat burglar named Night Twat. I've taken myself captive and I am attempting to prevent you from completing your mission which is to give me the perfect orgasm. Got it?"

Her so-called sitrep was complete nonsense but it vaguely sounded to me like we were going to play some kind of convoluted sex game where she wanted to fight me. I was supposed to fuck her to orgasm, but she was going to do everything she could to stop me. I had no doubt who would win that fight. I tried to hide my fear and kept silent. She pushed her big tits against my face and jumped up into my arms and wrapped her

So Many Maybes · 139

legs around my hips. I don't know what she could have been thinking. My legs buckled under the weight of her 275 pounds of solid muscle and I instantly fell forward and dropped her on her back like a bag of cement and I crashed down on top of her.

She pulled off her hood and glared at me.

"Jesus Christ Mr. Brown. You're a weak little shit. You should spend some time in the weight room."

I meekly said, "Yes SuperCop."

"God dammit Captain! My name is Night Twat."

I said. "Oh yeah. I'm sorry. I forgot."

"Don't let it happen again. It'll ruin the whole fucking game."

Taking care to get it right this time, I said, "Yes Night Twat."

She spread her legs wide and put her hands under my shoulders and pulled them up to boob level like she was curling a barbell.

She said, "Okay crawl up, line up, and take aim but don't pull the trigger yet."

I did as she told me to.

She raised her hips until her waiting wet-wonder-center barely touched the tip of my solid police battering ram. My well-armed Captain Commander Super Member burned with excitement, wanting to move in fast. But she stopped me.

She said, "You know the drill. Ram me hard. No sissy stuff. Ram me until you bust down the door to my hidden lair and knock me unconscious. Got it?"

With my strong and serious Captain Commander's voice, I said, "Yes."

Night Twat paused for a moment and wrapped her legs around me.

She shouted, "Go! Go! Go!"

I thrust into her and tried to kiss her.

She twisted her head away from me and wiped off her mouth

"Yeech! What the fuck are you doing Captain? Kissing a Super Criminal is inappropriate behavior for a Super Hero."

Evidently, kissing her was inappropriate, but fucking her was perfectly okay.

I lifted my head up and said, "I'm sorry, Night Twat."

She said, "Okay, Captain. You may proceed."

I tentatively began moving inside her and she quickly started my ramming engine by stroking my swollen power piston with the walls of her well-lubricated squad-car internal combustion chamber. I carefully moved in and out of her, but she stopped me again.

She said, "Oh for Christ's sake. I said no sissy stuff. Fuck me HARD, God dammit!"

She fiercely pulled me into her with her legs and shouted, "HARDER!"

I increased the downforce each time I rammed into her, but she kept shouting, "HARDER! HARDER! HARDER!"

So Many Maybes · 141

By the time she was satisfied with the force of my banging, I was pulling out of her completely between thrusts and yelling "Ahhh…" in preparation for the next hammering. Then I would drop my full weight down on her and flex my hips forward as far as they would go, and my body vibrated because I'd plunged down from a foot off the floor. Each time, Night Twat grunted "UNNH!" as if she was being kneed in the stomach.

The pair of us established a kind of vocal rhythm.

"Ahhh…"

"…UNNH!"

"Ahhh…"

"…UNNH!"

I continued to drive my heavy blunt instrument into her, over and over with momentary pauses each time I pulled my ram back in preparation for the next forward strike.

"Ahhh…"

"…UNNH!"

"Ahhh…"

"…UNNH!"

It was hard work. My back was fatiguing, and I was breathing hard and sweating heavily and I could feel the blood rushing to my face.

"Ahhh…"

"…UNNH!"

"Ahhh…"

"…UNNH!"

So Many Maybes · 142

Sweat poured from under my helmet and made my eyes burn and my sunglasses fogged up. I had almost nothing left.

"Ahhh..."

"...UNNH!"

"Ahhh..."

"...UNNH!"

And then I started to feel it. I thought, "Oh God no... Please no...She'll kill me!"

"Ahhh..."

"...UNNH!"

"Ahhh..."

"...UNNH!"

I thought, "I've got to hold back. If I don't, she'll break my back and use me as a carpet beater."

"Ahhh..."

"...UNNH!"

"Ahhh..."

"...UNNH!"

I began to panic, and I told myself, "Think of something, anything."

Out of nowhere, an infomercial flashed through my head and I thought, "That's it. That's it...I'll think of fucking a kitchen blender. That's it!"

"Ahhh..."

"...UNNH!"

"Ahhh..."

"...UNNH!"

So Many Maybes · 143

I could tell my time was running out. If I failed, I was doomed. I kept thinking, "Kitchen Blender... Kitchen Blender...Heeee...Hawww...I'm fucking a kitchen blender."

Of all things, an informercial saved me because Night Twat came before I did. Well sort of.

She let out a minor exclamation of pleasure, "Ummm, Ahhh...Shit!"

Then I collapsed on top of her again, gasping for air. She swore at me, "God dammit, Captain!"

She was obviously pissed. Her orgasm was much too weak and too short to satisfy Night Twat's Amazonian Sexual Hunger. She was disappointed in me and I sensed that she wanted to kill me on the spot. I weakly stood up and backed away in fear.

To my relief, instead of breaking my neck with some exotic cat burglar twisting choke hold, she decided to give me another chance. She said nothing and got on her knees and pointed her ass at me and silently signaled me to fuck her doggy style. Behind her, I struggled to catch my breath and my legs were wobbly. My dick was going limp, but I was afraid to disappoint her so I forced myself to continue. She was so tall that I couldn't enter her while I was down on my knees, so I stood up and squatted until I could line up my equipment with hers. But I couldn't hold that position without reaching forward and holding on to her shoulders like she was rescuing me out of a burning building with a fireman's carry.

Then I started again. I rolled my hips back as far as I could, then rushed into her gaping holding cell with my 12 Gauge riot gun. I rammed into her so hard that I drove her forward two inches with each thrust. I kept on going until my face turned red and my body was covered with sweat and I was afraid that I was going to lose control of my bowels. My spandex shirt was soaked, and snot was dripping out of my nose onto her back. Then I suddenly broke through her back door and shot my load like a blinding blue plastique explosion. I lost hold of Night Twat and flew clumsily off her back to the left and drove her hard to the right. Her head rammed against a chair leg and she laid on her stomach, semi-conscious.

I slowly stood up in back of her and leaned on one shoulder against the wall and attempted to catch my breath. My sinuses hurt from the strain of trying to breathe and a mixture of dribble and snot ran down my chest. My legs were so weak that I could hardly stand up, but when I saw her on the floor, not moving, I panicked and bent down to try and help her up. Since every muscle in my body was worked to failure, my fatigued legs buckled, and I fell down. I landed on top of her with my face placed perfectly in her ass crack and my nose drove violently into her asshole. The impact made her let loose with a long and wet thundering Super Fart that blasted directly up my nasal passage.

So Many Maybes · 145

I rubbed the rancid discharge out of my nose and tried to stand up, but my legs were too weak, and I toppled back on my ass. Night Twat sat up on one knee and looked at me with a disgusted smirk.

She said, "That was weak Mr. Brown, I didn't come. Next time put your back into it."

I rolled my eyes and shouted, "Christ!"

I stumbled out of her apartment as best I could, still wearing my Captain Commander costume with my child-sized Captain Commander toy pistol hanging out. Thankfully no one saw me, or I would have probably been arrested for indecent exposure and be faced with the impossible task of convincing the police that I was a Super Hero named Captain Commander who had failed to sexually satisfy a female Super Villain named Night Twat.

Michael finished, and the café was filled with applause. Camille and Robert's table again clapped the loudest.

Wolf said, "Such an amazing woman she is. Running this place is a round-the-clock job, but somehow, she finds the time to write too. And she's so good at both. What a team we'd make."

Baja said, "Have you proposed the idea to her?"

"Oh my statuesque green-eyed beauty, I've proposed it to her at least once a week for years."

Bonnie said, "What did she say?"

"That she doesn't want to marry a crazy playwright like

So Many Maybes · 146

me and run off to Tahiti. She's got things to do around here."

Will said, "Sounds like a weak excuse to me Wolf. She's probably lying. I think the real reason is that you're too exotic."

Camille said, "I like exotic men. That's why I'm here with Robert."

Robert squeezed her hand.

Baja said, "Me too. I think she's foolish not to run off to Tahiti with you Wolf. I would."

"Really my dear?"

"In a flash Mr. weird, but brilliant, playwright."

"Oh my beautiful Transylvanian Babe from San Francisco, my mind is racing. Will you wear body paint while we're there?"

"I will if you promise me to never wear Bermuda shorts. I think that sight would be horrifying."

Bonnie said, "I don't agree with you Baja. I think Wolf's naked legs would be really hot."

Robert said, "I don't think it would be such a good idea Bonnie. The astonishing bright light would kill all of the beautiful tropical vegetation."

Will said, "No doubt. It would be like the flash from an H-bomb blast."

Jenny walked over to their table and sat down next to Wolf. She had taken off her duck costume and was now wearing denim short-shorts and a sweat-soaked T-shirt. Her shorts rode up high into her crotch and ass, and her T-shirt had the sides ripped out from her armpits halfway down to her waist and revealed the profiles of her lovely breasts that were glistening with sweat.

So Many Maybes · 147

Wolf said, "Miss Woodward, I must say you were a very convincing duck. I gather the costume was hot. You look like you've just waddled out of the pond."

Jenny stood up and turned around and wiggled her ass at Wolf and said, "Duck you, Wolf."

Will quietly stifled a pained grunt when Bonnie stomped on his foot after she caught him staring at Jenny's tits and Wolf had to work hard to keep from reaching out and grabbing Jenny's ass.

Even though Jenny had shown Robert her naked tits and ass many times, he found her revealing outfit to be a very disturbing turn-on, and his reaction was predictable. His tail started to wag so fast that he was sure that everyone around the table could hear it go thwapity-thwapity against his pants. He crossed his legs to hide it from Camille.

Jenny asked, "So what did I miss."

Robert said, "An absolutely great short story that Brett wrote about a guy fucking a huge woman traffic cop to get out of a ticket."

Will said, "Robert, did you notice the striking similarity between the cop in Brett's story and Sgt. Clarkson?"

Camille said, "Who's Sgt. Clarkson?"

Jenny said, "The world's biggest police woman."

Camille asked, "How big?"

Wolf said, "What would you say Will, six feet six, and two-hundred and twenty-five pounds?"

Will said, "More like six eight, two fifty."

Camille asked, "How did you guys run into her?"

So Many Maybes · 148

Robert said, "That's an incredible story. I think Will should tell it because he was more involved that I was."

Will said, "I think Wolf should. Something tells me he's had some practice telling it already."

Robert nodded and smiled and said, "Oh, you know it didn't occur to me until you mentioned it Will"

Bonnie asked, "What?"

Will said, "Sgt. Mount and Sgt. Clarkson are too much alike for it to be a coincidence. I didn't tell Brett about her. Did you Robert?"

"Not me."

"How about you Bonnie?"

"Obviously not."

"Baja?"

"Nope."

"Camille?"

"Of course not."

"Jenny?"

"I hardly know Brett."

Then Will slowly pointed at Wolf who shrugged his shoulders and said, "I hoped that Brett would make passionate love to me in exchange for such good material."

Will asked, "Did she?"

Wolf said, "Will, my dear friend, that must remain a secret now that the beautiful Baja has agreed to go to Tahiti with me."

Camille said, "Wolf, please tell Baja and Bonnie and me the story about Sgt. Clarkson."

Wolf began the story. "In the ancient annals of the greatest

So Many Maybes · 149

book depository since the Library of Alexandria, commonly known as Grafton's Book Store, the events that I am about to relate stand without peer for absolute absurdity. It all began with a woman's child who wouldn't sleep through the night…"

Then Wolf told the entire story with such skill that he had everyone at the table laughing hysterically.

Hardly able to stop laughing, Camille said, "Robert, I'm sorry but there's one thing I have to know."

"What's that?"

"You didn't…ah…you didn't…?"

"Didn't what?"

Will said, "She means did you invade Night Twat's hidden lair?"

Robert's response was quick and definitive, "Oh God no."

Jenny said, "She wanted to though?"

Robert said, "Unfortunately."

Camille said, "How do you know that?"

Jenny said, "She kept inviting him down to the police station to get some special training to solve his clumsiness problem."

Wolf said, "How did you put it, Miss Woodword?"

"I said that I thought that Sgt. Clarkson saw Robert's big night stick and wanted it inside her special police unit."

Bonnie, Baja, and Camille laughed, and Robert smirked and feigned embarrassment while he said, "It's true."

Brett walked back up on the stage and said, "This next act is the last one for this evening and it sounds like it's going to be a really fun finale. It's called *Shoot The Hockey Player*.

Two men went up on the stage and sat down on stools. They

So Many Maybes · 150

were dressed exactly the same in cream colored sport jackets and pink turtlenecks.

> One of the men pointed at the other and said, "Good evening...He's Judge."
>
> The other man said, "And he's Jury."
>
> Then in unison, they both said, "And welcome to the Judge and Jury show."
>
> Jury said, "We're self-important film critics from New York, and each week we analyze and ruin our viewer's cinematic experiences by giving away the plot of every new movie that comes out."
>
> Judge said, "Tonight we're pleased to welcome the famous French filmmaker Depthcharge Below who has just shown his new film 'Shoot The Hockey Player' at the New York Film Festival."
>
> A man wearing very dark sunglasses and carrying a movie camera came out of the audience and sat down next to Judge.
>
> Judge turned to the filmmaker and said, "Monsieur Below, welcome to our show."
>
> Depthcharge said, "Canada has been bery bery good to me."
>
> Jury leaned over and said something in Judge's ear.
>
> Judge looked at Jury and nodded. Then he said, "I'm sorry for pronouncing your name wrong Monsieur Bowl-yeel-yuh. I don't speak French well."
>
> Depthcharge said, "Canada has been bery bery

So Many Maybes · 151

good to me."

Judge said, "I'm sure they have. Your films are brilliant... Tell me Monsieur Bowl-yeel-yuh, do they play hockey in France?"

Depthcharge took a deep breath and again said, "Canada has been bery bery good to me."

Judge said, "Monsieur Bowl-yeel-yuh, what was your inspiration for this film?"

"Canada has been bery bery good to me."

Jury leaned over and whispered to Judge again.

Judge nodded and said, "Now we have the privilege of being joined by Honoré 'penalty box' LaBleche, the star of 'Shoot The Hockey Player.'"

LaBleche walked up on the stage. He was dressed in a horrible plaid suit with a hockey jersey over it and he had hockey skates hanging around his neck. He sat down next to Depthcharge.

Jury said, "Good evening Mr. LaBleche. Thank you for coming on our show."

LaBleche said, "Glad to be here. Say I've got a question."

Judge said, "What's that?"

LaBleche leaned forward and spit on the floor, then he asked, "Why the fuck are you two dressed up like a couple of sissies?"

Both Judge and Jury gasped.

After a moment of uncomfortable silence, Judge said "Thank you for helping us out. We're having a tough

So Many Maybes · 152

time interviewing Monsieur Bowl-yeel-yuh."

LaBleche said, "That's no surprise. The stupid motherfucker can't speak English."

Judge said, "Oh no! Our producer told us that language wouldn't be a problem."

"Your producer was full of shit. Here, I'll show you."

The hockey player nudged the filmmaker and said, "Hey Depthcharge, I hear you like it when your mother shoves pine cones up your ass."

Depthcharge said, "Canada has been bery bery good to me."

LaBleche said, "See what I mean. But trust me. The cock sucker wouldn't have anything to say even if he spoke English"

Clearly annoyed by LaBleche's language, Judge leaned over and whispered in LaBleche's ear."

LaBleche said, "Why the fuck not?"

"Swearing isn't allowed on television, Mr. LaBleche. Please tone it down."

"I think it's stupid, but okay."

"Tell me Mr. LaBleche, what attracted you to this movie?"

LaBleche said, "My agent tricked my ass."

"How did he trick you?"

"He told me this monster pile of wet and steamy Men's Room diarrhea was from k-bec like me...Is that better Jud...I didn't swear?"

Judge's jaw tightened, and he didn't say anything.

So Many Maybes · 153

Jury jumped in and continued the interview, "So your agent tricked you and you didn't know that Monsieur Bowl-yeel-yuh was a legend in French cinema?"

LaBleche said, "What the fuck is...oh sorry... What is cinema?"

"It's another word for movies."

LaBleche said, "So why don't you just say movies?"

Jury said, "Cinema is what pretentious critics like me say."

LaBleche smirked.

Jury said, "Mr. LaBleche. Tell me. How was your working relationship with Monsieur Bowl-yeel-yuh?"

"It was horrible."

Jury said, "Why was it horrible?"

"Because he doesn't know shit about hockey."

"So Mr. LaBleche, why do you think that Monsieur Bowl-yeel-yuh wanted to make a movie about hockey if he doesn't know anything about it?"

"I'm not sure but I heard that the French pervert wanted to come to Canada and spend some time licking a husky's asshole while he jerked off on a dog sled."

Depthcharge quickly stood up and, in perfect English, shouted, "Shut the fuck up, you provincial back-woods Canadian Neanderthal!"

Then Depthcharge pulled out a gun from his pocket. He grabbed LaBleche's jersey and pulled it over the Canadian's head and he repeatedly hit LaBleche in the face with the butt of the gun. Then the filmmaker

So Many Maybes · 154

stepped back and shot the hockey player.

Judge and Jury applauded and shouted, "Bravo! Bravo! Another masterpiece!"

Depthcharge turned quickly and shot each of the critics twice.

He said, "I hate critics. They think they have the right to judge artists."

The actors stood up and they took their bows and the crowd applauded.

Brett walked up on stage and said, "That concludes the acts for tonight but we're still open until 2 A.M. So please stay around and eat a lot and drink a lot so I can pay my bills."

Bonnie said, "Camille, did I hear Robert say you were a model?"

Camille nodded and said, "For four years."

"What kind of work did you do?"

"I was a runway model."

Bonnie said, "I modeled a little too, but that was a long time ago before I grew up and got tits."

Will said, "I'm glad you grew up Bonnie. I think tits are good."

"We're all aware of that Will."

Camille asked, "What kind of modeling work did you do Bonnie?"

"I modeled clothes for teenage girls."

Camille said, "I think you could have done runway modeling too. The money can be good."

So Many Maybes · 155

Wolf said, "Bonnie doesn't care about money. She's so rich that thousand-dollar bills fly out of her ears when she sneezes."

Bonnie said, "Thank you Wolf for being so kind to me, but we all know you meant that I've got money up the ass."

Wolf said, "I was being polite my dear Bonnie. It would be crude of me to say that you fart money."

Jenny said, "It's the same thing. My mother used to fart when she sneezed."

Wolf said, "My dear Jenny, if you were to fart, you would create a wave of raw feminine sexuality that induces magic gonadal vibrations in all men within earshot and they would chase you like farm dogs going after a passing car."

Baja said, "Oh Wolf. What sensitive poetry."

Bonnie said, "Even if I could have done it, runway modelling was too big a hassle. When I traveled, I wanted to do it for fun, not work."

Baja asked, "So why did you quit Camille?"

"For several reasons. First I was twenty-two, and in the modeling business that's ancient."

Baja said, "What were the other reasons?"

Camille answered, "I have this deadly sense of humor and I kept embarrassing potential employers with deadpanned dirty jokes. I knew it wasn't a good idea, but I couldn't help it. Designers take themselves seriously which makes them easy targets. I got away with it for a while until my ex-husband fucked everything up."

Robert quickly interjected, "You never told me you were married."

So Many Maybes · 156

"He was my agent and it only lasted a year."

Robert asked, "Why did you break up?"

"I caught the twisted dick fucking a thirteen-year-old wannabe model."

Bonnie said, "Jesus!!! Did he go to prison?"

"No. He was a pervert but…what can I say? It's a man's world so they let him get away with it."

Bonnie said, "I'd have put his hot dog in a sausage maker."

Wolf said, "Bonnie, from what I know about you, I dare say that's an understatement."

Will said, "Bonnie doesn't take shit from any man. She's wanted in twenty-seven countries"

Bonnie said, "Twenty-six Will. If you remember, I was acquitted of the hit and run charge in Antarctica."

Camille laughed and asked, "Antarctica?"

"I ran him over with a bulldozer."

Will said, "They let her off on a technicality. It seems it's impossible to run from the scene of an accident on a bulldozer."

Wolf said, "Bonnie doesn't look like it, but she's an ice-cold bitch."

Bonnie said, "Very funny Wolf…Camille, did you at least get alimony?"

Camille looked at her and didn't answer immediately, then said, "No. I didn't want his money, but I didn't want him to casually walk away without suffering some form of punishment either."

Baja said, "No one could blame you. Did you hire a mercenary to break his fifth limb?"

So Many Maybes · 157

Camille said, "No. That would have been a good idea, but I've never met any mercenaries."

Bonnie said, "I hope you ran him over with a Land Rover?"

Camille sighed, and her face became serious and she stood up and methodically looked around the café.

Robert suspected that she was up to something, so he leaned back and shook his head and crossed his arms and quietly sighed.

Camille shut Robert up by putting her hand on his shoulder and squeezing then she leaned over the table.

She whispered, "Will you all promise not to tell anyone?"

Baja whispered back, "I promise."

Wolf said, "I swear to God."

Everyone else promised not to say a thing.

Camille sighed and kept whispering, "I temporarily lost my mind and did gruesome, horrible things to him."

Baja whispered, "Gruesome?"

Camille looked down and covered her eyes. She shook her head and whimpered, "I'm so ashamed and I'm scared that the police will come looking for me."

Baja repeated, "We all promise we won't tell anyone."

Camille nodded and scanned the restaurant again to see if anyone was watching.

Then she leaned over the table and said, "I kicked him in the balls, rammed a hammer handle up his ass, then pissed in his shoes and told him it wasn't right to fuck his little sister."

Everyone laughed hard, especially Wolf who started to slide under the table. A man in the next booth made a move to come

So Many Maybes · 158

to Wolf's aid, but Baja assured the man that Wolf was okay.

Wolf was still laughing when he got to his feet and dusted himself off.

Camille said, "I'm sorry Wolf. I didn't mean to make you fall out of your chair."

Robert said, "She can't help it. She's done it to me a couple of times."

Camille said, "After you get to know me better, you'll see what he means. It's a curse, but what can I say? I can't help it and, like I said, it's one of the reasons I didn't get modeling jobs anymore."

Bonnie said, "I'm proud of you Camille. You are a fellow master of feminine vengeance."

Will asked, "Did you really do those things?"

She laughed and said, "All of it except for sticking the hammer handle up his ass. I didn't have one handy."

Will said, "I thought you were just telling a joke. I had no idea it was true."

"The joke was really in the delivery and I think the addition of the hammer handle made it more fun."

Robert said, "I think it's time that we switch to our other planned topic for tonight's dinner."

Bonnie asked, "What's that?"

"Camille's painting."

Jenny asked, "You're a painter? So am I. I'm studying painting at U of M right now?"

Camille said, "I took classes for a semester, but I didn't like going so I went back to painting on my own."

So Many Maybes · 159

Bonnie asked, "When did you start painting?"

Camille answered, "When I was in the ninth grade."

Jenny said, "I started when I was twelve; when every boy I met started hassling me. Painting gave me a way to escape."

Brett walked over to them and said, "Do you remember the old Howdy Doody TV show that always began with Buffalo Bob asking, 'Hey kids, do you know what time it is?"

Robert said, "Vaguely, why?"

Echoing that TV show, she asked them, "Hey kids, do you know what time it is?"

Wolf said, "Alas. So we must leave. Lady Brett, will you accept my left nut for payment of our tab?"

Brett said, "Thank God that won't be necessary, Wolf. Bonnie has covered it."

Baja said, "That's so kind of you Bonnie. I want Wolf's left nut for myself."

Wolf said, "Be careful when you count Bonnie's money, Brett. It could be dirty money."

Bonnie said, "Fuck you Wolf."

Brett asked, "Bonnie, what's Mr. Crazy Man talking about?"

"He means I've got money coming out my ass."

Brett said, "Better than some things I can think of."

Robert turned to Camille, "What did you tell her?"

"Nothing. It must have been Wolf."

"Yes my dear. I take credit for any embarrassment, true or alleged, although Robert's farting skill is legendary."

Brett said, "Will you guys get the fuck out of here?"

So Many Maybes · 160

Chapter 11
Poltergeist

After the others turned and walked out of the Arcade, Robert and Camille stopped for a moment in front of the stairway to Camille's apartment. It was a tall narrow, fogged-glass paneled door, that was immediately to the left of the entrance to Maybe's. Unlike the rest of the Arcade, there was no number above the door, only a sign that said "Stairway." She took Robert's hand and froze him in place with her ethereal animalistic eyes, then smiled gently and kissed him. Her kiss was unlike any he'd ever experienced. It sent, not a chill, but a tingling warmth down from her lips through his entire nervous system to the tips of his limbs.

After that kiss, Robert was brain dead when they ascended the stairway to Camille's place. Her apartment was a small windowless efficiency that reminded Robert of his room on Thayer, except it had its own bathroom and kitchenette. It was spartan and mostly empty with no decorations except for a few unframed paintings. She had a chest of drawers and a large bed covered with a white, soft, and puffy comforter.

He said, "I only see a few paintings here. Do you have a studio or something?"

"I didn't paint these. Mine are in here."

She opened a door that Robert had assumed was a closet.

When she turned on the lights he faced a large room. It was about four times as deep as it was wide, which made sense because her apartment was directly above Maybe's which had a similar shape. Soft pure white light came from every direction projected by several dozen lamps mounted at the intersection between the sixteen-foot high walls and a peaked glass ceiling that covered the entire studio. Nice neutral gray rugs covered the hardwood floor. Off to his left was her easel and a work bench that held her paints and brushes. Down at the far end it was more like a small living room with a large Victorian couch and chairs and a bookshelf and a fireplace. Filling every wall from floor to ceiling were Camille's paintings.

Camille became quiet as soon as they entered her studio. She stood silently and leaned against the wall and was content to let Robert walk around and looked her paintings. All of them were landscapes. He recognized some of the locations as places around Ann Arbor, but most of them were of places he didn't recognize. There were dramatic mountain valleys and ocean coastlines with dark stormy seas and sailing ships riding over large waves in the distance. There were several of steep cliffs and green meadows and even a couple of small medieval castles that Camille said were in Ireland.

After he'd looked at a few of the paintings, Robert went over to her work bench and picked up her sketch book and thumbed through the pages. He noticed some sketches that appeared to be the basis for two of the paintings he'd seen hung on the walls. He carried the book across the room and held the paint-smudged sketches up next to the paintings

So Many Maybes · 162

themselves and marveled at how she had turned a simple pencil sketch into a color painting as beautiful as she was. Camille slowly approached him and with quiet possessiveness took the sketchbook out of his hands. It was obviously of great value to her.

Although he had only been to one art museum in his life, the one on the U of M Campus, Robert thought he recognized a few of the paintings.

He said, "I feel like I've seen some of these paintings before, or at least some that are very similar."

She nodded, "I have two on display downstairs at Maybe's and a couple are in books. You might have seen them at your bookstore."

Robert grinned and said, "So you're famous?"

She shook her head and said, "No, not really. But I have managed to sell a few paintings."

Puzzled now, Robert asked her, "So why are you tending bar at Maybe's?"

She smiled weakly and said, "Because I need the money. I'd never be able to support myself on my painting alone."

Robert nodded and asked her what her last name was.

She said, "O'Neil."

One large painting that was almost hidden in the back corner of the studio caught Robert's attention. It was different from the rest of her work. It wasn't a landscape. Instead it was some form of abstract picture. When Camille saw him head toward it, she suddenly became animated and tried to walk in front of him and block his view.

So Many Maybes · 163

"Don't pay any attention to that one, Robert. I painted it when I was furious with my ex and really fucked-up on wine, vodka and tequila. It was like I took out my frustrations on canvas. I don't know why I hung it up. It's not anything like my others."

Robert heard her pleas and stopped short of the painting. But he was still close enough to see it clearly. Her emotional state when she was painting was obvious by the way the paint was applied. In some areas the paint was splattered and looked as if she had begun by almost whacking the brush against the canvas. Then it appeared that she eventually calmed down and began to paint with more care. The painting was comprised of dozens of layers of colors and black lines all arranged into one giant spiral from the outer edges of the canvas toward the center. The colors at the outer edges were deeply dark and opaque and at the center they were pale light blue pastel washes. The opaque to pale color and line scheme combined with the spiral paint strokes created the illusion that you were looking up a spiral stairway to the sky.

*

THE JOURNAL OF ROBERT BAIN

I only stood there for a minute or two before my brain went into turmoil. I was desperately struggling to understand what I was seeing and feeling. Every layer, every different shape, every different color, simultaneously evoked different emotions and ideas all intertwined and superimposed upon one another and pulled me deeper into the painting. At first the

So Many Maybes · 164

image was only colors and lines on canvas. Then the world gradually darkened around me and the only light was coming from the center of the painting. I began to slowly rotate as a female heavenly body wrapped herself around me and lifted me off the floor and screwed me up the spiral staircase to sexual heaven. The pleasure grew continuously until I reached an orgasm of religious intensity and began ejaculating a huge load into my pants. I flew out of the top of the staircase and into the air like a depth charge from a destroyer. When I reached the peak of my trajectory, I fell toward the earth like a sky diver without a parachute and I hit the ground hard in a cold lifeless heap, unconscious.

*

Camille hurried over to Robert and bent down and shook him and said, "Robert? Robert? What's wrong?"

She felt his pulse and made sure that his heart was still beating then nervously called the ambulance.

*

THE JOURNAL OF ROBERT BAIN

When I finally woke up in the Hospital Emergency Room, Camille hugged me.

She said, "Oh Robert, thank God! What happened?"

I shook my head and said, "I don't know Camille. The last thing that I remember was looking at your painting and thinking that it was extraordinary. Then, after what felt like only seconds, I lost control of my entire being and the painting took hold of me and fucked me all the way up to heaven until I had a tempestuous orgasm and fell back to earth. Then everything went black."

Camille nodded and said, "You also filled your underwear with about a pint of semen."

I said, "That much?"

She nodded and said, "I'm not exaggerating. Anyway, the doctors can't find anything wrong with you, but they want to run more tests to be sure."

"I feel fine, Camille."

Camille leaned down and kissed me gently on the lips. Then she took off her clothes and put them on the chair next to the bed. I laid there motionless, watching her. Her body was mesmerizing: elegant breasts, a very narrow waist and an ass barely big and soft enough to make any man want to caress it. In the front, her hips and leg muscles formed a long triangle that pointed downward to what could only be described as the source of feminine mystery. When I saw Camille naked, I became so excited that my cock sprang up faster than a medieval catapult.

My groin was throbbing as Camille got in my hospital bed. She pulled the blanket up over us and wrapped her long legs around me. It was like a full body hug, a gentle loving embrace. It felt like every inch of her body was caressing every inch of mine and it was an experience that I had never imagined. I was in bed with a gorgeous woman without having sex

So Many Maybes · 166

of any kind. There was only intimate, loving, magic. An otherworldly creature was graciously sharing her supernatural spirit with me. I kissed her as lovingly as I could, and we drifted off to sleep together.

*

When Robert woke up for the second time, he was looking directly at his sister Dana and Camille was standing next to her. Off to his left, his friends from the bookstore were standing in a crowd. All had serious and concerned looks on their face except for Nort who was studying the ER equipment.

Dana said, "Oh thank God, Robert! What happened?"

Jenny breathlessly ran into the room and asked, "What's going on? Is Robert all right?"

In a hurry to be with Robert, she hadn't taken the time to change her clothes before she left her apartment and she was still wearing the same revealing outfit she had on when they left Maybe's.

Will quietly stifled another pained grunt when Bonnie put her full weight on his foot after she caught him staring at Jenny's tits again. Wolf, being Wolf, grabbed Baja's ass. She returned the favor.

Jenny went right to Robert's side and bent over him and took his hand in hers.

She said, "My God Robert, are you okay?

Camille quickly moved forward to stand next to her. She nervously ran her hand through her hair. Her voice quivered as she said, "It was terrifying."

Jenny said, "Holy shit, what happened?"

So Many Maybes · 167

Camille continued, "It was like the painting was a circus sideshow medium who conjured up a supernatural feminine poltergeist that grabbed Robert by his colossal male thunder muscle and made him shake like a paint mixer and come as violently as a high balling tractor trailer. Orgasmic shockwaves shot through his body and clamped down on his balls like an industrial vice that squeezed them so tight that enough milky white cum to fill a propane tank blasted from his dick like Old Faithful."

Camille stopped and grinned and waited for their reaction. Everyone but Dana and Terri started to laugh.

Wolf told them, "Camille has a gift for telling humorous stories."

Before Terri or Dana could say anything, a nurse entered the room and said, "You can go home now Mr. Bain. Your doctor can't find anything wrong with you."

Robert said, "Thank God."

He reached across his body and grabbed his blanket and rapidly whipped it off him. Everyone in the room shouted, "WHOA!!!" when his magic wand waved at them because he wasn't wearing any underwear.

Both Camille and Jenny quickly reached out and tried to grab his blanket to hide his exposed package. Their arms collided which resulted in Camille grabbing Robert's privates and holding onto them while Jenny pulled the blanket up over him. There followed an awkward pause while everyone watched nervously as Camille carefully, and much too slowly, pulled her hands out from under the blanket as if she was

So Many Maybes · 168

embarrassed. Only Robert could see her mischievous smile as she made sure to run her wiggling and caressing fingers over the entire length of his rapidly growing penis. Predictably, his small standard-issue pistol instantly became a full-sized masculine blunderbuss.

Robert's balls almost blasted, but he managed to control himself and he turned on his side to hide his erection.

He said, "Could you all please leave me alone for a minute while I get dressed?"

Will lingered a bit after the others left the room.

Robert said, "Could you leave too Will? I've got a hard-on the size of a solid fuel rocket booster. Camille's hand almost made me pass out."

Will nodded and said, "I can understand that. She's got nice hands."

After Will walked out in the hall, Robert got dressed but he left his shirt untucked to hide his erection. When he left the room and followed the others down the hall, he couldn't take his eyes off Camille's perfectly shaped ass.

Bonnie dropped Robert and Camille off at the Maynard Street entrance to the Nickel's Arcade and they walked hand in hand to Camille's door and up the stairway again. They went inside her apartment and she turned on a small red night light. She looked at him and he looked at her. Existing in a special dimension that included only them, they stood silently in front of each other and undressed. Her dark haunting eyes magically glowed in the soft light as she put her arms around his neck and they placed their faces close together and felt the soft touch of

So Many Maybes · 169

each other's cheeks. Then they tenderly caressed each other's ears and kissed each other on the lips and on their eyes and journeyed to their own special place in the universe by madly fucking the shit out of each other for over four hours. It was pretty romantic.

Bonnie was fascinated by Camille's painting that had, as Camille so colorfully put it, made Robert shoot a load in his pants big enough to fill a propane tank. She knew that it wasn't possible for the painting, now called *Orgasmic Poltergeist*, to have reached out and fucked Robert to a blackout orgasm. Obviously, the painting didn't come alive. It only made Robert imagine it did. For Bonnie, any painting that caused such a powerful hallucination was extraordinary and interesting. Therefore, she felt compelled to see it and she and Will went to Camille's studio.

The painting was on an easel to the right of the door and it was covered with a bed sheet. Camille led them over to the easel.

She said, "This is it."

Then she paused. She was apprehensive because of the effect that the painting had on Robert.

She asked Bonnie, "Are you sure you want to go through with this?"

"I'm sure."

Camille said, "I mean really sure?"

"Yes, Camille. I'm really sure."

"Okay if it's what you want…How about you Will?"

So Many Maybes · 170

Unlike Bonnie, Will wasn't sure of anything. But when he saw Bonnie glaring at him he said, "I'm sure too. How bad can it be? It's just a painting."

Camille took a deep breath and braced herself for their reaction and pulled the sheet away.

Bonnie shook violently, and her vagina vibrated faster than a buzz saw. Her face lit up like a flash bulb and her clitoris cracked like a bullwhip.

She screamed, "E-yowww!!! Holy-God-damned-fuck!!!"

Her body convulsed, and she flew backward and landed hard on her ass and back. Out of breath and trembling, she closed her eyes and gulped for air. She rolled onto her hands and knees and turned her back to the canvas, then she weakly crawled over to the couch and sat down. She bent over forward with her hands on her crotch and tried to recover.

Camille ran over to the couch and sat down next to her and asked, "Shit Bonnie, what did you see? What happened? Did the painting reach out and grab you like it did to Robert?"

Still gulping for air, Bonnie shook her head and said, "Unnnh…no, Camille…Ahh…Hunh... Ahh…Hunh…it…was…Hunh…Unh…was more like…Hunh…Unh…like…more like I stuck my clit in a light socket. Or maybe…like…a lightning bolt…gave me an orgasm."

"My God Bonnie! Are you hurt? Do you need to go to the hospital?"

Having caught her breath, Bonnie sat up in the couch.

She said, "Oh no Camille. It was a super-mother-fucking rush that I'll never forget. I'm as wet as a car wash sponge."

So Many Maybes · 171

Behind them, Will was still in front of *Orgasmic Poltergeist*. His eyes were transfixed on the canvas. His face turned red and his body began to shake, and he spread his arms wide and waved them back and forth like he was a soaring eagle. Then he slowly bent forward at the waist and his legs began to buckle as if a great weight was placed on his back and shoulders. He suddenly dropped to his knees then collapsed flat onto his stomach and started to flail his arms. He tried desperately to push his chest off the floor, but the weight continued to push him down. Will kept struggling until he suddenly rolled sideways and appeared to break free. He started moving across the floor on his stomach like he was a land-bound seal repeatedly arching his back up and down with his arms to his sides and shouted.

"Arnk, Arnk, Arnk!"

"Arnk, Arnk, Arnk!"

Camille and Bonnie turned around in time to see Will go back and forth across the studio several times like he was being chased. The weight caught him again and forced him down hard flat on his stomach. Then his hips bounced up and down violently.

He shouted, 'Oh no...no...PLEASE!!!"

His shouts turned to whimpers as he whined, "Ohhh… Nohhh. God, nohhh…."

Then he passed out.

Camille got up quickly and covered the painting with the sheet again and Bonnie rushed to Will's side to try and bring him back to consciousness.

So Many Maybes · 172

When Will came to, he stood up and walked around the room bowlegged and kept pulling at the seat of his pants.

Camille asked him, "What happened Will? Did the painting come alive and fuck you?"

"Not exactly."

Bonnie leaned over and said, "What does that mean."

"I really don't want to talk about it. It's embarrassing."

Camille said, "Please tell us Will. This is weird. First Robert, then Bonnie and now you."

Will kept walking around bowlegged and he was trying to straighten his pants as if he had crapped in his underwear.

Will said, "Camille, if I were you, I wouldn't show that painting to anyone again. It's dangerous."

"Come on Will. Tell me why it's dangerous. I need to know how. Tell me what happened. Please."

"Okay but promise me you won't laugh. It's humiliating."

Camille said, "We won't laugh. Will we Bonnie?"

Bonnie shook her head no.

Will kept pulling at the seat of his pants and said, "I was looking at the painting like you Bonnie, when it seemed like the world around me dissolved and I was transported in the nude to some desolate rocky sea shore where a huge bull walrus decided he liked me and attacked me and tried to mount me to mate. I managed to break free and run away but he eventually caught me and pushed me to the ground and crawled up on top of me and fucked me in the ass. It raped me Camille! I was raped by a walrus! It's fucking humiliating."

The women looked at each other and worked hard to stifle

So Many Maybes · 173

their laughter but they both lost it after Bonnie said, "Jesus Christ Will, I hope it didn't make you pregnant."

Will shouted, "God dammit, Bonnie!!!"

Over the next two weeks, Bonnie insisted that Terri and Wolf and Baja and Jenny stand in front of Orgasmic Poltergeist.

Bonnie didn't even consider Dilli O, because Robert warned that there was a risk that if Dill was exposed to the powerful eroticism of *Orgasmic Poltergeist,* she would spontaneously combust and burn the building down.

Bonnie didn't ask Nort either because she assumed he would be impervious to the painting's sexual powers. Besides, the idea of Nort having an orgasm freaked her out.

Each individual's experience was different, but everyone had a good time.

Terri asked Camille to leave her alone with the painting then she wouldn't reveal what happened. Wolf said it reminded him of getting fucked at Woodstock while he was high on acid.

Unlike the others, Baja laid down in front of the painting and entered a transcendental state of one continuous orgasm that hummed softly in harmony with her breathing. She could make it more intense by inhaling and relax it by exhaling. Either way, she remained in orgasmic bliss.

If Baja's experience was the most transcendental, Jenny's was by far the cutest. She imagined that she had a pulsating chain of multiple orgasms while she was masturbating on a soft bed of whipped cream spread on top of a chocolate layer cake. She wasn't sure exactly how many times she came because she lost count at nine when she unfortunately peed her pants.

So Many Maybes · 174

Chapter 12
Shopping

Robert's sister Dana invited the entire Grafton's crew to a cookout at her house in Brighton. Robert suggested to Camille that they should go up a couple of days early so Camille could get to know Dana. Camille and Dana had met at the hospital after *Orgasmic Poltergeist* had made Robert come like a tractor trailer and pass out, but they didn't spend any time together because Dana went home immediately after she made sure that Robert was okay.

Dana's house was a lovely, all brick, ranch style home with three large bedrooms and an oversized family room in addition to the living room. Off the family room was a cement patio and a beautiful green lawn and a swimming pool. Although he never went swimming (he didn't own a bathing suit or even a pair of shorts), Robert had always enjoyed sitting in a lounge chair next to Dana's pool and writing in his *Journal* and he planned on doing a lot of poolside writing during this visit while Dana and Camille spent time together.

After Dana gave Camille a tour of the house, Robert immediately grabbed his *Journal* and went out by the pool and the two women sat down on the patio.

Dana said, "I suppose Robert has told you that we grew up in an awful home and we were close."

"As a matter of fact, he's hardly mentioned it. He did tell me that Grand Rapids was hell and Ann Arbor is heaven by comparison."

Dana said, "What made you move to Ann Arbor?"

"The same thing that brings almost everyone there, U of M. I moved to Ann Arbor to study painting. What brought you here."

"Like Robert, I hated Grand Rapids and couldn't wait until I could leave. When I was a student at State, I went to Ann Arbor with a bunch of friends to see the Michigan-Michigan State football game, which I'm sure you've heard by now, is a big deal. After the game, I looked around and I liked the place. When I graduated, I looked for a job as a vet there. I wasn't able to find one, but there was a clinic up here that had an opening. So I moved here instead of Ann Arbor."

"Are you sorry you couldn't find something in Ann Arbor?"

"Not at all. I love it here. The people are great, and the real estate is a lot cheaper. I could never afford a house like this in Ann Arbor."

Camille said, "I think it's a dream house, but it brings up an obvious question?"

"What's that?"

"It's such a big place. Were you married once or something? I hope I'm not being too nosy."

"No, not at all. I've never been married. I'm too independent. Don't misunderstand me. I don't have anything against marriage, not at all, and I suppose that if I run into the right guy, I'd like to get married too. But right now, I just prefer to think of myself as married to my work, and bang anyone I want as often as I want."

Camille laughed.

She said, "Dana I never expected to hear you use the word 'bang.'"

"You'd be surprised. I guess Robert has never told you that I taught him everything he knows about swearing. But Robert takes it a step further than 'bang.' 'Fuck' seems to come more natural to him."

"I think it does, but recently he's been saying, 'make love,' instead of 'fuck.'"

"That might be a reflection of the way he feels about you."

"Maybe. I don't know."

Dana said, "I only used the word 'bang' to be polite. My favorite is 'screw the shit out of the mother fucker.' I just like the way it sounds."

Camille laughed hard.

Dana continued, "I think that your description of Robert's orgasm as 'coming like a high balling tractor trailer' was wonderful."

"Thanks. Actually, that was mild. I'm proud to say that I can have the dirtiest mouth in the world when I want to."

"What kinds of things would you say?"

"Ahhh…"

"Come on, Camille. You can't hold back now. You brought it up and now you've got me interested."

"Okay if you're sure you can tolerate the extreme."

"I can unless it's racist or disrespectful to kids or women

So Many Maybes · 177

or, I might add, to animals."

"You have nothing to worry about there. I feel the same way. Anyway, here goes. On the night of our first date, the same night he went to the hospital, I told Robert that I wanted him to jump me like a bull moose and pump my cunt until my clit exploded."

Dana laughed as hard as Camille had.

She said, "You're kidding? You said that to my brother?"

"I did."

"How did he react."

"He went into shock and fell off his barstool."

"I'll bet he did. I'll bet he did…Say, did you bring your bathing suit?"

"No. Robert didn't tell me you have a pool."

"He wouldn't. In all the time that he's been coming here, I don't think he's gone in the pool once. But that shouldn't keep you from going swimming. Why don't we go into town and see if we can find you a suit?"

They went over to the pool and told Robert they were going shopping to get Camille a bathing suit.

Camille said, "Why don't you come with us Robert? I think it'll be fun to go swimming, don't you?"

"I guess so, but I haven't been swimming in years. And if I remember right, the last time that I did, my dick shriveled up and my balls shrank to the size of raisins. I don't like it when that happens. You wouldn't like it either. No woman wants a man with a shriveled dick and balls the size of raisins."

Dana said, "Boy Robert, I think that your exposure to

So Many Maybes · 178

Camille has made your description of your genitalia more colorful than it used to be. I'm impressed."

Camille said, "Don't worry Robert, after the picnic I'll make your dick swell to the size of a fire hose and your gonads as big as confederate cannon balls."

Camille and Dana were both grinning broadly.

Dana said, "Nicely put, Camille."

Robert said, "Camille you know I like it when you talk dirty, but I'm still not sure I want to go swimming."

Camille said, "Oh come on Robert. Think of it. When we get in the water we can stand next to each other and blow big bubbles with our ass."

Dana laughed and said, "Not you, too?"

Robert said, "Oh yeah. She's wonderful. Farting was what brought us together in the first place."

Dana said, "How romantic...anyway Robert, it sounds to me like you have no choice but to go with us to get a suit. You owe it to all of the great gas blasters of the world. It's your duty to get into that pool and perform for the others at the picnic."

"Okay, but I can't promise anything. I've never been able to fart on cue. It just happens."

Camille said, "I know that. All I ask is that you try. I'll make up for the silent periods."

Robert got out of his lawn chair and went shopping with them. Over all, he enjoyed it, but at times he got tired of standing around while the women tried on one bathing suit after another, after another, after another. He would have gone out to the car and taken a nap, but they kept asking him for his

So Many Maybes · 179

opinion and he felt like it would have been impolite for him to leave. Of course they always ignored his opinion completely, but he felt like he was doing the right thing by staying. The process took even longer than it might have because Dana decided to buy a swim suit too. Eventually they found Camille an attractive reddish-brown bikini, and Dana found a screaming yellow one with a semi-transparent mesh that ran almost the entire distance between her nipples.

Although Robert thought Dana's suit looked great, he found it a little disturbing. He had never seen even a hint of his sister's breasts before.

He said, "Jesus Sis!"

Dana laughed and said, "What's wrong Robert. Remember, I'm your older sister and I took care of you when you were a kid. I've seen your dick more times that I can remember."

Robert said, "It's not the same thing. You've always been like my mother. No guy wants to see their mother nude."

Camille said, "I understand, Robert. I never saw my father naked, but I guess that might have disturbed me too."

Robert cringed and said, "Oh God Dana! Can you imagine how we would have reacted if we ever saw BadBob in the nude?"

"I would have gone temporarily insane and stolen his car and taken you with me and raised you in a commune in San Francisco."

Robert said, "In some ways, I wish you'd have done that anyway."

Just when Robert thought the women were done, Dana

So Many Maybes · 180

couldn't help but start shopping for shoes she didn't need.

She said, "It's a weakness I have. I've already got more than I have room for in my closet."

Camille said, "When I was modeling I probably would have too. Almost all of the clothes I have I bought when I was modeling and getting paid well."

Dana said, "Did designers ever let you keep the clothes you modeled."

"From my experience, models never get to keep the clothes, but there might be exceptions. I don't know."

After trying on what Robert perceived to be four hundred thousand pairs of shoes, Dana decided that she shouldn't buy shoes after all, and they left the shoe store and went looking for a bathing suit for Robert.

Dana said, "Okay Robert, what kind of suit do you think you'd like?"

"I don't know. Aren't men's bathing suits all pretty much alike?"

Dana said, "I'm not sure. But if I were to guess. I think you'd probably like something straight forward and conservative."

Camille said, "Oh wouldn't it be fun if we got you one of those little bikini bottom things that European guys wear?"

Robert said, "Fun to shop for, but not to buy. If you tried to get me to wear one of those at the picnic, I'd run away so fast that you'd have to chase me down in Dana's car."

The way Camille saw it, they had to find him something that didn't look like it was made for an old man but was conservative enough to not put him off. Their search began

So Many Maybes · 181

quite well. Each of them looked separately and found a few possibilities then Robert tried them on. This time the process was reversed, and the women stood outside the changing room door as Robert modeled the suits. Unfortunately, every time he showed them a suit that he himself had picked out, the women soundly rejected it. Unlike them however, he took their criticisms to heart.

He said, "I wonder if we'll ever find one. I know that at first I was reluctant to even go swimming, but now I'd be disappointed if I couldn't."

Dana said, "Don't worry. If worse comes to worse, we'll just get you a pair of khaki shorts to wear."

Robert said, "Why don't we just go with that idea and get supper. I'm starting to get hungry."

Camille said, "Let's keep looking a little while longer. Try these."

She held up a pair of women's yellow spandex short shorts.

Robert started to laugh and said, "Oh right. I'd look like a prostitute in downtown Detroit."

"Or how about these."

She held up a pair of pin-striped shin-length bloomers.

Dana said, "Where the fuck did you find those?"

"Believe it or not, they were hanging at the back of the discount rack. Either they were used for a costume in a play or something, or they've been hanging there for sixty years."

Dana said, "Makes you wonder doesn't it."

Robert said, "Okay that's enough with the silly jokes. Let's just go with the shorts and get out of here."

So Many Maybes · 182

Camille said, "Please Robert, just two more. Then I promise I'll stop."

Robert smiled and said, "Okay. Just two more. You promise."

"I promise."

"Okay bring it on."

She said, "Ta-da!" and held up the tiniest possible European bikini style bathing suit you could imagine.

Robert said, "Okay God dammit!"

He grabbed the suit and charged into the changing room and put it on. When he walked out in front of the women, his ass was bare, and his entire private package looked like it was enclosed in a thin fabric ball-sac. The women both laughed hysterically as he went through a series of poorly executed body builder poses.

Still laughing hard, Camille held up a pair of navy blue surfing baggies that had a wide white strip around the bottom of each leg and said, "Okay. I think you look great, but I guess it's time to stop the nonsense. Try these."

Inside the changing room, he put the suit on and looked at himself in the mirror. Robert liked what he saw. The suit looked perfect and he breathed a sigh of relief. At first the suit seemed a bit oversized or something because it fit a little loose, but then he remembered that baggies are supposed to be loose. That's why they're called Baggies. Surfers wear them because they don't constrict their movements when they're surfing. Besides, the suit had a draw string around the top, so he could tighten them up. In addition, when he got the inevitable erection from seeing Brett at the pool party in a bathing suit, he wouldn't look

So Many Maybes · 183

like he was wearing a throbbing tube sock.

They bought the suit and went to dinner.

*

THE JOURNAL OF ROBERT BAIN

It was fun to see the way that Dana and Camille and even I had bonded. It occurred to me that shopping together might serve the same purpose that the traditional game of catch did between a boy and his dad. Unfortunately, I never had that experience, but Dana and I had the Monopoly games and the Saturday morning cartoons.

*

Chapter 13
The Pool Party

On Sunday, the Grafton's crew along with Baja and Brett came up to Dana's for the picnic. Each person contributed pretty much the same thing to every group picnic.

Nort always brought an outrageously oversized grill. No one knew why he liked them so unnecessarily big. He just seemed to like big grills. This time it was a twenty-six burner Army field kitchen stove mounted on a riding mower. Terri always brought the weenies and the hamburger and the buns. Jenny brought watermelon and Dana contributed sweet corn. She also made barbecue baked beans and snuck them to Robert as his contribution because he could never think of anything to bring. Bonnie and Will brought their famous and hugely dangerous vodka and tequila punch. Also true to tradition, Wolf brought a jug containing a mystery tea made from some old family recipe. His family seemed to have an infinite number of recipes because Wolf brought a different concoction to every party. He called this one *Nietzsche's Concept*. When someone drank even a little bit of it, it made their groin and butt muscles twitch hilariously for about thirty seconds.

Since Camille and Baja and Brett were new to the group they were free to establish their own tradition. Brett said she could bring some Mother Maybe's Magical Mystery Strawberry

Kool Aid that her mom had taught her how to make. And Camille decided to bring pizza from Maybe's.

Baja had difficulty deciding what she wanted her contribution to be. She never cooked so she consulted her favorite grocery store clerk, Hondo, for suggestions.

Hondo was always eager to help Baja, probably because she was so good looking and was always complimenting him. It wasn't hard for her to do because he was very handsome and tall and muscular. He had broad shoulders and a thin waist and magnificent biceps that he proudly displayed by rolling up the sleeves of his white short-sleeved shirt with the name Hondo embroidered in red letters over the left front pocket. He was also a genuinely nice guy.

Hondo listened carefully as Baja went through the list of items that the others were already bringing, and he said, "Boy, I can understand your problem. It seems like all of the obvious items are taken," then he smiled and said, "How about pickled heart. My grandmother used to make that. It was great. I loved it."

It was obvious that he was kidding so Baja played along the best she could. "Where did she get the heart? I've never seen it in the store."

"You've got a point there. She only made it when my granddad shot a deer. Do you hunt?"

"Only for guys with bad attitudes and a big dick."

Hondo laughed nervously because his muscular member was starting to flex.

Then he said, "Baja, you never cease to amaze me with

So Many Maybes · 186

your clever comments."

"I try."

"Trust me. You could sit on the floor between the store's aisles and clean your ears with a cue tip and you'd still be amazing."

"Thank you for the odd compliment Hondo."

"You're welcome Baja. If you want, I'll show you where they are."

"What."

"Cue tips."

She laughed and said, "Not today Hondo, maybe some other time. Right now I have to figure out something to take to the picnic."

"Actually that's really not a problem. Take potato salad. A picnic isn't a picnic without potato salad."

"I don't cook, Hondo. How the fuck am I going to make potato salad?"

"We sell it premade over at the meat counter."

"Jesus Christ. Why didn't you suggest potato salad to begin with?"

"I just like talking with you Baja. You talk dirty and I like that."

While Nort cooked the food, Robert and Will placed bamboo Tiki torches around the perimeter of the pool. When they lit them, the candles flickered gently in the breeze. Everyone ate and drank slowly and talked about pleasant things. At twilight, they could see a thunderstorm in the distance and occasionally lightning struck from the clouds to the ground and from the

So Many Maybes · 187

ground to the clouds. Although the far-away clouds were dark and threatening, the sky above them remained a gradually fading friendly blue. At the beginning of the picnic, the crew tended to drink Bonnie's familiar vodka and tequila punch and they occasionally sampled Wolf's Nietzsche's Concept just for the outrageous fun of it. But as the evening wore on, everyone gravitated toward Brett's exquisite strawberry Kool Aid. It was irresistibly wonderful and seductive. Brett refused to tell anyone what was in it, but it didn't seem like alcohol because it didn't numb the brain. Rather it was some magic nectar that enhanced the senses. The more that people drank it, the better they felt, and the troubles of the world melted away and their love for their friends seemed almost visible.

The atmospheric humidity was very high, so as the day faded to darkness, the light from the flickering Tiki torches looked like twinkling stars reflecting off the droplets of moisture suspended in the air. Robert and Camille were sitting on a blanket they had spread out on the grass next to the pool. Robert was watching the reflections of the torches on the surface of the water, and he didn't feel the need to talk or do anything. It was enough to just be there, sitting next to the woman he loved and surrounded by his dearest friends.

Jenny broke the calm by suggesting they all go swimming.

Everyone but Will thought it was a great idea.

He said, "I'm not much on swimming. I'll just sit here in a lawn chair and admire the beautiful women parading around in their bathing suits."

Wolf immediately jumped into the pool with his clothes

So Many Maybes · 188

on, and to Terri's mock horror, Nort dropped his pants and went over to the pool in his navy-blue jockey shorts with Norton embroidered in red letters across the front. He ran off the diving board and did a cannon ball dive that splashed everyone.

Terri laughed and shouted, "Put your God damn clothes back on Norton. You're so pale you look like a skinny vampire out there."

Jenny, being Jenny, took off all her clothes and jumped in the pool naked. She was followed by Baja.

When Will leaned forward to get a good look at them, Bonnie moved quickly. She sat down hard in Will's lap both blocking his view of the naked nymphs and subjecting his genitals to maximum impact. Then the lawn chair collapsed. Bonnie stayed planted on top of Will. When Will tried to get free, Bonnie rose up slightly and dropped her ass down hard on Will's solar plexus. Will grunted and forgot all about looking at Jenny and Baja.

He yelled, "What the fuck are you doing Bonnie? Get off me."

Bonnie crossed her arms and smiled broadly.

She said, "Not until you stop staring at their naked boobs. It's not polite to stare at boobs."

Will continued squirming and said, "You know that's not possible. I like boobs."

Jenny looked over at Bonnie sitting on top of Will and shouted, "What's wrong Will. Does she remind you of the Walrus?"

So Many Maybes · 189

Still planted on Will's stomach, Bonnie suddenly unbuttoned her blouse then leaned back and took off her shorts and panties. She rolled over and grabbed Will's balls and kissed him hard on the lips. Then she grabbed his hand and stood up and pulled him to his feet. She kissed him again, then dragged him into the house and started banging his brains out on the couch in the family room.

Robert watched them run into the house and said, "It looks like Bonnie has decided to change the terms of their collaboration agreement."

Camille nodded.

Up to that point, Robert had maintained control of his famous hard-on in waiting by turning his back toward the pool so he couldn't see Jenny and Baja swimming naked. But then a much anticipated, at least among the men, event occurred. Brett emerged from the house wearing a magnificent white bikini that emphasized everything and hardly covered anything. Wolf put his hand over his chest and fell back and sank slowly under water, feigning a heart attack.

Even the women reacted.

Dana said, "Oh wow."

And Camille said, "Good God."

As soon as he saw Brett, Robert's dick sprang up so fast he almost got a genital aneurism. He quickly grabbed Camille's hand and said, "Come on Camille. Let's go get our suits."

Inside their bedroom, Camille saw Robert's hard-on.

She said, "Robert, you have an erection."

"You're right Camille. I do have an erection."

So Many Maybes · 190

"It appears to be a good one."

"I have to agree Camille."

Camille said, "I guess it's understandable. After all, Baja and Jenny were naked."

Robert said, "It was Brett's bathing suit that sent me over the edge."

"Isn't it interesting that two naked women didn't, but a woman in a bathing suit did."

Robert said, "It was an amazing bathing suit."

Camille said, "You're right it was, but it was Brett's body that made the package stand out."

Robert said, "Obviously, it made my package stand out too."

"That's a good joke Robert."

"Thank you, Camille. What should I do? I want to go swimming, but I can't go out there like this."

"Probably not. Maybe if we stay in here for a while, you'll lose it long enough for us to run out and jump in the pool."

Robert said, "That's a good idea. We can put on our suits while we wait."

As they dressed and his hard-on slowly subsided, he pulled his baggies up over his still stiff dork and tied the draw strings. Camille took longer than he did because she had to look at herself in the mirror and comb her hair. It always puzzled Robert when women did things like that. She knew she was going to run across the yard and dive in the swimming pool, yet she had to comb her hair.

When she finished, she said, "Okay, are you ready?"

Robert said, "Hold on a second," and he grabbed hold of

So Many Maybes · 191

his bathing suit's draw strings and pulled them tighter and knotted them.

Then he said, "Okay let's go."

When they walked out on the patio, they looked at each other and ran toward the pool.

Robert screamed, "YAHHHH…!!!"

For some reason, it hadn't occurred to either of them that is was a horrible idea for clumsy bastard Robert to even try to run across the yard. Miraculously he nearly made it to the pool. But when he got about five feet from the edge he tripped on one of Bonnie's sandals, hopped twice on one leg then entered the pool like he was trying to run across the surface of the water. His baggies dropped to his ankles and he fell forward and smacked the water in a spectacular belly flop. As soon as he was underwater, his suit slid down over his feet and floated to an undetectable location. He stood up fast and watched in horror as Jenny grabbed his baggies and swam as fast as she could to the other end of the pool where she held them up for everyone to see.

She shouted, "Hey everybody. Look what I found."

"God dammit, Jenny! Bring those back."

"Not until you show me your cock Big Boy."

By now, everyone was laughing hysterically.

Robert tried to remain calm and stood still in the navel deep water. He crossed his arms and thought about what he should do next.

Camille slowly moved over and stood beside him and calmly said, "Robert, it appears that you have a problem."

So Many Maybes · 192

"Yes Camille. I do have a problem. I'm considering my options. Any suggestions.

She said, "I have several."

Robert said, "I'm listening."

She said, "One. Stay in the water until everyone else goes inside. That might seem like a workable solution, but it could take hours and you'd get really cold. Besides you'd be subjected to maximum ridicule as soon as you walk inside."

He said, "Why don't you just go get my suit from Jenny or get me a towel to wear around my waist so I can go inside."

"That's probably the easiest, but personally I think it would also be humiliating because you're asking your girlfriend to bail you out."

"I understand, but what other choice do I have?"

She took his hand in both of hers and with a totally straight face she said, "Robert you're my man and I want you to turn this difficult situation into a chance to do the coolest thing possible."

"What's that?"

"I want you to walk over to that ladder and leave the pool totally naked. After all, Jenny and Baja and Bonnie are nude, why can't you be."

"I see your point. It does make logical sense. But don't you think it's different for me."

"You mean because your dick is going to get stiff?"

"It always does."

"That is a problem. Tell you what. If it comes up, dry it off with a towel and scratch your balls."

So Many Maybes · 193

Robert said, "That's certainly an interesting idea Camille."

"I think it is. If you stay cool and appear casual, you might even get a round of applause."

Robert knew she was joking but he was tempted to call her bluff like he had with the European Bikini bathing suit, but this was more extreme.

She said, "Are you man enough to do it or do you want me to get you a towel."

That was enough for Robert. He took a deep breath and went for it. When he emerged from the pool, all poolside conversation stopped, and he got a sudden burst of courage. He ran over to the picnic table and grabbed a hot dog then ran back and jumped back in the pool.

Jenny swam up to him and handed him his baggies.

She said, "Here Big Boy."

"Thank you Jenny."

She said, "Now was that so hard?"

"Unfortunately, it was hard."

Jenny said, "I saw. I wish I had my camera, but I guess I'll have to paint it from memory."

"Do me a favor and exaggerate the size."

"Don't worry Big Boy. I always give credit where credit is due."

Robert said, "Say Jenny. Show me your tits. Oops sorry, you already are."

Camille took off her top and said, "Robert, quit staring at Jenny's tits and look at mine. It's the proper thing to do."

"You're right Camille."

So Many Maybes · 194

Robert put his bathing suit back on and kissed her and said, "Camille?"

"Yes Robert."

"You've got gorgeous tits and I'm sure everyone here will enjoy looking at them, but I'm kind of possessive and I want to keep them for myself. Would you put your top back on and we'll get out of the pool and sit down with our friends and drink Brett's mystical Kool Aid and let the night fade away?"

"Okay. And Robert?"

"Yes Camille."

"It's been a great weekend."

"I know. But I'm worried."

"Why are you worried?"

"Well, you and Dana are now like sisters and that means I'm fucking my sister which, as I'm sure you know, is frowned upon by most people."

"I guess that's true, but you know what I say to that?"

"What?"

Camille turned and faced him and tenderly put her hand on his cheek and blew a long chain of huge bubbles out of her ass.

"I love you Camille."

"I love you too, Robert."

So Many Maybes · 195

Chapter 14
GaGa Land

Camille and Robert's relationship moved forward rapidly and they settled into a regular routine. Robert went over to Maybe's every evening that Camille worked. Some nights he sat at the bar, but other times he sat in his old favorite booth and wrote in his *Journal* and he was beginning to think that his life was as perfect as it could ever be.

Then, as it sometimes does, a crack in reality suddenly opened, and Robert tripped and fell down that proverbial rabbit hole and landed against his will in a unique place called GaGa Land. In GaGa Land logical conversation was next to impossible and unpredictable behavior was the norm.

He had returned to the stockroom after taking a stack of books out to the front of the store when a woman's voice angrily said, "Acka, I'm pissed at you. You didn't come over to fuck me like a corn dog."

Bunny was standing next to Jenny inside the stock room door. Both of them had their arms crossed and stern looks on their faces.

Jenny said, "Yeah Robert. Why didn't you go fuck her like a corn dog like you promised?"

Bunny said, "Jane, you just called Acka Robert."

Jenny said, "That's because his name is really Robert, not

Acka. Didn't he tell you that?"

Bunny said, "Robert, why did you tell me your name is Acka if it's not?"

Jenny playfully added to the confusion by saying, "Yeah Acka. What do you have to say about that? Why did you tell Bunny your name is Robert if your name is really Acka?"

Robert turned around and leaned forward and put his forehead against the wall and kept his back to Bunny.

He said, "Hi Bunny. It's really nice to almost see you."

"Same here Acka. Has anyone ever told you that you've got a nice ass?"

"No Bunny. But thank you for saying so."

"You're welcome Acka."

"Say Bunny?"

"Yes Acka."

"Remember the last time we met?"

"Of course I do. That's when you promised to come over and fuck me like a corn dog."

"You didn't give me your address or phone number, so I couldn't go over to your place and fuck you like a corn dog... Whatever that means."

"A corn dog. You know those cute little guinea pigs that live in holes out west. They fuck like rabbits."

"I think you mean prairie dogs."

"Of course not, prairie dogs live on the prairie. Everyone knows that."

"Where do corn dogs live?"

"In corn fields of course"

So Many Maybes · 198

"I see."

"Say Acka?"

"Yes Bunny."

"Do prairie dogs fuck like rabbits too?"

"Probably...Did you hear what I said?"

"About what?"

"About how I couldn't come over to your place because I didn't have your phone number or address."

"I heard you Acka, but why didn't you just look me up in the phone book?"

"I tried. You're not in the phone book."

"I don't know why. I had a phone once. I'll have to call them as soon as we get the phone turned back on. Well Acka, it actually worked out for the best."

"Why's that, Bunny?"

"I wasn't home that night anyway."

Robert was exhausted already. Like the last time he met her, Bunny had twisted his brain into knots. He turned around and faked the warmest smile he could.

He said, "Bunny?"

"Yes Acka."

"I can't talk to you now."

She seemed hurt and said, "Why won't you talk to me Acka? Is it because my boobs are too small?"

"No Bunny. Your boobs are just fine. I can't talk now because I'm at work. Let's meet at Maybe's later. That way I can introduce you to my friends."

"Okay. When we get there, will you show me your

So Many Maybes · 199

spring steel boner?"

"I'll think about it Bunny."

Bunny looked at Jenny and said, "Did you hear that Jane? Acka's boner is made out of spring steel."

Jenny raised her eyebrows and looked at Robert.

She said, "When did you see Acka's boner Bunny?"

Bunny said, "I didn't," and walked out of the stockroom and left the store.

Jenny said, "Acka?"

"Yes Jenny."

"Call me Jane, Acka."

"Okay Jane."

Jenny said, "I've told you that you've got a nice ass lots of times."

"Oh yeah, that's right. Sorry. I forgot. Bunny has that effect on me."

"So she's the famous Bunny?"

"That's her. Is she the way you imagined?"

"Well sort of."

"Why sort of?"

"She's certainly gorgeous, but you always said that she looked like she was in a state of grace."

"And you don't think she is?"

"Not unless The State of Grace is another name for The Land of Confusion. Why does she call you Acka?"

"I'm not sure, but I think it's because I told her my name was Robert, a.k.a. The World's Clumsiest Bastard."

Jenny grinned and asked, "So a k a became Acka?"

So Many Maybes · 200

Robert nodded and said, "I think so. Say Jane…"

Jenny interrupted him and said, "Please call me Jenny before I forget what my name is."

"Okay. Jenny would you go with me tonight when I go over to meet her at Maybe's? I need protection. I'm afraid that if I go by myself, I'll become as crazy as she is and join Dilli's church. I plan on inviting Will and Bonnie and Terri too."

Jenny said, "Oh I wouldn't miss it."

"Thank you Jenny."

"Call me Jane."

"Okay Jenny."

"Okay which?"

Robert said, "Neither. I'm not committing. Is it okay if I just call you Hot Stuff?"

"Absolutely Big Boy. Say Acka?"

"Yes Hot Stuff?"

Jenny ran toward Robert and reached toward his crotch and asked, "Can I see your spring steel boner?"

Robert slapped her hand away and said, "God dammit Jane!"

That evening, Camille was working at Maybe's, so Robert and Jenny went over early to explain to her that Bunny had shown up at Grafton's and she was coming over to talk with Robert later.

Camille said, "So she finally showed up. Why are you meeting her here?"

Robert said, "Bunny's almost impossible to have a sensible

So Many Maybes · 201

conversation with and I couldn't deal with her at work."

"What are you planning to tell her?"

"I plan to make it clear to her that I'm involved with you. Unfortunately, with Bunny, clarity can be the impossible dream."

Jenny said, "Camille, you can't imagine what she's like. She's sweet and a hoot to be around, but I swear to God, she's absolutely wacko. That's why Robert asked me and Will and Bonnie and Terri to come with him."

Camille said, "What are you guys going to do?"

Robert said, "They're going to help me from getting lost in GaGa Land."

"What does that mean?"

"It's hard to explain but you'll understand when you meet her."

Will and Bonnie walked in and Robert got up to go meet them.

When Jenny stood up to follow Robert, Camille said, "Keep him on track."

Jenny said, "Don't worry I've got it covered."

Robert and Jenny and Will and Bonnie and Terri all sat down in a booth to wait for Bunny.

She showed up half an hour late and said, "I could have been here on time but I decided to arrive late so I looked like a fashion model."

Everyone at the table looked at each other, baffled.

After Robert introduced Bunny, Jenny asked her, "Bunny, Robert tells us you're a dancer."

So Many Maybes · 202

Bunny asked, "Who's Robert?"

Robert said, "I'm Robert, Bunny."

"If your name is Robert, then why did you tell me it was Acka?"

Robert answered, "I didn't Bunny."

Then Robert realized that he was standing at the border of GaGa Land and resolved not to cross it. He was going to shut up until the time was right to tell Bunny about Camille.

Jenny rephrased her question, "Cindy didn't you say that you were a dancer?"

Bunny asked, "Who's Cindy?"

Jenny said, "You are."

"Oh I thought my name was Bunny, but I guess I misunderstood. In answer to your question, I was a dancer but I'm not any more. I'm a student at U of M now."

Terri asked her, "What are you studying?"

"Dance."

Everyone looked at each other again.

Bonnie asked, "What kind of dancing were you doing before?"

"My roommate Baja and I dressed up like Big Jungle Cats and wrapped our bodies around each other and looked a lot like we were fucking."

Will asked, "Baja is your roommate?"

"Of course she is. Why would we share an apartment if we weren't roommates?"

Bonnie asked, "Is your roommate from San Francisco?"

"She was when we lived there. Now she's from here like me."

So Many Maybes · 203

Bonnie said, "We know a woman named Baja."

"Wow! What a coincidence. I'll have to tell her…Now I'm studying to become a ballerina. I graduate at the end of the summer and I want to join a ballet company. I've already been going to auditions."

Bonnie asked, "Where have you auditioned?"

"In the last three weeks I went to St. Louis and Atlanta and Montana."

Bonnie said, "I'd never have expected that there's a ballet company in Montana."

Bunny responded quickly, "There's not."

Bonnie paused to process Bunny's answer, then she asked, "Have you tried New York? There are several ballet companies there."

"I'm going to New York in a few weeks, at least I think I am. I'll have to ask my teacher and get back to you on that."

"Make sure that you do…What company are you going to audition for?"

"I haven't a fucking clue, but I wrote it down."

Bunny searched through her purse to find the paper with the name of the ballet company on it. Then she said, "Here it is…It says Macy's and Company."

Everyone looked at each other again.

Then Bunny said, "Oh, of course that's not it. Macy's is a department store isn't it? Boy do I feel stupid. I wonder how a piece of paper with Macy's name on it got in my purse."

She returned to rummaging through her purse and eventually found the answer to Bonnie's question.

So Many Maybes · 204

"Oh finally...here it is...it's hard to read because my handwriting sucks donkey dongs but it says The Ballet Company of the City of Lincoln Center or something like that."

Bonnie politely said, "I've never heard of that one, but then I really don't know anything about ballet."

Bunny said, "Neither did I before I came here for school."

Bonnie said, "How about The Lincoln Center Ballet?"

"That's it. How did you know?"

"Just a guess."

"That's eerie. How could you know what's written on a piece of paper in my purse? It's like that magician guy on *The Johnny Carson Show*. You know that guy who holds up an envelope to his head and tells you what's written on the inside of it and when he reads it, it's a joke. What's his name?"

Without thinking, Robert entered GaGa Land and blurted out, "Carnac the Magnificent?"

"That's it. You're like Carnac, Betty, only a lot better looking. I remember seeing you on the cover of *Extreme Teen Magazine*. You looked fantastic. You're even more beautiful than I thought you'd be in person."

"Thank you, Cindy...I think."

Will asked Bonnie, "You were on the cover of *Extreme Teen*?"

"Yes I was Wallace."

Will asked, "Who's Wallace?"

Bonnie said, "You are."

Will asked, "Why didn't you ever tell me?"

Bonnie said, "I assumed you already knew your own name."

So Many Maybes · 205

Will said, "Very funny. No, why didn't you ever tell me that you were on the cover of *Extreme Teen*?"

"You never asked me. Besides, would you admit it if you were on the cover of *Extreme Teen* Wallace?"

Bunny said, "You should be proud Wallace. When were you on the cover of *Extreme Teen*?"

Will could only manage a single word answer to that question, "Ahhh..."

Bunny asked, "Say Tammy?"

Terri asked, "Who's Tammy?"

Now Robert lost total control and found himself deep behind enemy lines. He said, "You are."

Terri said, "I am?"

Bunny continued, "You know what Tammy?"

Terri answered, "Yes Cindy?"

"Who's Cindy?"

Bonnie said, "You are."

"Here all this time I thought my name is Bunny,"

Robert said, "It is."

"Thank God for that Acka. I was confused. Where was I? Oh yeah, Tammy you know what?"

"What Cindy?"

"You've got really nice, big boobs."

Terri smiled warmly and said, "Thank you Cindy."

"Call me Bunny."

Terri said, "Okay Bunny."

Bunny asked, "Are they real?"

"Are what real?"

So Many Maybes · 206

"Are your nice big boobs real?"

"Yes Cindy. They're all mine."

Bunny nodded and said, "That's good. I don't think it would be a good idea to borrow someone else's boobs. It wouldn't be healthy. How about you Jane? Your boobs are perfect for men to get a handhold."

"I think so. I've been trying to get Acka to grab my boobs since I met him, but he's chicken."

Bunny said, "Why are you chicken Acka. I think Jane has great boobs, don't you?"

Robert said, "Yes I do, but she shows them to me and then runs away."

Bunny asked, "Why do you run away, Jane? If I was you, I'd let him catch me and get a good handhold on my boobs and fuck me from behind like a corn dog."

Terri said, "Cindy, what do you mean when you say fuck like a corn dog?"

Robert explained, "They're like prairie dogs. They fuck like rabbits."

Bonnie said, "I didn't know that male prairie dogs fucked female prairie dogs from behind."

Will said, "You know, they just might. I'm not sure, but it makes sense don't you think?"

Robert said, "Why's that, Wallace?"

"I read once that it's easier for guys with tiny dicks to fuck a girl from behind and you have to admit that if corn dogs are anything like prairie dogs they have tiny dicks?"

Robert asked, "How do you know that Wallace? Have you

So Many Maybes · 207

been fucked by a prairie dog?"

Will's response was instant. "Fuck you, Acka."

Bunny said, "Anyway…A woman I knew got fake boobs. They didn't look too bad and I thought about getting them too because my boobs are too small, and men can't get a handhold but they're really expensive. Fake boobs I mean. I didn't pay anything for my own boobs because they're too small."

Robert felt he had to offer his less than expert opinion and said, "They're dangerous too."

Jenny said, "Mine aren't Acka, at least I don't think they are. I've had them a long time and nothing bad has happened."

Robert said, "I didn't know you've got false boobs Jane."

Jenny said, "I don't because I heard that false boobs can explode, and no one wants their boobs to explode."

Bunny said, "I think your right Jane. Exploding boobs would be bad news."

Jenny asked Bonnie, "Who's Jane?"

Bonnie pointed toward Bunny and said, "She is."

Bunny said, "No Betty, I'm Cindy at least I think I am. What's my name Acka?"

Robert said, "As far as I know it's Cindy and I think you've got great boobs."

"How could you think that. You've never seen them."

"I have X-Ray vision like Super Man. Don't I Jane?"

Bonnie asked Robert, "Who's Jane?"

Jenny said, "I am Betty."

Bonnie asked, "Who's Betty?"

Robert addressed Bonnie and said, "You are."

So Many Maybes · 208

Bonnie responded, "It's the first I've heard of it. Here all this time, I thought my name was Barbra Ann."

At that point, Jenny decided that the silliness had gone on long enough and it was time to get down to business before everyone became exhausted and decided to go home.

She said, "Bunny, Acka has something important to tell you."

Bunny said, "Oh I know, it's obvious."

Robert asked, "What is?"

"That you want to fuck me like a corn dog."

"That's just it, Bunny. I don't."

Bunny frowned deeply and sternly said, "Acka, most of the time you're a nice guy, but lately you've been pissing me off."

Robert didn't realize it, but he was stepping in a trap.

He asked, "How. We only met once then you were gone for weeks."

Bunny continued, "Never mind that...I offered to fuck you the first night we met, and you got a spring steel boner and said you would come over and fuck me the next night, but you never showed up. Never mind that I didn't give you my address and I wasn't home that night anyway. Now when you still don't know my address and I'm getting a phone but haven't given you the number, you're refusing to be honest with me."

She was moving much too fast for Robert. He said, "Hunh? What?"

Bunny suddenly became animated and she said, "Oh my God I just now got it. I'm an idiot not to have seen it before."

"What?"

So Many Maybes · 209

"That you're gay."

Robert shook his head. Like it or not, he had become that crazy knight, Don Quixote, in the Cervantes novel and he was fighting a windmill in pursuit of that impossible dream of a logical conversation with Bunny.

He said, "I'm not gay, Bunny."

"Oh."

Bunny frowned and thought for a moment and suddenly her face brightened again.

She said, "Now I finally understand. I'm so sorry Acka. It's so sad. You should have told me, but now I understand."

"I should have told you what?"

"That your balls were shot off in Vietnam. I saw a movie about a guy that had that happen. But that wasn't Vietnam was it?"

Will said, "If you're talking about *The Sun Also Rises*, no that wasn't Vietnam."

Bonnie elbowed Will for butting in. It was Robert's show now.

Bunny said, "So Wallace, where is this place that the Sun rises, and Acka got his balls shot off?"

Robert said, "Don't worry about the Sun, Bunny. It's not important. I've still got my balls."

Bunny said, "Then what. Tell me God dammit. No man has ever not wanted to fuck me. Some have even begged. It's fun when they beg. I can't think of any other reasons unless you're a virgin. Oh my GOD! You ARE a virgin. I've never fucked a virgin before. Don't worry, I'll be gentle when we fuck tonight.

So Many Maybes · 210

Tammy, why don't you come too. You've got nice big boobs, so it'll be real fun, won't it Acka?"

Robert said, "No it won't Bunny. Tammy's not gay."

Bunny asked, "Tammy, if you're not gay, why did you say that you wanted to come over and fuck me?"

Terri said, "What!? I didn't?"

Like Jenny, Robert finally decided it was time to get assertive and put an end to the nonsense and lay down his Quixotic windmill fighting lance.

He said, "Wait here a minute, Bunny."

He got up and walked over to the bar and invited Camille to come to their booth to meet Bunny.

He said, "Bunny, this is Camille. I make love to her every night, so I can't go over to your place and fuck you like a corn dog."

Bunny looked at Camille and her face almost exploded. She said, "Oh my wet womanhood, Connie! You're so beautiful that I'd fuck you too if I was gay but I'm not so I won't but you and Acka have to come over to our place and fuck on our couch so we can watch even though I won't take pictures isn't that right Betty?"

Bonnie said, "Ahhh…?"

Camille waited for her brain to catch up with Bunny, then she said, "Robert and I are very busy right now, but we'll get over to your place and fuck on your couch as soon as we can."

Bunny said, "Who's this guy Robert? Connie are you fucking around on Acka?"

Robert said, "I'm Robert, Bunny."

So Many Maybes · 211

Bunny said, "No you're not. You're Acka?"

Camille shook her head and even grinned. She now knew how easy it was for Bunny to take you to GaGa Land.

Robert said, "You're right Bunny."

Bunny asked, "So who is fucking you Connie?"

Camille pointed at Robert and said, "He is."

"What about Robert?"

Camille answered, "I've never heard of anyone named Robert."

"So where did I hear about him?"

"I don't know Bunny."

Bunny said, "Say Acka,"

"What's that Bunny?"

"Are you fucking Connie instead of me because her boobs are bigger?"

"No Bunny."

"Why then?"

"I'm making love to Camille because I love her."

Bunny said, "Who's Camille?'

Camille said, "I am."

Bunny said. "No you're not. You're Connie."

"I'm two people Bunny. I'm both Connie and Camille."

Robert said, "Who's Connie?"

Bunny said, "I thought she was."

Camille looked at Bunny and said, "Where did you get that idea?"

Bunny got to her feet and held out her palms in front of her to signal the others to halt the conversation and said, "Now, let's all slow down and take a deep breath. We can't talk about anything more until I get this straight."

Camille said, "Okay."

Robert said, "Okay."

Bunny said, "Acka, who is she?"

"She's Connie and Camille."

Bunny continued, "Connie and Camille is a weird name but whatever…and Acka, what's my name? I forgot."

"You're Bunny, Bunny"

"Oh good. That's what I thought…Now Acka, does Connie and Camille make your boner as hard as spring steel?"

"Harder, Bunny."

"Oh Acka, you told me my boobs don't matter?"

"I didn't even mention your boobs, Bunny."

"I noticed. Did you not mention my boobs because they're too small?"

"I think your boobs are just fine Bunny."

She smiled and bent over and kissed Robert on the forehead and said, "Oh you're so kind to me. I think yours are just fine too. Good night Acka."

"Good night Bunny."

And like she had done on the first night that Robert met her, Bunny walked out the door without telling him her address or phone number.

After the others left, Robert moved over to the bar and ordered his normal rum and coke.

Camille said, "You were right. She's a real trip. I was so confused I thought my name was actually Connie and Camille."

So Many Maybes · 213

"Bunny's like that. Things might start out making some sense but after a few minutes you're standing deep inside GaGa Land."

"I think she's basically harmless, but something tells me she didn't hear you when you said that you didn't want to sleep with her."

Robert nodded and said, "If that's true, I'll have to keep telling her and eventually she'll leave.

Like always, he stayed at Maybe's until she got off work and he accompanied her upstairs to her apartment. While she took a shower, Robert went into her studio and looked through her books. He found a book called *The Story of Art* by E.H. Gombrich and sat down on her couch to look through it. Since he was going with Camille and he was good friends with Jenny, he felt he should learn more about art.

Camille came out of the shower and sat down next to him and said, "That was my textbook for my Art History Class. It's wonderful."

Robert said, "I'll have to sit down here and read it some time. This is a nice place to read."

"It could be a nice place to write too, don't you think?"

"I think you're right. But I'd need a table."

"Maybe Brett has one you could use until you move your stuff over here. I'll ask her tomorrow."

"Okay. And I'll talk to Will and Nort about helping me move out of my room and move in here."

"Okay."

Later that night, when Robert and Camille were asleep in

So Many Maybes · 214

bed together, Robert woke up suddenly and sat up.

Camille said, "What's wrong Robert? Did you have that nightmare where you went to work without your pants?"

Robert looked back at her and said, "No I'm used to that dream. I have it almost every night. This was worse."

"What was it?"

"I dreamt that Bunny took me to a Christmas party and I woke up in a manger with a sheep licking my balls and I didn't have the slightest idea how I got there…"

Camille rolled over and said, "It's good you had that dream."

"Why?"

"Now you'll have time to prepare yourself."

"Prepare myself for what."

"I think she's already planning the party."

Chapter 15
Bunny's Story

Camille was right. Bunny didn't believe Robert when he told her that he didn't want to sleep with her. From Bunny's point of view, it was a foregone conclusion that Robert wanted to sleep with her. And it was also a forgone conclusion that he was in love with her too. After all, every man she'd ever met fell in love with her and wanted to sleep with her. But, no matter what, she was going away to join a ballet company and become a ballerina and she had no intention of getting serious with Robert. So she decided that the only kind thing to do was make that clear to him.

She went over to Grafton's and asked him to go to lunch with her because she had some important things to tell him. Although Robert figured it was probably best for him to avoid Bunny completely, he figured that no harm could come from having lunch with her, particularly since she suggested going to Dominick's Italian Restaurant just south of the Law Quad. Dominick's had a nice outdoor eating area where they would be in public view so Bunny probably wouldn't do something crazy like grab his crotch to feel his "spring steel boner."

On their way over, she stopped walking and turned and faced him. She didn't speak immediately. Robert didn't know what she was up to, but he knew he should be prepared for anything. She paused and looked at him and started to speak, then she paused again. She looked away from him for a moment and took a deep breath then turned back and looked him in the eyes then chickened out. Instead of saying what she wanted to, she put her hand down the back of his pants and rubbed his ass. Robert stopped dead. He liked the feeling of her hand down his pants, but it got embarrassing when two nuns walked by and chuckled.

Bunny gave them the finger and shouted, "Hey! He's got a nice ass, okay? You should be so lucky."

Having failed the first time, Bunny tried again. Two days later she called Robert at work.

She said, "Do you have a bike?"

Robert said, "Yes, but it has a flat tire."

"Oh that's too bad. I still have some important things to tell you and I hoped that we could go to the park by the river and eat our lunch together."

Then her tone turned more hopeful and she said, "Maybe I could ride my bike and you could run along beside me."

Robert smiled. Only Bunny would come up with an idea like that.

He said, "I could never run that far Bunny. Besides, whether I could or not, it would take too long. I only have an hour for lunch. How about inside the Law Quad? It's nice and quiet in there."

"No I don't think so."

"Why not?"

"I don't want to eat with a bunch of lawyers. Lawyers are

So Many Maybes · 218

fucking boring. That is except for my friend Lois. Lois isn't boring. You'll see that if you ever meet her."

"Do we really need to have lunch together today Bunny? I've got stuff to do here at the store."

"Please Acka. This is really important to me. I promise I won't grab my ass again."

Robert laughed at himself because he actually understood what she meant.

He said, "That's a relief."

"I'm curious though Acka, I grabbed my piece of ass. Why didn't you grab yours? Is it because my boobs are too small?"

"No Bunny. Your boobs are just fine."

"Thank you Acka."

"You're welcome Bunny…Why don't we just find a place on The Diag?"

"Okay, but do we really have to go that far?"

"Not necessarily…do you think we can find a closer place?"

"Sure…we can grab our asses on any street corner."

Robert stopped to catch his breath and decided it was time for him to take charge.

He said, "Meet me on the brass M at the center of The Diag."

She said, "Okay."

When he arrived at the M, he found Bunny sitting on a blanket under a tree. She offered him a peanut butter and jelly and macaroni and cheese sandwich and poured him a glass of wine. Robert grimaced when he peeled the bread back and looked at the sandwich's contents, but he didn't want to be impolite to Bunny who had obviously gone to some trouble

So Many Maybes · 219

to make him lunch. So he braced himself and took a bite. Surprisingly, it didn't taste too bad, but it felt really weird in his mouth. He took a drink of the wine, which was actually very good, and he silently waited for her to tell him the important things she wanted to talk about.

Bunny took a big drink of wine and swallowed hard.

After a long pause, she said, "Robert I want to tell you about myself."

He nodded, and with his mouth full of gooey, but oddly slippery macaroni, he asked her, "Why do you want to do that Bunny?"

"Because you told me all about your past and even though you were boring as fuck, I know more about you than you know about me. And I want you to understand why I'm going to leave Ann Arbor and join a ballet company no matter how hard your boner is."

Robert said, "Okay."

He mentally prepared himself. He knew that it was going to be fun listening to her but also a challenge because she was so disorienting. For short periods, Bunny was entertaining to be around if you could weather the confusion, but over the long haul she could be exhausting to talk to.

Bunny began.

"Robert, I grew up in Beverly Hills, California. It's a rich suburb of Los Angeles. You've probably heard of it."

Bunny paused and waited for Robert to react.

"Yes, I've heard of Beverly Hills."

Bunny continued, "Don't misunderstand me. I don't know

So Many Maybes · 220

if we were rich, but everyone else was so we probably were. I'm not sure. Maybe we weren't. I don't know. I'll have to ask my mother about that, if I ever see her again."

"Why wouldn't you see her again?"

"My parents threw me out after I offered the judge a blowjob if he would let me off the shoplifting charge."

"What did the judge say?"

"He said he couldn't accept my offer because I was underage, but he would let me go if my mother agreed to blow him while my dad fucked him in the ass."

"That's an odd offer."

"The judge was from San Francisco."

Robert nodded and said, "I see. Let me guess. Your parents didn't accept the judge's offer."

"No they didn't. Can you believe that? Personally, I think they were being really selfish. They wouldn't do it for me, their only daughter, that is, except for my sister."

"You have a sister?"

"As a matter of fact, I do. How did you know?"

"Just a guess."

"Anyway, when I got out of rehab I couldn't find a job."

"You were in rehab?"

"Of course I was. Why do think that I offered the Judge a blowjob?"

"You said you got caught shoplifting."

"You're right, I did say that didn't I? I was shoplifting for the coke."

"You were stealing cokes? That hardly sounds like a charge

So Many Maybes · 221

worth offering a blowjob for."

"Oh I wasn't thinking. Coke is wonderful, but it's so fucking expensive."

"Expensive...Ohhh...you mean cocaine not Coka Cola?"

"Of course not. I wouldn't offer a blowjob for a Coke, that is, unless the judge was really cute. Anyway, where was I?"

"You were looking for a job."

"Oh right. After I got out of jail, I…"

"Whoa…Ohhh…Ohhh. Hold on Bunny. You were in jail?"

"I thought I already told you that."

"You told me that you were in rehab."

"Oh rehab, jail, they're the same thing. They both have bars on the windows."

Robert wasn't sure whether rehab had bars on the windows or not, but he didn't stop her.

"Anyway, when I got out of rehab I didn't have a place to live and I didn't have a job, so they sent me to this lady to help me find a place to work. She asked me what skills I had, and I told her I was pretty good at shoplifting. She said that didn't count, besides I got caught so I probably wasn't that good at it."

"She made a good point."

"Then she asked me what other skills I had, and I told her I could dance. She said she didn't have any jobs for dancers, what else could I do. I couldn't think of anything and then I remembered that when I was in the joint I saw this movie or TV show or something where a woman became a stripper and went on to be a movie star and even though Lois said that movie was bullshit, I asked…"

So Many Maybes · 222

"Lois was your lawyer"

"No Lois was never my lawyer. How did you get that idea?"

"This morning, you said that Lois is a lawyer and she wasn't boring."

"Boy is that true."

Robert was starting to get confused now.

He said, "What's true. That's she's a lawyer or she's not boring."

"Both. She's a lawyer and she's not boring."

"Okay…if she wasn't your lawyer how did you meet her?"

"I met her at the theatre after Tank protected me."

"There was a tank in Los Angeles!?"

"I wasn't in Los Angeles any more. I was in Berkeley."

"So there was a tank in Berkeley?"

"Oh Acka. Berkeley is in San Francisco. There aren't any tanks there."

"But you just said that a tank protected you."

"He did."

'So Tank is a man."

"He's a man the size of a seven-foot-tall Coke machine. Oh. I guess I shouldn't say Coke."

"Don't worry about it. Just go on with your story."

"Okay, on my way into the theater, Tank threw the two drunks in the dumpster."

"Why did he do that?"

"They molested me and tried to grab me, but my boobs are too small, and the drunks couldn't get a handhold. Tank protected me. He beat the shit out of them and grabbed them

So Many Maybes · 223

by their collars and tossed them in the trash. That's when I met Lois."

"So you didn't meet Lois until after you went into the theater. But I thought she told you that movie was bullshit?"

"She did."

"So Lois advised you not to become a stripper before you met her."

"Oh Acka. How could you think that? That's not possible."

"I guess I misunderstood. Go on."

"Anyway, when I got out of prison the job lady told me that she did know…"

Robert interrupted again.

He said, "Wait a minute. Before you said rehab or jail. You didn't mention prison."

"Oh what's it matter? Like I said…"

Robert nodded and spoke in unison with her as she said, "They all have bars."

Then he said, "Okay. Please go on."

"Anyway…the job lady told me about Amanda. Amanda had her own modern dance company up in Berkeley."

"I thought you told me that you were a stripper."

"I know. That's a joke because we danced naked."

"Naked? I thought you said that you dressed up like cats."

"We did. We wore body paint."

Robert nodded. He had never suspected that Bunny was involved in modern dance. He had always taken her literally when she called herself a stripper.

"The job lady called up Amanda and Lois bought me

So Many Maybes · 224

a bus ticket to Berkeley."

"If it was Amanda's company, why did Lois buy you the bus ticket?"

"Lois was the company's business manager."

"I see. Go on."

"Anyway, I went up there the next day and auditioned for Amanda and she asked me to join her company. Amanda and Baja were dancing together, but Amanda wanted to retire from dancing and just choreograph, so she chose me to dance with Baja. Baja is really good at body paint and costumes and painting sets and that kind of stuff, so she and Amanda created a dance with two exotic Jungle Cats."

"How did it go?"

"Oh it went great. I loved dancing with her. Baja is wonderful. But I always felt bad."

"Why did you feel bad?"

"Because Amanda's got boobs."

"Why should that make you feel bad?"

"Amanda danced with Baja first, so I couldn't take her place."

"Who's place?

"Amanda's."

"Didn't you just tell me that you did take her place."

"I did."

"Okay Bunny. Please explain why you couldn't but you did."

"I did but I could never dance like Amanda. She's got boobs."

"I see."

"Anyway, Amanda's grant money ran out and the company broke up and Lois went back to being a lawyer. That's when

So Many Maybes · 225

Baja and I came here."

Robert shook his head and said, "Wow. In a way it is like the movies. It has a happy ending, but it starts out as a sad story."

Bunny nodded and said, "Well Acka, what can I say, I'm terrible at telling stories. You're a writer, maybe you can help me." Then she smiled and said, "There you have it Acka. Do you understand now why I have to leave Ann Arbor and why I can't let you fuck me?"

Robert started to remind her that she hadn't even mentioned that subject and besides, she had been pursuing him, not the other way around. But he stopped when he realized that her custom crafted logic had finally pointed her in the direction he wanted her to go.

He said, "Yes Bunny. Now I understand and thank you for being so kind to explain it to me."

Then he looked at his watch and began to stand up.

He said, "We need to stop Bunny. My lunch break is up. Come on."

Bunny said, "Okay, you can walk me back to the bookstore."

Again, Robert started to correct her statement.

He said, "You mean, you can…"

But he stopped because it wasn't important.

So Many Maybes · 226

Chapter 16
Wolf's Vampire

*Note: The play "Rilke's Dracula" is presented as a separate entity at the end of the book.

Wolf formed his own theater company soon after he moved to Ann Arbor. In the beginning, it was only a shell he used to apply for grants and sell advertising and to set up some semblance of a business. Over time he made dozens of friends and many of them joined with him to form the Wolf Rilke Theater Company.

Putting on a theater production can be a daunting, time consuming and exhausting enterprise but it can also be fun, and Wolf's productions were more fun than most. Wolf believed that everyone who was working with him should be allowed to perform whatever function they wanted to as long as it made sense. For example, Wolf wanted his productions to be well crafted and not everyone is skilled at lighting or sound or set design. However, if an unskilled individual wanted to take part, they were welcome to help in some way and maybe learn the skills as time went on.

As a theater producer, Wolf was a big Teddy Bear. He was always hugging people and thanking everyone profusely. This behavior was partly Wolf's natural affable personality, but it was also a matter of conscious philosophy. He had been around theater a long time and he thought that insensitive, unkind, and dictatorial theater producers, his father included, should be barred from theater for life and, if possible, undergo a forceful, well-televised enema.

By the time that his play *Rilke's Dracula* was in pre-production, everyone but Dilli O was a member of The Wolf Rilke Theater Company. Terri served as the company's business manager and head of publicity. Will did almost everything technical and, on occasion, would be a cast member. Jenny was a great actress and a natural comedian, and Nort was the company carpenter and electrician. Recently, Baja had joined them as costume and set designer. Robert had no real skills but writing and farting, so he was most valuable to Terri in writing advertisements. But if Wolf asked him for help in some other way, Robert would do what he could. And on a few occasions, he had even played a few non-speaking acting roles. However, because of Robert's clumsiness, Wolf was always careful not to let him get too close to the sets.

After their BunnySpeak discussion on The Diag, Robert hoped he could stay away from Bunny and get on with his life. Unfortunately, he had introduced Bunny to his friends and Bonnie really liked Bunny. She thought that Bunny was sweet and pleasant and her off-the-wall view of things original and fun. As it turned out, they both lived in the same apartment building, so they saw each other often and they became good friends.

So Many Maybes · 228

One evening, they sat down at the bar next to Robert. Bunny didn't say anything to Robert but said, "Connie, will you and Acka come over to our place on Friday night after the play and have dinner with me and Baja and Wallace and Bonnie and Whoa? We invited Jane and Bust too, but they can't come."

Robert leaned close to Bonnie's ear and said, "I know who Bust and Jane are, but who's Whoa?"

"Whoa is Wolf."

Camille said, "Why go to all that trouble, Bunny? Why don't we all come back here to eat?"

"That's what Baja said, but she changed her mind when I told her I thought the food here sucks."

Robert said, "How can you say that, Bunny? You eat here all the time."

"I know but that doesn't mean the food is any good. Anyway… I just told her that so you'd come over to our place. I want to show you my room."

Robert didn't respond. He was curious why she wanted to show them her room, but he was afraid to ask. Besides, going to her place was the last thing he wanted to do.

Bunny noticed his reticence and said, "Don't worry Acka. I promise to stay out of my pants this time."

Camille said, "Acka what is she talking about?"

Robert shook his head and said, "I'll tell you later."

Camille said, "I can't wait to hear about it. Anyway…we'd love to come…Wouldn't we Acka?"

"Oh sure…Absolutely."

Bunny said, "Oh good. I'll talk to Baja about what she

wants to have for dinner."

Robert said, "I knew you made sandwiches Bunny but I'd never have thought that you really cooked."

"I don't, so we might have to eat fish sticks and cheese whiz."

Robert tried his best not to react to her menu suggestion, but Bonnie made an ugly face.

Camille saw Bonnie's reaction and said, "Why don't we get Pizza delivered from Domino's instead?"

Bonnie quickly said, "Let's do that. It'll mean less work for you and Baja."

"Thank you Bonnie. Fish-sticks taste like shit anyway. I like Cheese Whiz though."

Camille said, "What's your address Bunny?"

"Oh, I guess you need that don't you? Wait a minute, my memory blows horse dicks and I can never remember it, so I wrote it down on a piece of paper."

She picked up her purse and started to look for it.

Bonnie knew that it would take a while for Bunny to find it, so she gently put her hand on top of Bunny's and stopped Bunny from looking any further.

She said, "She lives in Tower Plaza, the same building that I do, so just come over to my place and I'll take you to Bunny's apartment."

Camille nodded okay.

After the dinner arrangements were settled, Bunny returned to GaGa Land.

She said, "Acka, after dinner you and Connie have to fuck in my room and let me watch so I can see your boner. I think

So Many Maybes · 230

you owe me that much because you didn't come over that first night. Maybe we could all fuck each other, but on second thought I'm not gay so that wouldn't work Connie are you gay?"

"No Bunny, I'm not gay."

"That's good. I don't think Acka would like fucking a transvestite."

Camille looked at Robert and shook her head and said, "What?"

Two days before Wolf's adaptation of *Dracula* was to open, Bonnie dropped by Maybe's.

She said, "Camille, since this is the first time that you're going to see one of Wolf's plays, I have no doubt that you'll find it really weird, so I recommend you get severely hammered before you go. It would even be better if you were stoned or high on acid because once the curtain opens you're going on a trip that seems to start out making sense then quickly will take you to a place that makes a conversation with Bunny seem normal. But just give in to the absurdity and you'll have a good time. I'll meet you in the lobby before the play and chat a little before I have to go and change into my costume."

After Bonnie left, Camille said, "Robert, was she being serious? Are Wolf's plays really that weird?"

"She wasn't being entirely fair to Wolf. Unlike Bunny, Wolf's plays are easy to understand, but they're still off-the-wall crazy. You saw what he produced for Open Mic Night."

"It was a lot of fun."

So Many Maybes · 231

"That's really all he wants. He sometimes makes fun of things like he did with the hockey player, and other times he just acts insane like he did with the duck act. Sometimes he'll try things that turn out to be complete duds, but that's rare and if we follow Bonnie's advice and get hammered, we'll have fun."

Camille took Robert shopping this time. Like he did with Bonnie, they visited numerous thrift shops and Robert found another nice shirt. This time Camille ironed it for him. Camille's outfit was a little more formal than the one that she had worn for Open Mic Night. She wore a glistening brown and gold and black, one-shoulder top with close-fitting black pants and black patent leather heels. Of course, she took Robert's breath away and he worried that his time with Camille was only a perfect dream that was destined to end like all perfect dreams seem to do.

When they entered the lobby outside the theater, almost everyone turned to look at Camille. All the men smiled. The response from women was mixed. Robert had no idea why.

Camille and Robert looked around the lobby for Bonnie, but Bonnie found them first. Bunny was with her. A tall man in a black suit walked next to Bunny. Bunny looked absolutely stunning. She was wearing a mid-calf yellow dress decorated with several green branches of grape leaves, and a pair of red three-strap high heels. She'd gotten her hair restyled and it was now shoulder length and combed straight. When Robert saw her in such a beautiful dress, he realized that he'd never seen her wear anything but her dancer's tights.

So Many Maybes · 232

Bonnie said, "I'm so glad you're here. I'll feel better being up on stage knowing I have friends in the audience. I'm a poet, not an actress."

Camille said, "We wouldn't miss it for the world."

Bunny said, "I would. I get lost a lot. The world is a pretty big place."

She motioned to the man standing next to her and said, "This is my date, Cleft."

With a frown and a very stuffy Boston accent, the man said, "Although humorous, your ridiculous habit of changing everyone's name is offensive. Cleft is a vulgar name. I'm Clifton."

Bunny looked at Robert and Camille and loudly said, "Cleft is loaded, and he told me that his boner is huge. But he's also a huge asshole so I'm dumping him in the lobby after the play. Can I walk home with you guys?"

Clifton trembled with anger and glared at Bunny. Then he suddenly turned and quickly walked out of the theater.

Bunny said, "I think it's better to let them know where they stand before they get attached. That way I don't have to sit through a lot of boring breakfasts."

Robert said, "Where did you meet him? He didn't seem like your type."

"He's my gynecologist."

"Your gynecologist asked you out?"

"I went to see him yesterday and I guess he liked what he saw."

"No doubt."

Bonnie said, "Bunny and I are drunk. How about you?"

So Many Maybes · 233

Camille said, "To the max."

Bunny asked, "Did you take some acid?"

Camille said, "I don't know where to get acid."

Bunny said, "I do. I've got a lot of it back at our apartment. I use it all the time."

Bunny's comment about using acid caught Robert's attention immediately, and without thinking, he took the bait.

"You use acid Bunny?"

"When I was out in LA, the good housekeeping people told me it was the best."

"You mean in their magazine?"

"They have a magazine too? I thought they just worked for the hotel."

Bonnie could barely contain her laughter.

Robert whispered to Camille, "Do you have any idea what she's talking about?"

"I think she means that acid is good for cleaning or something."

Robert said, "You know Camille, I should know better by now."

"Yes, you should."

Bunny pulled a big bag out of her purse. It had large bold red letters on the side that said, "POPCORN."

"Do you guys want some popcorn? I snuck it in."

Camille said, "Bonnie you said that this play is really weird. What's weird about it?"

"It'll take too long to explain that but trust me. Did you get hammered?"

So Many Maybes · 234

"I already told you, yes to the max."

"Did you bring plenty of popcorn?"

"Bunny brought the popcorn."

"Did you wear panties?"

"What does that have to do with anything?"

Bonnie slurred her words as she said, "Nothing. But you have to admit that it's always fun to go without panties."

Robert said, "Bonnie do you think it was smart to get so drunk. You're in the play and you have a speaking role."

"In this play, being drunk will make my acting better."

"Oh…so you're playing a drunk in the play?"

"Nope, I just won't give a shit…See you, I have to go."

She left without letting Robert ask any more questions.

Camille and Robert and Bunny found three empty seats together and sat down. Robert looked down at the program. Terri had put it together by herself and he hadn't seen it.

RILKE'S DRACULA
BY
WOLF RILKE

Presented in Twenty-Six Acts
by
The Wolf Rilke Theater Company

Just kidding.
Why do you care how many Acts there are?
You'll probably leave early anyway.

So Many Maybes · 235

PRODUCED BY WOLF RILKE
LIGHTING AND SOUND BY WILL B. FREE
SETS, BODY PAINT, AND PROPS BY BAJA
MUSIC PLAYED BY THE GRUNGY HIPPYS
ORIGINAL MUSIC BY NOBODY

CAST OF CHARACTERS

JOSIA CARUTHERS..........................as Jonathan Harker

DR. JOHAN O'MALLEY................................as Hawkins

MICHAEL BROWN............................as Count Dracula

JENNY WOODWARD..........................as Lucy Hawkins

BAJA..as Alice Carroll

BONNIE HAINES....................................as Miss Partime

WOLF RILKE....................................as Plumber Houston

CONRAD WILLIAMS.................as Dr. Engine Snorkel

BRETT WINTERS.....................................as Do-Me Ruff

DR. ZITHER PLAYER..............Rich-American Bastard

DR. CLAMPED ORIFICE................as Collassa Bastard

The producers of Rilke's Dracula would like to thank the members of the University faculty who have agreed, albeit begrudgingly, to take part in this production. Since this is a Wolf Rilke play, Drs. Player and Orifice are pseudonyms. Dr. O'Malley didn't give a shit whether we revealed his real name or not. He's already collecting his retirement.

Robert reacted too quickly and said much too loudly, "Holy

So Many Maybes · 236

fuck! Twenty-six acts! What are you doing Wolf?"

Camille said, "Robert don't worry. See there where it says, 'just kidding.' Wolf is just being a smart ass. Let's make the best of it. Who knows? Maybe sometime before the end Wolf will fuck Baja."

Robert said, "Okay. But I'm putting my money on Brett and I'm praying that no one bangs Jenny. That would freak me out."

As the house lights went down, Camille reached over into Robert's lap and took Robert's hand and he felt warm all over.

And so began Camille's first journey into the Magic Land of Wolf. A place with unconventional staging techniques and where every room and building is covered with signs that not only announce where you're located but also make smart-ass remarks about the location and people who dwell there. A place where a horse-drawn carriage is simulated by a rocking-horse pulling an American Flyer Wagon. A place where hippies live in the 1890s and a place where a spectacular, totally unexpected ending can occur and convey obvious heavy handed social commentary.

And Robert got to see Baja naked again, but this time she was in body paint. As soon as she came on stage, he forgot everything else that was going on and just stared at her. And then suddenly he felt stupid and afraid and confused. He felt stupid because he was holding hands with a world-class beauty and lusting after another woman. He felt afraid because he thought that his lust could jeopardize his relationship with Camille. And he was confused because he had never lusted after a woman in this way before. In the past, his initial

So Many Maybes · 237

attraction to a woman seemed to come completely from visual stimuli, in other words, were they cute or beautiful. With Baja, it was different. Certainly she was beautiful, but his attraction seemed more primitive, biochemical, even hormonal, or maybe pheromonal. Consequently, he felt that he had no control over it and he desperately wanted to defeat it. In no way did he want this lust to persist. He loved Camille and he knew that she loved him.

Magically, Camille put his mind to rest.

After the play was over, she said, "I assume that you liked seeing Baja naked again."

"Was it that obvious?"

"Well, in a way."

"What do you mean?"

"Your hammer told me. If you recall, I had my hand in your lap."

"I'm sorry Camille. I didn't want to."

"I know. You can't help it."

As they left the theater, Bunny said, "I think we should wait here for Bonnie so she can meet you guys and show you where my apartment is."

Camille said, "I think you're right."

Robert started to say, "But Bunny, you…"

He stopped when he realized that, even though Bunny could lead them to her apartment herself, she knew that Bonnie was coming out into the lobby expecting to meet them, and it would be rude if they didn't wait.

So Many Maybes · 238

They only had to wait a few minutes until Will, Wolf, Baja, Jenny, and Brett and Bonnie arrived. Baja was still wearing her body paint but, of course, she was now dressed.

Bunny said, "Baja, why did you get dressed? I think Acka wanted to see your boobs up close."

Bonnie said, "He should've come to our rehearsals."

Camille said, "You went naked at the rehearsals."

Baja said, ""Wolf strives for realism."

Camille said, "I'll bet he does."

Bonnie said, "Most of the men in our cast and crew had a permanent hard-on."

Bunny said, "Oh Bonnie, I wish you'd called me. I would have come over to the theater and taken pictures."

Jenny said, "What kind of camera do you have Bunny?"

Bunny said, "It's a Canon and it's got a huge lens. I like huge cannons.

Jenny said, "I've got a Nikon."

Bunny said, "Doe's yours have a huge cannon too.

Jenny said, "No Bunny. It's only got a normal lens."

"That's too bad. Maybe if you sell a painting, you can buy a huge cannon like mine."

In fact, Robert had mixed feelings about seeing Baja dressed. He had to admit that it would have been great to see her naked painted body up close, but the last thing he wanted was to suffer the embarrassment that was inevitable when he got his hard-on in front of everyone.

Ultimately, Robert didn't have to worry about embarrassing himself because Bunny did it for him.

So Many Maybes · 239

She asked Will and Wolf, "Did you guys get boners tonight like Acka did when you saw Baja's boobs?"

Robert said, "Thank you for telling everyone Bunny."

"You're welcome, Acka."

Jenny said, "I've been waiting a long time for a chance to take a picture of Acka's boner so I could paint it later."

Brett said, "I'd love to put an abstract expressionist interpretation of Acka's boner on the wall over our stage at Maybe's."

Robert's terror was obvious in his face.

Camille said, "Relax Acka. Even if Bust did something like that, no one would know whose boner it was."

Brett said, "Don't be so sure. I would put a big label on it that said, 'Hail to the Glory of Robert Bain's Boner.'"

Bunny said, "Who's Robert Bain?"

Robert said, "No one really, Bunny. Bust was just making a joke."

Bunny said, "I don't get it. Why is it funny?"

Wolf said, "Don't worry about it Bunny. It's not important."

Baja said, "Whoa you didn't answer Bunny's question. Did you get a boner tonight?"

"Yes my dear, but I wore seventy-six jock straps to keep it from being visible to the audience."

Bunny said, "You didn't have to do that Whoa. Male ballet dancers wear a special stretching scrotal holster called a dance belt under their tights so the audience can't see their nuts. It would hide your boner too and it wouldn't make your balls sweat nearly as much as seventy-six jock straps. If you want,

So Many Maybes · 240

I can borrow one from one of the dancer's in my school. I'm sure at least one of them has an old one just lying around."

Bonnie said, "Wallace, please don't tell everyone about your boner."

Will said, "Boner? What Boner?"

Bonnie said, "Thank you Wallace."

"You're welcome Bonnie."

Bunny said, "As much as I like talking about boners, I want to get back to my apartment to change my clothes and take a shit."

Bonnie said, "Me too."

Bunny said, "Do you wanna' take a shit too Bonnie?"

Bonnie said, "Yes I do Bunny. I like taking shits."

Bunny said, "Me too Bonnie. Maybe we should take one together."

Bunny and Baja's apartment was three floors up from Bonnie's. It had two bedrooms, a big living room and there was a separate kitchen and dining room. Each bedroom had its own full-size bathroom.

When they walked in, Baja said, "Welcome to our little dancer's haven. Get your drinks then I'll give you the grand tour."

Bonnie said, "Show me the alcohol. I'm starting to sober up. I don't want to sober up."

Wolf said, "Try some of this. It will provide you with the lift you desire."

He handed her the two-gallon milk jug he had brought with

So Many Maybes · 241

him. It was labeled, "Wolf Man's 24 Carat Proof of Life" and the liquid inside tasted exactly like sweetened iced tea.

Bonnie removed the cap and chugged a significant amount.

Her eyes opened wide and she said, "Holy shit, Wolf! What is this stuff?"

"Miss Haines, it is the liquid expression of the primeval forest's conception of human perception."

"What the fuck does that mean?"

"Now that you have drank from its fountain of synaptic alteration, you will never see the world the same. Mere commercial alcohol will never measure up."

Robert said, "Is it moonshine Whoa?"

"Only in the sense that it's makers, my legendary namesakes, howled at the moon when they made it."

Robert said, "Let me try it."

"Be my guest my fellow composer of fictional fantasy. Join me and the brilliant poet Miss Haines on a trip down the rabbit hole."

"Are you saying it's got acid in it Whoa?"

"Oh no my dear man. I would never say such a thing. LSD is illegal. Let's just say that this is a magic elixir that stimulates the brain and the body to a higher state of consciousness not unlike good literature."

Robert took the jug from Wolf and drank. His lips went numb and he felt a strong tingling behind his eyes.

He hugged the jug and said, "I love this stuff Whoa. I declare it mine for the rest of the evening."

Bunny said, "Besides Whoa's literature, we bought some

So Many Maybes · 242

wine and tequila for tonight."

She knelt down on the floor in front of the sink and said, "I put the bottles under here with the acid."

Wolf said, "Oh my dear Bunny, You take Acid?"

Baja said, "Bunny uses acid to clean the grout in the bathroom."

Wolf said, "Thank God. I would have been dis-heartened to learn that her original and engaging view of life was the product of some illegal chemical."

Bonnie said, "Wolf, LSD doesn't bother me. I'm more shocked to learn that Bunny cleans the bathroom."

Bunny said, "If I don't, my knees get dirty when I throw up in the toilet."

Bonnie said, "I see your point."

Bunny removed several bottles from under the sink and handed them to Camille who put them on the kitchen counter.

Camille said, "Bunny why did you put the liquor down there?"

"It's the only place we had room. The cupboards are all full with my shoes."

"Your shoes?"

"I keep my shoes in the kitchen cupboard."

"Why don't you keep your shoes in your closet?"

"They're more organized in the cupboard. The cupboard has shelves."

"Where do you keep your dishes."

"When they're washed, I put them in the refrigerator, but mostly I just leave them dirty and store them in the sink."

So Many Maybes · 243

Robert leaned to Camille and said, "It's probably better that you stop the questions now. I suspect you don't want to know what she stores in the toilet."

Camille said, "I think you're right."

Bonnie rummaged through the kitchen drawers and said, "Bunny where do you keep your cork screw?"

Bunny opened the refrigerator and reached into the freezer and took out the cork screw and handed it to Bonnie.

Almost intuitively, Bonnie reached into the refrigerator and took out the wine glasses and put them on the kitchen counter next to the wine. Then she opened a bottle of White Chardonnay for herself and carried it with her as she left the kitchen.

She said, "Everyone get their own. I'm too busy getting drunk again to wait on you."

The apartment walls were covered with photographs of dancers. Several showed Baja and Bunny doing their Big Cat routine and others showed Baja with another woman.

Baja said, "These first three pictures are of Bunny and me doing our Big Cat dance and the others are of Amanda and me doing the same dance."

Wolf said, "Will you three beautiful kittens move in with me? I promise to frequently pet you wherever you wish."

Baja said, "Shush you Sexy Tummied Tahitian War Chief or I'll set your grass skirt on fire."

Camille said, "Who's Amanda."

Bunny said, "She was our choreographer. She's got boobs."

Wolf said, "Yes. Those certainly are boobs."

So Many Maybes · 244

When he looked up and saw Baja's frown, he added, "And they're almost as beautiful as Baja's."

Baja bent down and kissed him on the forehead and said, "So wise of you to say so Whoa."

Wolf said, "For a modern man, considerate wisdom with a woman is a fundamental requirement for civility and, I must say, survival."

Bonnie took a big drink of her wine and said, "I am a poet and I couldn't have said it better Whoa. Except for maybe adding something about kissing our ass."

Will said, "Recently I too have learned to appreciate the benefits of applying the aforementioned wisdom."

Robert took a big drink from his personal jug and said, "Personally, I like having my ass rubbed more than having it kissed."

Wolf said, "Acka, given your infamous skill at blasting rectal methane, I would think that rubbing your ass would be a much safer enterprise than kissing it."

Robert said, "You are very wise Whoa, but please don't try either."

Camille said, "I often do both. Rectal methane turns me on."

Bunny said, "I rubbed Acka's ass once. I think he liked it until I gave the nuns the finger."

Robert looked at Camille and said, "I'll tell you about it later."

Camille said, "Of course you will."

Whoa raised his glass of wine and said, "Here's to the joys of alcohol influenced conversation," and he took a big drink.

So Many Maybes · 245

Camille said, "Baja, did you do all of the body paint?"

Baja nodded and said, "And I designed the sets and all of the props too."

Bunny pointed to another picture and said, "We did other dances besides the cat shit too. Amanda made this one just for Baja,"

Baja said, "Amanda liked that I was tall and thin, so she choreographed a dance where I was a long serpent that was moving along a tree limb while I shed my silver reflected snake scales to reveal my naked body."

Bunny said, "Then I played a bunny rabbit with a cute little pink nose."

Camille said, "What did you do Bunny?"

"I stood still while Baja's snake strangled me."

"Ohhh! That's awful."

Baja said, "Amanda never told us why she had the snake kill the bunny."

Bunny said, "I think it was like Whoa's play."

Camille said, "Why is that?"

"I think she tried to read Alice in Asunderland and couldn't figure out how to follow the rabbit to Scandinavia."

Bunny's comment confused everyone, and the room became quiet while they all tried to understand what Bunny had just said.

Wolf finally broke the silence by saying, "Have we just heard how Bunny got her name?"

Bunny said, "No Whoa. Actually, the little bunny was named after me."

So Many Maybes · 246

The entire group became quiet again.

Baja broke the silence by continuing the tour.

"Besides me and Bunny and Amanda there are pictures of other dancers here too."

Bunny said, "My teacher got me these. The dancers signed their names on the pictures so we can tell who they are. This is Ivan Goodekov and here is Aglaya Stenova. They're the greatest ballet dancers in the world. If I get a chance to dance in New York, I want Goodekov to fuck me like a corn dog and have Stenova take pictures with my Canon."

Baja said, "Maybe Amanda would choreograph that into a ballet. She could call it *Afternoon of the Corn Dog* or maybe *Big Cannon in the Dark*."

Robert squinted drunkenly at the photo of Stenova and said, "For some reason, I feel like I've seen her before."

Camille put her head next to Robert's and looked carefully at the Russian Ballerina's picture too.

She said, "Bunny, would you do me a favor and come over here and stand next to Stenova's picture?"

Bunny stood next to the photograph.

Camille turned to the others and said, "Check this out."

Baja said, "Jesus Christ! I can't believe I haven't noticed before."

Bunny said, "What?"

Baja removed the picture from the wall and held it close to Bunny's face.

Bonnie said, "Bunny go get your Canon."

Bunny said, "Why? What's going on?"

So Many Maybes · 247

Wolf said, "It is truly astonishing."

Robert was still squinting drunkenly at the place on the wall where the picture had been.

Bunny returned with her camera.

Bonnie said, "Give Wallace the camera and Baja hold the picture next to Bunny. Now Wallace take a picture of Bunny next to the picture of Stenova."

Bunny said, "Baja please tell me what's going on."

Baja said, "You're identical."

"Who is."

"You and Stenova. You're like twins."

"That's not possible?"

"Why not?"

"I can't speak Russian."

Baja said, "You're right Bunny. I forgot."

Baja continued the tour of the apartment.

"And now…Ta-da…on to Bunny's famous room."

Everyone but Robert followed Baja. He remained motionless, staring at the wall. Camille grabbed his hand and pulled him toward Bunny's room.

When they entered, Bunny turned on the lights to reveal an amazing, bizarre place. Each wall was a complete jungle scene painted with black-light paint and the floor felt like grass. They could hear jungle birds. The room was damp and foggy, and the bed was a single grass covered mattress that rose a foot off the jungle floor in the center of the room. There were odd paintings of plants in wild greens and blues and yellows and the faces of lions and leopards and snakes and monkeys and

So Many Maybes · 248

things along with a perfectly round red sun.

Camille was amazed. She said, "I feel like I've entered an Henri Rousseau painting."

Robert was slowly spinning around and holding on to his jug. He was trying to understand what he was seeing.

Will said, "Who's Henri Rousseau?"

Bonnie drunkenly said, "He was a French 'naïve' painter."

Will said, "What's a 'naïve' painter."

Bonnie said, "A painter that doesn't know shit about art."

Camille said, "Bonnie means that he never studied painting or art history. He's best known for jungle scenes that are childlike and surrealistic just like this room."

Bonnie burped and slurred her words and said, "He was un...corrupted."

Camille said, "Where did you get the idea for this Bunny?"

Bunny said, "It's like the sets that Baja painted for our dance. Like the ones in the pictures, don't you think?"

Still walking around the room, Camille said, "I guess it is. It's wonderful Baja."

Baja said, "It was really Bunny's idea. I just helped her make it happen."

Robert was having trouble standing up, so he walked over to the bed to sit down and as soon as his butt touched the mattress there was an absurdly loud *MEEE-YOW!!!* It scared the shit out of everyone. Evidently Bunny thought Big Cats made Big Meows.

Robert shouted, "Yah!!!" and jumped up so fast, that he stumbled forward and rammed his forehead into the wall

So Many Maybes · 249

in front of him.

Wolf shouted, "Mother of God!" and fell backward onto his rump and held his hand to his heart.

Camille shouted, "FUCK!" and hid behind Bonnie.

Will looked suspiciously like he had pissed his pants.

Bunny and Baja laughed hysterically, and Bonnie giggled.

Baja said, "You're the first ones besides Bonnie that we've pulled that joke on."

Trying to catch her breath, Camille said, "Let me guess; it was Bunny's idea."

"She wanted to use an elephant's trumpet blast, but we decided that would give everyone a heart attack."

Wolf said, "It wouldn't have mattered. I'm having palpitations now."

With their journey into the jungle primeval over, Baja went into her bathroom to wash off her body paint.

Bonnie took her personal bottle of Chardonnay and sat on the couch. Robert maintained possession of Wolf's jug of magic sweet tea and sat down on the floor next to the coffee table. The others went into the kitchen to get the rest of the wine and tequila then walked into the living room to join Robert and Bonnie.

Wolf sat down on the couch next to Bonnie and everyone else sat on the floor next to Robert.

Wolf poured himself another glass of red wine and said, "It's a little-known fact that the first evidence found of the existence of wine goes all the way back to 7000 BC...I personally suspect that I am related to those primitive peoples. If not genetically, at

So Many Maybes · 250

least by their practice of indulging in the bad habit of drinking the fermented juices of grapes to excess. I also suspect that Miss Haines is my sister in this respect and if we were ever to mate, our child would come out of the womb a beautiful and brilliant alcoholic who shits gold bricks."

"Whoa, I admit that I am wealthy, but my money comes out of my trust fund and not my ass as you so often allege."

"I'll accept your word for it Miss Haines, but I'm still positive that my financial position would improve if you would let me stand behind you the next time you fart."

Robert drunkenly said, "People say I'm a fart smeller because I'm smart."

Everyone paused to look at Robert for a moment, then Wolf continued.

"It has also occurred to me that if our child was a boy, it would have a schlong as big as Babe Ruth's bat"

Bonnie said, "Whoa, if you agree to never display your bat while I'm in the room, I will agree to never shit gold bricks on your balls and crush them."

"I feel I must acquiesce, for I wish to have many bearded children."

Bunny said, "It just hit me. I forgot to take a shit."

Robert took a big drink from Wolf's jug and said, "I'm so glad you remembered Bunny. Can I watch?"

"I'm glad I remembered too. After a while it would have been bad news. You can come watch but you'll have to get a chair from the kitchen. There's not enough room for both of us to sit on the toilet."

So Many Maybes · 251

Bunny stood up to head for the bathroom.

Robert started to get up too, but Camille stopped him.

She said, "Acka sit back down and take another drink from Whoa's jug. It has to be better than watching Bunny take a shit."

"You're right. I wasn't thinking."

Robert took another drink then laid back prone on the floor.

Baja walked into the living room looking like her normal, non-painted self.

Robert looked up at her and said, "Baja I thought you were going to take off your body paint?"

Puzzled, Baja looked at Robert and said, "I did."

"I'm glad you didn't. You've got really nice breasts."

"Thank you Acka."

"What are they? About 43 double Ds?"

"What are you drinking Acka?"

"Whoa's stuff."

"You'd better be careful Acka. Whoa's concoctions are sometimes dangerous."

"I'll be careful. I still have to go watch Bunny take a shit."

Baja said, "Bunny did the pizza get here yet?"

"Oh…I forgot to order the pizza. I'll do it when I get out of the bathroom. Everyone think about what they want on it. I think we should start with dough."

Bonnie said, "I think that's a great idea Bunny, but why don't you let me do it? I'm an expert on pizza."

On her way to the bathroom Bunny said, "Okay Bonnie, I'm so glad you are. I don't know anything about pizza."

Bonnie got up and headed toward the kitchen where the

phone was. Baja sat down next to Wolf.

Wolf poured them all a shot of tequila and said, "Here's to the gorgeous women with us tonight. They bless our lives with their elegant presence."

Will said, "My God Whoa. How unexpected. A sincere toast without a trace of your signature sarcasm."

"Wallace my friend, sarcasm is inappropriate when one is describing beautiful women."

Baja said, "And lord knows, Whoa would never be inappropriate."

Bonnie walked out of the kitchen and said, "The pizza's ordered."

Baja asked, "What kind did you get?"

"I can't remember but I took Bunny's advice and started with dough."

"Makes sense."

Bunny returned from the bathroom and sat down on the floor again.

Camille said, "Boy that was fast."

"I was in a hurry, so I cut it short."

Robert said, "I'm glad I didn't go with you then. It wouldn't have been worth the walk."

Camille said, "Baja, how can you guys afford this place? It's huge."

"Bunny somehow got a ton of financial aid and I get a design job once in a while."

Bunny said, "Before Baja started making out with Whoa, she had a job working on a play in New York."

So Many Maybes · 253

Bonnie said, "What was the name of the play. I might have heard of it."

Baja said, "*Loosen My Bowels.*"

"Oh God. That play."

Baja said, "I was so disappointed. It closed in a week. It was supposed to be my big break"

"Why did it close so fast?"

"Ninety per cent of the cast quit. It had real live anal fist fucking on stage. That's where the title of the play *Loosen My Bowels* comes from."

Camille asked, "Didn't they know from the beginning what they were expected to do?"

"Oh they did. I guess they thought it would be fun to have someone shove a fist up their ass in front of a live audience."

"I gather it wasn't fun."

"I guess not. They all complained because they weren't having orgasms."

"You're kidding me! Orgasms?"

Baja shook her head and said, "No shit, orgasms…It's a weird world."

Camille said, "So Baja, I gather you're not in school like Bunny."

"I'm not the school type. I took a few classes at Berkeley when I was out there, but they were boring compared to doing the real thing."

Wolf poured Bunny and Bonnie a shot of tequila and they all touched glasses and repeated the ritual several times.

Bonnie said, "Wine stimulates the appetite for love."

So Many Maybes · 254

Bunny said, "I like wine. I like tequila too."

Camille said, "Three shots of tequila and I start to tell people my secrets."

Wolf said, "Would you share a secret with us tonight?"

"No Whoa. A secret is a secret is a secret."

"Okay my dear Connie. How about another shot."

Wolf filled everyone's glasses and held his high.

"Here's to Connie's secrets."

They all said, "To Connie's secrets."

Wolf said, "How about you, Miss Black and Blue Body paint? Do you have any secrets?"

"Not really Whoa. I'm pretty up front."

"Yes you are my dear. You certainly are. Don't you agree Acka?"

Robert didn't answer. He was asleep.

Camille said, "Whoa, from his previous comments, I think it's safe to say that Acka agrees that Baja is very pretty up front. He's just too unconscious to talk now."

Bunny said, "How do you know he's unconscious, Connie? He's asleep."

Robert rolled over on to his side and cradled his face in his hands and revealed to all of them that he had an erection under his pants.

Bunny said, "I think Acka is talking to us with his boner."

Wolf said, "How about you Wallace? Do you admire Baja's breasts as much as Acka and I do?"

"Ahhh…"

Bonnie said, "Good answer Wallace."

So Many Maybes · 255

Bunny said, "Connie, is your clitoris erect like mine? Tequila always makes my clitoris erect."

Camille's face flushed, and she didn't answer.

Bonnie said, "How many shots have you had now, Bunny?"

"I'm not sure, but I think forty-two…How about you Baja, is your clitoris erect?"

Baja said, "Yes Bunny. It's up, swollen and ready."

Wolf said, "I must pause for a moment in a short drunken reverie while I imagine what Miss Body Paint's standing and swollen clitoris looks like."

"Play your card's right, you mysterious bearded creature of the night, and I'll have Bunny take a picture of it for you, so you can hang it up on your ceiling over your bed."

"I will gladly play my cards and even bring my own dick… Ahhh…I mean deck."

Bonnie said, "Whoa how many shots have you had?"

Wolf said, "More than forty-two."

Bunny said, "Connie, can I take a picture of your erect clitoris too."

Camille said, "No Bunny, I don't think so. It wouldn't be fair to Acka."

"Connie are Acka's boner and your vagina seeing each other?"

"Yes Bunny."

"Are they going steady."

"Yes Bunny."

"Do they wear rings?"

"Rings?"

So Many Maybes · 256

"I saw in a magazine where people are getting rings in their vagina and boners. I guess it might be fun, but it has to hurt don't you think?"

Baja said, "Ahhh…what magazine was that, Bunny?"

Completely asleep, Robert stood up and began to undo his belt. Then he quoted a line from Wolf's play and said, "I can't help it Judy, all I've got is a woody."

Baja said, "Quick Bunny, go get your Canon again. Acka's boner is going to stand up and cheer for us."

"You mean Acka's going to give us a hand?"

Everyone paused a moment and looked at each other. Then Baja said, "I think so Bunny."

Bunny said, "Which hand Baja?"

Camille laughed and covered her eyes and shook her head.

Bunny got up as fast as she could and ran into the kitchen and grabbed her camera and ran back into the living room.

Before she made it, Robert had taken off all his clothes and stumbled towards Bunny's bedroom. She caught up with him just in time to snap a bunch of pictures of his naked ass before he plopped face down on her bed face first. As Bunny left her bedroom, she turned off the regular room light and flipped on the black lights and sound effects that turned her room into a psychedelic jungle.

Baja said, "Did you get a picture of it."

"No Baja. Before I could get there, it ran out of sight behind his ass. He's got a really fast boner."

Camille said, "Bunny, I have to go to work tomorrow and I'm tired. Is it okay if Acka and I fuck in your bed now? You

So Many Maybes · 257

can take pictures if you want."

"That's okay Connie. Thanks for inviting me but I think it would be rude if I took pictures, but I'll loan my camera to Baja if she wants to."

Baja said, "Thank you Bunny. That's very kind of you."

*

THE JOURNAL OF ROBERT BAIN

I don't know how long I slept before I woke up in Bunny's bed. I sat up and looked around. I was in a fabulous and beautiful glowing fantasy world. The room was completely bathed in black light. The walls were painted with surrealistic jungle scenes and I could hear jungle birds. The room was damp and foggy and smelled of jungle vegetation and sweating women.

The wall in front of me resembled a theater stage. A painted backdrop of jungle plants glowed with green fluorescent beauty. A mass of three-foot-tall jungle grass ran along the bottom of the entire wall to my left and jutted out about three feet. Barely visible in the grass, I could see the head of a huge standing cobra snake.

At the left side of the theater stage in front of me, a Black Panther was lying on a tree limb and stared at me with haunting green eyes. Other big jungle cats were hidden deeper in the jungle, only visible because of their bright glowing eyes that watched me carefully. Off to the right, a Golden Spotted Leopard squatted looking for prey, ready to pounce.

I laid there and tried to relax and listen to the birds

So Many Maybes · 258

and the wind, but I felt weird. The paint on the walls was growing brighter in the black light and made the jungle look three dimensional. A rich reddish orange light fell on my feet forming a golden tower in the mist. Now there was music and the show began. At first, I hardly heard it. Then it grew louder. It was jungle drums playing slowly over psychedelic rock.

There was a disturbing sound in the jungle and I could see the hidden Big Cat's eyes blink and turn their heads toward the door to see if someone had entered. High above me two howler monkeys made noises as they jumped from tree to tree. Then the haunting voices of the Jungle Sirens began to sing for me:

> *"Red brown colors in the darkness.*
> *Monkeys, monkeys laugh at me.*
> *Big Cats await their lovers*
> *and shining green eyes glare at me."*

I thought I heard more rustling in the high jungle grass to my left and wondered if someone was there. No one was. It must have been the monster snake.

The Jungle Sirens continued their song:

> *"No wind blows in the dampness.*
> *Blue green blades block my seeing.*
> *In the shadows things are moving*
> *and snakes were waiting near."*

So Many Maybes · 259

Then the Panther raised its head and loudly screamed MEEE-YOW!!! and suddenly jumped off the tree limb and scared the shit out of me. My body stiffened so violently that I bounced off the mattress and flew off the bed to my right with my arms and legs flailing. I hit the floor hard and rammed my head into the wall. The Black Panther saw what had happened to me and shook its head in disgust then returned to its limb. I clumsily crawled on my hands and knees back to the mattress and laid down again, waiting for something to happen.

As soon as I got settled, the Black Panther screamed MEEE-YOW!!! again.

That Panther's fucking scream scared the shit out of me again and I laid paralyzed with fear as the beautiful Golden Leopard jumped off its limb and landed at my feet and put its front paw on my bed of grass. She studied me. The Golden Leopard's naked body was sensuous and beautiful in the golden tower of light. Black ringed spots covered her body except for a light pink oval running between her breasts from her neck to the inviting darkness below.

The surprise of the Big Cat's pounce aroused me. I cocked my Big Cat Rifle and my muscles tensed for action. The sexy Black Panther was still watching me. The gorgeous Golden Leopard raised her paw and slowly walked on top of me. She leaned her head down and licked me in long slow strokes from my navel, over

So Many Maybes · 260

my chest and up to my lips where her swirling feline tongue assured me that I had nothing to fear.

Then the Black Panther took a quick step toward the Leopard. Startled, the Leopard jumped off me and onto a low tree limb in front of my bed. She sat there and looked at me. She was a human-like leopard vision. Golden spotted triangles on her face pointed to her dark mysterious eyes.

She leaned back and ran her long black Big Cat's claws slowly down her chest from the center of her delicate breasts and over her lovely nipples and past her abdomen to the dark triangular home of Big Cat wonder. She leaned her head back and opened her mouth and growled at me.

I moved to see her better. I got her close attention and she stopped the motion of her paw and stared at me. Then that mother fucking Panther screamed MEEE-YOW!!! again.

With amazing speed, the Leopard jumped and ran on all fours up on the bed and in between my legs and drove her knee squarely into my balls. Instinctively, I quickly raised my knees to protect myself and flipped the Leopard up into the air and drove the barrel of my big gun right into the Leopard's mouth. After that, things went really well.

I'm not sure but I think the Black Panther sat right next to us and watched everything that we did with glowing deep green eyes and laughed its ass off.

So Many Maybes · 261

*

The next morning Robert woke up on his jungle bed alone. He sat up with a start and looked around. His body was still shivering with excitement, even fear, as if he had returned from another dimension and he felt different from yesterday. Today, for some reason, his balls ached like hell.

He walked out of Bunny's bedroom into the living room.

He called out, "Hello...Hello?"

He got no response. He went further into the apartment and heard the shower running in Baja's room.

He opened the bathroom door a crack and hesitantly said, "Hello?"

Gloriously naked, Baja threw the bathroom door open and said, "Good morning Robert."

She was standing in front of a full-length mirror and struggling to wash her ass off with a wash cloth.

She looked at him and calmly said, "I have the damnedest time washing my rear end because I'm so tall and my arms are too short. Does Camille have this problem? She's even taller than I am."

He said, "Uhhh...I...a nubbla dink dink oh."

Baja shook her head and said, "What?"

Then she handed the wash cloth to the staring and stationary Robert.

She said, "Could you help me wash my ass crack?"

In the confusion of waking up in Bunny's weird room, Robert had forgotten that he was naked and when he was confronted with this sensuous naked beauty with the luminescent green

So Many Maybes · 262

eyes, his dick uncoiled faster than a party favor pumped up with a high-volume air compressor.

She looked down at his throbbing member and said, "Jesus Christ Robert!"

Without thinking, she reached out and tried to touch it.

In a panic, Robert turned and ran out of the bathroom, through the bedroom and into the living room and picked up his clothes and started to get dressed.

He'd just gotten one leg in his pants when she came out of the bedroom and moved toward him.

She said, "Shit Robert! I'm sorry. I didn't mean to scare you."

He tripped on his pants and stumbled forward and collided with her and knocked her backward onto the floor where she sat laughing at famously clumsy Robert as he hopped around the room in several directions trying to get his pants on. Then he fell forward and landed face down in a big potted plant.

Baja stopped laughing and got up and went to his side to help him up.

She said, "Jesus Christ Robert! Are you okay?"

Robert slowly lifted his face out of the black soil and wiped most of the dirt out of his mouth and got on his knees. With soil filled snot running down his chin, he looked up at her and said, "What the hell is going on? Why the hell was I in Bunny's bedroom?"

"Last night you got really fucked up and took off your clothes right in front of all of us and went into Bunny's room and laid down on the bed and went to sleep."

"It's a really weird room."

So Many Maybes · 263

"I think it's cool. But then again, I created it. That is, except for the sound effects. Bunny created most of those."

"I figured. Where is everyone now?"

"Will and Wolf went home, and Bonnie went downstairs to her apartment and Camille had to get up to go to work."

"Baja...did I sleep with Bunny?"

"No. She slept on the couch. But if the sounds coming out of her bedroom were any indication, you and Camille fucked like real wild animals."

"Why did you try to grab me. I'm Camille's boyfriend. You know that."

"I couldn't help it. I've never seen a man get hard so fast."

He said, "My mind was racing, and I couldn't think. Your naked body made all of the blood in my brain run down to my dick."

Robert stood up and went to pick up his shoes. One attempted step and an "Oh shit!" later, his face was buried in between the cushions on the couch. He had never completed putting his pants on.

Laughing and shaking her head, Baja helped him get to his feet again and steadied him while he finished putting on his pants and sat down on the couch to put on his shoes. Still naked, Baja went into the kitchen and started to make some breakfast.

When Robert finished dressing, he followed her and said, "By the way, could you give me your phone number in case we need to call you guys."

Baja looked up and asked, "She never gave you our phone

So Many Maybes · 264

number?" Shaking her head, she said, "Honest to God…
sometimes…"

She found a piece of paper and wrote down their number.

As she handed it to him, she aggressively scratched her naked crotch and said, "I'm sorry again about trying to fondle you."

Robert nodded and paused silently to watch her scratch her crotch then said, "Say Baja…"

She continued to scratch and interrupted him, "It feels like I didn't get all of the soap out of my crotch."

Robert nodded and smiled and said, "Miss Sunshine, standing here like I am now, watching you scratch your lovely crotch, I can't help but think of an old rock song by the Rivieras that went something like: 'Well, I'm going out West on the coast. Where the California girls are really the most'…"

"Clever. Now get out of here before I grab at your Muscle Beach Woody again."

"See you later Baja."

"See you Robert."

So Many Maybes · 265

Chapter 17
Lois and Amanda

Wolf called and said, "I'm sorry to bother you guys, but I can't get in touch with Baja. I'm writing another play and this time I'd like to include her from the beginning. Besides I'd just like to see her. I think she's hotter than a blast furnace in a Pittsburg steel mill."

Robert said, "I agree with you Wolf, I mean about the blast furnace thing."

"I've been trying to call her since last weekend. She didn't answer. Neither did Bunny. Have you seen either of them?"

Robert called over his shoulder and said, "Camille have you seen Baja or Bunny?"

Camille shook her head and said, "No."

"Wolf, did you try Bonnie. She spends a lot of time with Bunny?"

"I called Bonnie. She hasn't see them either."

Robert said, "Bunny is probably just at dance rehearsal, but I have no idea where Baja is."

"If you see either of them, would you have them give me a call?"

"Okay we will."

The next day, Sunday, Bunny called at about 4 P.M.

"I'm so sorry Acka. I had rehearsal and we went until after

2 A.M. this morning. Baja went out of town and I didn't see Wolf's note until this afternoon when I woke up."

"Wolf left a note?"

"He stuck it under our door and asked Baja to call him. She can't because she's not here."

"Where'd she go?"

"She went to New York to try and get another design job."

"Did she leave you the phone number where she's staying."

Bunny said, "It's probably in her note. I'll go get it."

"Okay."

Bunny came back on the phone and said, "Okay...let's see... Acka?"

"Bunny."

"Could you wait a minute, I'm having a hard time finding it?"

"Take all the time you need, Bunny."

Robert waited patiently while she searched. In the background, he could hear a lot of paper rustling, then a hard *KLABBA DABBA DING DING* followed by Bunny saying "Fuck...God dammit!"

She returned to the phone and said, ""Acka?"

"Bunny."

"Her note says...Baja says she'll call me with the number when she gets there. That's not much help is it?"

"No, it's not. Say Bunny?"

"Yes Acka."

Why did you call us? It's Wolf who's looking for Baja."

"Why? Don't you like Baja?"

So Many Maybes · 268

"We like Baja just fine Bunny."

"Then why won't you come over here tonight?"

"You didn't ask us to Bunny."

"I didn't? Why not?"

"Ahhh…Bunny are you really tired or something?"

"I'm exhausted Acka and I don't feel so good. I'm sick and I can't get ahold of Bonnie."

"Hold on."

"Camille. Bunny wants us to come over. She feels sick and she can't get ahold of Bonnie."

Camille said, "What about Baja?"

"Baja's out of town."

Camille said, "Okay. Hopefully Bunny's okay."

Robert said, "Bunny, we'll be over in a few minutes."

Bunny said, "Okay but you have to promise not to do any of that Big Jungle Cat shit in my bedroom."

Robert said, "Okay Bunny, I promise we won't."

Bunny asked, "Won't what?"

"That cat shit."

"Why would you do cat shit? You'd need a cat first and I don't have a cat. I had a cat once, but it was awful."

"Why was it awful Bunny?"

"It was dead when I found it and smelled like shit…Hey listen to me. I understand now. That was cat shit. Please don't do any of that."

"Oh I wouldn't think of it. See you in a little while."

"Thanks so much Acka."

Robert was proud of himself. It was the first time he'd ever

So Many Maybes · 269

gotten through a conversation with Bunny without letting her wrap his brain in dental floss.

When they arrived at Bunny's apartment and knocked on her door, she didn't answer.

Robert said, "Fuck! She probably forgot all about us."

Camille said, "I'm worried Robert. Maybe she is really sick and needs our help."

They walked down to the street to a pay phone and Robert called her. To his surprise, Bunny answered right away,

He said, "Hey Bunny, we just knocked on your door and you didn't answer."

"I'm sorry Acka. I was in the bathroom taking a shit."

"Oh."

"I've got a case of bombastic diarrhea. I can't stay out of the bathroom but I really want your guys company so would you still come over. Maybe we can watch TV or something."

"Okay Bunny."

"And Acka?"

"Bunny."

"Promise to cover your ears when I go in the bathroom."

"I promise."

They all sat on the couch together and watched *Ed Sullivan* and a bunch of other shows. Then he and Camille slept over and Robert thought it was nice even though Bunny woke them up every half hour by making loud noises in her bathroom.

Over the next week Robert and Camille saw Bunny a couple of times. Bunny liked being around them and she relaxed and didn't feel the need to talk so much. Robert became more

So Many Maybes · 270

relaxed around Bunny too, and he enjoyed her company. There was no longer any tension regarding whether to sleep with her and he'd gotten used to her unique form of conversation. In just a few days his view of their relationship calmed from a Bunny driven cyclone of confusing nonsense into a real friendship with no questions or illusions about what the future was to be.

On about the fifth day of this nice and quiet time, Baja walked into Maybe's and sat down at the bar next to Robert.

Surprised, Robert said, "Baja? I thought you were in New York."

"I was."

"Any luck."

"I'm not sure. The play's producer seemed interested. He said he'd get back to me but I'm not optimistic."

"What kind of play was it this time."

"It's a big-time Broadway musical. I probably don't have a chance. But I guess it was worth a shot."

"Have you talked to Wolf? He's been anxious to get in touch with you."

"I talked to him this morning. He's meeting me here."

Camille said, "He called us on Saturday looking for you."

Baja said, "Why would he call you instead of Bunny?"

"He said he'd been trying to call you and wondered where you were. Bunny wasn't there."

"The whole New York thing came up kind of fast. I got a call on Saturday that they wanted to see my portfolio and I didn't get a chance to even talk to Bunny before I left."

So Many Maybes · 271

Camille said, "By the way, how is she? She was pretty sick at the beginning of the week."

"Oh didn't she tell you?"

Robert said, "Tell us what?"

"She's at an audition in New York."

"Oh. I'm not surprised. She told us that she had an audition coming up in New York, but she wasn't sure when it was."

Baja said, "By the way, our old friends Lois and Amanda are coming to visit next Saturday and we're having a little get together for them. I'd like you both to come over and meet them."

Camille said, "We saw the pictures of Amanda but who's Lois?"

"She was our dance company's business manager."

Robert said, "What are they doing now?"

"Lois is a lawyer in San Francisco and Amanda works for her…Anyway, could you please come over? It would mean a lot to me. Bunny's got tons of friends from her dancing but you two and Bonnie and Will and Wolf are the only real friends I've got here. Unfortunately, Bonnie and Will can't come. They've got tickets to a Tigers game down in Detroit, and Wolf has to work."

Robert said, "I'd like to come. They sound like interesting people. What about you Camille?"

"I have to work, but I don't see any reason why you can't go. I know I can trust you even if Bunny does get weird again and pull your pants down or something."

Robert only grinned a little. Camille had laughed at his

So Many Maybes · 272

story about Bunny sticking her hand down his pants, but he had resolved to never tell Camille about his morning encounter with the naked Baja.

Baja said, "Oh thank you, thank you. Robert come over around 2 P.M."

On Saturday afternoon, as he walked over to Baja and Bunny's apartment, Robert was nervous. The last time he was there, he had made a fool of himself. First by getting hammered and taking his clothes off in front of everybody, then again the next morning by getting a humongous bare skinned erection in front of Baja when he saw her naked, and then again by stumbling around their living room and falling face first into a potted plant. He didn't want to repeat any of those performances, so this time he resolved not to drink.

But he still wasn't completely comfortable because he was meeting Amanda. He had an irrational fear that she would parade around naked in front of him like Baja had. However, he did take some comfort in the fact that Bunny's friends would be there, and their presence might discourage anyone from taking their clothes off. And fortunately, if anyone did strip and he got an erection as big as a Giant Sequoia, Camille wasn't going to be there to see it. He still found it embarrassing whenever he got one of his traditional spontaneous erections in front of her.

His visit didn't start out well. When Bunny answered the door, she was naked. Robert gulped and immediately turned his back to her.

So Many Maybes · 273

She didn't seem to notice and said, "Oh Acka, I'm so glad you came. I forgot to invite anybody, so you're the first one here."

Robert gulped again. That meant that he had no outside protection.

He said, "Say Bunny."

"Yes Acka."

"Why are you naked?"

She looked down at herself and said, "Oh you're right. I guess I forgot to put clothes on."

She left him standing in the doorway and headed toward her bedroom.

Robert turned around and walked into their apartment and looked for Baja.

He shouted, "Hey Bunny, where's Baja?"

"She's not here."

He started to say, "I can see that," but he stopped when he realized that it wasn't important. He had no doubt that Baja would come back soon.

Robert answered the door when Lois arrived because Bunny was still in her bedroom getting dressed. When he let Lois in, his eyes became as big as cue balls.

He said, "Ho...ohly...shit!"

His gaze instantly dropped to Lois's chest. She had the biggest tits he'd ever seen on an otherwise thin woman. Each one was significantly bigger than a large watermelon. It was obvious too, that she was self-conscious about them because she wore a business jacket and buttoned her blouse all the way

So Many Maybes · 274

up to her neck. But there was no denying her hummers. Even a thick mattress couldn't hide them.

Robert didn't move and dumbly stared at Lois's boobs.

After an uncomfortable pause, Lois shook her head with obvious impatience and stepped forward and gave Robert a hug and said, "Hi, I'm Lois."

Robert held his breath because the feeling of her huge breasts pressing against his chest sent a shockwave down to his groin, something he didn't want.

"Uhhh…Hi, I'm…Robert…Come in."

As Lois walked into the apartment, Bunny came out of the bedroom and greeted her old friend with obvious excitement by hugging her tight. Then Bunny looked at Robert because he had put his hands in his pockets to hide his uncontrollable wagging tail.

She said, "Lois has huge boobs. Men always like big boobs. It's part of the male anatomy."

Robert started to tell her that she had said that a little wrong, but he stopped when Bunny said, "Lois I can tell that Acka really likes you. Look at the size of his boner."

Red with embarrassment, Robert wasn't sure what he should do. For lack of a better idea, he walked quickly toward the kitchen and said, "Please sit down Lois. You and Bunny must have a lot to talk about. Would you like some wine or something?"

Bunny and Lois sat down in the living room and Bunny looked over her shoulder and shouted toward the kitchen, "Robert, open that new bottle of something or other that

So Many Maybes · 275

Hondo sold Baja yesterday."

While Robert searched the refrigerator for the bottle of "something or other," he gradually lost his erection.

Lois asked, "Who's Hondo?"

Bunny answered, "I'm not sure. I think it's a motorcycle. Lois are you still living in San Francisco and practicing to be a lawyer?"

Seemingly comfortable with BunnySpeak, Lois nodded and said, "Yes. My condo is just outside of Berkeley. It's too small for the both of us but it's all I can afford and it's where my practice is."

"I'm so glad you came here to see us Lois. We could never afford the time to drive to San Francisco, but it's so much faster than flying."

After Robert found Baja's wine, he hesitated and took a deep breath before he went in the living room. He was determined not to look at Lois directly until he could adjust to the extraordinary size of her breasts.

Lois said, "We're here to see Amanda's mother. She's in a rest home here. That's where Amanda is now."

Bunny said, "Why is Amanda's mother in a rest home here? Amanda's from Berkeley."

"Actually Bunny, Amanda's from Detroit."

"Oh that's too bad. Berkeley is so much nicer."

As Robert exited the kitchen and gave them their wine, Bunny said, "Is Amanda moving into her own place?"

"She's not moving right now, Bunny. It's an expensive part of the country."

So Many Maybes · 276

"Oh I know. Baja and I hired a guy with a van to move us here. It cost a bundle."

Lois smiled and said, "Where is Baja anyway?"

"I don't know. She must have gone somewhere because she's not here."

Lois didn't see the point in responding to Bunny's answer.

Bunny said, "Acka, did Baja tell you where she was going? Of course she probably didn't because she'd already left before you got here, isn't that right Lois?"

Lois just nodded.

Bunny said, "Lois where are you and Amanda staying while you're in town?"

"We're in a little hotel not far from here."

Bunny didn't like that answer.

She said, "Oh no, don't do that. Stay here with Baja and me. We've got two bedrooms and two bathrooms, so we won't have to shit together."

Lois's face went pale and she had only begun to respond to Bunny's outrageous invitation when Baja entered the apartment.

Baja said, "Oh Lois you're here already. I'm sorry I wasn't home. I was giving Hondo the clerk at the store a blow job in exchange for a free gallon of radiator fluid and it took longer than I thought it would."

Lois said, "I didn't know you had a car Baja."

Baja smiled broadly and said, "I don't."

Despite his initial nervousness, Robert was now loving this conversation. First Bunny had started to pickle Lois's brain in

So Many Maybes · 277

battery acid, and now Baja playfully added antifreeze to the engine of pleasant nonsense that Bunny always creates just by entering a room.

After she bent down and gave Lois a big hug, Baja stood up and said, "Lois you should see this guy's cock."

She held her arms out in front of her like she was a bragging fisherman and said, "Honest to God, I swear. It must be over fourteen-inches long. It's a God dammed ax handle."

Lois rolled her eyes and shook her head and said, "Wow Baja, I had no idea your mouth was that big."

Bunny said, "Oh it is Lois. She can get a whole Hostess Ding Dong in her mouth at the same time."

Baja smiled proudly and said, "I have many talents."

Baja walked across the room and leaned against the wall behind Bunny.

Bunny turned around and looked at her and said, "Baja... Lois and Amanda are going to stay with us. It'll be great won't it?"

Baja falsely grinned and paused a moment before she answered.

After Bunny turned back around, Baja looked at Lois and shook her head "No," while she verbally answered, "Oh sure Bunny. It'll be great."

Baja obviously didn't want to sleep in the same bed with Bunny.

Lois caught on and said, "No Bunny, we can't stay here. We've already paid the hotel, but we'll come over every day."

Bunny was disappointed.

So Many Maybes · 278

"Okay, I guess that's for the best anyway because Acka and Connie might come over and fuck in my room again. I told Connie they could."

Lois said, "Who's Acka?"

Robert said, "I'm Acka."

Even though she was sure what Robert's real name was, Lois was comfortable calling him Acka. She'd known Bunny long enough to know that Bunny always changed people's names.

She said, "Hello Acka. Nice to meet you."

Robert said, "Nice to meet you too Lois."

Bunny said, "Acka, do you like Italian food?"

Robert answered, "Yes."

"That's great Acka. We have so many things in common, don't we Lois?"

Seeing the confusion in Lois' face, Baja decided to change the subject.

"Say Bunny, why don't you and I and Lois go to the store and visit Hondo?"

Bunny said, "Okay. We need to get some food to cook for dinner before we go out to eat tonight."

Terror spread through Robert's body. If they left, it would mean that Amanda might arrive before they got back. If she took her clothes off, there was no doubt that his Giant Sequoia would reach for the sky.

He said, "Don't you think you should wait for Amanda to get here before you go to the store?"

Baja said, "If she gets here before we get back, just let her in. She's easy to get along with."

So Many Maybes · 279

He thought, *"I hope not too easy."*

As they walked out the door and left him in the apartment alone, Robert felt like a little kid left standing out in the mall in front of the woman's lingerie store. He knew Amanda was on her way and there wasn't a thing he could do about it.

*

THE JOURNAL OF ROBERT BAIN

When they left, I tried to amuse myself by watching the Tigers game on TV. I remembered that Will and Bonnie were going to it, and I watched closely to see if I could catch a glimpse of them in the crowd. Eventually though, I got bored and my mind drifted and I thought about the women I'd just been with.

Bunny is a very attractive woman. Men almost run to spend time with her. Certainly her looks and blatantly forward and uninhibited sexuality are important reasons for her appeal. But I think her wackiness is just as important. If you are willing to weather the confusion brought on by BunnySpeak and her unpredictable way of thinking, being with Bunny is so refreshing and out of the ordinary that she brings joy to your life. Even though BunnySpeak's unconventional sentence and paragraph structure makes only partial sense, it makes me feel free; free from the dreary habit of logical language that has been drilled into me since the time I learned to talk.

Baja is marvelous and second only to Camille as my dream woman. She is beautiful, talented, and intelligent and, in my experience, very mature and kind and has a great sense of humor.

Since I've only just met Lois, there's not much that I can say about her. Since she's a lawyer, I have to assume that she's very intelligent, and up to now she seems quite kind and tolerant of Bunny's unique wackiness. Strangely, as I write about her, I find myself reluctant to talk about her huge breasts. In our society, huge boobs will attract attention and it occurs to me that hers have received more attention than she liked.

*

As soon as Robert opened the door for Amanda, she stepped right into the apartment and French kissed him and said, "Hi, I'm Amanda...Let's fuck?"

Instead of being hypnotized like he was with Lois earlier in the day, Robert kept a calm head, but his lips became like Jello and he said, "Flubba dubba dubba."

Amanda was a beautiful and vivacious light skinned blond. She was about five-feet, five-inches tall and probably in her mid-thirties. She was wearing an elegant blue silk skirt that was so short that it barely covered her ass, and six-inch heels that made her legs seem like they were eight-feet long. Her white silk blouse was loose and draped downward from behind her neck to form a deep open Vee. It was joined in front by a single button at about navel level and did nothing to conceal her gleefully free-swinging breasts. Her long blond hair was curly and windblown and looked like she'd just been riding a wild stallion.

So Many Maybes · 281

Every aspect of Amanda impressed Robert as wild. From the moment she entered the room and kissed him and invited him to fuck her, he sensed he was about to witness even more uninhibited and outlandish behavior. And he did. She walked toward the couch to sit down and confirmed his worst fears by taking her clothes off. She wasn't wearing any underwear so her little skirt slipped easily down her legs, and her silky-smooth blouse melted away gracefully like vanilla ice cream sitting on a hot dish. She was naked by the time that she was only eight feet away from him. Amanda's clothes removed themselves from her, not the other way around.

Amanda sat down on the couch and struggled to take her shoes off.

She undid the strap on one of them and said, "I hate clothes. They're so uncomfortable?"

Robert attempted with all his might to keep from getting another hard-on, but he failed and a whopper blew up in his pants. He took a deep breath and managed to relax a little. But when she pulled her leg up by the ankle and spread her knees wide to take off her shoe, she gave him a blinding pink beaver flash and he had to go into the kitchen again.

When Lois and Bunny and Baja returned from the store and entered the apartment, none of them seemed to think anything of the fact that Amanda was naked.

Like she did with everyone, Amanda hugged Bunny and kissed her hard.

Bunny said, "Oh Amanda, you're so beautiful. I've always been jealous of you. You've got boobs."

So Many Maybes · 282

While the three other women were in the kitchen putting away the food, Amanda poured herself another glass of wine then pranced around the living room naked doing a few happy and slow and elegant, almost childlike twirls.

When she stopped, Amanda turned toward the kitchen and shouted, "Bunny would you mind if I fucked Flubba dubba? I think he's cute."

Bunny, Baja, and Lois walked out of the kitchen and into the living room.

Bunny asked, "Who's Flubba dubba?"

Amanda said, "I thought he was."

Robert said, "I'm really Acka."

Amanda said, "Why did you tell me your name is Flubba dubba?"

Robert said, "I'm sorry Amanda. Sometimes when I'm around Bunny, I get confused."

Amanda said, "Isn't she fun? Well Bunny, would you mind if I fucked Acka."

"No not at all Amanda, you're a dear friend."

Baja said, "But Bunny, don't forget that Acka's boner already belongs to Connie."

"Oh yeah, I forgot. I'm sorry Amanda. Connie has first dibs."

Amanda said, "Who's Connie?"

Baja said, "She's Acka's girlfriend."

Amanda looked disappointed and said, "Acka, do you think that Connie would let me use your boner if I promise to take good care of it?"

So Many Maybes · 283

Baja interrupted and said, "Acka, if Connie is going to let anyone borrow your boner, it should be me. After all, you pointed it at me and ran away before I could grab it."

Bunny said, "Baja, when did Acka point his boner at you?"

"The morning after he slept in your bed. He accidentally walked into the shower with me."

Bunny said, "I'm jealous. I fell asleep before I saw his boner the night before."

Amanda asked, "So Acka, you fucked Bunny?"

Robert answered, "No Amanda. I got drunk and passed out on her bed."

Bunny said, "By the way Baja, when you were in New York I got bombastic diarrhea and shit my brains out for a whole day."

Baja said, "Thank you for telling me that Bunny. Amanda, since you're my dearest friend, I'll loan you Hondo while you're waiting to see if Connie will loan you Acka."

Amanda said, "Who's Hondo?"

Baja said, "Hondo is the clerk down at the grocery store."

Bunny was confused and said, "You told me Hondo was a motorcycle."

"No Bunny, you got that a little wrong, Hon-DAH is a motorcycle, Hon-DOE is the cute guy you met at the store today. You know, the one with the big muscles."

Bunny said, "Oh I remember now. You're right. He is cute. And his boner is huge. It's over fourteen-inches long and as big around as an ax handle."

Amanda said, "How did you see Hondo's boner Bunny? Did you sleep with him?"

So Many Maybes · 284

"No Amanda. Baja told us about Hondo's boner."

Baja said, "That's right Amanda. She's telling the truth. Believe me. You won't regret it. Acka's boner, as cute as it is, is nowhere near as powerful as Hondo's."

Amanda said, "That's a kind offer Baja, but I'll wait for Acka."

*

THE JOURNAL OF ROBERT BAIN

On my way home I thought, "This day wasn't as bad as I thought it would be. Yes, two women did take off their clothes, and yes, I did get two long-lasting, bazooka-sized erections, but I managed to pleasantly sit through a really bizarre conversation centered around my boner and get through the afternoon without making a complete fool of myself.

*

Chapter 18
Bonnie's Movie

The next evening, Lois and Amanda and Baja joined Robert, Camille, Bonnie, and Will at Maybe's for dinner. Bunny was conspicuously absent.

Bonnie said, "Where's Bunny?"

Baja said, "I'm not sure. She just said that she had something to do and that 'we should have fun in spite of her.' Those are her words not mine."

Bonnie said, "I figured."

Will was uncomfortable from the moment they first sat down at the table because he was directly across from Amanda and Lois. Lois's humongous nosecone-shaped mammary monuments were pointed directly at him and extending across the table almost far enough to poke him in the eyes, and Amanda was wearing a T-Shirt that was cut off only a few inches below her breasts and it had, "Watch 'Em Bounce," printed in large letters on the front.

No matter how hard he tried, boob-obsessed Will couldn't help but follow the T-Shirt's command. He lost track of everything that was going on around him and he closely monitored the movements of Amanda's elegant braless breasts. He was so fixated that he didn't respond when Lois asked him where in San Francisco he was from.

Bonnie was sitting next to Will and when he didn't answer Lois's question, she noticed where his eyes were focused. She brought him out of his trance by reaching under the table and firmly pounding his crotch with the bottom of her fist.

She said, "Will, it's impolite to stare at Amanda's boobs. You should pay attention to the conversation."

Startled by the less than mild impact on his testicles, Will grunted and looked down at his menu.

Bonnie had been studying Amanda too, but for a different reason. When she agreed to collaborate with Will, Bonnie had also agreed to begin the frustrating search for film ideas again. And just like before, she couldn't come up with anything. But when she met Amanda, Bonnie was inspired. She spotted something that modeling scouts and Hollywood film producers looked for every day; a special quality that turns average people into movie stars or super-models. Amanda had a rare form of charisma that would produce magic when she was photographed and make people clamor to look at her picture. Then, while she was basking in Amanda's glow, Bonnie remembered Baja's amazing stage presence. The sum of the two women's charismatic power was enough to make Bonnie act impulsively.

Bonnie leaned forward and said, "Amanda, I want you and Baja to be in our next film."

Will looked up quickly. It was the first he'd heard of it.

Amanda smiled and said, "Really? How did you decide this? I've only just met you."

"I could tell as soon as I saw you that you both would be perfect."

So Many Maybes · 288

Amanda said, "I'd love to do it. It sounds like fun."

Baja said, "Me too. It would be like the old days when we danced together."

Lois asked, "Bonnie when are you planning on doing this? We have to leave right after Labor Day."

Bonnie answered, "We can start tomorrow."

Will, on the other hand, was aware of the technical challenges presented by rushing into production without the proper preparations and he started to object.

"But how can we…?"

He stopped when Baja enthusiastically said, "I can paint and design the sets too."

Bonnie said, "Fantastic Baja!"

Appearing uncomfortable, Amanda reached under her T-shirt with her right hand and scratched the bottom of her left breast and said, "Bonnie can I take my clothes off in the movie? Clothes make me itch."

When the bottom half of Amanda's breast escaped the cover of her shirt, Will gulped, and leaned forward to get a better look. Predictably, Bonnie hammered him again.

As quietly as he could, he grunted, "Unk…Fuck!!"

And so it was settled. Bonnie Haines' first film since the successfully presented misery of *Holding My Load,* would begin production immediately. However, Will didn't think anything was settled. The idea for this movie was entirely Bonnie's, and she hadn't discussed it with him. Consequently, he didn't know what she had in mind.

So Many Maybes · 289

Something else needed to be settled too.

Bonnie drove him home from Maybe's and when they pulled up in front of his apartment building, he decided it was time to bring it up with her.

He said, "Bonnie there are some things we have to talk about."

"I'm sorry Will. I know I should have talked this over with you before I talked to Amanda and Baja, but when they were sitting at the table with us and I saw how perfect they were, I figured I should bring it up then in case I didn't get another chance. But thinking back, I know that if we're going to collaborate, I have to at least give you a heads up."

"Yes you should, but that's not all. There's something else we have to talk about."

His serious tone concerned Bonnie.

"What's that Will?"

"You have to stop stepping on my toes or hitting me in the balls every time I look at another woman's tits."

Bonnie nodded and said, "I know you're right Will. But I can't help it. I want you all to myself and I do it without thinking. But you're right. I promise I'll stop."

"Okay, but please keep that promise."

"I will."

"And there's another thing."

"What's that?"

"Despite the fact that you bruised my testicular pride, I've got a hard-on the size of a water tower. Let's get in the back of the van and make it bounce up and down like a kangaroo

So Many Maybes · 290

until the police stop us?"

Bonnie said, "That's a great idea except for the police part. I know you don't want to have another encounter with Sgt. Clarkson."

As they moved to the back of the van, Will said, "Don't be so sure about that. She's quite the babe. We could invite her to join us."

Bonnie said, "We'd have to change our names. Who do you want to be?"

Will said, "I think I'll be Detective Defender. How about you?"

"I'll be Street Slut."

"Appropriate."

"Thank you. Now cut the shit and arrest me."

"Okay, put your hands behind your back and let me cuff you."

"Yes officer."

After Robert and Camille got home from the dinner, Bunny showed up at their apartment.

Camille answered the door and said, "Hi Bunny, how did you get over here?"

"I walked. You know it's not that far. You guys have walked over to our place lots of times."

"That's true Bunny, but we always made sure that we had our clothes on."

"I would have put on clothes, but I've changed my mind and decided to finally fuck Acka like a corn dog and I think

So Many Maybes · 291

it's more fun to fuck naked."

Camille nodded and said, "I have to agree with you there Bunny."

Bunny said, "Except when you're on a Greyhound."

Camille said, "You've fucked on a bus?"

"Only once?"

"Why only once?"

"It wasn't any fun. We couldn't relax?"

"Why? Were you afraid you'd get caught?"

"No not at all. It was just uncomfortable. The bus driver couldn't see around me because I was sitting on his lap. But I wasn't afraid. I'd do it on the grass in the middle of The Big House during the Ohio State game if the guy was cute."

Robert said, "You know that the U of M football stadium is called The Big House?"

Bunny said, "Of course I do, you can't live in Ann Arbor without knowing that...Acka, wouldn't that be fun? We could run out of the tunnel in the Big House and lay down on the 50-yard line and you could put your boner inside me and we could fuck like corn dogs."

Camille said, "You've really shocked me Bunny."

"Why Connie?"

"That you chose the Ohio State game instead of Notre Dame. You must know that my name is O'Neil and I'm Irish."

"Oh I know that, but I didn't think you'd mind because Ohio State is a bigger rival than Notre Dame, but you're right, I should have chosen Notre Dame because my parents were Catholic. At least I think they were. I would have probably

So Many Maybes · 292

known for sure if we ever went to church. Anyway, you're right. The Notre Dame game would be a better choice. Let's do that this fall Acka."

"I don't think so Bunny."

"Why not Acka. It would be fun?"

Robert glanced at Camille and said, "Some people wouldn't approve."

"Why? Fucking isn't a crime. Unless we were underage like the judge said."

"That's not what I meant Bunny."

Bunny looked at Camille and said, "Oh, I understand… Believe me Acka, you don't have to worry at all. Not at all."

"That's a relief."

"Connie can watch. I don't mind."

Camille said, "That sounds like a great deal to me."

Robert said, "Okay Bunny. With Connie's permission, I'm in."

"Of course you are. What guy wouldn't want their boner in me? So it's agreed. This fall at the beginning of the Michigan-Notre Dame football game, Acka and I will run out of the tunnel in The Big House and lay down at the fifty-yard line and Acka will put his spring steel boner inside me and fuck me until I scream like the student section…Oh I just remembered that we can't fuck on the 50-yard line in The Big House during the Notre Dame game."

Robert said, "Why not?"

"Because it'll be on TV and they don't allow fucking on TV."

"You're right Bunny."

So Many Maybes · 293

"Plus I won't be in Ann Arbor. I'll be in New York being a ballerina. They called me this afternoon."

Robert stopped breathing. Bunny had broken the exciting news in the only way she ever could. That is, from outer space. Camille broke into tears and hugged her. Robert told her he was overjoyed for her. Bunny's dream was going to come true.

When Baja and Amanda said yes to being in her movie, Bonnie was thrilled, but she knew that she had to get her act together fast. Amanda would be leaving soon. Writing faster than Jack Kerouac on mescaline and breaking three pencils in the process, Bonnie spontaneously spit out a screenplay in only about two hours.

While Bonnie was writing, Will drove her paisley painted VW microbus into Detroit and rented the necessary filmmaking gear that he and Bonnie didn't already own. And they began filming that evening.

Slowed down only by Will's insistence that their movie be well crafted and some difficulty finding props and arranging for places to work, the five of them blasted through the production in only five long days.

After filming ended, Bonnie began editing and no one heard anything about it until Will announced to Robert and Terri that the movie was done. Terri quickly suggested that they show Bonnie's movie in the loft over her garage during their upcoming store picnic out at her farm. Will wasn't sure that was a good idea. It was his first collaboration with Bonnie, and they had made a movie that was dramatically different

So Many Maybes · 294

from the sweet love stories he had always made before. He told Terri that, as you might expect, Bonnie's screenplay was kind of out-there, and it might not be appropriate for showing at a party that was meant to be light hearted and fun.

Terri said, "Nonsense. We all know what kind of movies Bonnie makes, but both of you are our friends and we owe it to you to watch your first collaboration. Relax Will, things will go better than you think, especially since we'll be eating hot dogs and I'll make popcorn."

Will felt mildly nauseous. He was very insecure about how people would react to the film, but he didn't know what else to say.

When Will told Bonnie about Terri's suggestion that the movie be shown at the store's picnic, Bonnie was thrilled. They had a good audience, not ideal, but good. Will kept his mouth shut, but he was worried that things wouldn't go well.

The picnic itself went great. Nort cooked on a small corner of a custom made twelve-foot-long charcoal grill he had over-constructed especially for the occasion and the feast began. Everyone made their traditional contributions: Terri's hot dogs and burgers, Jenny's watermelon, Camille and Robert's pizza, and Baja and Bunny's potato salad. Wolf also brought some exotic oriental dish that no one had heard of. It made their toes and ears numb.

The drink menu was traditional too. Bonnie and Will brought their dangerous vodka and tequila punch, Brett again brought her exquisite Mother Maybe's Mystical Strawberry Kool Aid, and Wolf brought another custom-made tea. This time he called it "Tropical Morning" and it made everyone but Nort's hair stand on end.

Just like the picnic at Dana's, a thunderstorm formed off in the distance and it became very humid. But this time, the storm moved over the farm and not too long after they finished eating, it started to rain heavily. Rather than being annoyed by the rain, the entire group was relieved because it forced the cancellation of Nort's planned after-dark fireworks display that had everyone terrified.

With their stomachs stuffed and their hair standing tall from Wolf's tea, they went inside and worked together to turn the loft into a mini-movie theater. Terri, Jenny, and Camille cleaned up the food that had been rapidly brought inside out of the rain, and Will tried to set up the movie projector. The others brought some chairs from Terri's house and arranged them in front of the projection screen.

Will was completely sloshed. He dropped the film reel on the floor and it rolled away on its edge like a perfectly balanced wheel without an axle while the film rapidly unwound behind it. Will wobbly gave chase. Jenny stopped it before it bounced down the stairs and she handed it to Will. Poor Will started rewinding the film and turned to walk toward the projector. After one step, he stumbled forward and began to fall down. Robert ran over to stop him, but since Robert was "The World's Clumsiest Bastard," he tripped on Will's feet and the two of them went flying across the room spinning and hugging each other like a couple at the beginning of a 1920s dance marathon. They crashed through the mini-theater of chairs, then rammed

So Many Maybes · 296

hard into the wall and fell on the floor and knocked the projection screen on top of themselves. Terri and Baja, both laughing hard, lifted the screen off them while Jenny pulled Will away from the disheveled pile of mini theater seats and leaned him against the wall.

He was babbling some drunken words about, "Humiliation the horror…the horror…and gonna' shit, gonna' shit."

Choreographer Amanda helped Robert up and said, "Impressive, but I think the routine could use a little polishing. Maybe next time you could add some tap dancing before you crash into the wall."

Robert nodded and said, "Thanks Amanda. I'll talk to Will about it."

Bonnie took over for Will and completed setting up the projector and screen. When she finished threading the film, She looked up at her audience and started to laugh, hard. Her best friends in the world were all seated in their make-shift mini-theater and staring at the screen with their arms crossed and their hair standing straight-up like threatened porcupines.

Baja asked her, "What's so funny?"

Bonnie shook her head and said, "Oh Nothing," and started the projector and walked to the back of the room to observe everyone's reaction.

The rainstorm that was raging outside the loft provided a dramatic opening to the film. Thunder boomed, and lightning flashed, just as the opening title of the film hit the screen. It was called *Flight of the Doves*.

FLIGHT OF THE DOVES

A beautiful bright yellow Sun rose over a dark urban skyline in front of an orange and yellow swirling sky. In the background were the sounds of singing birds and the river passing below. As the Sun rose, the camera slowly tilted down and looked across a large stone bridge.

Off in the distance, Baja and Amanda appeared. They were holding hands and running across the bridge toward the camera. They were both naked, and their mouths were wide open as they screamed in terror trying to get away from two preachers who pursued them and continually pushed Christian crosses towards them. As they approached and passed the camera.

Bonnie narrated the action by reciting a poem:

"Twas God's own male Serpents who ripped them
from their warm nests of kindness and love.
Then without guilt or honest repent,
tortured and raped the cute little doves.

The unholy churchmen's selfish ego and pride,
cast the doves out for loving their own kind.
Then charged them with seriously forbidden crimes,
and jailed them in a dark closet, to rot for all time.

So Many Maybes · 298

So the once peaceful doves became violent,
Blew the closet's door and came out of it,
Running and screaming, from hell's heaven sent."

Thunder boomed, and lightning flashed as the image dissolved to the inside of a stone-walled dungeon.

Baja and Amanda, still naked, were lying next to each other and bathed in dim red light. They were chained to the floor with their legs spread wide and their vaginas facing the camera. The preachers stood by them, one preacher next to Baja and the other next to Amanda.

Both churchmen raised their crosses high above their heads and paused in a momentary pose as a Moog-Synthesizer Version of "The Battle Hymn of the Republic" began to play.

Suddenly, as thunder boomed and lightning struck again, the preachers knelt down quickly and in one smooth motion they shoved their crosses directly into Baja's and Amanda's vaginas like daggers. The women screamed in pain.

Synchronized to the rhythm of the famous battle hymn, the preachers started rapidly plunging the crosses in and out of the two women as if the crosses were the handles of butter churns.

So Many Maybes · 299

The women began to writhe then thrust their hips upward and shook as if demons had possessed them while they shouted in unison with a wobbly wagon wheel jerky rhythm.

"Christ!...Christ!...Christ!

Continuing to churn the women with the crosses, the preachers both started singing:

*"Mine eyes have seen the glory
of the coming of the Lord;
He is trampling out the vintage
where the grapes of wrath are stored;
He hath loosed the fateful lightning
of His terrible swift sword."*

Thunder boomed, and lightning struck again, as the storm raged outside. The women continued to writhe and struggle to get free as the preachers continued pumping the women with their butter churn crosses. The women's vaginas began to smoke from the friction of the crosses rubbing against their flesh, and the preachers continued singing:

*"I have seen Him in the watch fires
of a hundred circling camps.
They have builded Him an altar*

So Many Maybes · 300

in the evening dews and damps."
At that moment, Baja and Amanda screamed in perfect harmony with the preachers,

"GLORY, GLORY, HALLELUJAH!"

There was more thunder and lightning and, suddenly, a huge explosion occurred and sparks and fire shot out of the women's vaginas like Fourth of July roman candles and set the preachers on fire and they burned until they melted into puddles of tar.

The fire melted the chains that had bound the women to the floor and they stood up and nakedly embraced and kissed.

The screen faded to black.

THE END

Nobody in the room moved.

Leaning against a wall off to the side, Will continued to blabber, "This is gonna be bad, really bad, just wait for it, wait for it."

Then absolute hell erupted. Amanda, Lois and Baja and Jenny and Wolf all applauded with enthusiasm at Bonnie's obvious talent. Camille and Robert applauded loudly too.

Bunny shouted, "Fannn...tastic!"

Robert winced at the same time that he applauded.

He shook his head slowly then turned to Camille and said, "It was a Bonnie Haines movie all right."

Camille nodded.

Bunny asked, "Acka, before you fucked Bonnie did your boner inflate?"

"What???"

"I never got to see your boner inflate. Isn't that right Lois?"

Lois turned to Bunny and said, "What's right, Bunny?"

Robert said, "Don't worry Lois. It's not important."

Lois sighed and nodded.

Robert said, "Bunny, I never fucked Bonnie."

"Oh Acka, of course you did."

"Why do you say that?"

"Because you never fucked me."

Robert facetiously said, "I fucked you Bunny. You must have forgotten."

"Oh thank God. You had me worried. But now you've made me sad."

"Why is that Bunny?"

"Because you're so bad in bed."

"I am?"

"You must be because if you were any good, I'd remember doing it. That brings me to my second question?"

"What's that, Bunny?"

"Why aren't you fucking Bonnie? She makes great movies and her boobs are perfect and will give you a monster boner."

"I think you're right Bunny, but I'm in love with Connie."

So Many Maybes · 302

"Acka, I'd be a bombastic shit if I didn't give you some advice."

"What kind of advice?"

"If your boner deflates, you should point your nice ass at Connie and beg her to fuck you from behind. It's fun when men beg."

Robert wasn't quite sure what Bunny meant, but he said, "Thanks for the advice Bunny."

"You're welcome Acka. I hear you're fucking Jane?"

"How did you hear that."

"A little bird told me. That reminds me. There's something I never understood."

"What's that Bunny?"

"How is it that birds can always hit people when they shit? I mean, it's like they aim."

Robert was patiently nodding while she talked.

He said, "You're right Bunny."

"And Acka?"

"Yes Bunny,"

"What is it about car windshields?"

"I don't know Bunny?

Bonnie's movie embarrassed Nort because the sight of naked women had given him an erection for the first time in years. He was nervously giggling and applauding loudly.

Terri clapped loudly too. She was happy that Bonnie and Will had produced such an interesting movie together. It made Terri sad when she saw the pain in Bonnie's face every time someone mentioned *Holding My Load*.

Will was puking his guts out in the corner of the loft.

So Many Maybes · 303

When the movie ended, Bonnie rushed out through the driving rain to her microbus and left quickly. It was an odd reaction for someone whose movie had just met with overwhelming applause.

Bonnie knew from the beginning that no one in the audience was going to give her a completely unbiased critical reaction to *Flight of the Doves*. After all, they were either involved in the making of the movie or her closest friends. But she had never expected the unanimous approval that she got. Ironically, she didn't see the movie in the same positive light.

It wasn't a new discovery for her. She had retired from filmmaking after she made *Holding My Load*. But a combination of factors made her decide to come out of retirement. First Will had suggested they collaborate and she agreed because she hoped he could help her make the kind of movie she wanted to. Then she found herself in front of Amanda and got inspired and made another movie she didn't like.

It made her angry at herself. She should have known better.

It wasn't until after Nort helped drunken Will down the stairs and left to take him home that Robert and Terri noticed that Bonnie's microbus wasn't parked in front of the garage. They both thought it was odd that Bonnie had left so quickly, and Terri suggested that they go look in on her.

Bonnie opened the door and gruffly said, "Go away. I need to think."

Then she shut the door on them.

Robert looked at Terri and said, "Well. What do you think

So Many Maybes · 304

that was about?"

Terri said, "I'm not sure, but if I had to guess, I'd say she was pissed off about something."

The next morning, a hung-over Will got a phone call from Bonnie.

She said, "Will, I can't stay in Ann Arbor anymore. I'm going back to New York where I belong."

"Why? You've always seemed happy here."

"Mostly I am, but I don't like what I've become since I moved here."

"What's that?"

"An artist that produces miserable, depressing and ugly shit."

Will didn't know what to say. He could understand her feelings in the case of *Holding My Load*, but not *Flight of the Doves*. Besides, Bonnie could not be fully characterized by the art that she produced. Although her films and poems were undeniably disturbing, Bonnie as a person was not. She was an extremely intelligent and beautiful woman who was kind to everyone and incredibly loyal and devoted to her friends.

He said, "Bonnie, what would be different in New York?"

"I don't know Will, but at least it would give me a chance to start again. A long time ago, my life got off track. I only came to Ann Arbor because of McSurly, and that's how that piece of shit *Holding My Load* came to be. I think *Flight of the Doves* is different, at least in an intellectual sense, but I don't think watching it is all that pleasant. Even you didn't like it."

So Many Maybes · 305

"Bonnie, I'm sorry I got drunk. I didn't think the movie was unpleasant. I was just afraid that the anti-religious theme was going to offend someone. As it turned out, I underestimated my friends. It's not unpleasant at all. It's a very original, surrealistic vision of the oppression of gay women by the church and their ultimate liberation."

"Maybe, but whatever, I'm still going home."

Will said, "Bonnie please reconsider. McSurly is gone. You have good friends here who love you, me included, and you have the resources to visit New York anytime you want for as long as you want."

Bonnie became silent. Will was afraid that they'd been cut off.

"Bonnie are you still there?'

He paused then asked again.

"Bonnie?"

She said, "Do you really love me Will?"

"Yes Bonnie, I love you?"

"Enough to go with me if I moved back to New York?"

"If you asked me to go with you, I would go. No hesitation."

"Are you sure Will? Would you really leave all your friends just to be with me?"

"Yes Bonnie. I couldn't bear to be away from you now."

She became silent again.

Then she said, "Will, do you mind if I call you back. I have to go out for a while. I need to think."

"Where are you going?"

"I don't know, but don't worry. I'll call you back in a few hours."

So Many Maybes · 306

Will hung up the phone and walked over to his couch and sat down. He had to do some thinking himself. A little while later, he called Terri and quit his job.

Although Will refused to give a reason for quitting so suddenly, everyone at Grafton's assumed that it had to do with what had happened at the picnic the night before. They assumed that Will was probably embarrassed about getting shit-faced then throwing up and passing out on the floor without even seeing the movie he helped make.

Since Will was his best friend, Robert asked Terri if he could leave work for a little while to go see Will. Terri understood completely and told Robert she was going with him.

When Will answered the door, he was pale and grubby looking. His hair stuck out in every direction, and he was still wearing the puke stained shirt that he had on when Nort brought him home after the picnic.

Will stepped back from the door and waved Terri and Robert in.

Robert said, "What's going on? Why did you quit your job?"

Will walked over in front of the window and blankly stared out with his back to them.

He said, "Bonnie's going back to New York and I'm going with her?"

Terri said, "Did she say why she's going back?"

"She told me that she was leaving because she didn't like what she'd become since she moved here."

Robert said, "What's that?"

Will said, "An artist who produces ugly disgusting shit, or something like that."

So Many Maybes · 307

Terri shook her head and said, "It doesn't make sense Will. She worked very hard to make a movie and everyone loved it, then all of a sudden she's so down on herself that she's decided to leave Ann Arbor and all of her friends? I think we should talk with her before she does something she'll regret later. Where is she now?"

Will shook his head and said, "I don't know. She said she was going out for a couple of hours to think."

Terri said, "I have an idea where she might be."

Robert asked, "Where's that?"

"The Forum."

Will said, "Of course, the Forum. Why didn't I think of that?"

Terri said, "Will, you smell like puke. Why don't you take a shower and put on some clean clothes then we'll all go over there and talk to Bonnie."

"Okay and I'll make it fast."

While Will was in the shower, Robert said, "Terri what made you think she went to the Forum?"

Terri answered, "Trust me. Women know these things."

Robert turned his back to Terri and threw his arms up in frustration. It made him crazy when women said things like that.

Since Bonnie was into radical art and far left politics, she spent a lot of time at Ann Arbor's most radical movie theater, The Fifth Forum. The Fifth Forum was an art house that showed unconventional and what some people might call pornographic films. In 1970 the Fifth Forum was the center

So Many Maybes · 308

of a big controversy when the city police stopped them from showing the movie *I am Curious Yellow*, a Swedish film that included scenes of nudity and sex.

Will and Robert and Terri found Bonnie sitting all alone in the back row of the theater watching a private screening of that horribly brutal martial arts movie called *Wah-zoo, The Feminine Karate Master From Hell* that Camille had told Robert about.

As they shuffled down the row of seats to where Bonnie was sitting, the feminine karate master shouted, "Hi-yee!" and Robert looked at the screen just in time to see Wah-zoo drive her knee into a man's balls. The impact made a horribly loud, *"THUNK!"* and the force of the blow sent the man six feet in the air.

Bonnie was drinking champagne out of the bottle and eating popcorn and she was clearly annoyed that they had found her.

She said, "Terri why did you tell them I'd be here."

Robert said, "Bonnie, how did you know it was Terri?"

Both Bonnie and Terri turned to Robert and, in perfect harmony, they said, "Trust us, women know these things."

Robert rolled his eyes and thought, *"Shit!"*

They sat down around Bonnie, and Robert tried to open a friendly conversation by giving her a compliment. He told her that he really liked her new movie. He thought it was beautifully made and the surrealist imagery was very original.

As Robert talked, Bonnie seemed to get more and more irritated.

So Many Maybes · 309

She said, "Oh shut up Robert. I'm not a dumb shit. I know it was good."

Another "Hi-yee!" came from the screen and Wah-zoo drove her fist into a man's head all the way up to his ears and ripped his face off.

Will said, "Bonnie, then why are you so upset?"

Bonnie said, "You shut up too Will."

Terri decided it was her turn to be snapped at.

She said, "Bonnie we just want to understand what's going on. We're your friends."

Bonnie paused and took a big swig of champagne from the bottle, then she handed it to Terri.

Terri took a drink and said, "Boy is this good. I don't usually drink champagne, but this is really good. Is it expensive?"

Bonnie nodded and said, "A hundred dollars a bottle."

Terri said, "Wow. I've never drank anything this expensive before."

"I have. Lots of times. Because I'm a spoiled rich brat."

Will said, "Is that why you're upset?"

Bonnie shook her head and said, "Oh for God's sake. Tell you what, why don't you two guys go someplace and play with yourselves and leave Terri and me here to talk. Will, I'll call you later. This movie makes me really horny and I want you to bang the shit out of me: front side, back side, top side, bottom side, every side, until we're so tired that we pass out."

Will was very surprised. Especially because she had just been so difficult. He didn't respond until Robert elbowed him.

With a hoarse voice Will said, "But I have to work."

So Many Maybes · 310

Robert stepped in quickly and said, "Terri, can Will have the day off to fuck Bonnie?"

"Of course. Will, consider fucking Bonnie to be your job for today and if you do it well, I'll pay you time and a half."

Again speaking for Will, Robert said, "Thanks Terri... Bonnie, Will is going home to wait for your call. Come on Will, let's get out of here."

As they got up to leave, Bonnie added one more thing, "By the way Will, I've decided not to move back to New York."

As they headed toward the exit, Robert looked at the screen as Wah-zoo knocked the man's head off with a sledgehammer then shoved her hand into his chest and ripped his heart out and ate it. Robert cringed and thought, *"Jesus Christ! That is one angry woman."*

Outside the theater, Will said, "Fuck Robert! Do you understand what just happened?"

Robert shook his head and answered. "Ahhh...no."

After Will and Robert left the theater, Terri said, "Bonnie, why are you watching this movie. It's awful?"

"I'm pretty down and this movie makes me feel good about myself. Compared to the sick bastards that made this piece of shit, I'm the Virgin Mary."

Terri said, "I don't know about you, but I don't feel comfortable talking here right now.

"I really don't either."

After they left the theater, they headed south on 5th Avenue toward Liberty St. and Bonnie's Apartment.

Bonnie said, "Terri, last night when I was watching my film,

So Many Maybes · 311

I had a moment of clarity that told me it was time for me to make a major change in my life."

Terri asked, "What kind of change?"

"I don't like my own art; my films, even my poetry. If anyone else had made *Flight of the Doves*, I would have said that it was an original and interesting creation that expressed anger and moral outrage at social injustice and as such, it was a valid maybe even very good work of art. But while I watched it with an audience, I realized that I didn't enjoy watching my own movie. I probably wouldn't even walk across the street to see it because it wasn't fun. And it wasn't the kind of film I want to make."

Terri said, "What kind is that?"

"If I could, I want to make romantic comedies; the kind of movies that you'd go to on a date before you made love in the back of your van. But even though I've tried for several years, I've never been able to come up with a decent idea for a romantic comedy. And even if I had, I probably wouldn't have known how to make it. Instead, I have this natural talent for making films and writing poetry that take the audience on tours of the dark world. A place that most people probably don't want to go."

Terri said, "But don't you think that some people do?"

"Maybe. But I don't. And being their tour guide makes me miserable. So it's time that I quit and do something else."

Terri said, "Like what."

"That's a question that I'm still struggling with. I didn't sleep at all last night, and by this morning I felt alone and helpless.

So Many Maybes · 312

My first inclination was to run and go back home and move in with my grandparents until I could get my head straight. But this morning, after I talked to Will on the phone and he was so supportive, I realized that I didn't need to go home to figure things out. I can do that here in Ann Arbor."

"You're right Bonnie, but don't put too much pressure on yourself. No one has everything in their life figured out. Pause the search for a while and give your brain a rest. Spend some time doing things that you know you like, even if they're just mindless fun."

Bonnie said, "That's probably good advice, but it's hard for me to do. The problem won't go away simply because I choose to ignore it."

Terri said. "Don't look at it that way. Think of it as doing something to clear your head so you can see things from a new perspective?

Bonnie nodded and didn't say anything more.

When they arrived at Bonnie's apartment building, Bonnie said, "Come on. I'll drive you back to the store."

Terri said, "You don't have to do that. I can walk."

Bonnie said, "Don't be ridiculous. The store is all the way across campus. Besides, I have to go out anyway. I have to go over to see Will and tell him that I'm in love with him."

So Many Maybes · 313

Chapter 19
Take Care Of My Cat

Immediately after Bonnie's movie was shown, it was time for Lois and Amanda to go home. It was also time for Bunny to go to New York, so she was riding to the airport with them in their rental car.

As they were about to leave, Lois and Amanda waited in the car while Bunny said goodbye to her friends. She seemed sad as she stood next to the car and addressed each of them individually.

She said, "Acka, I'm so glad I met you. You gave me almost all of my friends. I want you to promise to write me while you're gone?"

By this time, Robert knew that there was seldom any chance of correcting a BunnySpeak statement, so he just said, "I will."

"And Whoa?"

"Yes Bunny."

"I want you to come over here a lot and fuck Baja like a corn dog. She thinks you've got a nice boner."

"I promise."

"And Baja."

"Yes Bunny."

"Promise me you'll give Whoa blow jobs rather than Honda."

"I promise."

"And Bonnie."

"Yes Bunny."

"Promise me you'll bang Wallace's brains out every day."

"I will."

"And Wallace, keep kissing Bonnie's ass and make dozens of great movies together."

"I promise."

"And Baja."

"Yes Bunny."

"Take good care of my cat."

"You don't have a cat Bunny."

"Oh that's right, it was dead when I found it."

Bunny stuck her head through the open car window and said, "Lois can we wait a while before we leave to go to the airport? I might have to take a shit."

Lois said, "No Bunny. We have to leave now, but if you do have to take a shit later please tell me and we'll stop somewhere."

"Oh thank you Lois. I don't want to go in some theater to do it, isn't that right Baja."

Baja smiled and said, "Bunny, you promise all of us to be the best ballerina that the world has ever known and invite all of us to your opening night."

Bunny said, "I promise."

Bunny hugged each of them then stepped back.

She said, "Before we leave I have one more request."

She said, "Connie."

"Yes Bunny."

"Promise me you'll marry Acka when he asks you because

So Many Maybes · 316

he's great and he loves you."

"I love him too Bunny."

Bunny got in the car with Amanda and Lois, and they drove off.

Everyone stood in silence and watched their car until they turned the corner and went out of sight.

Then Camille said, "Baja, now that Bunny's left, are you going to move in with Wolf?"

Baja said, "That's the plan. But first I have to repaint Bunny's room."

Bonnie said, "It's shame you have to do that. I'll bet no other bedroom on Earth is like hers."

"No doubt that's true, but the building manager would shit her pants if she walked in and saw it."

Bonnie said, "I know you're right, but please let Will and me come over and take pictures of it before you paint over your art work."

Will said, "I think we should film it too. We could get a better sense of what the space looked like."

"Okay. But do it fast. I've only got two weeks before I have to move out."

Bonnie said, "How about tomorrow?"

Baja said, "Fine."

Robert said, "Camille, I'm exhausted. I think we should go to bed."

Camille said, "I agree."

He put his arm around her waist and Camille leaned her head on his shoulder. Then she put her hand down the back of his pants and rubbed his ass.

So Many Maybes · 317

Chapter 20
Jenny

A few days later, Bonnie surprised everyone by walking into Grafton's with Will when the store opened. She rarely came in the store, let alone so early in the day.

They stopped by the front counter and Will said, "Why don't you wait here and tolerate Wolf for a second while I go get Terri."

Wolf said, "Ah Miss Haines, my gorgeous scarlet-haired and well-financed love goddess, what brings you to Grafton's so early this morning? Darest I assume that you are here to compose a love sonnet to the delectable perfection of my full-bodied and oft-mentioned bat?"

"You're the only one who ever mentions it Wolf."

"Regrettably my lovely that is probably true, but I learned long ago that self-advertising is a vital component of successful monkey business with the fair sex. I would be selling myself short, so to speak, if I relied entirely on word-of-mouth."

Bonnie said, "Jesus Christ Wolf. You're sure in good linguistic form for so early in the morning."

Will and Terri walked up to the counter.

Bonnie said, "Terri, Will told me you wanted to talk to me about something."

Terri said, "Let's go back in my office?"

"Okay."

After they sat down, Bonnie said, "What's up?"

"I've been thinking about what we were talking about the other day, about how you needed a distraction, and I think I've found the perfect thing for you to do."

"What's that."

"I want to offer you a job."

Bonnie furrowed her brow and said, "Excuse me Terri, but I don't think I'd make a very good employee. I've never had a job. Not a normal one anyway."

"Don't worry about that. I think you're perfect for the job I have in mind."

"What are you proposing?"

"Come with me. I want to show you some things."

She showed Bonnie around the store. On every wall, hung above the bookshelves, were oil paintings.

"You've been here a few times. Have you ever noticed the paintings on our walls?"

"No. To be honest, I've never given them a second thought. Paintings in bookstores are always pretty much the same; just cheap art prints put in pre-made frames. But now that you mention it, the paintings in here are much more interesting."

Terri grabbed Dilli's step ladder and said, "Here, stand up and take a closer look."

When Bonnie got closer, she said, "No wonder they're more interesting. They're originals. At least this one is."

"All of them are original. I've hung them here to help the artist sell them."

Bonnie leaned closer and tried to read the signature.

So Many Maybes · 320

She said, "Who's the artist? The signature is illegible."

"I've talked to Jenny about that several times. It seems to me that a legible signature might be better for selling her paintings."

"Ideally, I think the signature should be entirely left up to the artist. However, I agree with you. If an artist is trying to establish a name for themselves, why not put it out there clearly for the public to see. Anyway, am I to infer from what you just said, that these are Jenny's?"

"Yes, they're Jenny's. What do you think of them?"

Bonnie got down off the ladder and stepped back. She walked around the store and looked at each painting. She stopped in front of one named *Nickels Arcade on a Spring Evening*.

Terri said, "Well?"

Bonnie said, "Paintings can affect me in different ways. They might interest me because of their technique, or their historical, political, or cultural significance. And of course I can just think they're beautiful. But these are different."

"How do these affect you?"

"Even though I love art of all kinds, I don't own a single painting. Paintings to me have always been something that you look at in a museum or in a book or someone else's home, but I've never had the desire to own one. But these are different."

Terri said, "Why are they different? Don't you think they're beautiful? I certainly do."

Bonnie said, "They are certainly beautiful, but that's not what I mean."

So Many Maybes · 321

Bonnie took a deep breath and pointed at the painting of the Nickels Arcade.

She said, "Take this painting for example. I think that it is like Jenny herself. It has her astonishing charisma and I'm drawn to it. I want to have it near me and, if you'll excuse the expression, I want to make love to it with my eyes. Every day, every night. In other words I want to own it."

"Do you think other people might feel the same way?"

Bonnie nodded and said, "I think so. People's taste in art is hard to predict. But these are easy to like."

"Do you think people would buy them?"

Bonnie nodded and said, "If they're priced right and they somehow reach the right market, yes."

Terri held out her hand and said, "Congratulations Bonnie. If you want it, the job is yours."

Bonnie was puzzled. She said, "What job is that?"

"To be Jenny's agent. With her approval of course."

Bonnie smiled and nodded and said, "Do you think Camille needs an agent too?"

"I don't know. You should ask her."

Bonnie said, "I'm going to, and Terri?"

"What?"

"Thank you for helping me sort things out."

"Don't mention it. It's what I do."

After her discussion with Terri, Bonnie formally assumed the role that Terri had been playing ever since Jenny had come to work at Grafton's. Jenny had never had any ambition or

So Many Maybes · 322

desire to be famous or financially successful, so she wasn't inclined to be a self-promoter. But Terri adored Jenny and she adored Jenny's paintings and she thought that Jenny deserved to profit any way she could from her work. So Terri became Jenny's self-appointed agent.

She applied for grants on Jenny's behalf and entered her work in contests in hopes of winning her a little money because a little money might buy more paint or even a studio for her to work in. She also hung Jenny's paintings up for sale on the walls of the bookstore.

Thanks to Terri, Jenny often won the contests and she got a lot of grants and now and again someone would buy one of her paintings. This all pleased Jenny, but it wasn't necessary to keep her painting. She was going to continue even if she didn't win contests or get grants or sell pictures.

Although she was casual about winning prizes or selling her work, she did understand how the money could help her pursue her art. With Terri's help, Jenny had quietly hidden the money she earned from her paintings from Jack.

Jenny didn't trust Jack with her money. Their relationship and their finances had been strained since they moved to Ann Arbor. Jack's salary from *BRAAAK'S!* was a pittance, yet he was spending a lot of money on beer and running up huge phone bills calling his buddies back home. Consequently, Jenny had to support them with her small income from the bookstore.

When they moved to Ann Arbor, Jack and Jenny had been sweethearts since childhood. They grew up as next-door neighbors in a small town near Cadillac, Michigan. They

So Many Maybes · 323

often played in each other's yards, and every so often Jenny's mother would take them to the movies or the Dairy Queen for ice cream cones. By the time they reached junior high school they were a couple.

In high school, Jack was the most popular guy in the school. He was handsome, and he excelled in every sport, particularly basketball. All the guys envied him and wanted to hang out with him, and all the coolest women wanted him as their boyfriend.

Jenny was different from Jack. In high school she was uncomfortable with her strong charismatic appeal, and she chose to downplay it. Although she had several good friends whom she appreciated, she chose them carefully, and she used her relationship with Jack as a shield to protect herself from the endless and mostly unwanted male attention that she naturally attracted.

Jenny was a good student in general, but she was an outstanding painter. Her talent was recognized when she was twelve years old and cultivated since then. But Jenny didn't paint to earn compliments from her teachers or parents or anyone else. She painted because she loved it and was exceptionally modest about her gift. After they graduated from high school, Jenny was given a scholarship to the University of Michigan Art School to study painting, and she and Jack moved to Ann Arbor together.

From the moment that she arrived, things went well for Jenny. Her teachers praised her paintings and she easily found a job that she liked.

So Many Maybes · 324

Unlike Jenny, Jack floundered when he left his home town. It was Jack's tragedy that his social popularity and athletic excellence in high school fueled his failure after he graduated. His lack of intelligence and horrible performance in class was intentionally hidden by his teachers and coaches and administrators so he could maintain academic eligibility to take part in high school sports. Therefore, Jack never received the help he needed to overcome his mental deficiencies and he left high school barely able to read. In Ann Arbor, Jack's natural gifts of athletic talent and good looks were worthless. He was a mediocre jock when compared to the world class athletes that Michigan recruited, and he wasn't intelligent enough to be accepted by any college as a student or to find and keep a decent job. It was humiliating, and he slowly lost his self-respect. Self-hatred spread through his once swollen ego until he hated everything. He hated Ann Arbor and he hated the University. He also hated Jenny's friends, even though he'd never met any of them. To compensate, he drank too much, and relived the glory of his past athletic achievements by calling one of his old high school teammates to talk for hours rehashing their great games.

As Jack became more and more despondent, Jenny and Jack's childhood romance faded away and they became nothing more than two people sharing the same apartment. Jenny spent most of her time in her bedroom where she slept and painted, and Jack slept on the couch in the living room and watched sports on TV or played basketball with his friends. They seldom talked to each other except when Jack felt the need to

So Many Maybes · 325

complain about something Jenny did that annoyed him. And as time went on, his complaints became more frequent and unkind and sometimes hurtful. The more unkind that Jack was, the more that Jenny tried to ignore him. She retreated to her room and painted and painted and painted.

Eventually painting by itself didn't offer Jenny adequate escape from Jack, so she started leaving their apartment to get away from him. She spent her time with her friends from Grafton's or acted in Wolf's plays. But Jenny never confided in her friends. She kept her problems to herself because she couldn't see past her sentimental affection for Jack. She had grown up with him and seen him at his best and she didn't feel comfortable saying bad things about him.

Then Jack committed the ultimate sin. Jack and Pat, one of his basketball buddies, went searching for a basketball in Jenny's closet. Jenny knew the basketball wasn't in there because the closet was where she stored her paints and canvases and many finished paintings. She stood back and leaned against the wall with her arms crossed and knowingly watched them while they callously rummaged through her things.

After a few minutes, Jack became frustrated.

He said, "This is stupid. Look at all this shit! We'll never find anything in here until we get rid of Jenny's fucking paintings!"

Then he started throwing her artwork across the room.

Jenny shouted, "What are you doing?!" and ran frantically around the room to recover her beloved paintings.

When she saw that one of them had landed on a bed post and gotten torn, months of imprisoned frustration, unhappiness

So Many Maybes · 326

and pain broke through her wall of sentimental restraint and Jenny became purple faced angry.

She screamed at him, "STOP...STOP! You've no right! Get your vacuum filled basketball brain out of my things!"

Jack looked up from his crouch in front of Jenny's closet and said, "Huh?"

He was confused. Jenny never got mad about anything.

She continued her string of insults.

"And take your urinal-cake covered hands off my paintings!"

At first, Jack almost laughed because he didn't take her seriously. But as she continued to insult him, his anger began to show.

His ears became red and he stood up and tried to respond, "Oh yeah? You..."

But Jenny was far too intelligent for him and he couldn't keep up.

She said, "You're a stupid worthless peon who can't find a decent job and licks up *BRAAACK'S!* puke with his tongue."

Jack flinched at that insult and tears formed in his eyes.

Jenny saw Jack's tears, but she no longer cared whether she hurt him or not, and she continued to shout at him.

"You smell like the brainless puddle of smoking Crisco grease that you are. You're a cruel worthless piece of men's room diarrhea...which reminds me, you need to wash your teeth. Your breath smells like the shit you eat at work every day!"

Then to just keep her string of insults going, she lied to him.

"And your boss told me he caught you using mouse droppings as sprinkles on their ice cream and munching on

So Many Maybes · 327

deep fried cockroaches while you cooked."

Jack's pain turned into rage and he screamed back at her.

"What's it to you if I did, and what gave you the right to talk to my boss?"

Jenny shook her head and screamed, "My God! You repulsive moron! And no one complained to the health department? I'm surprised you didn't get fired!"

Jack took a step toward her and said, "What are you gonna do if I did?!"

He took another step toward her, and Jack's buddy Pat realized what Jack had in mind. Pat reached out to stop him, but Jack pulled free. Now furious, Jack clenched his fist but then had doubts about what he should do.

He hesitated and looked like he was going to turn and leave, but then Jenny committed the ultimate sin. When Jack hesitated, Jenny found extra courage. She stopped backing away and paused her continuous string of insults and crossed her arms again and grinned.

She suddenly shouted, "And even worse for me, your cock is too small. You hear that Pat? Your jock friend here has a weenie the size of a tiny pickle, and in all these years he's never made me come. Not once."

That was enough for Jack. It was one thing to insult him about his job or hygiene but revealing the size of his cock in front of Pat was unforgivable. He suddenly stepped forward and took a swing at her.

With her face tensed in terror, Jenny managed to partially deflect his punch with her stack of paintings, but he still

So Many Maybes · 328

knocked her backward, and she hit her head against the mirror on top of her antique bedroom vanity. The mirror shattered and cut the back of Jenny's head. She screamed in fear and pain.

Jack started to move forward to hit her again, but Jack's buddy Pat stepped in more forcefully this time and stopped Jack.

He said, "Come on Jack. This is no good. You shouldn't hit a woman. I've got a ball at home. She'll calm down in a while."

After they left the apartment, Jenny got up off the floor and sat down on the couch and struggled to control herself. She knew she had to stop shaking and think. She knew that she had to leave Jack right away. She had to leave right then, before he came home from playing basketball and hit her again. But where would she go and what about her things?

She called Terri and asked for help.

"Terri. I'm scared. Jack's been awful and now he hit me. I have to leave him but I'm afraid of what he'll do. I have to leave, and I have to do it now before he comes back, but I don't know how. All of my stuff is here, and all of my paints are here. Some paintings too. But I have to get out. I have to do it."

Terri said, "Where is he?"

"He's playing basketball with his buddies."

"Listen to me. Don't worry about your stuff and don't worry about Jack. You have good friends who love you and will protect and take care of you. Grab your purse and walk out the door. Don't hesitate. Just do it and meet me down at the store in twenty minutes."

"Okay."

So Many Maybes · 329

"Promise me you'll do it right now."

"I promise."

Terri said, "See you at the store."

Jenny hung up the phone and and took a deep breath. For a moment she sat motionless, frozen in a state fear, then she courageously did exactly what Terri told her to do; she walked out of the apartment. The blood was still running down the back of her neck.

When they met at the store and Terri saw the blood on Jenny's head, Terri said, "Oh my God Jenny! How could he do this to you?"

Terri immediately escorted Jenny into the bathroom and pressed a damp paper towel on the cut to stop the bleeding.

Still shaking while she talked, Jenny told Terri what had happened.

Terri said, "Where are your paintings now?"

"They're scattered all over the bedroom. He threw them all over."

They walked to the front counter and Terri phoned Bonnie and Will.

"Bonnie, Jenny needs your help."

"What kind of help?"

"Jack hit her."

Clearly pissed off, Bonnie said, "Fuck! Should Will and I go over there and beat the shit out of him?"

It was a predictable response from Bonnie. Bonnie hated men who didn't respect women.

"No, as much as I'd like that, that's not what she needs.

So Many Maybes · 330

Jenny had to leave her apartment fast and she left some of her paintings there and she's worried about them. Can you and Will go rescue them?"

"Of course we can. Where does she live? I've never been there. I don't think Will has either."

Terri said, "Hold on."

Terri turned to Jenny and asked, "Where do you live?"

Jenny gave her the address then said, "But the door's locked."

Terri said, "Do you have your key with you?"

"I think so."

Jenny looked in her purse.

She said, "Yes, I've got my keys."

Terri turned back to the phone and said, "Jenny's got her keys here. We're at the bookstore. You'll have to come down here and pick them up."

"We're on our way."

Bonnie and Will drove to the bookstore to pick up the keys. When Bonnie saw the blood on Jenny's collar, she tenderly touched Jenny's hand and thought, *How could he do this? Sweet Jenny. It was like hitting a little girl?"*

Bonnie said, "Don't worry Jenny, we'll protect you. He can't even imagine what's going to hit him now."

Will didn't say anything, but he was worried about what Bonnie had in mind. Despite what he had told Bonnie, he didn't really want to see Sgt. Clarkson again.

Terri said, "You two go. We have to get her paintings before Jack gets back from playing basketball."

Thankfully Jack hadn't returned when Bonnie and Will

So Many Maybes · 331

entered Jenny's apartment. When she saw the broken stack of paintings that Jenny had used to defend herself and the other paintings thrown all over the room and the blood covered broken mirror where Jenny had hit her head, Bonnie became enraged. While Will gathered Jenny's paintings, Bonnie didn't hesitate. She phoned Robert and firmly said, "Robert, find Nort and you two bring his truck over here fast. Jack hit Jenny and her life is in danger. We don't have much time."

Robert said, "Shouldn't we call the police?"

Robert's response wasn't what Bonnie wanted to hear.

She said, "Robert don't argue with me. The police won't help us soon enough. We need to act now."

Will was standing still and staring at Bonnie. He didn't know what she was doing because Jenny was safe with Terri and he had already gathered up Jenny's paintings.

Bonnie looked at him and started shouting commands.

"Will, quit staring at me and give me a hand..."

If Jack had been paying close attention while he was on the basketball court several blocks away, he might have heard thunder because he was about to enter the maelstrom of Bonnie Haines' feminine vengeance.

Three hours later when Jack returned to his apartment, there was nothing inside but a hollow echo. Everything was gone: furniture, dishes, drapes, rugs, everything. Even the light bulb in the refrigerator was gone.

Jack stopped in the doorway, confused.

He said, "What the fuck!!!?"

So Many Maybes · 332

In a state of shock, he quickly checked the apartment number on the door and confirmed that it was his apartment. Then he slowly walked around and looked in every room. He sighed and shook his head. Someone had cleaned them out.

He called the police to report the robbery. Then it hit him like a burning bag of shit. Jenny was gone too. Somehow she had taken everything and left.

When the police arrived, Jack explained that his girlfriend had stolen all of the furniture.

The police officer shook his head.

He said, "Sir did you buy the furniture together?"

Not understanding what the police officer was getting at, Jack stupidly answered, "Yeah...except for a few antiques that her grandmother gave her."

The police officer frowned and shook his head again.

He said, "I'm sorry sir but there's nothing we can do. Your girlfriend has as much right to the furniture as you do, particularly those antiques. So technically she didn't steal anything, she only moved it which she has a right to do."

After the police left, Jack went into the bathroom to take a leak. When he opened the toilet, he became both heartbroken and nauseous. His precious basketball was in the toilet. It was completely deflated by numerous violent knife punctures and was floating in a toilet full of piss and shit.

That night, Jenny went home with Terri. Nort slept in his recliner and Jenny slept in his bed. Jenny felt safe and loved and the horror of the day faded enough for her to get some sleep.

It broke Jenny's heart to hurt her childhood friend but it

So Many Maybes · 333

was necessary. He was making her life miserable and he had become violent.

It was best for Jack too. He spent the next two nights after their fight at Pat's place, then he left Ann Arbor and hitchhiked back to Cadillac. Back there, Jack did okay. He got a job with an old teammate mowing lawns in the summer and shoveling snow in the winter. And he would occasionally go to the bar and tell stories about the great games of his past.

The next morning, Jenny woke up eager to get her life back together. She sat at the breakfast table with Terri and they discussed what Jenny should do. Bonnie and Will and Robert and Nort had put Jenny's things in the loft above Terri's garage where it was safe, but she had to deal with the problem of her old apartment. She had no intention of going back there, and she knew that without a job, Jack couldn't afford the rent by himself. That meant she had to either break her lease or get her landlord to let her out of it. Unfortunately, her landlord was a notorious prick. Since Jack's income was next to nothing and Jenny's income from the bookstore was limited, they were forced to live in a cheap place run by a slum lord named Mathew Ress.

Hoping for the best, Jenny and Bonnie first tried to get in touch with Agatha Snut, who was Ress's agent in Ann Arbor. Jenny wasn't optimistic because Snut was a crass bitch. Predictably, Snut was never in her office and she never returned their phone calls. Bonnie wanted to hang around outside the bitch's office and scare the shit out of her with a Filipino machete, but Jenny wasn't eager to try such an extreme

So Many Maybes · 334

solution.

They decided to go see Ress in person at his office in Detroit. Their visit didn't go well from the beginning because Bonnie walked right past his secretary and stood in front of his desk.

She said, "Are you Mattress?"

Ress hated being called mattress. He was the victim of that teasing joke since he was in the fourth grade.

His response was not civilized.

He said, "Who the fuck are you?"

Bonnie started to answer but couldn't get a word out before Ress screamed at her.

"Get the FUCK out of my office!"

Civilized attempts having failed, Bonnie had another solution. She called Lois.

Lois said, "Don't worry. I'll take care of it. When I'm done, this guy Mattress will be licking the soles of Jenny's shoes by mid-morning tomorrow."

Bonnie and Jenny and Terri and Baja met Lois and Tank O'Henry at the airport that evening and they drove back to Ann Arbor. Tank O'Henry was the vending-machine sized bouncer that watched over Amanda, Baja, Bunny and Lois at their dance theater. He now worked full-time for Lois's Law Firm. They had dinner at Maybe's and discussed their plans for their assault on Mattress.

The next day Bonnie and Baja began the operation by going to the pet store and picking up as many mice and other rodents as they could buy. Then they went to Jenny's old building and distributed the animals throughout every washer and dryer

So Many Maybes · 335

and toilet and the other public rooms and hallways and took Polaroids of the mice infested areas. Then they went to Ress's office.

What followed was a scene right out of a Humphrey Bogart movie. They barged in unannounced and Tank, dressed in the proverbial fedora hat and a brown suit with a black shirt and white tie, walked around the desk and stood next to the sitting slum lord.

Ress was intimidated by the appearance of the vending machine sized Tank, but he still gave them the same greeting that he had given them before.

"Get the FUCK out of my office!"

Lois didn't move but Tank grabbed the back of Ress's collar and twisted it tight. Lois handed Ress a phony business card and introduced herself.

"Mr. Ress, I am Selena Singsing, attorney at law, and this is my associate Mr. O. We are here representing Miss Jennifer Woodward."

Lois gestured toward Jenny and said, "Miss Woodward is a tenant in one of your buildings in Ann Arbor."

Ress's face turned red and he choked slightly as he tried to pull Tank's hand away. Predictably he couldn't budge the giant's hand and Tank twisted Ress's collar even tighter.

Lois laid the Polaroids out on Ress' desk he looked at each picture. Fortunately, Lois spotted the Polaroid of what was obviously a cute little guinea pig before Ress got to it. She surreptitiously removed the photo from Ress's desk and passed it back to Terri who put it in her back pocket.

So Many Maybes · 336

Then Lois said, "Mr. Ress, as anyone can see, you have obviously violated the terms of your lease with Miss Woodward by failing to maintain your property up to current Ann Arbor health standards. Frankly, the place is disgusting. Since you have violated the terms of the lease we demand that you release Miss Woodword from any obligation to continue paying you rent. Furthermore, we demand that you return her entire damage deposit."

Ress continued to resist and managed to spit out a couple of impolite words.

"Ach...FU...K...ach, you!"

Lois nodded at Tank and Tank lifted Ress right out of his chair by his collar and held him off his feet and let Ress start to strangle. After a moment, Lois nodded again, and Tank lowered Ress back into his chair, and loosened his grip on Ress's collar slightly. Ress gasped for air.

Lois continued, "If you don't comply with our demands, we will show these pictures to the Health Department and shut your building down, plus Mr. O will pay you another visit, but he won't be as gentle then as he is being now. Do you understand me?"

With Tank's grip slightly lessened, Ress was able to speak.

"This is blackmail and I wanna' see that other picture you took away!"

Jenny and Terri swallowed hard. That silly guinea pig could screw everything up. Lois however, didn't let it phase her.

She said, "The picture is irrelevant Mr. Ress, and don't think of it as blackmail, think of it as your normal crooked way of

So Many Maybes · 337

doing business."

Lois reached into her briefcase and took out a copy of Jenny's lease and placed it on Ress's desk. She wrote the words, NULL AND VOID on it in black marker and dated it. She handed the lease to Ress and told him to sign it.

Ress signed it and Terri witnessed it.

Then he said, "Now get the FUCK out of here!"

Tank tightened the collar again and Lois didn't budge.

She said, "And the damage deposit?"

Barely able to move his arms while subjected to Tank's twisting force, Ress reached into his desk drawer and pulled out his checkbook. He started to write the check, but Lois stopped him.

She said, "Just sign it and I'll fill in the rest."

Ress signed the check and Lois grabbed his checkbook and held on to it.

Lois said, "Remember, if you make any attempt to renege on this agreement including stopping payment on this check, we will turn over the photographs to the Health Department and Mr. O will pay you an unpleasant visit. Do you understand me?"

Ress nodded yes.

Lois said, "Answer verbally please."

Ress weakly said, "Yes."

Lois and Tank and Jenny and Terri and Baja calmly walked out of his office and quietly drove to Ress's bank and cashed the check. They didn't celebrate but they did breathe a sigh of relief.

Now that she was out of her lease, Jenny needed somewhere

So Many Maybes · 338

to live. Terri emphasized that there was no hurry for her to move out, but Jenny wanted her own place. She watched the Apartments for Rent sections of both the *Ann Arbor News* and *The Michigan Daily*, and she routinely checked the bulletin boards in the Michigan League and the Michigan Union. But she couldn't find anything that she could afford and had enough space for her to work on her paintings. She concluded that, although it wasn't ideal, her only alternative was to find a roommate in the Art School.

But at Bonnie's suggestion, Mother Terri came up with a wonderful and generous solution for Jenny. If all of the Grafton's friends worked together, the loft over Terri and Nort's garage could be converted into a perfect apartment and studio for Jenny.

Terri refused to let Jenny pay any rent, so it seemed as if it was a dream deal for her. However, the out of town location was a problem. Terri and Nort's house was several miles outside of Ann Arbor. It was about a thirty-minute bicycle ride during good weather which meant that she would be away from Ann Arbor and her friends and work. The ride in the summertime would probably be pleasant, but during the cold Michigan winter it would usually be very uncomfortable, if not miserable. Although Jenny knew that she could always depend upon Terri and Nort for rides, she valued her independence, so she was leaning toward turning Terri's offer down. But Terri immediately solved the transportation problem too. She asked Nort to let Jenny use one of the cars that was stored out in the pole barn Wilderness.

Nort sincerely wanted to help Jenny, but his cars were

So Many Maybes · 339

precious too him, and he was hesitant to even uncover the cars. He only relented when Terri threatened to change the official Bookstore Maintenance Man's uniform to a yellow-ribbed, navel-length muscle shirt along with pink satin short-shorts, a light blue sailor's cap, and a pair of high top Red Ball Jets basketball shoes. Even Nort thought her threat was funny.

He smiled and said, "Okay Terri. I get the point and I just happen to have a car that would be perfect for Jenny."

Since everyone was already familiar with the loft, Terri led the Grafton's crew out to the pole barn and they boldly ventured into The Wilderness.

When Terri and the others walked over to the covered car, Nort stood next to it with a sad and mournful face. He reached toward the car's cover then stopped and quickly pulled his hand back and shook his head.

He said, "Please Terri, I can't do it."

Obviously prepared for this situation, Terri held up a pair of pink short-shorts and Nort flinched.

Terri said, "Oh, for Christ's sake Norton, it's not a Ferrari!"

For the first time since they all crowded around the car, Nort smiled and suddenly beamed with pride.

He said, "No everyone, it's not a Ferrari, but it's my prized possession so I was hesitant to let it be used by anyone, but it's different with you Jenny. You're the most wonderful young woman I've ever known, and I'm so happy to be able to give it to you."

Nort grabbed the car's cover, paused to add drama, then pulled it off with the flourish of a matador.

So Many Maybes · 340

He said, "It's a 1947 Plymouth Special Deluxe Woodie Station Wagon in mint condition."

When California born Will saw the iconic car he shouted, "No way! A Woodie!"

Everyone in the pole barn but New York bred Bonnie knew what a Woodie was.

She asked, "Besides a morning hard-on, what's a Woodie."

Delighted that Bonnie had asked, Nort began slowly walking around the car and proudly described it's features.

"Bonnie, a Woodie is an old station wagon with real wooden paneled sides. It was a famous part of the Southern California surfing culture of the 1960s. At the time, surfing movies like *Beach Party* and *Beach Blanket Bingo* were shown at all of the drive-in movie theaters here in Michigan, and popular rock groups like The Beach Boys, Jan and Dean, The Safari's and The Rivieras celebrated the surfing culture and the warm Southern California winter weather. To us frozen Michiganders, the warm weather and the beach life that supposedly offered continuous views of well-built bikini-clad babes, was romantic heaven. The Woodie Station Wagon was probably second only to surf boards as the essential symbol of that romance. While the Ford Woodie Station Wagons were the most famous, the Plymouth Woodies like this one were just as 'bitchin.'"

When Nort said "bitchin," Terri, who was normally bored with Nort's technical lectures, turned her head and looked at him in surprise. The others noticed it too. Nort never used expressions like that.

Nort continued his lecture. "The main body structure is

So Many Maybes · 341

steel, but the rest is made from a combination of white ash and mahogany. Both are very strong and look cool."

Now the Grafton's crowd were aware that they were seeing a bizarre, outlandish side of Nort that wasn't normal. Only Will and Bonnie ever used the word "cool."

Nort continued, "It's powered by a 217-cubic-inch flathead straight-six engine with a small single barrel Carter carburetor. It has only 95 horsepower and when you consider all of the heavy wood, it's a dog and you'd be severely undergunned if you tried to drive it any distance on the highway. But it's great to just drive around town."

Then Nort paused his narrative and walked around the car and stood in front of Jenny and held out the car keys to her.

With a Camille-like straight and unemotional face, he said, "And Jenny, you couldn't ask for a better station wagon to ride in when you moon or flash your tits at a bus load of high school football players or to hide in when you get fucked in your itsy bitsy teeny weeny yellow polka-dot bikini."

Terry smiled and shouted, "God dammit Norton!"

Robert and Jenny laughed so hard they doubled over.

The rest stood still and tried to understand what had just happened. The only explanation they could think of was that they had entered *The Twilight Zone*. But whatever place it was, it was deeply humorous and wonderful and Nort, the most boring person on earth, had created it. After she was done laughing hysterically, Jenny hugged Nort warmly and they all entered a new period in their lives.

With the transportation problem solved, the Grafton's crew

So Many Maybes · 342

turned their attention to building Jenny's studio in the loft. It was a large empty space with an unfinished plywood floor, a high ceiling and a roof that was supported by bare steel beams. It had enormous potential as a future studio for Jenny, but they faced a large project.

Their first step was to develop a floor plan. Nort had pointed out that, since the plumbing and electrical had to be installed first, a complete plan for the space had to be formalized before they began any construction. So Jenny and Terri and Bonnie sat down in a booth at the back of Maybe's and discussed what kind of studio space that Jenny needed. Jenny also invited Camille to take part in the planning because she was very impressed with Camille's studio.

That said, Jenny's needs were different from Camille's. Camille worked exclusively in oils and, although she was initially inspired by her sketches, she painted pictures of imaginary places. Throughout the creation of one of her paintings, Camille often sat down on her couch or reclining chair in her studio and stared at the fire or browsed through books to develop a vision of what she wanted to put on canvas.

In contrast, Jenny worked in a variety of media including oils, acrylics, water colors, toy model enamels, house paint or any other kind of paint that she happened to come across, and unlike Camille's, Jenny's paintings were abstractions of real places. When she wasn't at work at Grafton's, she carried her used 35mm Nikon camera wherever she went, and she snapped color pictures of anything that caught her fancy. Then she put one or more of her photographs on a clip board next

So Many Maybes · 343

to her easel and faced the canvas. She didn't spend a lot of time worrying about what medium or techniques to use, she just started to paint; sometimes with a brush, sometimes with whatever was around or felt good in her hand, or sometimes with just her hands or feet or other parts of her anatomy. The painting that eventually emerged on the canvas was an intuitive interpretation of what was on the photograph. Unfortunately, her improvisational style meant that she needed to have many kinds of paint, brushes and other raw materials close at hand. If she had to wait until she could buy what she needed, the creative moment might be lost. Consequently, her style of painting required that she had sufficient studio space to store the materials but no need for the contemplative living room.

Therefore, Terri suggested that they divide the loft space into three separate sections. Nearest the steps down to the garage, would be a small apartment similar to Camille's, but because the layout of the loft permitted it, Jenny's apartment could have two large windows facing the fields in back of the farmhouse. Her painting studio would be the next section behind the apartment and it would be followed by a store room at the back.

It seemed like a workable set-up, but Bonnie had a different suggestion.

She asked, "Jenny, do you really need the entire center section of the loft as your work area?"

"Not really. What's important is that I have good light and enough space for my easel and a workbench along with a lot of shelves around me to put my paints and tools that I might

So Many Maybes · 344

want to use, and maybe a movable bulletin board to hang my photographs on. It would be nice to have a darkroom too, so I can develop my pictures without having to take them to the camera store. Otherwise the rest would just be open space."

Bonnie sketched her proposal on a napkin and said, "Here's what I think would be cool. First, we move your apartment to the rear of the loft. Next, we divide the center section in half, one part for your painting area, and the other part for the storeroom and darkroom. Then, and here's the cool part, we turn the area at the top of the stairs into a gallery complete with movable panels to show off your work to potential buyers. We could even put in a nice beautiful Victorian desk and chairs, so Terri and I could discuss business with the visitors."

Terri and Camille thought it was a terrific idea, but Jenny hesitated.

Eventually she said, "Okay, but only if we include Camille's work in the gallery too That is, of course, with the exception of *Orgasmic Poltergeist.*"

Camille simply said, "Thank you Jenny. Of course you'd get the majority of the space."

Jenny said, "Don't worry about it. We'll do what makes sense. From now on we're a team. Me, you, Terri, Bonnie, Robert, Will, Wolf, Baja and Nort will work together. Agreed?"

Everyone said, "Agreed."

With the floor plan established, they turned over supervision of the construction project to Nort, and with everyone's help, Jenny's studio was completed quickly. They intentionally left the gallery section to the end because Nort had never been

So Many Maybes · 345

inside an art gallery and he needed Bonnie's help to formulate the final plans.

So, whether she knew it or not, seventeen-year-old Jenny had laid the intellectual and emotional foundation for what could eventually be an artist's cooperative.

Chapter 21
The Art Fair

Every summer, Ann Arbor puts on a Street Art Fair. Artists from all over the world come to Ann Arbor to display, and hopefully sell, some of their work in booths set up down the center of South University Avenue. Both Jenny and Camille wanted to show their work in the fair and Bonnie, now officially acting as their agent, thought it was a great idea.

To get things rolling, Bonnie held a Sunday evening planning meeting in her apartment to formulate plans for the exhibits.

Bonnie said, "We need to talk about *Orgasmic Poltergeist*. It's had strange and unpredictable effects on everyone but Camille."

Terri said, "That's true Bonnie, but everyone enjoyed themselves."

Jenny chuckled and said, "Except for Will…Tell us Will. Does a Walrus have a big cock?"

Will smirked and gave Jenny the finger.

Robert said, "But that's the problem isn't it? I can't think of any reason why Will would get raped by a heavy mammal, but the rest of us would have fun. If Camille shows *Orgasmic Poltergeist* at the fair, we don't know what to expect."

Bonnie said, "True, but it's Camille's most exciting painting. I think it's worth the risk."

Terri said, "I agree Bonnie, we should show it, but since Robert and Will both passed out and Baja went into a trance, maybe we need to set up some place where people can sit or lie down and collect themselves before they try to leave our booth and walk down the street. I know Norton has plenty of cots and things to outfit it."

They all agreed that was a good idea.

Bonnie said, "The next thing we need to address is whether or not to show Jenny's paintings in the same booth with Camille's."

Wolf said, "They should be shown separately and some distance apart. Although it is well known that I am an ardent supporter of some forms of outrageous art, I find *Orgasmic Poltergeist* to be problematic. As Robert has so clearly stated, it has the potential to cause a bit of a stink, especially if Will's beloved walrus makes another appearance. In contrast, Miss Jenny's paintings are like her: playful and beautiful and, although spirited, quite harmless. If her work is in the same booth with Camille's and *Orgasmic Poltergeist* makes someone's balls explode like a ruptured inner tube, it would assuredly draw attention away from Jenny."

Bonnie laughed and applauded.

She said, "Wolf, you certainly can say the most mundane things with an excess of style. But your point is well taken. Let's display them as far apart as we can."

They decided to reserve one booth for Jenny and three booths for Camille. Jenny's set-up would be a single tent open to the street with three folding chairs and a small table. The paintings were to be hung along the walls of the tent.

So Many Maybes · 348

Camille's set-up would be more complex than Jenny's. It would consist of three tents connected in a line. Her primary exhibit would be in the tent that is at the right end of the line and would be arranged like Jenny's. Immediately to its left would be the recovery tent, and a tent dedicated to *Orgasmic Poltergeist* would follow. The primary exhibit tent would be open to the street and the other two wouldn't. So to get to *Poltergeist*, the guests would have to first go into the primary exhibit, then turn left and go through the recovery tent.

Since Bonnie was interested in how *Orgasmic Poltergeist* would affect people, they decided that she and Robert would work in Camille's exhibit, and that Terri and Baja would work with Jenny. That left Wolf and Will to keep Grafton's open.

Everyone but Camille voiced their approval of Bonnie's plan. Instead, Camille sat quietly for the whole meeting.

As Robert and Camille walked back to their apartment, Camille said, "Robert, I don't want to show *Orgasmic Poltergeist* in my exhibit."

Surprised, Robert said, "Why not?"

"It's a horrible anomaly and I hate it. I should never have let you see it to begin with."

"Why do you hate it? Didn't you hear Bonnie say that it was the best painting you'd ever produced. Bonnie's an expert. She knows about these things."

"Robert, I didn't say anything because I didn't want to argue with her, but I took offense when she said that. I want to be an artist who's known for painting beautiful landscapes, not some abstract expressionist piece of shit that gives people orgasms."

So Many Maybes · 349

Robert said, "I can see your point, but *Poltergeist* could make you famous."

"That may be true, but at what cost? It will distract people's attention from the work that I'm proud of. I'd rather be a bartender for the rest of my life than let that happen."

"Okay. What do you think we should do? Everyone else liked Bonnie's plans and they'd be very disappointed if *Orgasmic Poltergeist* isn't in the show."

"You're right I guess. I'll give in for the Art Fair, but after the fair is over, I want to burn it."

"I understand Camille. It's your painting, and let the others be damned. I'll help you destroy it."

Camille smiled and put her arm around Robert's waist and said, "Maybe we could have a ceremony."

Robert said, "I think we should. Let's think about it. I'll call the director of the Michigan Marching Band again. He might give us a discount this time."

Camille said, "Offer him a penny per band member. If we blow the painting up with dynamite, it's possible he would take the deal. Guys always seem to like explosions."

"You're right we do. I have no idea why, but we do."

The first day of the Art Fair at Jenny's booth began like everyone expected it would. The majority of the visitors loved her paintings, but they were often puzzled by what they were looking at. Jenny had chosen to display paintings of well-known places around the Ann Arbor area, but she had severely abstracted the shapes of the buildings and foliage by turning

So Many Maybes · 350

them into mostly colors and mixed media textures, so that the locations were sometimes hard to recognize without some help. Therefore Jenny and Terri and Baja spent much of their time explaining the paintings and pointing out the features of the locations.

Early in the morning, a nice middle-aged man stopped by. He had grey eyes and a medium non-athletic build and his light-brown hair was cut short and business like. He was dressed conservatively in a white short-sleeved summer shirt, dark blue pants, and simple Hush Puppy shoes. He greeted them with a warm smile and said his name was Henri Roberts. He was very intelligent and well-spoken, and Terri suspected that he was a professor at U of M. However, she wasn't sure because he lacked the pretentiousness that is so often true with academics. He was interested in Jenny's painting entitled the *Nickels Arcade on a Spring Evening*.

He said to Jenny, "Nickels Arcade is one of my favorite places in Ann Arbor. You've captured its spirit perfectly."

Henri was so relaxed and nice that Jenny felt as if she'd just been praised by her father.

Terri said, "Do you teach at U of M?"

He shook his head no and said, "I live in Chicago now, but I went to school at U of M. I'm here this week for the Art Fair. I'm looking at some real estate too. I'd like to move here."

"What do you do in Chicago?"

"I own a small art gallery...Terri, I gather you're Jenny's agent?"

Terri shook her head and said, "No Henri. Jenny's agent is working in a booth down the street with another one of her

So Many Maybes · 351

clients. I'm just helping out because I love Jenny and I love her paintings and I want her to keep working."

Henri said, "I can see why. They're lovely. A combination of strong technique and a sensitive nature."

Terri nodded and continued, "Jenny's still a college student right now and she has a job in my bookstore to pay her living expenses, but she needs money to buy paint and other materials. I've done what I can to help her for the time being. Ultimately though, I think Jenny will be able to live off the income from her art alone. Of course we're aware that painting is a tough business, but her agent is from New York and has a lot of influential friends in the art world so we're hopeful."

"What's her agent's name? As you might imagine, I have contacts in New York too."

"Bonnie, Bonnie Haines."

Henri only nodded.

He moved on to the next painting and said, "Jenny I would like to hang a couple of your paintings in my gallery. Would you consent to that?"

Jenny didn't answer. Instead, she looked at Terri.

Terri smiled and tried to restrain her enthusiasm. Inside she was as excited as a five-year-old at Christmas, but she felt she had to make sure that Henri would treat Jenny fairly.

She said, "Henri, I'm pretty sure that we could work out some sort of agreement with you, but you should talk to Bonnie. Are you busy this evening?"

"Not really. I just planned to have a quiet dinner at The Old German. Would you care to join me?"

So Many Maybes · 352

Terri smiled and said, "Yes I would Henri, very much, but we're all getting together at a place called Maybe's tonight. Why don't you join us?"

"Does Brett still own Maybe's."

"You know Brett?"

"Very well. For years in fact."

Terri said, "Why don't we meet at eight. Bonnie and another painter you should meet will be there too."

Henri turned his attention to Jenny's other paintings. When his back was to them, Terri smiled at Jenny and gave her a thumb's up.

As the day went on, a crowd formed around Jenny and blocked the front of the booth. Panting men wanted to talk to her and to touch her. Jenny thought that most of them were boring and creepy, and she didn't like being touched. But although it was a strain, she tried to be polite.

The crowd slowly grew, and it got hotter in the booth and the air stopped moving. Jenny felt like the people were inching closer and closer to her and she found it hard to breathe and she was on the verge of a panic attack. Then an asshole wearing a photojournalist's vest and toting an expensive camera, began relentlessly taking her picture.

He loudly said, "Hey Miss, could you open your blouse a couple of buttons."

Jenny's near panic turned into rage, and she grabbed one of her booth's metal folding chairs and charged through her table of brochures and went after the photographer.

She swung the chair at him repeatedly and shouted, "Get away from me, you limp-dicked piece of pig shit!"

So Many Maybes · 353

Then another guy with a Sony Portapak video recorder noticed the action and he began taping her.

He said, "Go on beautiful, let him have it."

Baja took after the videographer. She grabbed his recorder and pulled him backward across the street to the sidewalk where she smashed the camera against a telephone pole. Then she nearly crippled him with a brutal dancer's kick in the balls. He bent forward, and she kicked him in the face and knocked him on his ass where he rolled around holding on to his groin.

Terri pulled the reel of videotape out of the Sony recorder, then she ran to keep Jenny from killing the wannabe photojournalist.

Meanwhile, Jenny had caught up with him. With a powerful forehand sweep of the chair, she hammered his camera and knocked it thirty feet away where it landed on the pavement and shattered the camera lens. Horrified, the photographer took a step toward it, but Jenny wildly slammed him across his back with the chair and knocked him forward on to his knees.

Baja ran over to his camera and removed the film, then she raced back to Jenny who was repeatedly hitting the man across his back with the chair. Terri and Baja both grabbed Jenny around the shoulders and stopped her from slamming the photographer over the head with the chair and potentially killing him.

Baja shouted at the humiliated and injured photo snapper, "Get out of here you pathetic vulture, or I'll grab the other chair and both of us will turn your head into a smashed watermelon."

So Many Maybes · 354

The man ran away, and Jenny picked up the chair again and threw it at him. Trembling, she stopped and took a deep breath to get control of herself. Without looking at either of the two other women, she returned to her booth and turned the table upright, then picked up her brochures that had been scattered all over the street. She carefully stacked them on the table then quickly walked away from the booth.

After Jenny left, Terri and Baja recovered the chairs and sat back down and waited for the next visitors. About fifteen minutes later, Wolf arrived at the booth and sat down next to Baja.

He said, "Baja, my tall and sinuous object of fervent sexual desire, I am quite curious. Could you tell me why Jenny blew through the front door of the store with the look of a natural-born killer on her face, then disappeared into the Ladies Room? She was surrounded by such a brilliant aura of violence, that I expected to see as many mangled bodies out here as the battlefield at Gettysburg."

Baja said, "Wolf, you might say that Jenny was pissed."

The first visitor to Camille's booth was a pleasant enough, hauntingly pale-skinned, blue-haired woman named Deidra Dada. Dada was dressed like the clichéd schoolmarm of 1950s movies. She had on a grey mid-calf skirt, and a loose long-sleeved blouse; the antithesis of Miss Pullit. Dada spoke with a strong accent that none of them could place.

While she walked around the booth and looked at Camille's paintings, Robert, Bonnie, and Camille watched Dada carefully.

Robert whispered to Bonnie, "Do you think she's Amish?"

So Many Maybes · 355

Bonnie smiled and said, "No. As old fashioned as she looks, her outfit is definitely not Amish. She looks to me like she's just someone's sweet old aunt."

Curious why this Auntie Em was interested in Camille's work, Bonnie stood up and said, "Good morning Miss, what made you stop at our booth?"

Dada answered in a sweet old lady voice.

"Die dam dook ding dor dum ding do dough dith die dowch."

For everyone but Camille, the charming old lady's multi-dee'd accent made her answer to Bonnie's question impossible to understand. But Camille immediately knew that the deceptive old witch had said, "I'm looking for something to go with my couch."

Camille hated those words. It meant that Dada was only concerned with how the painting's colors harmonized with her home decor rather than looking at the beauty and quality of the paintings themselves.

Bonnie said, "Hi, my name is Bonnie, and this is Camille. Camille is the artist who made these paintings."

School marm said, "Die dam Deidra Dada."

Bonnie didn't quite understand so she said, "I'm sorry. My hearing's not so good. Did you say Dada?"

Charming Deidra chuckled and said, "Dahhh, Dada."

"Dadada?"

Deidra shook her head and said, "Doe. Dada."

Bonnie responded with, "Dohdada?"

Obviously becoming a little annoyed like she was talking

So Many Maybes · 356

to a disobedient child, Dada slowly said, "Dahhh…dahhh."

Bonnie nodded and said, "Dohhh…Dada," then felt ridiculous. It was like she was speaking an odd form of pig Latin.

Dada gave up. She nodded but didn't say anything more.

After looking at all the paintings on display in Camille's primary exhibit, and apparently rejecting them all, Dada pointed toward the *Poltergeist* tent.

She asked, "Dot diz dare?"

Camille hesitated to answer. She didn't want to show *Orgasmic Poltergeist* to anyone, let alone this tasteless country bumpkin.

Bonnie felt differently. She was perversely curious what would happen when you subjected aging frigidity to the power of artistic sex primeval.

She said, "There's a very special painting in there. You just have to see it."

Camille frowned, and her face sank.

Robert noticed Camille's disapproval and he said, "Bonnie do you think that's a good idea?"

Bonnie didn't answer, but she grinned with a twinkle in her eye and guided Dada into the recovery tent. Robert and Camille reluctantly followed them.

Once inside, Bonnie said, "Please Camille. She wants to see your painting."

Camille glumly gave in, and she led Dada into the next tent. When Dada was in front of *Orgasmic Poltergeist*, Camille pulled off the sheet that was covering the painting and quickly walked into the recovery tent and sat down.

So Many Maybes · 357

Dada stood still in front of the painting for a few seconds, then her body began to tremble and shake. She slowly spread her arms out like she was about to be nailed to the cross, then turned her palms up as if she was a Saint opening herself to the light of God. She leaned her head back and looked up at the sky then suddenly dropped to her knees. Her sweet old lady's eyes rolled up and glazed over and she started to pray in perfect English.

"Oh yes, oh yes. Come to me. Come to me, my dear lord. Transform yourself into human form. And thrust yourself into my open back door; ramming your grandest of all grand dorks, into me, into me, into me. And unload your high and mighty cock. Filling me my God, keep filling me, with creamy...white...bubbling...snot."

Robert's and Bonnie's eyes opened wide, and their heads jerked back at the language of the prayer.

Bonnie faced Robert and silently mimed, "Holy fuck!"

When the kneeling Dada was done reciting, she slowly rolled forward and slammed her forehead against the hot asphalt street and knocked herself out. Bonnie and Robert rushed to Dada's side.

Camille shouted, "GOD DAMMIT!!!" and covered up the painting.

Bonnie rolled Dada over and shook her. As Dada began to regain consciousness, all three of them helped the wobbly old religious pervert up and led her to one of the cots in the recovery tent.

After Dada became fully conscious, she reached up and grabbed Camille by the throat and started strangling her.

So Many Maybes · 358

Dada shouted, "Doo darr dah dev dull! DOO DUDDA DUCKKING DWITCH!!!"

Gasping for air, Camille turned as blue as Dada's hair, and she desperately tried to get free. Robert grabbed the old lady's shoulders and with some difficulty pulled her away from Camille.

Dada turned around and brutally hit Robert in the jaw. Then she fiercely kicked him in the balls and waddled out of the tent and down the street.

Laughing, Bonnie looked down at Robert who was rolling around on the pavement and holding his crotch.

She said, "I guess it would be accurate to say that this was unexpected."

Robert looked up at Bonnie and hoarsely said, "Bonnie please, it wuz…unht…it wasn't funny."

Bonnie put her hands over her mouth and tried to control herself but couldn't stop giggling.

Still trying to catch her breath, but with her amazing expressionless face, Camille said, "Doely Dudder Duck!!!"

With that, Bonnie couldn't control herself anymore. And while Robert rolled around on the ground holding his balls, Bonnie rolled around on one of the cots laughing her ass off.

The next visitor to Camille's booth was an art critic from New York named Saliesin Willi. Bonnie knew Willi well. She was a brilliant and eloquent writer and Editor in Chief of *Art Vision Magazine*. *Art Vision* was the most influential journal in the art world, and Willi was famous for writing scathing articles that crucified artists and their work.

So Many Maybes · 359

When she saw Willi coming toward them, Bonnie said, "Oh fuck! What's Willi doing here?"

Robert said, "Do you know her?"

"Yes, I know her. She's a famous art critic from New York and she's trouble. She gets off by trashing artists."

"Why would she be here in Ann Arbor?"

"I have no idea but stay cool. She seems nice at first, even charmingly weird, but when she reviews art she's a monster. Sali trashes almost everything and seldom praises anything?"

Robert said, "Oooh boy."

Camille didn't react, at least not openly. Inside she was hostile. She didn't like people like Willi who set themselves above the rest.

To most people, Sali Willi had an odd and flamboyant charm. She was a strangely attractive woman in her mid to late fifties, with a curvaceous, full breasted figure like Terri's. But Willi wore too much make-up and she couldn't seem to get control of her gray-streaked dark-brown hair. It looked as if it hadn't been styled since 1962, and it stuck out on the side because of her habit of rolling a pen in it. Bonnie had never seen Willi dressed in anything but a knee-length navy-blue skirt and vest combination, and a white blouse that was overly snug and button-stretching because she had gained weight in the sixteen years since she bought it. She topped off the outfit with a four-foot-long white silk scarf that she repeatedly tossed over her shoulder with a 1940s-movie-star flourish. Willi's nylon stockings always had a run in them somewhere, and it wasn't uncommon for her to have forgotten to zip up her skirt completely so that a portion of her white blouse stuck out. Willi

So Many Maybes · 360

spoke with an affected, pseudo-French accent, even though she was from The Bronx and she called everyone, "dahlink."

When Willi arrived in front of the booth, Bonnie and Robert stood up from their folding chairs to greet her. Camille stayed seated.

Willi instantly recognized Bonnie and said, "Ah, if it isn't Bonnie Haines, the wonderfully wicked woman who humiliated Jack McSurly. I commend you dahlink. McSurly was a nobody who acted like somebody, so he could sleep with children. I never could understand why you stayed with him. You're much too intelligent and ravishing for that fraud."

"Well Sali, everyone makes mistakes."

"Yes dahlink, yes they do, particularly artists. Most of them should have chosen a different profession. Speaking of which, did you know that McSurly has recently been commissioned to paint a giant mural inside the gymnasium of a girls finishing school in Upper Manhattan?"

Bonnie shuddered and said, "No I didn't, but it scares me to think about it...So Sali, what brings you to Ann Arbor?"

"I was invited by a group of university faculty to look at the paintings that are being shown, and maybe write about them in my magazine."

Bonnie thought, *"Oh Fuck. What a stupid thing to do."*

Sali continued, "Personally I think they were foolish to invite me. They must not have ever read one of my articles. If they had, they would know that I will most likely give negative reviews of everything that I see here. It's my duty. I have my fans to think about."

So Many Maybes · 361

Bonnie turned her head to hide her smirk.

Sali examined Camille's brochure then looked down at her and said, "Very nice to meet you Miss O'Neil. I'm Saliesin Willi. As I'm sure you can tell, Bonnie and I have known each other for some time."

Obviously unimpressed, Camille nodded and said, "Yes Miss Willi, I can see that. Did you stop by to visit Bonnie or are you interested in seeing my paintings?"

Bonnie cringed. Camille's painfully direct question wasn't what Sali was used to being asked. Sali Willi expected artists to blatantly kiss her ass. But down deep, Bonnie knew that Camille would kiss no one's ass.

Sali frowned and said, "Unfortunately Miss, as happy as I am to see Bonnie, I'm here to review your paintings, a fact that will probably displease you. I am proud to say that I'm an evil witch when it comes to art criticism."

Camille said to herself, *"According to the blue-haired bitch, I'm a witch too. Maybe we could start a coven."*

Camille nodded and said, "However true that might be, Miss Willi, I think my art will speak for itself."

Now Bonnie started to tremble and thought, *"Jesus Christ! Why would Camille blatantly declare war on the most powerful art critic in the world? Forget the review. I hope Sali doesn't slug Camille."*

Sali was now speechless. She thought, *"She is a tough one, but so incredibly beautiful. I'm not sure whether I want to crucify her or make love to her."*

After coming out of her puzzled reverie, Sali looked at

Robert, then unabashedly walked around behind him and studied his rear end.

She said, "Bonnie dahlink, who is this young man with the nice ass?"

Robert almost jumped out of his shoes, but he took Bonnie's advice to stay cool and he casually turned around and shook Sali's hand.

He said, "Hi Sali, my name is Robert."

Sali moved her gaze from Robert's butt to his face and threw her scarf over her shoulder.

She said, "Robert dahlink, we should talk later."

Even though it was coming from a peculiar older woman, Robert enjoyed her compliment, so he smiled and said, "Sali. It would be a privilege. I seldom get the opportunity to have an intelligent discussion with such a brilliant and beautiful woman as you are."

Sali said, "Thank you for the compliments Robert, even if they are pure bullshit. A woman with my reputation and looks needs any kind of praise she can get."

When Sali turned her attention to the paintings, Bonnie elbowed Robert's side and whispered in his ear, "Be careful. She's smarter than God dammed Socrates."

As Sali walked around the booth and carefully examined each painting, Camille sat down in one of the folding chairs and turned her back to the critic and watched the passersby. Bonnie and Robert fearfully waited for what they thought was going to be a string of murderous condemnations lightly disguised with polite language.

So Many Maybes · 363

Instead, Sali said, "How nice...Reminiscent of Turner or maybe Conrad Martens...Very dramatic and beautiful."

Sali's apparent approval of Camille's paintings made Bonnie and Robert hopeful that Camille had escaped the brutal crucifixion that Sali was known for. After she'd examined the last painting in the primary exhibit tent, Sali stepped back, paused, then revisited a few of the paintings and made some notes. Everyone, even Camille, waited for Sali's final verdict. Then Sali approached Camille who felt as if she was facing her last judgement.

Sali said, "Camille dahlink, do you have any photos of your paintings that are suitable for publication?"

Camille looked at Bonnie and guardedly said, "No Miss Willi, I'm sorry but I don't."

Sali said, "You really should you know."

Bonnie boldly said, "Sali if you promise me that you're not going to piss and shit all over Camille's work in your magazine, I'll have some photos taken and send them to you."

"Don't worry dahlink, I love her work. If anything, I'll have to restrain my praise lest I disappoint my readers. They enjoy it when I eloquently call someone's paintings worthless garbage."

Camille and Robert and Bonnie wanted to scream with joy, but then Sali raised everyone's anxiety level again when she asked about *Orgasmic Poltergeist*.

She said, "Bonnie, there's a painting mentioned in Camille's brochure that I didn't see displayed here. Did someone buy it?"

"Sali I assume that you're talking about *Orgasmic Poltergeist*. No, it hasn't been sold yet. In my opinion, it is Camille's finest

So Many Maybes · 364

work so far, but it's so different from what most people are used to seeing that we were afraid that they'd find it profoundly disturbing. Consequently, we put it in its own special viewing area, so it wouldn't divert attention away from Camille's other work."

"How do you mean disturbing, dahlink? Is it ugly and horrible like Shock Art?"

Feeling grateful that Sali hadn't seen *Holding My Load*, Bonnie said, "No Sali, it's not at all like Shock Art."

"Then I must see it dahlink."

Camille decided that it was time for her to quit sulking. She led Sali into the *Poltergeist* tent and she said, "This is it."

Sali walked over and stood in front of the painting. When Camille pulled away the sheet, Sali turned red and started to sweat like she had just bit into a raw jalapeño pepper.

She said, "Oh my...Bonnie dahlink, do you have something to drink?"

Bonnie smiled. She knew what was happening to Sali because it happened to everyone. Sali was getting terrifyingly aroused.

Bonnie said, "No Sali, but there is a bar across the street. What would you like?"

"For some reason, I desperately want a Screaming Orgasm."

Bonnie said, "Don't we all? How about a Coke?"

Sali's body began to tremble and shake and she struggled to stand upright. Her lower abdominal muscles began to involuntarily contract rhythmically. In an effort to stop the contractions, she crossed her legs and put her hands firmly against her crotch.

So Many Maybes · 365

THE JOURNAL OF ROBERT BAIN

Still trembling, Sali leaned her head back and shouted, "Holy mother of line, shape and color! The damn painting is fucking me!!!"

Then there was a loud rumble of thunder and a bright orange halo of static electricity surrounded the painting. A sizzling blue-green electric flame suddenly shot through the air toward her like a thunderbolt from Thor's hammer. As if it was a viscous fluid, the continuous flow of energy entered her body through her vaginal opening and it pumped up her muscles until she was a female-body-builder version of a men's blow-up sex doll. Then, in a trance, Sali flexed her now huge biceps, and the arms of her white blouse split in half and fell to her wrists. Her leg and hip muscles grew so big that the waist of her skirt tore, and it dropped to her ankles. Her panty hose ran and split quickly from her now smoking vagina, down and under her crotch, and up the crack in her ass. Then she turned around and faced me and put her hands on her hips and flexed her massive back, shoulder, and chest muscles. Her vest split up the back and her bra exploded, and her tits blasted out the front and blew out the buttons of her blouse. Then she pounced on me and knocked me on my back...

*

When Sali woke up she was lying on top of Robert who was splayed out flat on his back. She slowly raised her head and looked at him.

So Many Maybes · 366

She said, "My God dahlink, your good! What an experience. I came so hard, steam came out of my ears and my eyeballs nearly popped out."

Robert said, "As much as I'd like to take credit for that Sali, I can't."

Sali said, "Don't be modest dahlink. That was the strongest orgasm I've ever had. I feel like I've been fucked by the Incredible Hulk."

Bonnie said, "Robert isn't trying to be modest Sali. He didn't give you an orgasm. It was the painting. It does that to everyone. That's why it's called *Orgasmic Poltergeist* and why we have to display it separately."

Sali stood up and suddenly realized that her blouse was ripped open and her bra was gone.

She said, "Dear God! Why are my tits hanging out? Certainly the painting couldn't have torn open my blouse."

"You did it yourself Sali. You were pretty excited."

While Sali and Bonnie were talking, Robert wasn't listening. Without really wanting to, he was checking out Sali's matronly naked tits and his tail was wagging perversely. Very embarrassed, he slowly rolled over on his stomach then stood-up and left the tent as fast as he could.

Sali tried to hold her blouse closed and said, "I've never even heard of a painting that could induce such strong mental and physical reactions. I proclaim it to be a masterpiece."

Camille stood silently. Her fears were being realized. The beauty of her precious landscapes had been lost behind the sexual fireworks of *Orgasmic Poltergeist*.

So Many Maybes · 367

Sali slowly walked into the recovery tent. She stopped next to a cot, but she didn't sit down.

She said, "Bonnie dahlink, could you come over here please?"

Bonnie walked over next to Sali, and Sali bent forward and whispered in Bonnie's ear.

She said, "Bonnie dahlink I need your help."

"What's the problem Sali?"

"I seem to have messed myself. Do you think you can help me get some clean clothes and clean up? I obviously can't leave this tent like this."

Bonnie said, "Of course Sali. You wait here, and I'll get you something to wear."

Bonnie quickly left the tent. Sali stood still and weakly smiled at Camille.

Camille quickly walked out and silently sat down next to Robert in the primary exhibit tent.

Robert reached over and squeezed her hand.

As Bonnie ran down the street to get Sali some clean clothes, she laughed and thought, *"How fitting. After devoting her entire career to shitting on artists, Sali Willi, has finally pissed and shit on herself."*

Bonnie bought Sali an official U of M T-shirt and sweat pants and returned to the recovery tent.

Camille and Robert couldn't help laughing at Sali as she slowly walked bowlegged across the street. Sali didn't notice them. She went into the Jug where she cleaned up and changed her clothes. When she returned to the booth, Sali looked like

So Many Maybes · 368

an attractive older woman instead of a caricature in *The New Yorker Magazine*. Robert thought her high heels worn with sweat pants were an interesting touch.

Another enthusiastic fan of Robert's, Sgt. Clarkson, was called to the scene to respond to the complaint filed by Deidra Dada. Dada alleged that *Orgasmic Poltergeist* was evil and pornographic.

Clarkson said, "Ahhh…Mister Bain. So we meet again. I'm glad you're not sitting on your ass this time. I still wish you would reconsider my offer. I'd be happy to drop by your place tonight and begin your physical training. I'm told that I'm a very skillful trainer. We could do some body curls and pushups and squat thrusts, then I could show you a few maneuvers that would make you feel satisfyingly powerful and masculine."

Unlike Sali's compliments which Robert actually enjoyed, Clarkson's advances made him uncomfortable, even afraid. In no way did he want to get involved with this Amazon, but she was so physically imposing and aggressive that he found it terrifying to say no. Fortunately, he somehow found the courage to dodge the issue yet again and said, "I'm still thinking about it Sgt. Clarkson."

Clarkson looked down at her police officer's notebook and asked the group, "Which one of you is the plaintiff…let's see here…Miss Deidra Dada?"

Dada said, "Die dam dur. Dank dod doo dot deer dough doon."

So Many Maybes · 369

Clarkson's jaw immediately tightened because it sounded to her like this foreign woman had just called a Police Sergeant, "Damn sir."

Clarkson said, "Did any of you understand what she said?"

Robert and Camille and Bonnie and Sali played dumb and shook their heads.

Dada pointed at Camille and said, "Dee diz day dwitch. Dur dainting diz deevul dand dorno."

Clarkson shook her head and said, "I can't understand a word she's saying, but in her written statement she alleged that you have a painting here that is evil and pornographic."

Robert said, "Her assessment of the painting is not fair, Sgt. Clarkson."

"Why aren't her allegations fair, Mr. Bain?"

"Because the painting isn't evil in anyway. It's just kind of disturbing."

"What do you mean by disturbing, Mr. Bain?

"It's an unforgettable experience to look at, Sgt. Clarkson. Once you see it, everything in your life will seem boring by comparison. Maybe Miss Dada thinks that means it has some supernatural powers or something."

"Mr. Bain, that sounds like nonsense if you don't mind me saying so."

Sgt. Clarkson thought for a moment then asked, "Now Mr. Bain, Miss Dada also alleged that the painting is porno. Is the painting pornographic?"

"Oh not at all. It's just extremely pleasurable to look at. Miss Willi thinks it's a masterpiece."

So Many Maybes · 370

"Who is this Miss Willi?"

"I am, Sgt. Clarkson."

"What is your full name, Miss Willi?"

"It's Saliesin Willi, Officer. But you can call me Sali."

Clarkson paused and looked up from her notebook. Then she shook her head and said, "No, I don't think so. Sali Willi sounds silly to me."

Clarkson grinned for a moment while she took pleasure in her rhyme.

She said, "I'll just call you Miss Willi if you don't mind."

Clarkson wrote Sali's name in her notebook.

"And Miss Willi, are you an art expert?"

"Yes Sgt. Clarkson. I am the most respected art critic in the world. I'm familiar with almost all of the significant art ever created, and I've studied many of the most famous artists of our time. I am often invited by gallery owners everywhere to give them my opinion on whether a painting is any good or not. I also have a Doctorate in Art History from Cambridge University."

Clarkson said, "That's interesting Miss Willi. However, you don't look like an art critic to me, but then again I've never been to Massachusetts."

Sali frowned at Clarkson's ignorance.

Robert jumped in and said, "Sgt. Clarkson, Miss Willi's baggage was stolen at her hotel in Detroit. Her U of M T-shirt and sweats are the only clean clothes that she has to wear until she can go shopping."

Sgt. Clarkson nodded.

So Many Maybes · 371

"Okay, Miss Willi why do you think the painting is a masturbatory work of art? Isn't that the same thing as pornographic?"

Sali tried to keep calm but she thought to herself, *"Oh Christ! This cop is a moron."*

"Sgt. Clarkson the painting isn't masturbatory, it's exceptionally well done. It's masterful. Miss O'Neil is a master of painting."

Dada yelled, "DAT DIZ DULLSHIT! DAT DIZ DULLSHIT! DIT DIZ DORNO!"

Then she calmed a bit and pointed to the tent opening and said, "Doe dook dat dit."

Sgt. Clarkson said, "Mr Bain, I think she's asking me to go look at the painting and see for myself. She's right. I need to see it. Show me the painting."

Although Camille was very worried about what would happen, she knew that she had no choice but to let Clarkson see *Orgasmic Poltergeist*.

So Camille began to walk into the tent and slowly said, "Okay Sgt. Clarkson, follow me."

Sgt. Clarkson opened her notebook again and asked Camille, "What is your name miss?"

"My name is Camille O'Neil, Officer."

"And how are you involved here, Miss O'Neil?"

"I'm the artist that painted the picture."

Sgt. Clarkson said, "Okay Miss O'Neil. Show me the painting."

Camille led Clarkson inside the tent and Robert and Bonnie

So Many Maybes · 372

and Sali followed them. As it had been all day, *Orgasmic Poltergeist* was on an easel in front of the righthand wall of the tent and it was covered with a sheet. Robert and Bonnie and Sali stayed back to watch how Clarkson reacted, but they were careful not to get a glimpse of the painting.

Camille said, "This is it."

After Camille pulled the sheet off the painting, she quickly walked across the tent and stood next to the others and took hold of Robert's hand as they all nervously waited for the painting to work its weird magic.

Clarkson stood motionless in front of the painting for about thirty seconds. Unlike the other women, she didn't start to tremble and shake. She just studied it carefully. She tilted her head back and forth, then stepped closer and bent over to get a better look.

She shook her head and said, "That old lady is crazy. As you know, an experienced law enforcement officer encounters crazy people from time to time."

Camille and Bonnie felt relieved.

Robert said, "I'm glad you agree with me Sgt. Clarkson."

"Well I can't say that I agree with you entirely, Mr. Bain."

"Why is that, Sergeant?"

She pointed toward the easel and said, "While I don't see anything pornographic or evil about this painting, I don't see anything life-changing about it either…but I guess everyone is entitled to their taste in art. I myself, prefer the more humanistic Renaissance painters like Michelangelo and da Vinci."

Puzzled, Bonnie looked at Sali. Clarkson mentioning

So Many Maybes · 373

Michelangelo and da Vinci was extremely odd.

Clarkson used her index finger to call attention to the paint strokes on *Orgasmic Poltergeist* and said, "All these formalistic squiggles and spirals make me dizzy."

Clarkson turned to the right and looked down and opened her notebook to write down her observations. She took two wildly wobbly and unbalanced steps, then stumbled forward as if she was slipping on ice. She seemed to recover her balance by arching her back and taking another two steps, but then crossed her left leg in front of her and did a perfect imitation of Robert by tripping over her own feet.

She shouted, "Ohhh…what the fuck? GAAAD DAMMIT!" and slammed her massive body face-first into the wall of the recovery tent, and made it collapse.

Fortunately, Clarkson landed with her head sticking out into the primary exhibit tent, and she stood up and called for help on her police radio. While they waited for the Police and Fire Departments to come to their aid, the others struggled to find their way out from under the heavy canvas. Bonnie and Sali managed to crawl under the front of the recovery tent but Camille and Robert were trapped under two layers of canvas and tangled up in ropes. It was miserably claustrophobic and hot. They used their legs to push up the canvas and made some room for air to breathe.

With astonishing composure, Camille took Robert's hand and said, "So that was the famous Sgt. Clarkson?"

Robert said, "In all her Amazonian glory."

Camille said, "She's big."

So Many Maybes · 374

"Yes, she's big"

"Do you regret it now?"

Robert said, "Regret what?"

"Not invading her hidden lair?"

"No"

"You're sure? I'll bet it was big."

Robert said, "As big as a mine shaft."

Camille said, "No doubt."

Robert said, "Slippery too."

Camille said, "Like snot.

"Camille?"

"Yes Robert."

"I've got a hard-on."

"Of course you do."

After that, The Fire Department rescued them.

Deidra Dada was shaking with fear when the huge, sweaty Clarkson approached her.

Clarkson shouted, "You're wrong, you crazy old witch. It's not evil and it's not pornographic. Go home and take off those silly clothes. Don't you know it's the 20th Century? And, oh yeah, trim your nose hair."

Dada looked at Clarkson and angrily ran away.

When Clarkson passed Robert, she said, "Mr. Bain, one word to anybody about what went down here, and I'll shove a stick of dynamite up your ass. Get my drift?"

"Yes, Sgt. Clarkson."

Robert and Camille and Bonnie and Sali sat down on the curb and watched Clarkson walk away.

So Many Maybes · 375

Bonnie said, "You know Robert, something tells me that Clarkson is going to stop telling you that she can solve your clumsiness problem."

Robert nodded and said, "Maybe."

Then all four of them decided to close the booth for the day. They were exhausted. They carried Camille's paintings to Bonnie's van and drove over to Maybe's where they discussed how the day had gone. Everyone including Bonnie agreed that it wasn't wise to show *Orgasmic Poltergeist* again for the rest of the fair.

Not too long after that, Terri and Jenny and Baja and Wolf and Will showed up.

Bonnie said, "This is Sali Willi. She's an art critic from New York. Sali this is Wolf, Will, Baja, Jenny, and Terri. Wolf is an insane playwright, Will is a filmmaker, Baja is a dancer and a muralist and set and costume designer. Jenny is a painter and Terri is the only sane one amongst us."

Sali shook their hands and said, "Please excuse my outfit. My normal clothes were ruined."

Bonnie interjected, "Sali stood in front of *Orgasmic Poltergeist* today."

Terri asked, "How'd it go?"

Bonnie said, "Well…you might say it was interesting."

Wolf asked, "So tell us my mysterious braless, T-shirt-clad New York woman, how is it that you are so beautiful and an art critic at the same time?"

Baja said, "Shut up Wolf."

So Many Maybes · 376

Sali giggled and said, "Oh I can see why you are a playwright. You do have a natural gift for words, especially poorly veiled insults."

Baja said, "Oh you have no idea."

Robert said, "Jenny, you've been really quiet. How'd your day go."

Jenny responded, "Pretty much the way my day always goes."

Terri said, "Well, not exactly. I'd say that today reached a new level of Jenny Woodward inspired feminine action."

Bonnie asked, "What does that mean?"

Jenny said, "It all started when about fifty people crowded into my booth and started pawing me."

Terri said, "Then a couple of photographers started to hassle Jenny and she lost it. It ended with all three of us kicking the shit out of the two guys. Jenny almost killed one of them by hitting him over the head with a folding chair."

Baja said, "It was very stylish. I'm proud to say I was part of it."

Will said, "It sounds to me like old-fashioned professional wrestling."

Wolf said, "I'm so sorry I missed it. Jenny promise me you'll reprise your performance again tomorrow."

Terri said, "Wolf...I think Jenny should stay away from her booth tomorrow."

Jenny said, "You'll get no argument from me Terri. You know enough about my work so that you and Baja can handle things. I'll stay back at the store with Wolf and Will."

So Many Maybes · 377

Henri Roberts walked into Maybe's and hugged Brett and they talked briefly. Brett handed him a beer and he walked over and sat down next to Terri.

Sali said, "Henri dahlink! What are you doing in Ann Arbor?"

He said, "Hello Sali. Still walking around with a gun in your purse to protect yourself from enraged painters?"

Sali said, "Henri, you beautiful man. Have you changed your mind about making love to me in the intelligent manner that I deserve?"

"Sali, you know I can't. If I did, you might visit my gallery and review some of the art and destroy my business."

"Oh Henri dahlink, you say the nicest things."

Henri said, "Hello Bonnie. I wondered where you ended up."

Bonnie said, "Hello Henri...I came here with McSurly. He taught at the Art School here for a short time several years ago. When he left, I debated whether to go back to New York or not, but I liked it here, so I stayed."

"So you two broke up."

"I caught him banging one of his students, so I kicked the deadbeat out."

Sali said, "The way I understand it, Bonnie was a little tougher on him than that, dahlink. Rumor has it that she ripped McSurly's balls off. I could hear the sound of tearing flesh all the way in New York."

Henri laughed and said, "I never thought that McSurly was such a bad guy and I've heard he is a good teacher. He just can't keep his hands off the young women in his classes."

So Many Maybes · 378

Bonnie said, "I hate him, but you're right. His students love him."

Sali said, "Loved. He's not teaching anymore."

Henri nodded.

Terri said, "Obviously all of you know each other."

Henri said, "Sometimes the art world is pretty small. I met Bonnie when I worked at the Museum of Modern Art in New York, and everyone knows Sali."

Sali said, "Henri, you haven't answered my question. Why are you here?"

"I'm here for the fair, and I'm looking for a place to live."

"You're moving to Ann Arbor?"

"I hope so. I'm sick of Chicago?"

Sali asked, "Are you going to sell your gallery there?"

"I don't know. For sure not right away. It's a big city so the art market is better there, but I'm hoping there's enough here to support a small place like mine if I specialize in local artists."

Terri said, "Henri is interested in putting some of Jenny's paintings in his gallery...From what you're saying Henri, I assume you mean in your gallery here."

"Primarily yes, but also in Chicago as long as I keep the place there."

Sali said, "You should check out Camille's work too. It's wonderful."

"Coming from you Sali, that's a huge compliment."

"I'm not kidding Henri. It's that good."

"I'll stop by your booth tomorrow, Camille...Say Sali, why are you dressed like a poverty-stricken college student."

So Many Maybes · 379

Camille said, "That's kind of a complicated story..."

That night, Bonnie drove Camille, Robert, and Will out to the farm where they were going to meet Terri and Nort and destroy *Orgasmic Poltergeist*. Even though Bonnie was still curious how an abstract image on canvas could induce orgasms, she had no problem seeing it destroyed. The painting belonged to Camille and it was up to her what should be done with it. Besides, after only a single day at the Art Fair, Bonnie realized that the painting should never be shown in public again without a medical team in attendance. They were just plain lucky that no one had a heart attack.

They set *Orgasmic Poltergeist* on fire on the top of an Indian burial platform that Nort had hastily constructed. As Camille watched her unintentional creation go up in flames, she felt no sadness or remorse. She felt only relief.

Chapter 22
The Holes

One Friday afternoon, a weird guy named Tilblit came by the bookstore and asked if he could put a poster in the store window. Terri said no immediately. She thought that posters made the windows look trashy. But just for the hell of it, Will asked Tilblit to show them the poster. As soon as he saw it, Will started to laugh. It was an organizing poster encouraging people to join a protest march against the existence of a rock band named The Holes.

Terri looked at the poster and asked the guy, "Who are The Holes?"

Will answered for Tilblit. "They're an extreme punk-shock-rock band from New York. They play their instruments badly on purpose, and they write songs with titles and lyrics that are sometimes offensive, and they do disgusting things on stage. But they're basically harmless."

Tilblit frowned angrily and shook his head and said, "Oh come on, their music is rude and filthy and…and they're spreading their universally regarded bad attitudes around the world. One of their songs even tells people to shit on every Beatles and Elvis and Buddy Holly album that they can find, then eat them for lunch."

Terri made a disgusting face and looked at Will.

She said, "You're kidding me?"

Will said, "I haven't heard that song. Where did you hear it?"

"I didn't hear it. I read about it in *The Village Voice*."

Will said, "Anyway, he's sort of right, but The Holes aren't exactly what they seem at first glance either. They do what they do to be shocking and outrageous and sometimes even funny, but they never advocate crime or violence or racist behavior, and they don't display Swastikas or other Nazi symbols like some shock-rock bands have.

Tilblit said, "Yes they do. Just look at their song 'Vatican Storm Troopers.' It's an obvious reference to the Nazi Stormtroopers who were trained to torture and murder my people."

Terri now felt sorry for Tilblit, and she was beginning to feel guilty for rejecting his request to put the poster in the store window.

She said, "Oh my God, that's horrible. Did your relatives live in Europe during the war?"

"No, they lived in Mukluk, Manitoba."

"When was the SS in Manitoba?"

"They weren't, but they could have been if things were different. That's my point."

Terri rolled her eyes and threw the poster at him.

She shouted, "Oh for God's sake! You moron. Pick up your poster and get the hell out of my store…Will, if he tries to come back in here, shove an unabridged dictionary up his ass."

Will said, "Gladly."

Tilblit angrily picked up his poster. He wanted to say something further, but as soon as he opened his mouth

So Many Maybes · 382

to speak, Will grabbed the four-inch-thick, twelve-pound Webster's and ran at him. Tilblit's eyes opened wide and he split as fast as an atom in a nuclear reactor,

Laughing, Terri said, "Will, how do you know about this awful band?"

"I know Bonnie Haines."

Terri nodded and said, "Are The Holes going to perform around here anytime soon."

"Not that I know off."

Terri said, "I wonder why Tilblit would think that Ann Arbor is a good place to stage a demonstration?"

"Beats me. They have a few fans in New York, but I'd be surprised if twenty people here have even heard of them."

Terri said, "Have you heard their music?"

Will said, "Unfortunately. The music is worthless, but the album that I listened to does have songs with clever titles and lyrics."

"What's the title of the album?"

"*The Sanctification of Christian Defecation*. I think the titles and lyrics are what interests Bonnie. It's the radical poet in her."

That evening, Robert and Camille and Will and Bonnie met at Maybe's for dinner.

After dinner, Bonnie signaled Mike the bartender and ordered five shots of tequila each.

Will asked, "You're kidding me? Five?"

"I think five is about right for a good buzz, don't you?"

"Maybe for you, but in my case three is more than enough."

So Many Maybes · 383

Bonnie handed Robert a record album and said, "Will told me about the demonstration tomorrow. I couldn't find the *Village Voice* article about The Holes, but I brought their album so I could show you guys the cover."

Mike arrived with the tequila and Bonnie said, "Line 'em up Mike."

"Okay. Let me know if you need more, but please don't drive home."

Bonnie said, "Don't worry Mike. We only live a block away. Besides, after we leave here tonight, I plan on taking a detour to bang the shit out of Will on The Diag before we walk home. Fucking in the fresh air should be a good way to sober up don't you think?"

Mike smiled and shook his head and set down the twenty shot glasses in front of Bonnie.

Bonnie drank three shots in succession and put each empty glass upside down on the table as she went.

She said, "I love tequila. It makes me wanna fuck. How about you Camille. Does tequila make you horny?"

Camille reached across the table and picked up a shot and said, "Always."

She drank it and stylishly put it upside down on the table.

Even though he was strongly anti-religious, Robert flinched when he saw The Holes album cover. It showed the naked band members riding a huge wooden cross together like it was a hobby horse."

He reached forward and drank one of the shots himself.

The album obviously had a religious theme. It was entitled

So Many Maybes · 384

The Sanctification of Christian Defecation and the songs on the album were: "Vatican Storm Troopers," "Presbyterian Emasculation," "Masturbatory Confessional," "Blow Me to Heaven," "Pulpit Dry Hump," "Compulsory Christian Compliance," "Southern Bible Belch," "Evangelical Money Maker" and "Banging in the Pew."

He looked on the back and read the description of the band. They had adopted stage names that made humorous use of the word hole. The lead guitar player was Bung Hole, Blow Hole played bass and Dripping Hole played rhythm. Their drummer was Gaping Hole

Robert immediately noticed that the obvious name, Ass Hole, was left out and he thought that maybe the band felt it was too obvious and wouldn't get any kind of reaction.

Robert said, "Interesting. They obviously try to offend people. Dilli O would shit bricks if she saw this."

Will nodded and said, "I thought about showing it to her, but I was afraid she'd use the record like a discus to cut my head off."

"No doubt."

Bonnie reached forward and drank a fourth shot and said, "I think it would be fun to go over and talk to some of the demonstrators. I'm curious why people here would bother protesting an obscure band like The Holes."

Robert drank another shot then said, "It might, but from what Will says, maybe only two or three people in Ann Arbor have even heard of them."

Bonnie said, "They were all art students at New York

So Many Maybes · 385

University and they hung out together at a night club called HeeBeeGeeBee's which was in the East Village just down the road from NYU."

Camille reached forward and picked-up her second shot. She gulped it down then wiped off her mouth with her hand and said, "That's where I saw them."

Bonnie said, "You saw The Holes?"

"I was working in New York and one of the other models suggested that we go see them. It was appealing because we spent all day trying to look glamorous and we thought that indulging in a little ugliness would be a release, but it wasn't really. We couldn't relax because people kept staring at us."

Robert drank another shot then said, "Understandable don't you think? Beautiful models in a grungy place."

"I guess."

Bonnie continued, "All of the bands that played there were non-mainstream punk rock or shock rock groups like Cruel, Loud Phart and Anal Magic..."

Robert held up his hand to signal her to pause for a moment. He downed another shot then said, "Wait a minute, Loud Fart?"

"Isn't it a cool name? And Phart is spelled with a P h."

Camille said, "We should contact them Robert. We could add sound effects to their show."

Bonnie downed her fifth shot and said, "Anyway, they thought it might be fun to form their own band. And since conventional musical talent appeared to be irrelevant, they went for it. So Camille, besides feeling uncomfortable in the club, what did you think of them?"

So Many Maybes · 386

"They impressed me as nice suburban kids trying too hard to act like badasses; all show, no dicks."

Finally feeling the effects of the tequila, Bonnie's mind started to drift toward the magic land of drunken creativity where she often had great ideas. Unfortunately, she seldom remembered them when she sobered up."

She said, "You know what Will?"

"What Bonnie?"

"I have an idea."

"What kind of idea?"

"A good idea."

Robert drank another shot and, with mock formality, he said, "Ah yes, it is often said that a good idea is better than a bad idea."

Bonnie responded with equal formality.

"You are quite right Mr. Bain, but the problem is not what is better but instead what is good or bad in the first place."

Robert nodded in agreement.

"Yes Miss Haines, your point is well taken. But I think there is no one answer to that problem. It depends on how the fuck you look at it,"

Bonnie said, "You're quite right Robert. I don't know about men, but for women fucking is the primary problem."

"Why is that?"

"Just like men, women want a good piece of ass. But for some reason they always think that the badass is better than the good ass, and they inevitably get fucked in the ass by the badass."

So Many Maybes · 387

Will said, "Well said."

Bonnie said, "Here here! Will said, 'Well said well said.'"

Camille drank her third shot and said, "I agree Miss Haines, I agree. You are a true poet."

Will laughed and said, "You know Robert, I feel sorry for you."

"Why's that?"

"Women always say you have a nice ass, which means that you're not cool and will never be a good piece of ass."

Robert drank his sixth shot and said, "Kiss my nice ass Will."

Will said, "So Bonnie, what was that good idea you had?"

"Ahhh…ahhh…God dammit Robert. You made me forget my idea."

Camille said, "Let me help. You were saying that you needed to get badly fucked in the ass."

"Right. But I'm thinking I'm going to wait until I find a real badass."

Camille said, "Good idea."

"That's what I had, but I forgot when Robert interrupted me."

"What was that?"

Bonnie said, "A good idea."

Will said, "Bonnie I think it would be a good idea if you and I made a movie about that demonstration tomorrow."

Bonnie scared the shit out of everyone by standing up fast and pointing at the ceiling and shouting, "That's it!"

After getting control of his colon, Robert said, "What is?"

Bonnie sat down and said, "That was the good idea I forgot."

So Many Maybes · 388

She drank another shot and said, "Thank you Will for reminding me."

Will continued. "The Holes are a controversial group and a movie about them might get some attention at film festivals."

Bonnie drunkenly said, "That's a great idea Mr. B. Free. After we film tomorrow, we could go to New York and film them butt fucking and maybe even share a taxi with them."

Camille drank her fourth shot and said, "Robert was going to butt fuck me on the sidewalk for our first date, but we couldn't afford to hire the Michigan Marching Band."

Will ignored their silliness and tried to keep the movie planning on track. He said, "Can you finance it Bonnie?"

Bonnie smiled and said, "I don't know. How much was the band going to cost Camille?"

Will rolled his eyes and said, "I was talking about the movie Bonnie. Can you finance it."

Bonnie said, "No sweat Mr. Mekas."

Robert asked, "Who's Mr. Mekas?"

Bonnie said, "Jonas Mekas. He's a famous underarm cock-u-men-try film shooter in New York."

Now excited about the project, Will said, "Let's do it. I'll do the camera work."

Bonnie said, "I'll blow the sound."

Camille said, "I'll hire the band."

Will asked, "What? Why do we need a band?

Camille and Bonnie and Robert all answered him together, "To accompany the butt fucking!"

Will said, "Shit! Come on you guys. I'm serious about this.

So Many Maybes · 389

Camille, do you have a camera?"

Camille nodded and said, "It's kind of old, but it's good enough to take pictures of butt fucking."

Will asked, "What kind of camera is it?"

Camille said, "As Deidra Dada would say, it's a dittle Dodak."

"Who's Deidra Dada?"

"A crazy school marm."

Bonnie drank her seventh shot and said, "God blew snot up her ass."

Will said, "What the fuck are you two talking about!!?"

Robert was definitely feeling it now too. He said, "Butt fucking. It happened at the art fair."

Will loudly said, "What!!!? Someone got butt fucked at the art fair?"

Bonnie shook her head and said, "Of course not Will. Don't be ridiculous."

Will looked up at the ceiling and took a deep breath, then he asked, "Camille, does your camera take good pictures?"

Bonnie said, "Are you thinking she could shake kills?"

Will said, "You mean take stills?"

"That's what I said."

"No you didn't."

"I didn't? What did I say?"

"Shake kills."

"Oh. I meant shake tits."

Robert asked, "How did tits come up?"

Bonnie said, "Will likes tits. Don't you? I think every guy likes tits."

So Many Maybes · 390

Camille said, "Robert likes Bunny's tits."

Robert said, "Bunny doesn't have any tits."

"So why are you always telling her that her boobs are just fine."

Bonnie said, "I don't think boobs and tits are the same thing."

"Why not?"

"Tits are for flashing. Boobs are for getting a hand hold."

Robert said, "Now you're talking like Bunny."

Bonnie looked sad and put her elbow on the table and said, "I miss Bunny."

Will continued, "We need stills and if Camille has a good camera, she can take an active part in this adventure instead of standing around watching us work."

Bonnie said, "But Will, you've got a big Canon that she can fuck up the pictures with?"

Robert shook his head and smiled and thought, "*Bonnie sure is charming when she's hammered.*"

Bonnie said, "It's a really big Canon too. Will, show Robert your big Canon."

Now even Will was having trouble keeping a straight face. He said, "Maybe later. It takes some time to learn how to use my camera, and there's probably going to be a lot of hub bub at the demonstration. I think it's better that she uses one she already knows how to use."

Bonnie said, "Bunny's got a big Canon too. I miss Bunny's Canon."

Camille suddenly said, "I'll go and get my Dodak so I can show it to you."

So Many Maybes · 391

She drank her fifth shot and got up from the table and ran out to go up to her apartment.

Robert said, "Will, what am I going to do?"

Bonnie said, "You're going to help me with the sound by grabbing my crotch and holding on tight."

Robert opened his eyes wide and smiled broadly and drank another shot. He wiped his mouth off and said, "Boy that sounds like fun. Maybe I should be a filmmaker rather than a writer."

Will said, "Sound is really a two-person job. One person holds the microphone and the other carries the recorder."

Robert nodded and said, "So why do I have to grab Bonnie's crotch?"

Bonnie said, "Because I like having my crotch grabbed."

Robert nodded again.

Camille returned with her camera. It was a Kodak Pony 135.

Will looked at it with a fondness that the others didn't expect.

He said, "I love these little cameras. They're simple and work great and take good pictures. They're perfect for traveling. My grandfather had one. Camille, we want you to take as many pictures of the demonstration that you can."

Camille said, "Okay. Thanks you guys for letting me take fart."

Will said, "You have to be there. You're one of us…Okay, we're on. Let's all meet at our place at 8 A.M."

There was one shot of tequila left on the table and Will reached for it, but Bonnie slapped his hand and grabbed it

So Many Maybes · 392

herself and quickly downed it.

Bonnie said, "And don't forget to go without panties."

Now exasperated Will raised his voice again and said, "God dammit! What the fuck do panties have to do with it?"

And again, Bonnie, Camille and Robert answered in harmony, "Nothing. But you have to admit that it's always fun to go without panties."

*

THE JOURNAL OF ROBERT BAIN

The assembly point for the Anti-Holes March was in front of the Student Union on State Street. When we got there, only about twenty people had shown up for the march. I guess I should have expected it. This demonstration was a silly idea."

For the last decade, someone in Ann Arbor was protesting and marching against something or other. Usually it concerned serious issues like the war in Vietnam or the arrest and imprisonment of John Sinclair who was sentenced to ten years for the possession of two marijuana cigarettes. John Lennon even showed up for that one. But protesting against The Holes, no matter how offensive and outrageous they were, could hardly be compared to those causes.

When Bonnie saw the pathetic turn out for the demonstration, she said, "Fuck! This sucks!"

Will said, "Don't worry Bonnie. We're documenting what is, not what should be. That's what documentary cinema vérité is. Besides more people will probably

So Many Maybes · 393

show up before the demonstration starts."

I said, "What's cinema vérité?"

Will answered, "It's a French phrase that translates literally as truthful cinema. The meaning has changed over the years, but basically it means that we're only going to film what goes on here and not stage anything."

We unloaded the gear from Bonnie's van. Then Will put several loaded film magazines in his and Camille's back pack. Bonnie put the strap holding the sound recorder over my shoulder and connected me to her microphone with a ten-foot cable.

While we were waiting for the demonstration to start, Bonnie suddenly moved over and sat down on the curb. Since I was connected to her by the cable, she nearly jerked me off my feet. She opened her back pack and removed a metal Roy Rogers lunch box and a bottle of Southern Comfort.

I smiled and thought, "Who the hell has a Roy Rogers lunch box?"

Camille said, "What's in the lunch box?"

"Lunch."

Then she held up the bottle and said, "And pain killer."

Inside the lunch box were four huge marijuana brownies. She handed one to each of us, then scarfed down the other one herself.

With her mouth still full, she said, "It wooks to ma that we'll have to be hah to get through this stupid thing."

So Many Maybes · 394

Camille and I nodded in agreement.

Bonnie took a large gulp from the bottle of Southern Comfort and handed it to Camille. Camille took her gulp and handed it to me. I took a double gulp and offered it to Will.

Will frowned and said, "No thanks."

He gave his brownie back to Bonnie too and said, "I have to be clear headed when I'm filming."

Bonnie gave him a questioning look and said, "Okay. But feel free to come back to me when the gunfire starts."

While they were discussing the Clear-Headed vs. Fucked-up dilemma, more and more people had been showing up to take part in the demonstration. It was amazing how big the crowd eventually became. By my guess, they numbered over a hundred.

I said, "I never expected this."

Bonnie said, "Me neither."

As people continued to arrive, Will said, "Man alive. This is great. We're smart to film this. We'll get more film than we can handle."

Tilblit walked out in front of everyone and we got up and moved into position to begin filming.

Speaking through a megaphone, Tilblit said, "We're going to start the march in about twenty minutes, but first I want everyone to go to my van over there and pick up a protest sign."

As the protestors went over to Tilblit's van, we

followed along. The protest signs were four-foot-long, wooden one-by-twos, with poster board stapled to them. On the poster board was painted the words "DOWN WITH THE HOLES" in bright red letters. There must have been a hundred signs in Tilblit's van. It was obvious he was expecting the size of the crowd that actually showed up.

When everyone had their sign, Tilblit set the protest in motion and the demonstrators walked down State Street toward the State Theater.

They chanted, "Down with the holes. Down with the holes. Down with the holes."

We followed them and filmed the action. Although people were laughing at the protesters and shouting insults, things went okay at the beginning.

But when we reached the middle of U of M's Angel Hall everything went insane. Horse mounted wild Indians in Apache Headdresses and shouting war hoops attacked from three sides and methodically hit the demonstrators with stone tomahawks. Some of the Indians grabbed the protester's signs and smashed them over the head. A flatbed truck carrying The Holes came out of nowhere and drove right into the crowd. Bung Hole, Blow Hole and Dripping Hole jumped off the truck and swung their guitars back and forth and smashed the marchers across the face, cutting them with their guitar strings. Gaping Hole, with his drum set mounted on the truck, drove past and shoveled piles of green horse shit at everyone. The rhythm guitar player, Dripping Hole, tried to hit Bonnie, but she used the microphone cable to whip me around like a Scotsman's hammer until I drove the top of my head squarely into Dripping's dribbling mouth. Dripping flew backward onto his back, and Bonnie moved in and stomped her heel into his groin.

Miraculously, Will managed to remain untouched and he calmly filmed the entire slaughter in detail. While Dripping rolled around on the ground and held onto his balls and screamed in pain, Bonnie pulled the recorder off my shoulder and ran to join Will.

I tried to stand up, but Blow Hole ran past and smashed me over the head with one of the protest signs and knocked me down. When I tried to get up again, several protesters ran over me and knocked me on my back and another one tripped and kneed me in the stomach and another one stepped on my face. I rolled onto my knees and had just managed to get to my feet when one of the horse mounted war hooping Indians rode past and hit me on the back of the head with a stone tomahawk and I flopped face down into a large pile of horse shit, unconscious.

When I came to, the air was filled with tear gas as the police moved in to break up the melee. The tear gas was awful. I could hardly breathe, and I coughed, and my eyes burned, and it got worse when I tried to rub them.

So Many Maybes · 397

Most of the protesters were sitting on the ground and some were crying. Tilblit was running around in a panic from protester to protester and calling for ambulances and apologizing to everyone.

He shouted, "We will get vengeance! They have declared war on the wrong man! Tilblit will get even! The Holes are history."

As things calmed down, the police went from protester to protester to take their statements. I was sitting on the curb attending to my wounds when Sgt. Clarkson walked up and blocked the Sun as she stood in front of me.

With her deep, raspy voice, she asked, "Mr. Bain, why are you sitting on your ass again?"

"Once you get to know me, Sgt. Clarkson, you'll understand that I spend a lot of my time on my ass."

"Why is that Mr. Bain?"

"Because I'm clumsy."

"So you've told me before. I told you then that a little training could solve your clumsiness problem. I'd be happy to give you that training myself."

"I'll think about it, Sgt. Clarkson."

"Please do. I think you'd enjoy being a cop. Come down to the station sometime. I'd like to show you my private office."

I had to stifle a laugh because I remembered Jenny's sarcastic comment about Sgt. Clarkson's special police unit.

I said, "Okay, Sgt. Clarkson."

"Did you fall down today Mr. Bain?"

"No. Today wasn't a normal day. Today, a man hit me over the head with a sign, about ten people ran over me and an Indian on a horse knocked me out with a stone tomahawk. My entire body is bruised, and my head is bleeding and my eyes are burning from your tear gas and I smell like shit."

Clarkson leaned forward and looked at my bleeding tomahawk wound. She pushed on it roughly and made me flinch then she stood back up and wiped her dung covered finger on her pants.

"You do need a bath Mr. Bain, but you'll live."

If I wanted sympathy for my suffering, it was obvious that Sgt. Clarkson wasn't the one to ask.

She removed a silver pen from her chest pocket that was tightly stretched by a huge, well-shaped breast and opened her famous policeman's notebook and looked down at me.

"Please tell me what happened Mr. Bain and, for God's sake, explain that Indian crap. It's not wise to try and bullshit a police officer."

"I'm part of a documentary film crew. We were here filming a demonstration that was protesting the existence of The Holes. Evidently The Holes heard about the demonstration, so they and their Indian thugs attacked us."

"We'll need to look at that film Mr. Bain. Who

should we contact to do that?

"You should contact Will B. Free, Sgt. Clarkson. You've met him before. That's him over there with the camera."

Sgt. Clarkson looked over at Will who was still moving through the crowd with his camera. She wrote in her notebook.

She said, "Mr. Bain, you two sure have a knack for getting entangled with crazy people."

I nodded and frowned.

"Anyway, Mr. Bain, who are these Holes?"

"The Holes are a punk-rock band from New York."

Clarkson wrote in her notebook then looked up and said, "I hate punks."

She reached into her other, equally stretched chest pocket, and took out another one of her police officer's calling cards and wrote on the back then handed it to me.

She said, "By the way Mr. Bain, do you like my tits?"

I froze. That sure wasn't a question I expected during an interview with a police officer. I shook my head to make sure I heard her right.

I said, "Uhhh...what, Sgt. Clarkson?"

"You heard me, Mr. Bain. If you're a real man and have big enough balls, come home with me after we get done here today and I'll give you a great look at my tits. Then we'll jump in the shower together and I'll wash your scrotum with my big Amazon hands then fuck

So Many Maybes · 400

your brains out. Get my drift?"

I shook my head again and said, "I'm sorry, Sgt. Clarkson. I'm having a hard time concentrating. I got hit on the head pretty hard."

"I understand Mr. Bain. We're forming a special police unit to look into what happened today. The number is on the back of that card. Give us a call if you have anything to add to your statement."

"Okay Sgt. Clarkson, I certainly will."

Clarkson firmly said, "Good"

She closed her notebook then went to interview some of the other protesters.

I watched her walk away and thought, "I wonder if she was going to try and fuck a few of the other marchers too."

I shook my head again when I realized what I was thinking, and I put my hands over my face. I promptly pulled my hands away because they were covered with green horse manure.

After Sgt. Clarkson left, Camille walked up next to me and sat down.

I looked up at her. She looked seemingly untouched and was as neat and beautiful as ever. I shook my bloodied and horse shit covered head and thought, "How is it possible that she went through this weird riot and came out looking so gorgeous?"

I swear to God, it was like she took a stroll in the park in a driving rainstorm and didn't get wet.

She examined my bleeding head wound, but unlike Sgt. Clarkson she was gentle and concerned.

She said, "Robert are you okay? Do you think we should go to the hospital?"

"No, I don't think so. Besides feeling ridiculous, I'm okay. If my head keeps bleeding or something, then we should."

She nodded and said, "You know, despite the fact that you look and smell like shit, I'm really happy that I was here today. It was a hoot?"

I said, "Maybe later I'll look back at it and feel the same way. But right now, I hurt all over..."

*

Chapter 23

The Commie Putz

Robert was just finishing up his *Journal* entry when Bonnie and Will walked into Camille's studio.

Bonnie flopped down on the couch and said, "Uhhhg…How can you write this morning? I feel like shit?"

"I was inspired. I did feel like shit earlier, but since it's four in the afternoon my hangover has pretty much subsided."

"It still morning as far as I'm concerned."

Camille said, I gather you guys didn't go over to the demonstration this morning."

Will said, "No. We didn't get our act together soon enough."

"Oh that's too bad. You seemed really excited about it last night."

"I was, but we didn't get to sleep until seven this morning. We only woke up an hour ago."

"Did you guys really go out on The Diag?"

Bonnie said, "No. I wanted to, but Will insisted we go home."

Will said, "I may be a hippie from San Francisco, but I don't like fucking in public."

The phone rang, and Robert answered it.

A man with a heavy Slavic accent was calling. He rudely said, "Who are you? Is phone yours."

"I'm Robert, and yes it's my phone. Who are you?"

"I am Platikov. I am greatest dancer in world. I am famous. You have heard of me, yes?"

"No I haven't, and I know for a fact that Goodekov is the greatest dancer in the world."

Platikov hated it when people said that, and he angrily responded.

"NO! You are one barbarian fucker of mother! Platikov is best. Goodekov is short little boy. He is weak. Platikov is strong."

Robert jumped back at the insult. Although it was obvious that this Russian guy had no idea what he was saying in English, Robert couldn't help but counter with an insult of his own.

Doing his best to imitate a Russian accent, Robert said, "You are stupid farmer who fucks cows."

"Is not true. Have never been farmer."

Robert almost doubled over laughing and said to himself, *"This guy really is an idiot!"*

"Is true. Why you laugh?"

Robert asked, "Why are you calling me?"

"I call because American Stenova is Platikov's woman now. You have lost her because Platikov is strong lover. You are weak, yes?"

"What are you talking about? Who are you really?"

"I am Platikov. I am greatest dancer in world."

Platikov's arrogance and poor grasp of English gave Robert an idea for how he could have a little fun with this Russian dipshit.

He said, "No. You are stupid fucker of cows. Fred Astaire is greatest dancer in world."

So Many Maybes · 404

"Who is Fred Astaire?"

"Fred Astaire fucked your mother while dancing cheek to cheek with Ginger Rogers."

"What is Ginger Rogers?"

"Ginger Rogers is greatest dancer in world."

"I am confused. You say Fred Astaire is greatest dancer in world."

"He is."

"What company he dance with?"

"Macy's."

"Macy's is not company."

"Yes it is. Ask Acka."

"Who is Acka?"

"I am. Who are you."

"I am Platikov."

"No you're not. You're Pissoff."

"I am? Have never heard of Pissoff."

"Pissoff is dead man. Fucked Stalin."

"That mean I fucked Stalin."

"You did."

"No. Stalin was man. Platikov fuck woman, except once but I was very young. Now Platikov fuck American Stenova because you are weak."

Robert rolled his eyes and looked at the ceiling. It seemed that a BunnySpeak conversation was exhausting no matter which end of it you were on.

He finally lost patience and yelled, "Platikov, go fuck Goodekov."

So Many Maybes · 405

Platikov tried to respond, "Goodekov is…"

Robert hung up on Platikov with the zeal of a charging Cossack.

He shook his head and said, "I guess Bunny taught me well."

Camille asked him, "What was that all about?"

"I'm not exactly sure. He was some Russian idiot who first insulted me then told me that American Stenova is his woman now because he's a better lover than I am, or something like that."

Bonnie said, "Robert, even though that makes no sense and the guy was an idiot, I'll bet that the woman he's calling American Stenova is Bunny because they look alike. I think we should call her and make sure she's not in trouble. Hopefully this guy hasn't made her pregnant or something."

Robert said, "You're right Bonnie, but I don't have her phone number. Do you?"

"She didn't give you her number?"

"She never remembers to give it to me and my brain is usually so twisted from talking to her that I forget to ask for it."

"Bunny does have that effect on people…but she did give it to me."

Bonnie called Bunny's New York apartment and there was no answer.

Camille said, "I'm getting worried. You know her. She's capable of doing almost anything. She could have fucked a KGB agent without knowing it. She could be anywhere, even Russia for all we know."

Bonnie said, "I'll find her. Even though it's Saturday, she's probably just rehearsing."

So Many Maybes · 406

Bonnie dialed information for Manhattan and got the phone number for Bunny's practice studio and called it. A female voice with a French accent answered.

Bonnie said, "I need to talk to Bunny."

"What is Bunny?"

"She's one of your dancers, you idiot."

"Oh. Attendez."

"I'll wait but don't take long. This is critically important. Tell her a friend of hers is dying."

Camille asked Will, "What's going on?"

Will looked down and put his hands over his eyes and slowly shook his head.

"Don't ask. Just go with it."

Bunny was out of breath when she answered the phone and she sounded upset.

She said, "This is Bunny."

"Bunny, this is Bonnie."

"What's going on Bonnie? Who's dying?"

"Well Bunny, all of us are dying?"

"Oh no! Did you catch Aids."

"No Bunny. We didn't catch Aids."

"That's good. I've heard Aids is bad news."

"Yes it is…Say Bunny, can you tell us why some Russian idiot from your dance company just called Acka."

"Which Russian idiot was it?"

"His name was Platikov."

Bunny said, "Platikov wants to fuck me, but I don't want to have breakfast with him so I won't. Don't get me wrong,

So Many Maybes · 407

I think fucking in Russian might be fun, But not with him. But he won't go away, even when I farted on him."

"You farted on him?"

"I tried, but I'm not as good at it as Robert is and I shit my tights. It was bad news."

"Oh shit!"

"Exactly. But he still wants to fuck me. Yesterday, he grabbed my crotch. I slugged him in the balls and he said he'd get me thrown out of the company if I didn't give him a blow job. I told him no because he's not cute. This morning he showed me his boner."

Bonnie handed the phone to Robert and he described his whole conversation with Platikov.

"Acka...I'm not his woman and he has never fucked me because my boobs are too small."

"Bunny ballerinas are supposed to have small boobs."

"Really? Oh Acka. You're so nice to me. Now I feel better. You always make me feel better about my little boobs."

Robert said, "So tell me more about Platikov."

"He thinks that because he's famous, all of the ballerinas will kiss him and shove their fist up his ass to get tips."

"I didn't know ballerinas got tips."

"We don't Acka. You know that."

"Do the ballerina's sleep with him?"

"Some do. I don't know why. He's got an ugly boner."

Robert asked, "Ahhh...How do you know that, Bunny?"

"He showed it to me this morning."

"Good God! Did you report him to the police?"

So Many Maybes · 408

"Of course not Acka. Why would the police care whether his boner was ugly or not?"

As always, Robert was getting exhausted.

"You're right Bunny. I guess they wouldn't"

"Everyone here hates him. They call him the Commie Putz."

"What's a putz Bunny?"

"It's radish for a worthless dick."

"From the conversation I had with him, that sounds appropriate."

Bunny said, "Did Platikov want you to be his woman?"

Robert said, "No Bunny. He thought you were my woman."

"Oh Robert, I thought we settled that."

"Settled what."

"That I can't be your woman because I'm going to New York to be a ballerina."

"Bunny, you're already in New York and you're already a ballerina."

"Thank God you finally understand. When did you give Platikov your phone number?"

"I didn't. Didn't you?"

"I couldn't. I can never remember it. Besides, I know you're not gay and you wouldn't want to fuck him. Maybe he looked you up in the phone book. Are you in the phone book?"

"Yes Bunny, I'm in the phone book, but I'm listed as Robert."

"You are. I knew I'd heard the name Robert somewhere. I must have looked you up in the phone book."

Robert started to explain to her how that couldn't have happened, but he decided that it wasn't important.

So Many Maybes · 409

The important thing was that Platikov was harassing her.

During Robert's conversation with Bunny, Bonnie's anger festered until she finally grabbed the phone out of Robert's hand and said, "Don't worry Bunny, this Commie Toad is going to pay."

"He's not a toad. They call him the Commie Putz because his boner is ugly."

Robert said, "Bunny told me they call him the Commie Putz."

Will asked, "What's a putz?"

"Bunny says it's radish for a worthless dick."

"Radish?"

Camille said, "She means Yiddish."

Bunny said, "Thank you Bonnie. If you make him pay, I'll tell Acka to fuck you like a corn dog. I'd do it myself if I was there but then I'm not gay so I guess that wouldn't work anyway. Maybe I could fuck Will for you…anyway make him pay Bonnie. How much do you think we should charge him?"

Bonnie said, "We'll worry about that later. I'll be there in New York on Wednesday."

"Why are you coming here Bonnie? I already told you I'm not gay."

"I heard you Bunny. I'm not coming to New York to fuck you. I coming to New York to kick Platikov's ass."

"Good. But don't shove your fist up it because he'd probably like that."

Bonnie hung up the phone.

So Many Maybes · 410

Robert said, "What do you have in mind Bonnie, I mean we can't really beat the shit out of him?"

Bonnie said, "Well, actually we probably could, but I think we should kick him where it hurts the most."

Camille said, "In his balls?"

"No, although that might be fun, I mean his ego."

Camille said, "How?"

Bonnie said, "I'll figure something out."

After confirming the dates that Platikov would be in New York, Bonnie called Lois and Amanda. She explained the situation and told them that she wanted to publicly humiliate Platikov and that she needed their help. Both women immediately agreed to take part and their three-woman mission of feminine vengeance began.

Bonnie knew they had to work fast because Platikov was performing with the Lincoln Center Ballet Company on Friday night, only six days away. In order for Bonnie's plan to work, she needed some information about Platikov's habits, so she called Bunny back.

"Other than the ballerinas, does Platikov go out and try to pick up women?"

Bunny said, "I don't know. He's busy rehearsing like all of us, but I guess it's always possible that he might have enough free time to go out and pick up chics in bars and show them his boner, don't you think?"

"God dammit, Bunny! We need to find a predictable way to get to him. For my plan to work, we have to use Lois to turn

So Many Maybes · 411

him into a horny dribbling dick. Is there any way we can meet on Thursday and talk about this?"

"Gee, I don't know, Bonnie. I'm busy all week with rehearsals."

"Shit Bunny."

"There is a party on Friday. A bunch of rich people who give us money will be there. Satyrikov is making all of us go to meet the donors but they'll only want to meet the stars like Platikov and Stenova. No one will pay any attention to me. We can sit down and talk then don't you think."

"Who the fuck is Satyrikov?"

"He's the ballet company's Artistic Directordemon."

"What's an Artistic Directordemon?"

"He's our boss, but everyone here calls him the Directordemon because he's evil."

"Why is he evil Bunny?"

"He's mean to us and calls us fat and ugly and he won't let us eat."

"Oh, I'm so sorry to hear that Bunny."

Bunny continued, "And he lets Platikov do whatever he wants to."

"Sounds like we should make him pay too."

"Okay. But we have to do it right."

"What do you mean?"

"Because he likes it when women do awful things to him."

"What kind of things."

He pays ballerinas extra to piss on his face."

"Holy shit!"

So Many Maybes · 412

"I wouldn't call it Holy Bonnie, although I've heard that it feels divine to let go on your boss."

"I guess I can understand that. Anyway, are you telling me that Platikov will be at the party on Friday?"

"Yes, but he'll be too busy to sit down and talk with us." Bonnie's face brightened.

"What's the name of this group that the party is for?"

"Hold on I wrote it down."

Bunny rummaged through her purse and, as always, Bonnie waited. Generally impatient Bonnie had gotten used to Bunny's quirk of writing everything down then not being able to find her note.

Bunny said, "No this isn't it…No, not this either…I'm sorry to make you wait so long, Bonnie. I know my memory sucks, so I write everything down but then I can never find my mother fucking notes. Maybe I should send them to Lois for safe keeping. Do you think that would help?"

"Not really Bunny. Just keep looking. I'll wait."

"Oh here it is, it's called The Ballet Foundation."

Bonnie said, "The Ballet Foundation…Okay Bunny we'll meet you there."

Bunny said, "I'm not sure why we're holding a fund raiser for the theater foundation. I hope the building isn't collapsing. It would be bad news if it did."

Bonnie rolled her eyes. She liked Bunny but now Bonnie was in a hurry to formulate her plan of action.

She said, "We'll see you there, but you'd better lay low at the party. Remember that you look exactly like Stenova.

So Many Maybes · 413

The donors might mistake you for her."

"Okay Bonnie, I'll lay in the closet where they can't see me."

Bonnie thought, *"Fuck Bunny! Just this once leave GaGa land."*

"Don't do that Bunny, just stand off to the side of the room until we get there."

The next day, Amanda and Lois flew to Ann Arbor and met with Bonnie.

Bonnie said, "Lois, on Friday evening before the ballet I want you to get near enough to Platikov to show him every detail of your bare cleavage. I'm sure that once he sees it, his dick will be dribbling and up and ready and he'll do whatever you want him to. Then we can set him up for ultimate humiliation in front of the Ballet audience."

Lois said, "I can see the logic to your plan. My tits always get attention. But I've never been comfortable with it and I've certainly never been comfortable with showing cleavage, so I don't have a bra or any clothes that will."

Bonnie said, "Trust me. Between Camille and me, we have enough friends in the clothing business to take care of that problem. What are your measurements?"

"76PP-26-36."

Bonnie said, "Jesus!"

"Do you understand now? My bras are custom made. They have to be really strong to keep my boobs from bouncing against my knees."

Bonnie said, "I repeat, Jesus! Have you ever considered breast reduction surgery?"

So Many Maybes · 414

"I've tried. But every surgeon that I've gone to wants a ton of money to do it."

Amanda said, "I think that's understandable. After all, it's a really big job."

Lois said, "Fuck you Amanda!"

Bonnie said, "It's obvious that we have some work to do before we go to New York."

She picked up the phone and called Terri.

"Terri, we need Nort's help and we need it fast."

Lois said, "Oh shit."

Terri said, "Got it covered."

Bonnie said, "Lois, grab one of your bra's and you and Amanda come with me."

They rendezvoused with Terri and Nort out in Nort's pole barn workshop, and they explained what they needed.

Nort looked a trifle embarrassed, but he nodded and said, "Okay, but since we don't have much time, you'll have to cooperate and do what I ask."

Bonnie looked at Lois and said, "No problem. Right Lois?"

Lois grudgingly said, "Okay. Since it's for Bunny."

Bonnie handed Lois's bra to Nort.

He looked at it in amazement. Each cup looked like a fabric-covered mold for a battleship artillery shell.

He said, "Interesting."

He measured every detail of the bra and made a sketch showing a frontal view, then he put the sketch down on his work bench and said, "Here's the way it looks now. How do you want it to look when I'm done?"

So Many Maybes · 415

Lois took Nort's pencil, and she sketched an opening that she thought would show enough cleavage to get Platikov excited, but still be decent in public.

Bonnie said, "I'm sorry Lois, but I think you're being too conservative. At best, we'll only have a few minutes with Platikov, and we need a fail-safe device to capture him. I think we should go for something like this."

Bonnie took the pencil from Lois and drew an opening down the middle of the bra that went all the way from the top of it to the bottom. It was barely wide enough to cover Lois's nipples."

Amanda said, "Now, that's sure hot!"

Lois said, "Amanda, if you like it so much, you wear it. There's no way I'm going to."

Bonnie said, "Knowing Amanda, she'd have no problem wearing it, but Amanda doesn't have the boobs we need. Remember, it's for Bunny."

Lois said, "Okay, Nort if you think you have the engineering talent to make something like Bonnie's design work, go for it."

Nort said, "No problem, but now comes the hard part."

Bonnie asked, "What's that?"

"I've got the dimensions I need, but in order to put together something that will work, I'll need to weigh Lois's breasts."

Lois said, "Not on your life Nort!"

Bonnie again said, "But it's for Bunny, Lois."

"I don't care. Measuring my bra and developing a design is one thing, but weighing my tits is another. I've gone along with everything so far but weighing my boobs means that

So Many Maybes · 416

he has to feel me up and I'll never allow that."

Nort said, "I promise I'll be gentle."

Lois said, "Fuck you Nort! Fuck you all!" And she stormed out of the pole barn and into the house.

Amanda made a move to follow Lois, but Terri stopped her and said, "I think this is a job for Mother Teresa."

Terri walked out of the pole barn and went into the house while Bonnie and Amanda and Nort waited inside the pole barn. Barely twenty minutes later, Terri returned with the weights of Lois's breasts measured at various points along their length.

She said, "Is this what you need?"

Nort carefully examined the weights.

"Yes. I can definitely work with this."

Then he went to work in typical Nort style. He made more sketches and looked through his reference books and calculated the stresses that Lois's breasts would put on her new bra. Then he sat down and thought.

He took too long for Terri to endure,

She said, "God dammit Norton! Get to work."

Nort nodded and walked out into the Wilderness and located different pieces of pseudo-junk and returned to his work bench.

He put on his goggles and said, "You all need to stand back."

He moved over to his industrial grade saw and cut the raw materials into pieces with the proper dimensions. The saw blade made a terribly loud "*WANNANHG!*" noise and sparks flew everywhere. Then he moved over to his welding bench.

So Many Maybes · 417

He said, "Everyone turn around. 'This arc welder is going to be too bright for your eyes."

When he was done, he said, "Okay, you can turn around."

When they saw Nort's masterpiece of industrial garment fabrication they all gasped.

Bonnie said, "Holy shit."

With a proud smile, Nort said, "I think this will do it. Of course, I'll have to add a little padding here and there to make it comfortable to wear. But before I do that, I think Lois should try it on. I might have to make a few alterations."

Nort handed it to Lois who held it up in front of her and stared at it as if it was a big rat that she was holding by the tail. It looked like it was made of heavy grade platform steel supported by two high-tensile suspension bridge cables.

Terri said, "Oh thank you, my dear crazy engineering genius brother."

Nort said, "Of course. It was for Bunny."

Terri and Lois went into the bathroom and discovered that the bra fit perfectly, then they gave it back to Nort who added what he thought would be enough padding. Then the three women went over to Maybe's and told Camille that they needed her help getting special evening wear made for Lois. Camille called an old friend in New York who fabricated clothing for designers. Camille's friend agreed to help.

On Wednesday, the three women flew to New York and checked into the Plaza hotel. On Thursday, they went to see Camille's friend.

So Many Maybes · 418

Bonnie said, "Now Lois, it's important that you go through with this and not get a conservative dress. Remember, it's…"

Lois completed the sentence.

"It's for Bunny. I know. I know. Don't worry. I'll get a dress that will definitely turn the putz on and might even make the front of his pants explode."

Bonnie said, "That's the spirit."

While Lois was getting her dress made, Bonnie and Amanda went shopping on Third Avenue where Bonnie bought them both the most beautiful and sexiest evening attire that they could find.

Coincidentally, the dance company's reception was being held at the Plaza, the same hotel where they were staying. However, Bonnie didn't want to just go downstairs and walk into the reception. She wanted to arrive in style and make it seem logical that Platikov would leave with them later.

She hired a stretch limo, then she contacted an old friend of her Uncle Judd's and asked him for help. Antonio, "Bronco," Calabrese owned a great Italian Restaurant and a well-known numbers and off-track betting establishment in Brooklyn and he had several old-fashioned gorilla tough guys working for him to protect the money and deal with unruly patrons. Bonnie asked if she could borrow a couple of Bronco's big dudes to right a terrible wrong committed by an evil Russian commie bastard. Bronco said he'd give her all the help she needed.

Then Bonnie called another friend who was the editor of New York's most notorious tabloid newspaper, and she told

So Many Maybes · 419

him to make sure that his photographers were ready to catch a lot of good action inside the theater during The Lincoln Center Ballet Company's performance on Friday.

With Bronco's two big dudes posing as their limo chauffeurs, Bonnie, Lois and Amanda arrived in front of the Plaza hotel fifteen minutes after the reception was scheduled to begin. When the three shockingly beautiful women got out of the limo, they were greeted by dozens of photographers. Lois had her humongous bazoombas on full display, and Bonnie of course looked like a magazine cover-girl, but it was Amanda who created the greatest excitement. All decked out with perfect make-up, six-inch heels and a wonderful long white dress that was slit up the side and cut deep in the front, she looked like the most vivacious movie star alive. As soon as she got out of the car, she posed for the photographers as if she was entering the theater to accept her Academy Award. Every one of the paparazzi struggled to get in front of the others to get a shot of her.

The three women walked inside and looked for Bunny. Bonnie was the first to spot her. Bunny was doing her best to hide from the donor's. She was standing behind a monster artificial fig tree that was in the corner of the room and she was drinking from two glasses of champagne at the same time.

Amanda and Lois sat down at a table, and Bonnie headed in Bunny's direction.

Amazingly, a little girl dressed in a ballerina dress had discovered Bunny and asked for her autograph.

So Many Maybes · 420

The little girl said, "Oh please Miss Stenova, will you sign your picture for me and let my mother take a picture of us together."

Bunny smiled warmly and signed the little girl's picture. The mother moved in front of them and pointed her camera at the two ballerinas and said, "Say cheese."

Bunny said, "Cheese…Does little girl's barbarian fucker of mother have a huge Canon?"

The mother's jaw dropped in shock.

Bonnie grabbed Bunny by the arm and pulled her away and said, "Please excuse Miss Stenova. Her English is not good."

The little girl said, "Mommy, what's a fucker?"

As Bunny and Bonnie rushed across the room to join Lois and Amanda at their table, Bunny said, "Hi Bonnie. Did you like the way I spoke Russian?"

"Very impressive Bunny, but please don't do it again."

When Bonnie and Bunny sat down at their table, Lois was concerned about Bunny. Bunny was pale, and her eyes were bloodshot, and she looked older than she had before she left Ann Arbor. The hard work of a professional ballet dancer had obviously taken its toll.

After they sat down at the table, Bonnie told Bunny what they were going to do to Platikov. Bunny smiled and nodded. Even though she knew that Bonnie's plan would destroy her ballet companies opening night, Bunny loved the idea of humiliating Platikov.

The four of them spent a short time together, then Bunny pointed out Platikov to Lois.

So Many Maybes · 421

Platikov was talking to one of the potential donors when Lois walked up to the Russian.

The donor said, "Is that right? I thought Goodekov was the best dancer in the world."

Platikov scowled in annoyance. He was tired of people saying that.

"No! You are stupid barbarian fucker of mother! Goodekov is short and weak. I am strong and tall. I am greatest."

Platikov was so into himself that he didn't notice that the donor was severely insulted and had decided to never give any money to the Lincoln Center Ballet Company as long as Platikov danced with them. The donor excused himself and ran out of the reception as fast as he could.

Lois said, "Platikov, my name is Lois. I'm a big fan of yours."

Platikov turned and looked at Lois. He smiled broadly, and his gaze immediately dropped to her cleavage.

"I am Platikov. I am greatest dancer in world. I am famous. You love me, yes?"

"No, Platikov. I love your dancing. How could I love you? We just met."

"You show me big tits. You want to fuck me, yes?"

Lois moved closer to Platikov and pushed one of her mammoth breasts against his arm.

"I might fuck you. Would you fuck me strong like a real man or are you weak like a little boy?"

Platikov's face tensed. He didn't like that question. He puffed up his chest and said, "Platikov is man. Fuck strong. Platikov's cock is strong, yes."

So Many Maybes · 422

Lois stepped back and crossed her arms and tilted her head back and forth and studied his crotch and shook her head and said.

"If your cock is so strong, why can't I see it?"

She paused again and moved forward and pressed her tits and hips against him, She reached down and grabbed his crotch and felt around as if she was attempting to get a good mental picture of his Slavic package. Then she shook her head again.

"Nope you're still a weak little boy?

Platikov was angry.

He bluntly said, "Platikov fuck woman with big tits now. Show woman with big tits Platikov is real man, yes."

Lois nodded and said, "Okay Platikov. Come with me and prove you're not a little boy."

She turned and walked toward the door.

Platikov's monster ego forced him to follow Lois. He had no choice. He mumbled to himself, *"Platikov is not weak little boy. Platikov will fuck woman with big tits strong. Make her come like howling Siberian Wolf."*

As Lois passed them, Amanda and Bonnie and Bunny got up from their table and walked out behind Platikov. Bronco's two big dudes met the four women and Platikov outside the hotel and provided a body guard escort to the limo and they pulled away. Inside the limo, Lois grabbed Platikov's right hand and pulled it across her chest and put it on her left breast. When Platikov turned his body toward Lois, Amanda pounded a huge needle into his right thigh and shot him full of racehorse

So Many Maybes · 423

tranquilizer that they'd gotten from Bronco. Platikov jumped and turned quickly to look at Amanda. He started swearing at her in Russian, then his eyes rolled up and his face went white, and he collapsed on the limo's floor like a half-empty sack of potatoes.

When they arrived at the back of the theater, the two goons grabbed the unconscious Platikov and pulled him out of the car and carried him, feet dragging, through the stage door. Bunny led them to Platikov's dressing room, and Bonnie and Amanda and Lois followed them.

While Lois and Amanda undressed Platikov, Bunny handed Bonnie his tights.

Bonnie said, "Bunny, wait here a minute," then she took the tights from Bunny and disappeared into the bathroom.

Lois poured pink tinted massage oil all over Platikov's crotch. When Bonnie came out of the bathroom with Platikov's white ballet costume, the two big enforcers roughly dressed him.

Bonnie said, "Bunny does this Satyrikov have an office or something?"

"Yes Bonnie, it's on the other side of the stage."

"Take me there."

Bunny led Bonnie to Satyrikov's office, and Bonnie started searching through his desk drawers.

"What are you looking for Bonnie?"

"Oh it's just an idea I have. Sometimes these Russian bastards drink a lot of vodka. Look around and see if you can find his bottle…Oh never mind. I found it."

So Many Maybes · 424

Bonnie opened a small bottle of liquid that she had brought with her, and she poured its contents into Satyrikov's vodka bottle.

Then she said, "Come on Bunny, let's get out of here."

They returned to Platikov's dressing room where Bunny picked up Platikov's dance belt and put it in her purse.

When Platikov was dressed in his tights, Lois poured more pink massage oil on his crotch, then the tough guys threw him on his bed like the bag of dirt he was.

After Bonnie set the dancer's clock forty-five minutes slow and turned off the alarm, Amanda started to give Platikov another shot of horse tranquilizer, but Bonnie grabbed Amanda's wrist and stopped her.

"We only want him out of it for a while. We don't wanna' kill him."

"Your right. Would be fun though."

"Oh believe me, I agree with you. I hate men like him."

Bunny went to her dressing room and the others escaped to the limo and returned to the Plaza Hotel to wait until it was time to go to the ballet.

Fifteen minutes before the ballet was to begin, they met Bonnie's Uncle Judd in the theater lobby. After her Uncle gave Bonnie a warm hug and made her feel guilty for not calling him more often, they all walked into the theater and took the seats that Judd had "procured" for them. The opening night had been sold out for months. Uncle Judd didn't explain how he got the tickets and Bonnie didn't ask, although she suspected that Bronco had something to do with it.

So Many Maybes · 425

Being mostly unfamiliar with ballet, Judd and the three women studied their programs to get some clues about what was going to happen. The program said that the night's performance was of *Giselle*, a classic romantic ballet with a libretto by Jules-Henri Vernon de Saint Georges and Théophile Gautier adopted from works by Heinrich Heine and Victor Hugo with music by Adolph Adam along with Jacques Offenbach and other traditional sources.

Uncle Judd leaned over to Bonnie and quietly asked, "What's a 'libretto'?"

"It's the ballet's story."

Judd nodded and then asked, "Why don't they just come out and say story instead of using a word that nobody understands?"

"I don't really know. Dancers live in their own world."

The evenings performance of *Giselle* by the Lincoln Center Ballet Company was a greatly anticipated event and everyone in the dance world along with many dignitaries were there, even the Mayor. It was going to be televised live on public television because it was staged by the famous Vasaly Nagurski, and it featured two of the greatest dancers in the world: Vladimir Platikov as Duke Albrecht of Silesia and Aglaya Stenova as Giselle.

The house lights dimmed, and the orchestra began to play a soft rendition of the overture. A spotlight fell on the tuxedo-clad Nagurski as he walked onto the stage to loud applause. He spoke to the audience in Russian, with a short woman dressed in a cheap polyester pink dress acting as his interpreter.

Nagurski said a few words and paused for her to translate.

So Many Maybes · 426

She must not have known English well because her translation was oddly humorous and stupid.

The PinkLady shouted, "Good night you inferior limp-dicked capitalist barbarians."

The offended audience began talking amongst themselves.

The interpreter continued, "Tonight I am pleasured to ram up your ass my bland but brilliant masturbatory piece of French drivel, a thoroughly wretched version of a boring classic named *Giselle* or something similar."

As she was talking, a formally dressed woman in red ran out onto the stage and said something to Nagurski. Nagurski's body stiffened and the veins in his neck swelled as he turned and looked harshly at the PinkLady. He bowed formally toward the audience and said one last sentence.

The PinkLady interpreted it as, "Thank you, you ignorant sluts."

The theater erupted in laughter as the RedLady roughly yanked Nagurski and the PinkLady off the stage.

The embarrassed Nagurski surreptitiously returned to his front row seat next to his friend Ivan Goodekov. Goodekov was Platikov's bitter rival and Stenova's boyfriend. Once the audience settled down, the ballet orchestra began to play.

As the time approached for Platikov to make his grand entrance, the stage manager was getting nervous. He turned to one of his assistants and said, "That awful Commie Putz should be here by now. He's probably fucking some poor ballerina and forgot the time. Go get him."

After knocking repeatedly on the Commie Putz's door,

the assistant went in and saw Platikov lying in a disheveled ball on his bed with his white tights covered with limp lipped drool and pink massage oil. The assistant ran over to the Russian and grabbed him by the shoulders and shook him violently.

He shouted, "Hey you Com…uhhh…Mr. Platikov wake up. It's time to go on stage."

Platikov sat up suddenly. He was horribly dizzy and disoriented, and his right leg was numb. He looked at the clock, confused.

"You are stupid. Clock says not time."

"The clock is wrong. You must hurry."

Platikov jumped out of bed in a panic and his legs buckled and he fell on the floor.

The assistant helped him up and said, "Go go go!"

Platikov ran thru the open door and rammed his face hard into the wall on the other side of the hallway and he fell down again. He shouted something in Russian that the assistant couldn't understand but assumed meant "SHIT!" or "FUCK!" or something like that. The assistant laughed hard as the Putz slowly got to his feet again and limped toward the stage as fast as he could.

The curtain opened showing two cabins, one on the left side and one on the right side of the stage. In the background was a painted backdrop showing distant grape fields visible through an opening in a forest. The chorus of supporting dancers entered from both sides and danced around with hops and twirls and stuff like that to simulate the celebration of the joy of a sunny-fall grape harvest. Then the chorus surprised

So Many Maybes · 428

everyone by forming a line and beginning high kicks to the music of the French Cancan. The audience, most of whom knew the ballet by heart, was outraged and began booing. They were not happy with what Nagurski had done to their favorite romantic ballet.

After the Cancan, the chorus returned to the ballet's traditional choreography. But it didn't last long. After only a moment, the chorus again veered from the traditional to the outrageous.

Eight male dancers ran on the stage. Four of the men were dressed in cowboy outfits and four were dressed in drag as cowgirls. They began a Western Square Dance to heavily Russian accented calls of Do-si-do's and Promenade's and Right and Left Grand's then they formed a line facing the audience and one by one from left to right they ripped off their own pants and ran off stage swinging their trousers over their heads like male strippers.

Then a guy with a bad haircut entered from the right carrying a stick with two pheasants hung on it. He stopped and hung one pheasant by the door of the cabin on the left and then walked away into the forest.

It was now time for Platikov to make his grand entrance. When he reached the left edge of the opened curtain, he paused to try and regain his balance, but the stage manager put his foot on the hated Russian's butt and roughly pushed him forward. Platikov stumbled onstage and down a ramp from left to right, and he started to execute one of his famous leaps to express the strength of life of the young Duke Albrecht.

So Many Maybes · 429

He loudly inhaled like a bodybuilder preparing for a deadlift and he threw his left leg high into the air. Then he attempted to raise his right leg and tap his toes together when he was high above the floor. But his horse tranquilized right leg collapsed, and he crashed down hard on his right side with a boom that was as loud as a bass drum inside of a Rest Room stall. He laid on the floor motionless, groaning in pain.

At a loss for what to do, the orchestra director stopped the music. After a moment, he ordered the orchestra to start playing again to fill the silence even though there was no dancing to go along with the music.

Stenova emerged quickly from the door of the cabin on the left, and she hurried next to Platikov. She reached down and grabbed Platikov's hand and angrily pulled him to his feet and swung him around to her left side to dance arm in arm with her facing the audience.

Gasps swept through the theater because Platikov's cock and balls were boldly outlined and highly visible under his oil-soaked tights. Normally his private package would have been hidden by his dance belt that Bunny had put in her purse. Camera flashes came from everywhere and the audience started laughing.

Confused, Platikov's face became pale and he stopped moving and allowed the photographers to get an even better and longer series of shots of his Slavic nads and wang.

Stenova slapped him into consciousness and told him why everyone was laughing. Platikov looked down at his center of attention and quickly turned his back to the audience.

So Many Maybes · 430

Then another commotion erupted because the heat of Platikov's body had melted the shaved chocolate that Bonnie had spread all over the inside of the back of his white tights. The brown slop soaked through the fabric and made it appear as if he had shit his pants.

Even the normally stuffy New York ballet audience laughed hysterically. Goodekov in particular was having a great time watching his rival go down in a ball of melting shit.

The stage manager should have dropped the curtain when the reporters started taking pictures, but like everyone else, he hated Platikov and was savoring the Russian's humiliation.

Furious at having his masterpiece defiled, Nagurski stood up from his front row theater seat and started to run toward the stage. Goodekov "accidentally" tripped him and the choreographer flew through the air and directly into the orchestra pit. He knocked over the drums and cymbals making a cacophony of loud *booms* and *thuds* and *clangs* and *bawanga-wang-wang-wangs* and *thuddle-dud-dud-duds*, followed by a string of Russian obscenities.

Meanwhile, Stenova shouted at Platikov and he turned around fast and faced the audience again and when the laughter intensified he looked down again then he turned sideways. He should have just run off the stage, but embarrassment and confusion overwhelmed him, and he stood motionless. He looked sick to his stomach and about to cry as he desperately held his hands in front of his crotch. He stood still in a panic because he didn't know what to do.

Most of the ballerina chorus was standing behind Platikov

So Many Maybes · 431

and were laughing and enjoying the arrogant putz's humiliation. But Stenova was enraged. Platikov had ruined her big opening night. Simply humiliating him wasn't good enough. She wanted to hurt the bastard. She did a series of rapid spins up to the paralyzed young Russian dancer, then she slugged him with a wild round-house haymaker that knocked the hated Commie Putz sideways.

Bunny did a similar series of spins until she was ten feet in front of him. Then she leapt high and did the splits and drove the point of her wooden-toed ballet shoe into his nuts.

When Platikov bent forward to grab himself, Stenova knocked him on his ass with a brutal windmill uppercut. He laid there, unconscious.

The two beautiful ballerinas who looked like identical twins, moved side by side. They took each other's hand, and together they did a beautiful ballet reverence bow to the audience. Then ran off stage where Stenova ordered the stage hand to lower the curtain.

The theater boomed with the sounds of the audience stomping their feet and shouting, "Bravo, bravo!"

Two stage hands picked up Platikov and dragged him down the hallway to his dressing room. They grabbed him by his arms and legs and swung him back and forth and heaved him through the dressing room door like a big bag of Russian horse shit. He crashed onto the floor and slid across the room and rammed into the wall. He didn't regain consciousness for an hour. When he did, the first thing that he saw was writing on the wall.

So Many Maybes · 432

It said, "Go back to Russia you Commie Bastard or this will happen to you every night."

It was signed, "The Alliance of Weakly Fucked Ballerinas."

After the curtain was dropped, the three sexy members of the Bonnie Haines Alliance for Feminine Vengeance remained in their seats astonished at how things had gone down. Their initial goal had been to only temporarily humiliate Platikov. Instead, they had most likely publicly destroyed him. However, they felt no remorse. They had sent an abusive and cruel man a message; treat a woman poorly and you will pay, big time.

Before they left for the airport, Amanda and Bonnie and Lois waited outside the theater to say goodbye to Bunny. She took longer than they thought she would. Lois was about to go inside and try to find her when Bunny emerged walking next to Ivan Goodekov. She handed him picture after picture to autograph. Goodekov signed politely and nodded every so often as Bunny talked to him non-stop. Lois called for Bunny and Bunny turned and saw her three friends. She smiled broadly and said good night to a relieved Goodekov who got into a waiting limousine and drove off. Bunny ran over to Bonnie and Lois and Amanda and hugged every one of them. She was laughing and crying at the same time and it took her a minute or two before she turned to Lois and with more emotion than would be expected.

She said, "I'm really tired Lois, will you take me home? I wanna go home."

"Of course Bunny. Where do you live?"

So Many Maybes · 433

Bunny excitedly said, "Bonnie is from New York Lois, she'll know how to get me home."

Bonnie said, "I will if you tell me where home is."

"You already know Bonnie."

"I do? What's the address?"

"You really need the address?"

"It would help. It's a big city."

"Not really that big, but okay, I wrote it down. I keep it on a piece of paper. Just a minute, I'll find it."

While Bunny rummaged through her purse, Bonnie turned to Lois and Amanda and grinned and rolled her eyes and silently mimed, "FUCK!"

With tears in her eyes. Bunny said, "Here it is," and handed the paper to Bonnie.

The paper said, "555 East William St, Ann Arbor, MI 48104."

Bonnie said, "Okay Bunny. Let's go home."

Bonnie showed Lois the paper. Lois nodded, then handed the paper to Amanda. Amanda nodded and put her arm around Bunny's waist. Bunny leaned her shoulder against Amanda as they all walked to the waiting cab.

So Many Maybes · 434

Chapter 24
Smiles of a Snowy Night

The next day, Nagurski was told to either redo his choreography or go back to Russia where he would undoubtedly be sent to a work camp in Siberia.

Satyrikov mysteriously came down with a violent case of bombastic diarrhea that didn't stop for days and forced his hospitalization for dehydration. When he was in the hospital, he received an anonymous letter that read, "Let this be a lesson. If you allow a ballerina to be abused again, the Specter of Feminine Vengeance will kick the shit out of you again...literally."

Platikov was fired from the Lincoln Center Ballet company for the embarrassment he caused. He left New York to look for another company that would overlook his hilarious antics of the night before and invite him to dance with them. He was confident that some company would because he knew that despite what had happened, he was still one of the greatest dancers in the world. However he was deeply embarrassed. And as he boarded the airplane, he hoped that, *"He was not famous, yes,"* and no one would recognize him.

Amanda and Lois and Bonnie helped Bunny move out of her apartment, then they took a cab to the airport. Once there, Bonnie went into the gift shop and bought every newspaper they sold.

All of the papers, even the traditionally stuffy New York Times, featured front page photos of Platikov in his pink oil-soaked tights. His cock and balls were as visible as a nude stripper's vaginal hair under a clear plastic raincoat, and there were dozens of articles detailing his hilarious performance. Nagurski's nose dive into the orchestra pit even made the headlines.

Back in Ann Arbor it was snowing, the first snow of the year. The snow kept the customers away, so the five Grafton's friends took the opportunity to change out a few of Jenny's paintings. Jenny had lived in Ann Arbor for a full year by that time, and she had a collection of paintings for every season. Her fall creations used the vibrant colors of the hardwood's falling leaves, and her winter works captured the translucent blue-gray of snow swirling around the vague shadowy outlines of the buildings around town.

When they finished hanging the pictures, Robert grabbed a few of the fall paintings and carried them back into the stockroom to be stored until they could be returned to Jenny's studio out at the farm. Terri and Wolf followed Robert carrying the rest of the paintings. When Robert turned to leave the stockroom, Camille was standing in the doorway waiting for him.

He said, "Oh what a wonderful surprise!"

He walked up to her and kissed her and said, "What made you venture out on this cold and snowy evening?"

"Actually it's not cold at all, and the snow is beautiful,

So Many Maybes · 436

so Baja and I thought we'd meet up with all of you here and walk back to Maybe's to celebrate the coming of the first snow."

When they left the store and Terri locked the door, they were standing in a world of Middle Western delight. An October snow is always the best in Michigan, and this night was no exception. The flickering reflections of the city lights hitting the big white snowflakes covered Ann Arbor with a soft dome of light

As they left the store, Jenny said, "I'll have to meet up with you guys later. I'm going over to the grocery store to see Hondo for a minute."

Robert smiled broadly and looked at Baja and they responded in unison.

"HONDO?!"

Baja said, "If he's the same Hondo I'm thinking of, he's a friend of mine."

"It's the same one. I met him last summer at the Art Fair when he stopped by our booth to see you."

Baja said, "Oh that's right. I remember."

Robert said, "I've never met him, but Baja told me he's the guy to see there for special personalized treatment."

Terri grinned and said, "Are you going out with him?

"Not tonight. He hasn't asked me out yet, but I like him so I'm going over to see him and show him I'm interested. Hopefully he'll get the hint."

Robert said, "He will. Just go stand next to him and that famous Jenny Woodward magic will have him panting in about five minutes."

So Many Maybes · 437

"I hope your right. See you guys later."

Baja said, "Tell Hondo that I said he'd be an idiot not to take you out."

After Jenny left, Baja leaned over to Robert and whispered, I may have exaggerated just a little to have fun with Lois and Amanda. I've never even seen him naked."

"I figured."

Baja said, "But I have talked to him a few times and he seems like a nice guy."

Robert nodded then asked, "How about you Terri?"

Terri said, "I'm just going home in case the roads get bad. Henri Roberts is staying out at the farm with us. He's helping Norton put the finishing touches on the loft's gallery."

Robert said, "Drive safe."

On their way over to Maybe's, they passed the Campus Theater where Ingmar Bergman's movie *Smiles of a Summer Night* was showing.

Robert said, "Ironic for a night when it's snowing outside."

Since Will liked Bergman movies, they crossed the street to check the show times.

While the others looked at the movie poster displayed inside a brass and glass case next to the theater entrance, Robert asked Camille, "Do you want to see this movie?"

Camille said, "I might, but I've seen it already."

"What's it about?

"It's an old-fashioned comedy of manners. The plot is almost impossible to summarize, but it's about a group of people who get together on a summer night, and every one of them wants

So Many Maybes · 438

to go to bed with everyone else, but they never do because they're too hung up or too polite to try."

Robert smiled and said, "Sounds more tragic than comic."

Camille smiled back and squeezed his hand and said, "Maybe. But sometimes it's good to laugh at tragedy."

They crossed South University Avenue and walked through the arch in the West Engineering building and entered the Central Campus Diag. As they headed northwest through the tunnel of street lamps that lined The Diag sidewalk, the five close friends were surrounded by a beautiful golden aura of mutual affection that followed them like a warm cloud of mist.

Robert held Camille's hand, and Baja held Wolf's hand, and Will was lonely and worried.

He said, "I wonder how things went in New York. I haven't heard from Bonnie all week."

Robert said, "I'm sure she's okay. We'd have heard if she wasn't."

Will said, "I guess."

About halfway across the campus green, Camille stopped and stood on the large brass block letter M that marked the center of The Diag. She looked up at the heavens and let the snow fall on her face and threw God a kiss.

She said, "Oh thank you God for such a beautiful snowy night."

Then she looked at Robert and reached out toward him. Unsure of what to do, Robert stood still.

She said, "Robert don't just stand there. Take my hand."

So Many Maybes · 439

Robert smiled and did what she asked. Camille pulled him to her and put her arms around him and kissed him warmly and passionately.

Just like their first kiss in the Arcade, their kiss that night, standing on the big brass block M, sent a tingling of warmth from her lips through his entire nervous system to the tips of his limbs. But unlike that first kiss, the tingling he felt was no longer a supernatural mystery to him. He recognized it as a clear message from her heart to his, telling him that she loved him.

The others quietly watched them and basked in the lover's warmth until Wolf said, "Ah, the definitive romantic movie kiss."

Baja turned to Wolf and said, "Shall we?"

She faced him, and they gently held each other close and began to gracefully waltz in circles around the kissing Robert and Camille.

Baja said, Wolf, do you think they waltz in Tahiti?"

Wolf said, "It's highly doubtful. But I have researched the subject of Tahitian dancing and I've discovered that they do have one dance that I find appealing. It's called the Ote'a and is essentially ass shaking to drums."

He backed away from Baja and turned his back to her. Then he held his arms over his head like a female flamenco dancer and proceeded to rapidly wiggle and shake his oversized rear end in her direction.

Baja laughed and began the same dance. After they established a common rhythm, Baja and Wolf again began moving in circles

So Many Maybes · 440

around the two kissing lovers. Camille and Robert stopped their kiss. They began laughing and started clapping in accompaniment to Baja and Wolf's primitive dance that probably had nothing to do with Tahiti but allowed Baja to show her extraordinary dancing ability. And no one could doubt that Wolf's shaking butt added immensely to the overall celebratory atmosphere that the coming of the first snow had inspired.

Will watched for a while, but he finally lost patience and said, "Oh for Christ's sake you crazy people. Let's get going. I want to check the newspaper to see if there's anything about what they did to Platikov in New York."

They walked away from the big brass M and headed toward the entrance to The Nickels Arcade and Maybe's.

Robert said, "Wolf, I wish Jenny had been here with her camera to take a picture of you when you were shaking your not-so-nice ass."

Wolf said, "I would be happy to repeat the performance for her at any time. I must practice diligently so that I may excite the semi-naked native Tahitian women."

Baja slapped him on the butt and said, "You will do nothing of the kind sweet buns, your ass is mine."

After they crossed State Street, Will stopped at a newspaper stand and bought the Detroit Free Press. He would have liked to get a New York paper, but those wouldn't arrive in Ann Arbor until Monday. They walked down the Nickel's Arcade and went into Maybe's and sat down in Robert's booth and Brett joined them. After they ordered their drinks, Will looked through the Press.

So Many Maybes · 441

Brett said, "Camille, with all of the stuff that's been going on, I never got to ask you what you thought of our production of Wolf's play?

Camille's initial response was noncommittal.

She said, "Ahhh…"

Brett said, "That's what everyone says."

Wolf said, "No need to be kind my runway wonder. I have learned to thrive on abuse."

Camille said, "Honestly I had a great time. It was fun and full of surprises. Almost nothing was predictable. Especially the ending."

Brett said, "Did getting drunk help."

"Since I actually was drunk, I can't be sure. All I can say is that it probably didn't hurt."

Wolf said, "I wish we could sell alcohol in the theater like they do at baseball and football games. No doubt it would improve our gate. It seems like people will pay anything for a beer at a ball game. In addition, given the nature of my plays, I think public drunkenness would make a positive addition to the absurdist comedy. But alas, the theater won't let us. However, I have given considerable thought to opening a hot dog stand that we could park off the theater property and sell fifty cent hot dogs and $25 beers."

Baja said, "Wolf, I'm sorry to break it to you, but no one would pay $25 for a beer."

"Regrettably you are probably right my dear lady, but I am confident that we could find a suitably outrageous price that the public would tolerate."

So Many Maybes · 442

Camille said, "Do you think the city would really let you set up a hot dog stand in the street?"

"It's highly doubtful, so my current plan is to try and strike a deal with various liquor stores around town, then put a discount coupon in our advertisements."

Robert said, "Hot dogs make me fart."

Wolf said, "Sir Robert, as we have discussed many times before, I would be very grateful if you would discharge a few of your superb intestinal outbursts during some of my plays. It is a well-established fact that loud farting in public will almost certainly get a laugh."

Robert said, "I'm sorry Wolf. I would if I could, but you know I can't fart at will. My farts just happen."

Wolf said, "Yes I know, but I think it would be a real gas if you could."

Brett said, "Clever Wolf."

Baja said, "Not your funniest joke, but amusing just the same."

Wolf said, "I'm saving my best for Tahiti."

Camille said, "Wolf does it bother you when people don't laugh at the jokes in your plays?"

"I'd like to say no, but I would be lying. Yes it does. I and everyone else put a lot of work into our productions, and to have the audience just sit there is a painful experience for us."

"Have you ever asked people what they didn't like."

Wolf said, "Seldom, because it makes for an embarrassing conversation. But people do occasionally feel compelled to seek me out and tell me what they didn't like."

So Many Maybes · 443

"What do they say?"

"They say that my work isn't serious comedy, it's merely 'infantile' nonsense."

Camille said, "Maybe it is, but watching children play can be a treat."

Brett said, "That's a perfect description of Wolf. He's just one great big lovable kid creating new and elaborate children's games for people's amusement. It's up to anyone in the audience to decide to either let themselves have a good time watching or to leave with a scowl on their face and shit all over what is really a children's game like hop scotch."

Wolf said, "You are right my dear friend with a framework as perfect as the Mackinac Bridge. But please remember that I am a kid playing with my giant balls and bat."

Baja said, "Did you say butt?"

"I did not, but people often say that I am a genuine smart ass."

Robert said, "Wolf, I've known you a long time and I would tell anyone who bothered to ask, that you are indeed a smart ass."

Baja said, "Not only smart, but cute too."

Wolf said, "Thank you truly, my talented master of insincere flattery, but although quite remarkable, my ass is definitely not cute."

Brett said, "Is it actually true Baja; about Wolf's bat I mean?"

"The biggest I've ever seen. It's at least fourteen inches long and as big around as an ax handle."

Baja winked at Robert.

Brett said, "I don't believe that for a second, but if it was,

So Many Maybes · 444

I assume that some forms of oral sex would be impossible."

Robert said, "Don't be so quick to assume that. Bunny told me that Baja can get an entire Hostess Ding Dong in her mouth at the same time."

Baja said, "It's true."

Brett said, "That is amazing. Can I come over to your place sometime when you do it and take pictures?"

Camille said, "I've got a camera you can use."

Brett said, "Terrific. How about tomorrow night."

Wolf said, "Do you want to take pictures of Baja practicing the ancient art of fellatio on my bat, or of her putting a Hostess Ding Dong in her mouth?"

"Wolf, like all serious artists, I want to record the most important and exciting event. So obviously I mean the Ding Dong."

"I am quite relieved. Unlike Robert who seems to do it frequently, I am generally uncomfortable dropping my pants in front of my friends. I care about them too much to subject them to such an awesome but disturbing experience."

Jenny walked up to their table. As it always was, her Nikon was hanging around her neck.

She said, "Wolf I have to agree with you. If I pointed my camera at your allegedly giant bat, it would probably cause my lens to explode. On the other hand, Robert's cock is as perfect as my tits."

Wolf helped Jenny move an empty table so that it was next to their booth and she sat down.

Robert said, "How'd it go with Hondo?"

So Many Maybes · 445

Jenny nodded and said, "I'm going out with him on Friday night."

Baja said, "What are you planning on doing?'

Jenny said, "I don't know what he has in mind, but I plan on following Nort's suggestion."

Baja said, "What was that?"

"I'm going to flash my tits at him and get fucked in the back of my Woody...Now I have to figure out how to get an itsy bitsy teeny weeny yellow polka-dot bikini in October."

Robert said, "Maybe Terri could help you make one, I think she's got a sewing machine?"

Camille said, "Nort made a bra for Lois. Maybe he could help too."

Jenny said, "A bra for Lois? That must have been something to see."

Camille said, "I didn't see it, but Bonnie said it looked like two oil drums held together with metal reinforced cargo strapping."

While the others talked, Will wasn't listening to what they were saying. He was sitting in the back corner of the booth and scouring the newspaper for any hint of what went on at the ballet the night before.

Camille said, "Wallace, have you found anything?"

Frustrated because he hadn't found any mention of it, Will was now methodically scanning every single line of the paper.

He continued to scan but said, "No. Not a thing. I know most people here in Michigan don't care about what happens at a ballet in New York, or any ballet for that matter, but you'd think there would be something."

So Many Maybes · 446

Camille said, "Have you checked the Arts section?"

"I tried, but there wasn't one."

Brett said, "It might be called the Entertainment section. Try that."

"I found that section, but it was only movies and other stuff taking place in Detroit and what was showing on TV tonight. Nothing about ballet."

Camille said, "How about the gossip columns?"

Will frowned and said, "No God dammit, and I didn't check the Sports either."

Camille said, "I'm worried now. Maybe they didn't do anything to Platikov. They could have been arrested or something. Maybe that's why Bonnie didn't call. Or OH MY GOD! MAYBE SOMETHING HORRIBLE HAPPENED TO THEM!"

Will quickly looked up and said, "Like wha...?"

He stopped mid-sentence when he saw Bonnie and Bunny standing next to Wolf with snow in their hair and big grins on their faces.

He said, "Bonnie!"

Robert said, "Welcome home."

Will was completely surprised. Camille had set him up well.

He said, "Bonnie…Bunny?

Bonnie said, "It's good to be home. Now everyone get up and move and let me sit next to Wallace."

The others moved and made room for Bonnie. Wolf pulled up another chair for Bunny.

Will kissed Bonnie.

So Many Maybes · 447

He said, "I'm so glad you're back. I missed you. You didn't call all week."

"I was busy. Anyway, I'm back now."

Bunny said, "It's good to be home too. Boy am I glad to get out of that place."

Baja said, "Why are you so happy you left?"

"I couldn't sleep."

"Was New York too loud."

"Not really, except maybe when the Subway train would go through my building's basement."

Baja said, "Are you kidding me!? The Subway ran through your building's basement!?"

"Of course not. I'm not stupid. I would never rent an apartment like that."

Baja paused to absorb Bunny's answer, and everyone else looked at each other.

Then Baja said, "So why couldn't you sleep?"

"Because it was fucking boring."

Baja said, "New York is boring? I've never heard anyone say that before. Usually people complain that there's too much going on."

Bunny said, "Oh New York is probably not fucking boring, I don't know. I never got outside of the studio because of all our rehearsals."

"So what was boring?"

"The dance company was fucking boring. All we did was work so I never got fucked. I don't think I had over two hundred orgasms since I moved there."

So Many Maybes · 448

Baja said, "Two hundred orgasms sounds like a lot to me."

"I guess. But masturbation is never as much fun as getting fucked like a corn dog. When I was here, I got fucked every night but Acka wouldn't fuck me because he was in love with Connie and Camille, but Connie never heard of Robert."

Brett said, "Who's Camille."

Baja said, "Camille is Connie but who's Robert."

Wolf said, "It sounds to me like Camille is Camille and Robert is Robert."

Brett said, "Who'd have guessed?"

Baja said, "How the fuck would I know?"

Bunny said, "That's why I couldn't sleep."

Baja asked, "Why couldn't you sleep."

"Because I wasn't getting fucked."

Everyone paused and took a deep breath again.

Bonnie said, "Bunny, tell them what happened with Platikov?"

Bunny said, "Bonnie made him pay, big time."

Will said, "Was my mistress of feminine vengeance at her best?"

"Absolutely. She really overcharged him."

Baja said, "So tell us what happened."

"On Friday afternoon, Platikov was with our company at the party for the Ballet Foundation. When Bonnie and Amanda and Lois came in to the party, Lois had on a green dress with her boobs hanging out."

Bonnie said, "Not really, but almost."

Bunny continued, "Lois went over to the Commie Putz

So Many Maybes · 449

and his eyes got bugs in them and he stared at her boobs. She talked to him for a minute, then she grabbed his crotch. Then she walked to the door and he walked behind her like he was her little weenie dog, but he begged her to fuck him like a corn dog…It's fun when they beg…anyway, we got up and followed them. When we walked out of the hotel, these two big vending machines were at the door, and we got in the limo."

Camille said, "Vending machines?"

"Oh Connie, you know what vending machines are. They're those big things you get stale cheese sandwiches from at the hospital."

"So it wasn't a very nice hotel?"

"No it was a great hotel and it cost a bundle. Bonnie's rich you know that. Isn't that right Whoa."

Wolf started to answer. "So rich that…"

Bonnie interrupted him and said, "Don't say it Whoa. Connie, it was The Plaza."

"Then I'm confused."

Bunny said, "Why are you confused Connie, you must know what The Plaza is? Isn't that right Bust."

Brett nodded slowly and said, "Most likely."

"I know what the Plaza is Bunny. But it's one of the best hotels in New York. Why were there cheese sandwich vending machines outside."

"Oh they weren't real vending machines, they were just as big as vending machines."

"What was."

"The two Tanks."

So Many Maybes · 450

"There were tanks outside The Plaza?"

"Oh Connie, how could you think that? We were in New York. There aren't any tanks in New York."

As amusing as it was to watch Camille fall down the same rabbit hole as he had, Robert decided it was time to step in."

He said, "She means men that were as big as Tank."

Baja said, "Tank was our bodyguard when we danced in San Francisco."

Jenny said, "Trust me. Tank is big, real big. Vending machine is a good description."

Bunny said, "Jane, when did you meet Tank?"

"He came here with Lois."

Bunny said, "He did. I'm so sorry I missed him, but now I'm mad because he didn't come over and say hello when Bonnie showed her movie."

Jenny said, "I'm talking about another time Bunny. Tank came here with Lois to help me deal with Matt Ress."

Bunny smiled and said, "Isn't Tank great? Not many men would come all the way from San Francisco just to help you move your mattress?

Jenny smiled broadly and said, "You're so right Bunny. Tank is great, and I couldn't have asked for anyone better to help me."

Bunny said, "But Bonnie, now I have a question."

"What's that Bunny?"

"If Tank came here just to help Jane with her mattress, why didn't he come to New York with you guys? It only makes sense that Lois would need a bodyguard when her boobs were hanging out. Guys would want to get a hand hold."

So Many Maybes · 451

Will said, "From what I saw it would take four hands."

Wolf said, "I have to agree with you Wallace. Four hands might even be an understatement."

Baja said, "Shut up Whoa."

Wolf said, "I shall try. I shall try. But now you have put me in a difficult situation my dear. I find it enormously stimulating to be ordered around by a beautiful woman and I feel a strong urge to continue making objectionable comments."

Baja smiled and reached under the table and grabbed his crotch.

Wolf's eyes opened wide and he straightened up.

He said, "Bunny, my radiant ballerina, I am now in dire need of one of those specialized genitalia paraphernalia that dancers use to cover their erections. What are they called?"

"Dance belts. They're cooler than seventy-six jock straps."

"Yes, a dance belt. It's too bad you didn't get me one."

"But Whoa I did. I just haven't had time to give it to you."

Bonnie said, "Oh God! Bunny you didn't."

Bunny reached in her purse and took out Platikov's belt and proudly held it up to show Wolf.

She said, "It was Platikov's, but he didn't need it. Besides he had pink oil on his nuts."

Bunny handed Platikov's belt to Wolf who marveled at it. Bunny didn't seem at all phased about giving him another man's dirty underwear to use.

Wolf was sincerely moved that she had thought of him, and without a trace of sarcasm he said, "Thank you so much Bunny. It was very thoughtful of you to think of me

So Many Maybes · 452

when you were so busy."

Wolf stood up and began to put the dancer's belt on over his pants.

Baja said, "Oh my God Whoa!"

Everyone at the table started laughing.

When he finished putting on his pre-owned dancer's jock strap, Wolf moved away from the table and turned his back to them and began rapidly shaking his butt like he had out on the diag. This time it was Jenny who stood up and began to dance with him.

Baja kept reaching to grab his ass, but Wolf deftly sidestepped her and continued shaking his butt until he was out of breath and sat back down.

Robert said, "Dammit Jenny, you should have gotten a picture of Wolf doing the shake rattle and roll."

Bunny said, "Acka who's Jenny? And who's this guy Wolf? I feel like I've heard their name somewhere."

Robert said, "Don't worry about it Bunny. It's not important. Just continue your story. I'm anxious to hear what happened."

"Okay…Anyway, the two Tanks took us all to their limo and inside the car, Amanda gave Platikov a shot in the leg with a huge needle and it knocked him out on the floor.

"Bunny, what was in the needle?"

"I don't know Acka. I guess I should have asked. I mean it's a critical part of the story don't you think? But like you said, I'm a sad storyteller."

Bonnie said, "It was horse tranquilizer."

So Many Maybes · 453

Will said, "Bonnie, where the hell did you get horse tranquilizer?"

"I got it from an old friend of my Uncle Judd's named Bronco. He owns a great Italian restaurant in Brooklyn."

Robert said, "Why would he need horse tranquilizer?"

Bronco occasionally bets on the horses and he said horse tranquilizer can sometimes be useful."

Robert started to ask why Bronco found horse tranquilizer useful for betting on the horses, but Bonnie interrupted him and said, "I have no idea why he needs it. Bunny go on."

Bunny said, "When we got to the theatre, the two big Tanks dragged the knocked-out Putz into his dressing room and took off his clothes and Lois poured pink oil all over his crotch. Bonnie took his tights into the bathroom and did something with them and that's when I took his dancer's belt. Then Bonnie and I went to Satyrikov's office and Bonnie poured some stuff in his vodka bottle. When we were done, I went to my dressing room and Bonnie and Lois and Amanda went back to their hotel."

Camille said, "Who's Satyrikov?"

Bunny said, "He's the company's Directordaemon. He's evil like Platikov so Bonnie made him pay too."

"What's a Directordaemon?"

Bonnie said, "Satyrikov is the company's artistic director. Except for the money people, he oversees every aspect of the company's dancing. Bunny and the other dancers added the daemon part because he was cruel to them."

Baja said, "What was the stuff that Bunny mentioned that you poured in his vodka bottle?"

So Many Maybes · 454

"It was a super-laxative. From what Bronco said, Satyrikov will have uncontrollable diarrhea for days. The papers only said that he was hospitalized for an unknown illness."

Robert said, "So what would your friend Bronco do with a super-laxative?"

"Besides the restaurant, Bronco runs a private gambling establishment where some of the patrons occasionally misbehave. If they do, he slips the laxative in their drink and they become permanent toilet fixtures and stop making trouble. The two big Tanks that helped us also work for Bronco. If customers get too unruly, the Tanks diffuse the situation quickly."

Wolf said, "Bronco seems like a useful man to know."

Bonnie said, "He definitely is."

Bunny continued, "The first part of the ballet went like Nagurski wanted."

Will said, "Who's Nagurski?"

"He was the ballet's choreographer."

Will nodded, and Bunny continued, "When Platikov came out on stage, he was limping because of Amanda's shot, and when he tried to do a leap, he fell flat because his leg wouldn't work. He fell really hard and he didn't move until Stenova came out of Giselle's little house and grabbed his hand and pulled him up off the floor.

Jenny said, "Who was Giselle?"

Bunny said, "Giselle was Stenova."

When Bonnie saw the puzzled look on Jenny's face, she said, "Giselle was Stenova's character in the ballet."

So Many Maybes · 455

Bunny said, "Giselle is a great ballet Wallace. It's a beautiful love story. I think you'd really like it because you're so romantic."

Will said, "Why do you say that Bunny?

"Because I've seen how you look at Bonnie? By the way Wallace, has Bonnie been banging your brains out every day like I told her to do when I left?"

"Yes Bunny."

"That's great Wallace. I wish I could have been here to take pictures of you two with my Canon."

Baja said, "What happened then Bunny?"

"I don't know Baja. You'll have to ask Bonnie and Wallace."

"I meant what happened next with Platikov?"

"Oh Baja, I knew that. I was only making a joke. Anyway, when Platikov stood up, all the people in the audience started to laugh because they could see his ding dong with nuts."

Wolf laughed heartily, and everyone followed.

Over the laughter, Bonnie said, "The pink oil that Lois dumped on him made Platikov's tights more transparent that a wet T-shirt."

After Wolf and the others stopped laughing, Bunny continued her story.

"Platikov turned around and faced his ass at the audience and showed everyone he'd shit his pants. He must have tried to fart like Acka. It's never a good idea to fart on stage, but it happens sometimes. Even ballerinas fart...It's lucky the orchestra hides the noise. Otherwise it would be really funny and whoever farted would have to stop dancing and take a bow."

So Many Maybes · 456

Bonnie said, "I put shaved chocolate all over the back of his tights and his body heat melted it, so it only looked like he shit his pants."

Bunny said, "Oh Bonnie, it wasn't chocolate. He really shit in his tights. I could smell it."

Camille said, "Oh my."

Will said, "I'll bet those tights would be worth a fortune on the black market. From what I understand, Platikov is a big star."

Bunny said, "Why would anyone wear tights that are full of shit? It wouldn't be healthy."

Will said, "Oh you'd be surprised…"

Bonnie interrupted him.

She said, "Bunny don't pay any attention to Wallace. He's interested in things no one else is. Just go on with your story."

Bunny continued, "Stenova got really pissed off at Platikov for ruining her performance, so she hit him and knocked him back. Then I ran over and kicked him in his chocolate covered nuts. When he bent over to grab them, Stenova knocked him down and he didn't move."

Bonnie said, "Stenova hit him under the jaw with the wildest uppercut you'll ever see. It knocked him up off his feet. When he hit the floor, he was probably unconscious.

Bunny said, "Then Stenova grabbed my hand and we faced the audience and did a reverence bow together and we both left and that's what happened. Bonnie did I tell the story right. Acka told me I'm a sad story teller."

Wolf said, "My dear, don't listen to Acka. You are a brilliant story teller."

So Many Maybes · 457

He held up his glass and said, "Here's to you Bunny, and here's to you Bonnie."

Everyone else held up their glasses and said, "Here's to Bunny and Bonnie."

Bunny smiled and held up her glass and said, "Thank you so much everybody and here's to you Wolf. You're a great butt shaker."

Wolf raised his eyebrows and said, "Oh my dear Bunny, did you just call me Wolf?"

"Of course I did. I know your name is really Wolf and I know Jenny and Brett and Will and Camille and Robert too. I just like to change people's name's because I think it's fun. I like having fun. Don't you?"

*

THE JOURNAL OF ROBERT BAIN

After Bunny made her rather charming admission, I realized that I'd always been unfair to her. Bunny wasn't crazy, she just saw the world differently from others and she freely offered her fresh perspective to all those with the patience to listen and willingness to put forth the effort to understand. It was this special and original quality that Bonnie had recognized before everyone else. Bunny was probably the greatest artist of all of us because she changed the way we looked at the world.

As I looked at Bunny and the other artists who were sitting around the table that night, I thought about why we spent our time producing a painting or a story or a drama or a dance that might enrich the life of

So Many Maybes · 458

others. There was nothing profound about our reasons. We did it because we liked doing it and we could. We were lucky enough to be in good health and live in a place and time where being an artist was possible. If we were fighting a serious illness in some way, or if we had others demanding our full attention, or if we were starving in some third world hell or living through a brutal war like the Vietnamese people, some of us might not have had the courage or drive to persist. However, some of us might have. There's simply no way to tell.

When I moved to Ann Arbor, my life changed in the most profound way possible because I learned what was truly important to me. Surprisingly, it wasn't my writing. It was the phenomenal friends that I'd made. For me, being alive is having great friends and looking forward to making more. With every new person that comes into my life, comes the opportunity to share and exchange ideas and hopes and dreams. If I keep my heart and mind open to those encounters, I will be alive. But if I retreat solely into memories of the past, I will slowly kill my spirit and end up like BadBob; miserably sitting at the dining room table and tragically staring through that imaginary porthole to what I thought was a better time.

Thankfully, I learned that lesson early in my life and I resolved to never follow my father into the hell of self-inflicted spiritual death. Instead, I would embrace the future and follow the path toward being alive.

So Many Maybes · 459

Then I looked at Camille and I knew that I desperately wanted her with me as I traveled down that path.

*

Impulsively, Robert took hold of Camille's hand.

He said, "Camille you're the most beautiful woman in the world and I love you deeply. I'm so lucky to have met you. Will you marry me?"

Camille paused and sat motionless. She appeared to be stunned. She directed her dark and mysterious gaze straight into Robert's yearning and tear-filled eyes. Then she looked down at the table for moment then returned her gaze to his.

She took a deep breath and shouted, "FUCK NO!!! Never again!"

Robert was so shocked at her unexpected answer that his body spasmed like it had so many times before, and he slid under the table and onto the floor.

Camille bent over and looked under the table and said, "I mean yes. I'm sorry Robert. I just couldn't help it. My jokes will be the death of me yet."

Robert said, "Jesus Christ Camille. Me too."

To be continued…maybe.

BOOK TWO: Rilke's Dracula

RILKE'S DRACULA

A Play In Twenty-Six Acts
by
Wolf Rilke

Just kidding.
Why do you care how many Acts there are?
The audience will probably leave early anyway.

Contents

ACT ONE

Scene 1	471
Scene 2	475
Scene 3	479
Scene 4	483
Scene 5	487
Scene 6	489
Scene 7	493

ACT TWO

Scene 1	495
Scene 2	499
Scene 3	503
Scene 4	507
Scene 5	511
Scene 6	519
Scene 7	521
Scene 8	525

ACT THREE

Scene 1	532
Scene 2	537

LIST OF CHARACTERS

JONATHON HARKER..a young lawyer.

COUNT DRACULA..................................a Transylvanian vampire.

HAWKINS...senior partner of the law firm.

LUCY...Hawkins' daughter.

ALICE CARROLL..a beautiful actress.

MISS PARTIME....................................an office temporary worker.

PLUMBER HOUSTON..........................a law firm problem solver.

DR. ENGINE SNORKEL.......................................a mass murderer.

DO-ME RUFF..a prostitute.

RICH-AMERICAN BASTARD.............................seller of a house.

COLLASSA BASTARD................wife of Rich-american Bastard.

*Note To Producer: Throughout the play, the stage is divided down the middle by a partition into two equal halves; left half-stage and right half-stage.

With only a few exceptions, all of the action will take place on a single half-stage and the other will be dark and covered with a curtain.

On a few occasions the entire stage will be used and will be designated as such. It is a device used to move forward quickly from one scene to the next and keep this thing from being six hours long

ACT ONE

Act One Scene One
Setting: Left half-stage. Hawkins' Office.

An elevated desk sits in the left-hand rear corner and two comfortable chairs are in front of it. To the right side is a wooden door with a sign on it saying, "MR HOUSTON." Painted on the backdrop, are signs; saying things like: "HAWKINS ESTABLISHMENT," "DISHONESTY IS OUR SPECIALTY" and "MAKING DEALS SINCE 1850."

Hawkins is sitting behind the desk. He is elderly and is dressed in an 1890s knee length double breasted formal business jacket. He is writing.

> JONATHON: (from offstage) "Mr. Hawkins, you called for me?"
> HAWKINS: "Come in and sit down."

A young man, Jonathon Harker, dressed the same as Hawkins, enters from the left and sits down in one of the chairs in front of the desk.

> HAWKINS: "Harker, I called you into my office because

Rilke's Dracula · 471

we need to discuss your job performance."

JONATHON: "Yes sir."

HAWKINS: "From this firm's perspective, you are a total loser. I personally chose you to defend two high-profile clients that were accused of murder. The prosecution humiliated you in court and both of your clients were found guilty and given severe, inhumane sentences. Your performance was so bad that the *Law Journal* did a special issue on you. They called you the worst lawyer in history."

JONATHON: "I'm sorry sir but there were extenuating circumstances."

HAWKINS: "What circumstances were those."

JONATHON: "They were both obviously guilty and they both confessed."

HAWKINS: "Harker, a defense attorney's job is to get their clients off, no matter how guilty they are."

JONATHON: "I tried sir. I tried my damndest to convince my secretary to give them a blow job, but she refused."

HAWKINS: "What the fuck are you talking about Harker?"

JONATHON: "Getting them off sir."

HAWKINS: (smacking his forehead) "You idiot! Anyway, since you're engaged to my daughter Lucy, I've decided to give you one last chance. Fail this time and I'll have Plumber work you over and fire your ass and make sure you don't get unemployment."

Rilke's Dracula · 472

JONATHON: "I could never collect unemployment sir. I'm an unpaid 'intern.' Isn't that what you called it, an intern?"

HAWKINS: "Oh right. Because you were my daughter's fiancé, I let you intern here for nothing. Most interns here pay to work for me."

JONATHON: "Thank you for the opportunity sir, I won't let you down this time, I promise. What would you like me to do?"

HAWKINS: "We have been retained by a Transylvanian Count to find him a house in London. He's one of this firm's most important clients both because he's an old friend of my family and because he's so loaded he shits pound sterling. What I want you to do is find him a house and work the deal."

JONATHON: (starting to get up) "Yes sir. I won't fail you."

HAWKINS: "And Harker…"

JONATHON: "Yes sir."

HAWKINS: "Bilk the rich sucker for as much as you can."

Act One Scene Two

Setting: Right half-stage. Lucy's apartment living room.

*Hanging across the top of the room is a banner saying,
"LUCY'S HIPPY HAVEN."*

*On the right side of the room is a large puppet theater. Across
the top of the puppet theater is a sign that says, "PUT AN END
TO VIOLENCE."*

*To the left of the puppet theater is a large wooden door with
a peace sign on it." In the puppet theater, two puppets, Punch
and Judy, are arguing.*

> JUDY: "Punch, you worthless limp dicked piece of shit.
> Have you been having wet dreams about Lucy again?"
> PUNCH: (Looking away from Judy and putting his
> hands over his face in shame and shaking his head)
> "Ahhh…of course not my dear."
> JUDY: "So why is it that every morning I catch you with
> a monster Woody?"
> PUNCH: "I can't help it. All I've got is a Woody. I'm a
> wooden puppet."
> JUDY: "Okay, I'll give you that, but why don't you make
> love to me anymore? When we were newlyweds, you
> banged the shit out of me every night."
> PUNCH: "You've changed dear."
> JUDY: "How have I changed?"
> PUNCH: "Well for one thing, you're a nagging bitch."
> JUDY: "So What? That's my job. I'm your wife."

Rilke's Dracula · 475

PUNCH: "Then there's the other thing…"

JUDY: "What other thing? Is it because my boobs are too small?"

PUNCH: "No Judy. Your boobs are just fine."

JUDY: "So what is it?"

PUNCH: "When we got married, we were twenty-years-old, but since then, our puppet master has upgraded to the newest model and now we're only two, so we're under age."

JUDY: "FUCK!!!"

PUNCH: "Sorry. We can't. We have to wait fourteen years.

Excuse me. I'm going in the bathroom and polish my Woody."

Punch turns to walk off the puppet stage and Judy starts chasing him around and hitting him with her puppet bat.

There is a knock on the apartment door. Lucy, Hawkins' daughter, enters from the right and walks toward the door. She is strikingly beautiful and is obviously a hippie. She is barefoot and is wearing an Indian head band to keep her long wavy hair in place. Her low-rise bell bottom jeans barely cover her ass. Her bikini top is made of suede leather and it has cowboy fringe along the bottom. She opens the door and let's Jonathon in.

LUCY: "Jonathon, why are you here?"

JONATHON: "Because I love you Lucy. I just wanted to see you."

LUCY: "Well I guess it's good you came over because

Rilke's Dracula · 476

we need to talk."

JONATHON: "About what my love?"

Lucy walks over to the puppet show where Judy is still chasing Punch around and hitting him with the bat. Lucy pulls a lever on the puppet theater and both puppets fall to the floor along with their strings and controls.

LUCY: "Jonathon I'm calling off our engagement."

JONATHON: "But my dear Lucy, why?"

LUCY: "Because you're a despicable, thieving, evil mother fucker."

JONATHON: "I'm sorry Lucy I'm only trying to be like your father."

LUCY: "Oh trust me I know. You've become just like him. You're a stinking capitalist establishment pig and a corporate stooge. You're anti-union, and your politics are further right than Napoleon's."

JONATHON: "I'll give you that, except for the pig part, but I work for your father's firm and he has well established and successful policies."

LUCY: "I hate my father and I hate you."

JONATHON: "If you hate me Lucy, why did you say that you would marry me?"

LUCY: "I've changed Jonathon. Over the New Year's holiday I took a trip to California and I saw the play Hair. It changed my life. I don't want to marry an establishment pig. I want to move to California and

Rilke's Dracula · 477

start a commune."

JONATHON: "I've never heard of that play. Is it being performed here in London? If I went and saw it, would you reconsider marrying me?"

LUCY: "You can't see it anywhere. My father hated the play's anti-establishment ideas, but it was making money, so he bought it and had it re-written. Of course, they butchered it. It's such a shame. The original was way ahead of its time."

JONATHON: "Please reconsider Lucy. Your father has given me a second chance. Why won't you?"

LUCY: (opening the door for him) "Jonathon, you IDIOT. If you can't understand what a stupid thing you've just said, there's no hope for you. Now get the FUCK out of my apartment!"

Jonathon walks through the door and leaves. Lucy slams the door.

LUCY: "Pig!"

Rilke's Dracula · 478

Act One Scene Three

Setting: Left half-stage. Hawkins office.

Hawkins is sitting behind his desk. Jonathon is sitting in front of the desk.

> HAWKINS: "Harker, have you found a place for the Count?"
>
> JONATHON: "I have sir. It's a very nice three-story, 15-bedroom, 17-bath house in West Bromton. It has 36,000 square feet of living space, a full basement, and a 10-stall garage."

He pauses as their office worker, Miss Partime, enters carrying a tray with a coffee pot and two coffee cups. She has gorgeous long red hair and is good looking enough to routinely cause carriage wrecks in front of their office building. She has on a short, tight skirt. She bends over to put the tray down and both Hawkins and Jonathon lean way over to look under her skirt. She notices them and stands up quickly and puts the tray down so that it is hanging over the edge of the desk. It crashes to the floor then she quickly turns to exit. Just before she leaves the stage she turns and gives them a two-handed middle-finger salute, then exits.

> JONATHON: "Wooh...eee! Who is she sir?"
>
> HAWKINS: "Her name is Miss Partime. She's our new office temporary hire."
>
> JONATHON: "When I saw her I wanted to run into the

Rilke's Dracula · 479

Ladies Room and play with myself."

HAWKINS: "You mean Men's Room."

JONATHON: "Oh right. Of course I did. I don't know what I was thinking."

HAWKINS: (looking suspiciously at Jonathon) "Isn't she amazing? I just wish she could do something besides look good. Like maybe answering the telephone."

JONATHON: "What's a telephone sir."

HAWKINS: "Never mind. It's not important. Go on with your description of the house."

JONATHON: "Let's see…where was I? Oh…The lot covers a total of 20 acres that is surrounded by a sixteen-feet-high stone wall topped with concertina wire. Watch towers with search lights and gun emplacements are positioned at each corner. In front of the wall on all sides, is a sixty-feet-wide, thirty-feet-deep moat that is occupied by alligators. Except for the road approaching the drawbridge across the moat, the rest of the surrounding property is extensively mined."

HAWKINS: "It sounds like it's a good house. Why do they want to get rid of it?"

JONATHON: "They have two houses sir. They want to live in their California house full time."

HAWKINS: (nodding) "Alright…Although it's a little small, I think we can con Dracula into believing it is the best we can do. He's not too bright. At least the house does sound fairly secure."

Rilke's Dracula · 480

JONATHON: "It is sir."

HAWKINS: "What is the asking price."

JONATHON: "That's the best part sir. The Bastard's have lowered the price to eight million pounds in cash, two hundred sheep, two hundred wolves and one beautiful twenty-six-year-old Transylvanian babe with loose morals who runs around naked except for blue and black body paint."

HAWKINS: "Harker, you're too new to this business to call people we're doing business with bastards. It takes experience to be able to insult your clients and get away with it."

JONATHON: "That's their real name sir. Mr. and Mrs. Rich American Bastard. They're from San Francisco."

HAWKINS: "Harker, don't you think everyone is tired of that joke by now?"

JONATHON: "I'm sorry sir."

HAWKINS: "Where ever they're from, that name makes me suspicious. Have you checked their references?"

JONATHON: "Yes sir. They're not illegitimate Bastards."

HAWKINS: "Okay. I'll take your word for it, but I'm still suspicious...Anyway, by some people's standards the Rich-American Bastard's asking price is reasonable but we have to get our piece of the deal. Offer them half and tell Dracula double. Except for the babe of course."

JONATHON: (with some hesitation) "Ahhh...But that isn't...."

Rilke's Dracula · 481

HAWKINS: (interrupting) "Once the Bastards accept our offer, you leave immediately for Transylvania and tell the Count that we've found him a house. We need to push this deal through before that stupid Transylvanian sucker figures out we're screwing him."

JONATHON: "Yes sir, I will contact the Bastards today and if they accept our offer, I will leave tomorrow for Transylvania."

Jonathon stands up and exits to the left.

Act One Scene Four
Setting: Right half-stage. The outside of an inn.

The outside of the inn is made of large stones. A door is at the left, and a lighted window is in the center. On the door is a sign that says "DOOR." On the backdrop above the window is a neon sign that says, "VAMPIRE COUNTRY INN AND SUITES."

Directly in front of the window is a red American Flyer child's wagon with a rocking horse attached to the front. A tall man in black holds on to the horse's reins. Jonathon emerges from the door followed by a plump red cheeked old lady dressed in a puffy screaming red and white candy cane patterned dress.

OLD LADY: "Oh young Herr, must you go to the castle."

JONATHON: "Yes I must. It is my duty."

OLD LADY: "If you must go, take this. It will protect you
    from Dracula."

The old lady hangs a huge gold crucifix around Jonathon's neck. It is so heavy that it makes him bend quickly forward until the cross hits the floor with a loud "CLUNK!" and he almost falls down.

JONATHON: "Why should I need protection from the
    Count?"

OLD LADY: "Oh you might not, sometimes he's mellow
    and as cuddly as a puppy dog, but he suffers from
    a serious mental condition and he can be unstable.

Rilke's Dracula · 483

Legend has it that when he is off his medication, he's a real maniac to be around."

JONATHON: "Thank you for your kind hospitality and your generous gift and warning. Fortunately, I am not without experience in dealing with manic-depressive clients including a member of the Royal Family who beheaded members of Parliament just for the fun of it, and one doctor named Engine Snorkel who wandered the streets of London at night and strangled at least eleven prostitutes."

OLD LADY: "Oh my lord. Were they hung?"

JONATHON: "Uhhh…I don't know. I never saw them naked."

DRIVER: (In a horse gravelly voice) "Oh for Christ's sake, you idiot! She means were they hanged, like strung up?"

JONATHON: "Oh. No, they weren't put to death. The Royal was placed under house arrest in Buckingham Palace for the rest of his life and forced to eat nothing but plain hot dogs that have been sitting on concession stand rollers for a week. Dr. Snorkel was sentenced to 99 years of cleaning manure spreaders with his tongue in a maximum security Dairy Farm and Mental Institution outside of London. He's not particularly fond of the place."

OLD LADY: "Why would anyone want to spread manure around. We clean it up around here."

Rilke's Dracula · 484

The rocking horse's tail lifts and it drops a big load of manure on the wagon driver's foot.

> DRIVER: (In a horse gravelly voice) "Hey speaking of manure, this little bastard just crapped on my foot! Could you get in the wagon, so we can get going?"

The wagon driver gets in the wagon and Jonathon gets in behind him. Jonathon tries to put his arms around the wagon driver for stability, but the driver slaps his hands away, so Jonathon leans back to hold onto the back of the wagon. Just as he does, the wagon takes off with a lurch and Jonathon falls off and has to chase after it as it exits to the right.

Act One Scene Five

Setting: Left half-stage. The outside of Dracula's Castle.

The outside of Dracula's Castle is made of ginger bread. In the center is a dark brown wooden door. Over the door is a sign with large letters saying, "DRACULA CASTLE." On the door are the numbers "666" written in yellow frosting. On either side of the door are signs written in white frosting saying, "GO AWAY, YOU BOTHER ME" and "SUCK YOU."

Jonathon enters from the left and stands in front of the door and looks at a piece of paper.

> JONATHON: "Let's see…666. Well, if the address Mr. Hawkins gave me is right, this is Dracula Castle."

He knocks on the door and a little girl's voice says, "Oh yeah!" every time he knocks.

> DRACULA: (obviously annoyed from behind the door) "WHAT!!!?"
> JONATHON: (raising his voice to be heard through the door) "I'm Jonathon Harker. I was sent here by Mr. Hawkins."

Dracula opens the door. He is sweat covered with a five-day old beard, dreadlocks, and a patch over his left eye. He has on a tight, black sleeveless-T-shirt with a green luminescent hand flipping the bird on the front. His bloused purple and lime green

Rilke's Dracula · 487

camouflage pants are tucked into black knee-high NAZI storm trooper jack boots. Tied along his right thigh is a long-barreled .44 magnum revolver in a black leather half holster.

DRACULA: (in a horse gravelly voice) "Come in Asshole… take your shoes off. That God dammed mother fucking horse dumped a pile of shit in front of my door."

Jonathon looks down and examines the bottom of his shoes.

Act One Scene Six
Setting: Right half-stage. Inside Dracula's bedroom.

Dracula's bedroom walls are covered with farm scenes with cute lambs, puppies and kittens. Dracula's casket is in the middle of the room and tilted toward the audience. It is made from a modified clawfoot bathtub with a naked mermaid ship's figurehead on the front. On the wall over the casket is a sign saying "DRACULA SORT OF SLEPT HERE." To the left of the casket is a floor standing gong.

Dracula is sitting in his casket. Clearly annoyed, he is madly going through papers that are on his lap desk. He reaches to his left and hits the gong with a polo mallet, DONGGGG!!

DRACULA: (shouting) "Hey Asshole. GET the FUCK in here."

Jonathon runs in from the right and trips over the edge of the gong and knocks it down. It hit's the floor with a loud DONGGGG!!...Dong, Dong, Dong. After he trips Jonathon keeps on moving and stumbles across the stage and goes off to the left. Without moving Dracula watches him and continues to look offstage until Jonathon runs back on stage and stops in front of Dracula.

JONATHON: "Yes Count."

Dracula silently glares at Jonathon then shakes his head.

Rilke's Dracula · 489

DRACULA: (continuing his horse, gravelly voice and looking at Jonathon with a stern face) "Call me Sucker."

JONATHON: (pausing before he speaks) "Ahh...Count, I..."

DRACULA: (interrupting) "Sucker."

JONATHON: "Sorry...Sucker...I don't think that Sucker is a good name to go by."

DRACULA: "Who cares what you think. I'm a vampire. Besides, Sucker is my name."

JONATHON: "Yes, Sucker."

DRACULA: "Asshole, I've been going over these papers and I don't like the deal you made on the house."

JONATHON: "I'm very sorry Count..."

DRACULA: "SUCKER! God dammit!"

JONATHON: "Sorry...what don't you like about the deal...uhh...Sucker?"

DRACULA: "I can't afford it."

JONATHON: "Oh I'm so sorry. Mr. Hawkins knew your family and he assumed you were a rich Sucker."

DRACULA: "I am a rich Sucker. I have plenty of money and I have plenty of wolves and I even have plenty of sheep, although that sounds like a perverted request to me. But now that I think about it, who am I to talk? I suck people for a living. Anyway, you've been here for a couple of days. Have you seen any babes around the castle?"

JONATHON: "No Sucker. I haven't."

Rilke's Dracula · 490

DRACULA: "Of course you haven't. That's because there aren't any. The babes won't come back to my place any more. I haven't gotten laid in approximately 156.4618 years."

JONATHON: "That's too bad Sucker. Why do you think that is?"

DRACULA: "I'm not sure, but I think it's because my balls are too small."

JONATHON: "Oh surely that's not true. A rough tough Sucker like you must have huge balls and a monster bat to go along with them."

DRACULA: "My bat doesn't have anything to do with the size of my balls. It spends all day just hanging around. But it's true. My balls are too small. Come over here and I'll show you."

Dracula opens his fly.

JONATHON: (holding his hand in front of his eyes) "That's okay Sucker. I don't want to see your balls. I believe you."

DRACULA: (still holding his fly open) "You're sure? I've got three of them."

JONATHON: "Three? Well surely that counts for something. I mean, perhaps three small balls would add up to two big ones."

DRACULA: "Unfortunately they don't. They just freak the Babes out. Tell me Asshole, do you know any

Rilke's Dracula · 491

babes?"

JONATHON: (wistfully) "Yes Sucker. I know a babe."

DRACULA: "What's her name?"

JONATHON: "Lucy."

DRACULA: "Do you think Lucy would be my Babe, so I can give her to those Rich-American Bastards from California?"

JONATHON: "She just might Sucker. I know for a fact that she wants to move to California."

DRACULA: "Okay, if you want this deal to go through, take the fastest boat that you can find back to London, grab Lucy and give her a black and blue paint job, then offer her to the Bastards. I'll take care of the rest."

Dracula looks down at his papers again. Jonathon doesn't move.

JONATHON: "But Sucker…"

DRACULA: (interrupting) "Why haven't you left yet Asshole?"

JONATHON: "Lucy's not Transylvanian."

Rilke's Dracula · 492

Act One Scene Seven
Setting: Entire Stage. The English Channel.

The bottom of the backdrop has large waves. In the blue sky above the waves, a skywriting airplane has written "ENGLISH CHANNEL." On the far right of the stage is a mountain scene and a large sign that says, "LEAVING TRANSYLVANIA." On the far left is the London Bridge and a sign that says, "ENTERING LONDON."

A rock band begins to play and sing "Row row, row your boat, gently down the stream..."

Jonathon enters from the right. He is seated in a toy row boat on wheels, and he is feverishly rowing. The boat is pulled quickly across the stage from right to left and exits.

END OF ACT ONE

ACT TWO

Act Two Scene One

Setting: Right half-stage. Lucy's apartment living room.

There is a knock at the door. Lucy enters from the right and opens the door and Jonathon is there. She pauses momentarily then slams the door in his face. Another knock at the door.

> JONATHON: (shouting from behind the door) "Lucy please let me in. I have to talk to you. It's really important."
>
> LUCY: "Go away. I don't want to see you."
>
> JONATHON: "Please Lucy. It'll only take a minute."
>
> LUCY: "Okay. One minute."
>
> JONATHON: "I'm sorry Lucy. I lied. Make that ten minutes."
>
> LUCY: "Of course you lied. You're a lawyer."
>
> JONATHON: "Please Lucy."

Lucy opens the door and Jonathon enters. Lucy turns over an hourglass and crosses her arms to wait.

> LUCY: "You've got ten minutes. What is it, you

establishment pig?"

JONATHON: "Lucy, why do you talk to me like that now? When we first met, we made love in the park."

LUCY: "Get with it Jonathan. This is the 1890s. People don't say we made love any more. They say we fucked. Besides I was high on acid."

JONATHON: "What's acid?"

LUCY: "If you'd read Alice in Wonderland like I told you to, you'd know."

JONATHON: "I tried. Honest I did. But I got lost in the beginning. How could Alice go down a rabbit hole. I mean the hole is too small."

LUCY: "Go ask Alice…"

JONATHON: "Okay, I will. Where does she live?"

LUCY: "Oh for God's sake. Why do you need to talk to me?'

JONATHAN: "I've found a way for you to get to California and make money for your commune at the same time."

LUCY: "How?"

JONATHON: "It's a win-win situation. I save my job and you get a California Commune."

LUCY: "You still haven't told me how."

JONATHON: "It's simple really."

LUCY: "Tell me God dammit!"

JONATHON: "All you have to do is occasionally make… uh…excuse me, all you have to do is occasionally fuck a Rich-American Bastard."

Rilke's Dracula · 496

LUCY: "WHAT!!!! Get the FUCK out of my apartment!!!!"

Lucy grabs Jonathon by his sleeve and swings him around toward the door then kicks him in the ass. He flies through the door opening. Lucy slams the door and then walks off the stage to the right

Act Two Scene Two
Setting: Left half-stage. Hawkins' office.

Hawkins is sitting at his desk.

JONATHON: (from off the stage to the left) "Mr Hawkins it is imperative that we talk."

Hawkins looks up and looks off stage toward Jonathon.

HAWKINS: "Harker, so you're back. You were gone longer than I thought you'd be. Come in and please don't tell me you fucked up again."

JONATHON: "I'm sorry sir. It is a long trip and the boat back to London was slower that I hoped it would be."

HAWKINS: "So what happened with the Count? Did he bite."

JONATHON: "No thank God. Dealing with a vampire is hard enough, if he bit me, it would have made things a whole lot more complicated."

HAWKINS: "You idiot. I meant did he go for the deal."

JONATHON: "Oh…Well, not exactly…"

HAWKINS: Why not. You didn't say something stupid like maybe that we intended to screw him?"

JONATHON: "No sir. I presented the deal to him just the way you told me to."

HAWKINS: "So why didn't he go for it?"

JONATHON: "Well, first, Sucker…ahhh…Count

Rilke's Dracula · 499

Dracula is a bit eccentric."

HAWKINS: "I don't think eccentric is the right word. I'd say crazy is more like it. The whole Sucker family is crazy."

JONATHON: "So Sucker is really his name? I thought he was messing with me."

HAWKINS: "It's true and to make things worse, his first name is Sour."

JONATHON: "You're kidding me. Sour Sucker? No wonder he's so foul tempered. Where did the name Dracula come from?"

HAWKINS: "I'm not sure but I think it's a pseudonym he used when he wrote his memoirs. But of course, he has to use his real name when he buys the house."

JONATHON: "Unfortunately, sir, it looks like that deal may fall through."

HAWKINS: "Why? Is the house too small?"

JONATHON: "No the house is just fine…"

Jonathon pauses as Miss Partime enters from the left and walks across the office and goes out the wooden door to the right.

JONATHON: "I'm sorry sir, but I need to excuse myself for a minute and go to the Ladies Room…uhhh…I mean Men's Room."

HAWKINS: "Hold on to it until we're done here."

Jonathon grabs his crotch.

Rilke's Dracula · 500

HAWKINS: (puzzled) "What are you doing Jonathan?"

JONATHON: "I'm holding on to it like you told me to…
Anyway, like I said, the house is just fine but Sour
Sucker won't agree to the terms we negotiated for
him. He says he can't afford it."

HAWKINS: "That's bullshit. The Count is a real rich
Sour Sucker."

JONATHON: "That's true sir. But the problem isn't with
the money or the sheep or the wolves. It's the babe.
He doesn't have any."

HAWKINS: "So the Count is a Babe Poor Rich Sour
Sucker?"

JONATHON: "I'm afraid so sir."

HAWKINS: "So we've got a problem."

JONATHON: "I'm afraid so sir."

*Hawkins sits silent for a while. He is thinking. He gets up
from behind his desk and walks over to the door on the right
and opens it slightly and looks in.*

HAWKINS: "Houston, we have a problem."

Rilke's Dracula · 501

Act Two Scene Three
Setting: Left half-stage. Hawkins' Office.

Hawkins is seated behind his desk. Jonathan and Plumber Houston are seated in front of it. Plumber is a short rotund man with a beard dressed in a modern business suit and carrying a long-barreled .44 magnum revolver in a shoulder holster.

> HAWKINS: "So there you have it Plumber. If we don't do something fast, the deal will fall through. I'm afraid Sucker will get generally annoyed and fly here and hang around upside down from one of our coat racks until we find him a place he can afford. That might scare our clients away and all of us, including you, will be out of a job."

Plumber removes his revolver from his holster and uses its long barrel to imitate an obscene metallic middle finger and he gestures slightly upward.

> PLUMBER: "If he won't leave when you ask him too, I'll shove all ten and a half inches of my personal enforcer up his ass all the way to his balls and turn his dick into a smoking blow hole."
> JONATHON: "He has three."
> PLUMBER: "Three what?"
> JONATHON: "Balls. And they're small."
> HAWKINS: "Please tell me how you know that?"

Rilke's Dracula · 503

JONATHON: "He told me sir. He wanted to show me, but I told him I'd take his word for it."

PLUMBER: (nodding slowly) "It sounds to me like that Sucker has a weakness; three of them in fact. Maybe he'd drop his drawers for you again Harker, so I could spike his balls to the floor with a ping pong paddle."

HAWKINS: "Plumber, I know how much you like hurting people and most of the time I enjoy watching you work, but as crazy as Sucker is, he is an old friend of my family. I'd rather solve this problem peacefully."

PLUMBER: "Why don't we take the alternate route and muscle the sellers into accepting a deal without the babe."

JONATHON: "I proposed that to Rich Bastard. He said that he's willing to forgo the sheep and the wolves but he's adamant that the deal has to include a babe. He said that once I meet his wife, I'll understand."

PLUMBER: (holding up his gun again) "Just let me talk to him. He'll come around."

HAWKINS: "I've no doubt he would, but we can't risk having the police sniff around our business affairs. They could bring down our whole organization. Like I said we need to do this peacefully."

PLUMBER: "Okay, okay. It'll bore the shit out of me, but I guess we'll have to find him a babe."

JONATHON: "How about a prostitute. Our old client Dr. Snorkel seemed to know how to find them. Maybe we could offer him some kind of deal to help us"

Rilke's Dracula · 504

PLUMBER: "That's an excellent idea Harker. Why don't you pay him a visit and see what you can work out?"

JONATHON: "Ohhh…no…not this time. I went to see him last. Remember?

PLUMBER: "Hawkins, if you want avoid violence, keep me away from Snorkel. The last time that I went to see him, he tried to lick my nose."

HAWKINS: (flinching) "Harker, I can see why Plumber doesn't want to go. Why don't you?"

JONATHON: "For one thing the guy is creepy."

PLUMBER: (with a trace of disgust) "Of course he is you chicken shit! He's a mass murderer."

JONATHON: "The problem isn't that I'm a chicken shit Plumber. It's that Snorkel smells like cow shit."

HAWKINS: "So wear a clothes pin on your nose! Get over there before I tell Plumber to shove his pistol barrel up your ass and blow your teeny weenie inside out."

Act Two Scene Four

Setting: Right half-stage. Inside of a jail interview room.

On the left side of the jail interview room is a steel door. The door has a window with bars. The walls of the room are covered with multi-colored graffiti like: a man strangling a woman, a man chopping another man's head off with an ax, a man in front of a firing squad, a man fucking a sheep from behind and other similar things. To the far right in the room is a table with a chair. Another chair is to the far left and faces the front of the table.

Jonathon is sitting in the left chair with his legs crossed and a yellow legal pad in his lap. He is wearing a gas mask. The door opens and two huge orderlies, also wearing gas masks, escort Dr. Snorkel into the room. Except for the masks, the orderlies are dressed entirely in white. A third orderly, carrying a shotgun, follows. Snorkel is dressed in orange coveralls and he is covered with shit. He is wearing handcuffs, chains and leg irons and has to shuffle into the room. The orderlies lead him to the chair behind the table and chain his hands and feet and forehead to the table.

> SNORKEL: "Hello Jonathon. If my face wasn't chained to the table, I'd say you're looking fit. The gas mask harmonizes well with your suit."
> JONATHON: "Thank you Engine. Frankly, you look like shit."
> SNORKEL: "What can I say? It goes with the territory.

Rilke's Dracula · 507

But we semi-human sociopathic monsters have a way of adapting to our circumstances. I've learned to love my grunt grinder."

JONATHON: "What's a grunt grinder?"

SNORKEL: "It's a joke name for a manure spreader. that my grand mother used. To understand, you simply have to think of the sound you make when you're having difficulty taking a shit."

JONATHON: "Oh. I see…Unnnh!"

SNORKEL: "You've got it."

JONATHON: "I might be able to help your situation Engine. That is, if you cooperate with me."

SNORKEL: "What can I do for you Jonathon?"

JONATHON: "My law firm needs to hire a prostitute and if I remember right, you're very good at finding prostitutes."

SNORKEL: "That's true. And I admit that I did in fact kill a few of them but I had to. It's just the way I am."

JONATHON: "I know Engine. Because of that, you should have been given a less severe sentence. I feel bad because I handled your case poorly. But you didn't help yourself by pissing off the judge."

SNORKEL: "I know. He hated me because I fucked his twelve-year-old daughter. But you have to believe me Jonathon. At first she said it was consensual, but she changed her story later after she got pregnant. If you recall she wanted child support."

JONATHON: "Whether it was consensual or not

Rilke's Dracula · 508

Engine, she was still only twelve."

SNORKEL: "Details…details."

JONATHON: "Anyway, if you help us, the warden has agreed to move you to a luxury apartment in the farmhouse and relieve you of your shit-licking duties."

SNORKEL: "Is he making me have a roommate?"

JONATHON: "That's the only down side. You'll have to share it with a huge python named Big Mouth Serpent and change your name to Nighttime Prey."

SNORKEL: "Oh…oh well. What choice do I have? While it's not a perfect offer, it's truly an offer I can't refuse. It might even be fun sharing a place with a fellow strangler. When do we start?"

JONATHON: "We start tomorrow night. I'll pick you up around six. Do me a favor and take a shower and I'll have the warden arrange for you to get some clean, not nut-house clothes."

SNORKEL: "Okay. Bring plenty of cash."

JONATHON: "Won't that be risky. We're going into some bad neighborhoods."

SNORKEL: "It might, but you're going to be dealing with some tough business women. In their world, money talks. You'll see."

JONATHON: "Okay. How much?"

SNORKEL: "A lot…Ten thousand will probably cover it."

JONATHON: (very loudly) "TEN THOUSAND!!!"

SNORKEL: "Hey…You want this to work or not?"

Rilke's Dracula · 509

JONATHON: "Okay. Okay. I'll talk to Mr. Hawkins."

The orderlies take Snorkel out of the room and Jonathon gets up to follow them. As he does, the orderly with the shotgun leans toward Jonathon.

ORDERLY: "Be careful sir. Dr. Snorkel can be a real handful."

Jonathon loosens his collar.

HARKER: "I've heard that too. But don't worry, I know how to handle him.

Act Two Scene Five
Setting: Left half-stage. A city street at night.

Painted on the backdrop are numerous models of 1950s cars and up in the sky is a helicopter. In front of the curb are parked several child's pedal powered play cars.

Two blond prostitutes are leaning against a store with a sign on the front that says, "STORE." Jonathon and Snorkel enter from the left. Snorkel is dressed in a multi-colored court jester outfit complete with the stupid double pointed hat and curved up-pointed toe shoes.

SNORKEL: "God dammit Jonathon! What kind of clothes are these? How do you expect me to pick up a babe dressed like this?"

JONATHON: "I'm sorry Engine. The Warden told me this was the best he could do."

SNORKEL: "The Warden was fucking with you. He's a real mother fucker. I mean that literally. I know. He's my twin brother."

JONATHON: "That must have been really traumatic for you. How did you deal with it?"

SNORKEL: "I strangled her...Don't tell anybody I told you"

JONATHON: (shaking his head) "I won't...remember we need a woman that looks Transylvanian."

SNORKEL: "You're being awfully picky for someone who's so desperate to find a woman. What's a Transylvanian

Rilke's Dracula · 511

babe look like anyway?"

JONATHON: "I'm not sure, but let's look for a tall thin woman with jet black hair who's so beautiful that she makes you want to strangle her immediately."

SNORKEL: "Gotcha."

Snorkel points toward the two women standing in front of the store.

SNORKEL: "How about those two? I admit they're not tall and they don't have black hair, but they're good looking and they look like sisters. If we work it right, we might get two for the price of one. That way, you'd get the woman that you need, and I'd get one to strangle. It's a win-win situation."

JONATHON: "I'm sorry Engine. I understand your needs, honestly I do, but we need a babe that looks Transylvanian."

Do-Me Ruff enters from the left. She's definitely a babe but she's not tall and thin. Rather, she is movie star curvaceous with nice, large heavy breasts. She is wearing a jump suit with an unzipped front that reveals more than ample cleavage. She walks directly up to Jonathon and grabs his crotch and holds on to it.

DO-ME: "Hey you boys wanna' party?"

She continues to hold on to Jonathon's crotch while she looks

Rilke's Dracula · 512

down at Snorkel's shoes. Jonathon tries to pull her hand away.

DO-ME: "Hey I really like your shoes. Do you mind telling me where you got them?"

SNORKEL: "I'm not sure. My brother got them for me, but I think he got them at Bloomingdales in New York."

DO-ME: (nodding) "The next time I'm there I'll look for them."

JONATHON: (slowly pulling her hand away from his crotch) "Miss, we would like to purchase your services. Do you take credit cards?"

DO-ME: "What the fuck are credit cards?"

SNORKEL: (pushing Jonathon aside) "Oh for Christ's sake Jonathon shut up. I'll take it from here."

JONATHON: "Okay."

SNORKEL: "We have a full-time job for you. The pay is great, and you'll get to live like a rich woman in San Francisco, and only fuck an old man once and awhile…the down side is that you'll have to wear black and blue body paint all the time."

DO-ME: "I'm not too worried about what I wear? However I am concerned that the paint will damage my skin, not to mention my vaginal opening."

SNORKEL: "I'm a medical doctor and I assure you that we'll use a vaginal opening friendly body paint."

DO-ME: "How much will I get paid?"

JONATHON: (pushing Snorkel aside) "Twenty thousand

Rilke's Dracula · 513

pounds a year with benefits."

DO-ME: "I want a carriage and driver too."

JONATHON: "What kind of carriage?"

DO-ME: "A brand new canary yellow, 1898 Cobble Stone Kamikaze with an all leather interior and a bed in the back."

JONATHON: "Okay, but are you willing to be flexible on the color? Canary yellow is only available by special order and it could take us several weeks to get one."

SNORKEL: "How do you know that Jonathon?"

JONATHON: "I sell carriages on weekends. Hawkins doesn't pay me anything."

SNORKEL: "Nothing. I bet he calls it an internship."

JONATHON: "How did you know?"

SNORKEL: "It's happening everywhere. Internships are a huge source of unpaid labor. Employers are using the idea to exploit people who desperately need a job."

DO-ME: (continuing) "I really wanted a canary yellow one, but okay, I'll go with basic black until the yellow one comes in."

JONATHON: "So do we have a deal?"

DO-ME: "Deal."

JONATHON: (taking her arm) "Good. Come with me."

DO-ME: (pulling her arm away) "Hold on there, you upper class capitalist bastard. What about the down payment?"

JONATHON: "Down payment?"

Rilke's Dracula · 514

DO-ME: "Yes down payment. You don't expect to get a girl in this day and age without a down payment, do you?"

JONATHON: "How much of a down payment do you need?"

DO-ME: "I think we could get away with 20 pounds. He's pretty stupid."

JONATHON: (taking his wallet out of his pocket) "Who is?"

DO-ME: "My pimp."

JONATHON: "You have a pimp?"

DO-ME: "A prostitute has to have a pimp these days."

JONATHON: 'Why is that?"

DO-ME: "For protection. A few years ago, some maniac mass murderer walked the streets and strangled prostitutes. Since then, we have to have a pimp."

Jonathon slowly turns and looks at Snorkel and glares at him.

SNORKEL: (mugging to the audience) "Sorry. Like I said, it's just the way I am."

DO-ME: "Personally I don't want a pimp to protect me from getting strangled but, what can I say, the Union requires it."

JONATHON: "You have a union?"

DO-ME: "Yes. When we started needing a pimp, we formed a union to protect us from the pimps. It's

Rilke's Dracula · 515

called IBLOE, the International Brotherhood of Ladies Of the Evening."

JONATHON: "That's an interesting acronym but the word Brotherhood isn't appropriate for an all-woman union. Wouldn't International Womanhood of Ladies Of the Evening make more sense?"

DO-ME: "Probably. For a while we did consider the Professional League of Prostitutes, but the acronym PLOP wasn't as flattering as IBLOE. Besides, we're going to change the union's name to the Womanhood of Womanhood or WOW, because we're expanding to include woman workers of all professions. Women today need a union to protect themselves from the tyranny of men."

JONATHAN: "I don't agree. Women are not treated poorly. They are simply asked to accept their proper place in our society. Besides, unions result in higher prices of goods and services and lower business profits."

DO-ME: "But unions have been responsible for protecting workers worldwide. In our case they've protected us from being exploited by our pimps."

SNORKEL: "Are we going to talk socio-economic theory here, or do you want to make a deal?"

JONATHON: "I'm sorry. Economic theory is one of my hobbies. I'll shut up so we can get down to business."

DO-ME: (continuing) "...The only down side with our Union is that they're keeping me from having orgasms."

Rilke's Dracula · 516

JONATHON: "The union prevents you from having orgasms?"

DO-ME: "I get off on being strangled. The last time a man strangled me, I had a whole night of almost continuous orgasms."

JONATHON: (pausing momentarily) "Ahhh…"

DO-ME: "I was screaming all night. You know things like, 'UNNNH!!!, UNNNH!!!, UNNNH!!!' and OH YEAH!!!, YEAH!!!, YEAH!!!, and STRANGLE ME BABY!!!, STRANGLE ME BABY!!!, and I'm gonna come, I'm gonna come. Things like that."

While she's speaking, Snorkel mugs a smile to the audience then suddenly grabs Jonathon's wallet and then grabs Do-Me's sleeve and pulls her off stage leaving Jonathon staring dumbly in their direction.

JONATHON: "FUCK!!!"

Act Two Scene Six
Setting: Right half-stage. A hotel hallway.

The hotel wall is green with the paint peeling. In the middle of the green wall is a door. Across the top of the wall is a sign that says, "CHEAP ASS HOTEL CIRCA 1898." On the floor, blocking the door is a passed out drunk.

DO-ME: (shouting from behind the door to the hotel room) "UNNNH!!! UNNNH, UNNNH!!! OH, YEAH!!! YEAH!!!, YEAH!!! STRANGLE ME BABY!!! STRANGLE ME BABY!!! I'm gonna' come, I'm gonna come!!! UNNNH!!! UNNNH, UNNNH!!!"

Jonathon enters from the right and runs past the door, then moves back in front of it when he hears Do-Me's shouts. He opens the door, leaps over the drunk, and rushes into the room.

SNORKEL: (from inside the room) "Helloooh Jonathan."

There is a loud crashing of furniture in the room.

DO-ME: (yelling from inside the room) "Get away from me, you stinking woman hating capitalist pig!"

Jonathon screams in terror and pain from inside the room.

Rilke's Dracula · 519

Act Two Scene Seven
Setting: Left half-stage. Hawkins Office.

Hawkins is sitting behind his desk and Plumber is sitting in front of it.

HAWKINS: "Plumber. I'm worried that Harker has swindled us. He came in here yesterday and asked me for ten thousand pounds to get a babe. Against my better judgement I gave it to him. Now he's disappeared with my money."

PLUMBER: "Harker is too stupid to swindle anybody. Something else must have happened."

There is a big commotion off stage then two policemen in motorcycle helmets drag an unconscious Jonathon in front of Hawkins desk and drop him on the floor.

COP: "Does this guy belong to you. We found him in the middle of the street, unconscious and face down in a pile of horse shit."

HAWKINS: "Unfortunately he does. Thank you officer We'll take it from here."

COP: "Wait a minute. What about our finder's fee?"

HAWKINS: "You want a finder's fee?"

COP: "We have to. The conservative Parliament has cut off our money. They say that public funded police protection is a form of socialism. From now on we

Rilke's Dracula · 521

operate on a cash only basis."

HAWKINS: "What's socialism?"

COP: "I'm not sure but people keep telling me it's bad."

HAWKINS: "I see. Plumber, will you take care of this?"

PLUMBER: (standing up from his chair) "Officers come with me."

Plumber walks off stage to the left followed by the two police officers. Four gunshots are heard then Plumber walks back into Hawkins office and sits down.

PLUMBER: "Done."

HAWKINS: "I said no violence."

PLUMBER: "I only did what was necessary. Don't worry. I'll put cement overshoes on them and throw their bodies in the Thames. No one will be the wiser."

HAWKINS: "What are cement overshoes."

PLUMBER: "Haven't you seen them? They're all the rage right now. I'll show you a picture sometime."

Awakened by the noise from the gunshots, Jonathon starts to stand up then falls down again. Plumber stands him up and moves him over to a chair. Jonathon's suit jacket is gone, his shirt tail is hanging out and the seat of his pants has been completely ripped out and a peace sign has been painted on his ass. His face and head are covered with shit. Plumber sits him down in a chair.

PLUMBER: "Who smells like shit now?

Rilke's Dracula · 522

HAWKINS: "So tell me how you fucked up this time Harker."

JONATHON: "Snorkel betrayed me and stole your money and kidnapped our babe."

PLUMBER: "Oh great. She's probably lying in a gutter somewhere."

JONATHON: "Don't be so sure. It seems that she found being strangled sexually stimulating, so she and Snorkel hooked up for the night. I rushed into their room to get her, but they knocked me unconscious. When I woke up I was being beaten from all sides by women wielding protest signs. Our prostitute was one of them."

PLUMBER: (laughing) "So a bunch of women beat the shit out of you, so to speak."

HAWKINS: (also laughing) "That is funny Plumber, but unfortunately we still have a problem."

PLUMBER: "I'll take care of it."

He gets up and goes into his office.

JONATHON: "I assume I'm fired?"

HAWKINS: "Don't jump to any conclusions just yet Harker. We still need your help to make this deal go through. You're the only one who has dealt with both parties."

JONATHON: "I won't let you down again sir."

HAWKINS: "Just don't say anything stupid."

Rilke's Dracula · 523

Act Two Scene Eight

Setting: Entire Stage.
Left half-stage. Plumbers office.
Right half-stage. A hallway.

Plumbers office is a mirror image of Hawkins' office. The desk is in the right rear corner and has two chairs in front of it and a wooden door is to the left. The sign on this door says, "MR. HAWKINS." Across the top of the backdrop is sign saying, "PLUMBERS FUCKING OFFICE." Painted on the back drop is a giant, long-barreled .44 magnum revolver. Under the big gun is a sign that says, "GIVE ME SHIT AND I'LL STICK THIS UP YOUR ASS." Other signs on the wall say, "I'LL FUCK YOU UP," and, "FAILURE IS NOT AN OPTION," and, "WHEN ITS TIME, TURN TO CRIME" and, "EXCESSIVE FORCE IS MY MOTTO."

The backdrop of the hall way is covered with wall paper. Painted on the wallpaper are different kinds of bullets. Across the top of the backdrop is a large sign that says, "HALLWAY TO HELL."

On the left half-stage, Plumber is sitting at his desk.

On the right half-stage, Miss Partime and Alice Carroll enter from the right. Alice is very tall and beautiful with jet black hair and is naked except for black and blue body paint. She is carrying her purse. They walk toward the left and stop just to the right of the center partition.

PARTIME: "Wait here a moment Miss Carroll."

Rilke's Dracula · 525

Alice waits in the hallway while Miss Partime enters Plumber's office.

PARTIME: "The young actress is here to see you sir."
PLUMBER: "Oh…hold on."

Plumber takes off his shoulder holster and revolver and puts it in his desk drawer.

PLUMBER: "You can bring her in now."

Miss Partime returns to Alice who is standing in the hallway.

PARTIME: "Come with me Miss."

Miss Partime brings Alice into Plumber's office.

PARTIME: "Mr. Houston, this is Alice Carroll."
ALICE: "Very nice to meet you Mr. Houston."
PLUMBER: (looking up at her) "Yes…ahhh…HO… OH, HOLY SHIT!"

Alice remains standing in front of Houston's desk. Miss Partime walks out of his office and down the hallway to the right and exits.

PLUMBER: "Uhhh plubba…pah…pubba pubba… please sit down."

Rilke's Dracula · 526

Plumber stands up and pulls up a chair for her. Alice sits down and puts her purse on the floor next to her chair.

ALICE: "The agency sent me. They said you needed an actress wearing nothing but black and blue body paint."

Plumber walks over to the door to Hawkins' office and opens it a little and sticks his head in.

PLUMBER: "Hawkins, you should come in here."

Hawkins enters through the door and stops suddenly as soon as he sees Alice.

HAWKINS: "Holy shit!"
PLUMBER: "Mr. Hawkins, this is Miss Carroll."
HAWKINS: (nervously) "Hello Miss, I'm Stringent Hawkins. I'm the Senior Partner of this law firm."
ALICE: "Nice to meet you sir."

Plumber returns to his desk and Hawkins sits down next to Alice.

PLUMBER: "Miss Carroll you have the perfect look we want and if we can come to terms, we would like to hire you for a single day."
ALICE: "What character will I play."

Rilke's Dracula · 527

PLUMBER: "We don't have an actual character name, you will simply be called Miss Body Paint."

ALICE: "What do you want me to do?"

PLUMBER: "It is a very simple role. This afternoon, Mr. Hawkins and I are meeting with some clients to propose a possible advertising campaign to them."

ALICE: "I gather it's a television campaign?"

HAWKINS: (interrupting) "What's a television?"

ALICE: "Don't worry about it sir. It's not important."

PLUMBER: "Anyway...when you're called, all you have to do is go into that office through this door and join us."

ALICE: "Okay."

PLUMBER: "When you get through the door, I want you to remain silent and slowly turn around once like a fashion model so they can get a look at you and your body paint. Then you will immediately exit back to this room without speaking."

ALICE: "So it's just a walk-on?"

PLUMBER: "If that's what actors call it, yes. Your silence is the most important part of this role. Under no circumstances will you speak."

ALICE: (sounding indignant) "You mean I rode over here in The Underground with my tits hanging out for a measly walk-on?"

PLUMBER: "Is that a problem?"

ALICE: "Not really. I like being naked."

HAWKINS: "As you should Miss Carrol. You look

Rilke's Dracula · 528

terrific."

ALICE: "Thank you sir."

HAWKINS: "It must have been difficult finding shoes to go with your body paint."

ALICE: "It was. Fortunately, I had an old can of spray-paint in the garage that my father used to paint the lawn furniture."

PLUMBER: (interrupting) "Hawkins what's spray-paint?"

HAWKINS AND ALICE: (In unison) "Don't worry about it. It's not important."

PLUMBER: (shaking his head) "Anyway...Once you're back in here, just sit down and wait for us to complete our meeting. When we are done, I will give you ten thousand pounds in cash and you're free to leave. Will you do that for us?"

ALICE: (barely able to contain her excitement) "Of course."

PLUMBER: "Fantastic. I'm so glad you could come over here and help us on such short notice."

ALICE: (her voice shaking) "It was my pleasure. Mr. Houston if your proposal is successful, is there any chance that I might get to act in your advertising campaign too? I could really use the work. Acting is a tough business."

PLUMBER: "Yes Miss Carroll, if you perform well today, there's a very good possibility that could happen."

ALICE: "Oh thank you sir. I won't disappoint you."

Rilke's Dracula · 529

Plumber stands up and leans forward and they shake hands.

PLUMBER: "I have faith in you Miss Carroll. You can wait out there with my secretary until she brings you in here to wait for us to call you into our meeting. There is some milk and cookies for you to munch on, but please take care not to mess up your body paint while you're eating."

ALICE: "Thank you for the excellent opportunity sir."

Alice leaves the office and walks down the hallway to the right. She stops and pauses just before she exits the stage.

ALICE: "Shit! I forgot my purse."

She walks back up the hallway toward Plumber's office and stops at the partition and starts to knock on the door jam. She doesn't knock because she hears Hawkins and Plumber talking. She stops and listens.

HAWKINS: "Did you have to offer her so much?"

PLUMBER: "I had to make the deal attractive. Besides, it doesn't really matter. We're not going to pay her anyway?"

Alice turns around and drops her head in disappointment then runs down the hallway to the right and exits.

Rilke's Dracula · 530

HAWKINS: "How are we going to handle Rich-American Bastard when he realizes Miss Body Paint in there isn't going with him."

PLUMBER: "Trust me. I'll get him a suitable substitute. At least this maneuver will buy us some time."

HAWKINS: "It won't be easy to replace her."

PLUMBER: "It would be impossible. Miss Body Paint is perfection. Thankfully we don't need perfection. All we need is good enough."

HAWKINS: "What do you have in mind?"

PLUMBER: "Don't you have a beautiful daughter?"

HAWKINS: "Forget it Plumber."

PLUMBER: "Getting soft Hawkins?"

HAWKINS: "She's much younger than twenty-six. Besides, she'd never do it. She's gone radical."

He holds up his hands and uses his fingers to gesture as quotation marks.

HAWKINS: (continuing) "She's got principles. It breaks my heart. I thought I brought her up right."

PLUMBER: "I'm sorry to hear that Hawkins."

Plumber takes his gun out of his holster and holds it up to show it to Hawkins.

PLUMBER: "I'm sure I could convince her."

Rilke's Dracula · 531

HAWKINS: "No doubt. But remember I don't want the police involved in our business. Let's leave the threat of deadly force off the table until we really need it."

Miss Partime and Alice enter the hallway from the right. They stop at the far right

.

PARTIME: "Wait here. I'll get your purse then we'll get out of this place. Trust me. These mother fuckers are going to pay for betraying you and all of the other evil things they've done to other people."

ALICE: "I hope so. I'm so broke and I was hoping for this money to pay my rent."

PARTIME: "Trust me. I know some people who will help us."

Miss Partime leaves Alice standing at the far-right end of the hallway and walks to the left and enters Plumber's office.

PARTIME: "I'm sorry to interrupt you sir. Miss Carroll forgot her purse."

Miss Partime bends over to pick up Alice's purse off the floor and both Plumber and Hawkins lean way over to look under her skirt. She notices them and stands up quickly and gives them the finger. Then she storms out of Plumber's office and enters the hallway from the left and walks down the hallway to the right. When she is next to Alice, she stops and turns around and both

Rilke's Dracula · 532

of them give the middle finger towards Plumber's office. Then they exit to the right.

END OF ACT TWO

Rilke's Dracula · 533

ACT THREE

Act Three Scene One
Setting: Right half-stage.
The front of Hawkins' office building.

PROTESTERS: "Stay away. Hawkins is a crook. Spend your money somewhere else. Dealing with evil, makes you evil. Fund a pig, you're a pig. Stamp out corporate greed. Give to WOW and feed a child. Hawkins hates women."

Collassa Bastard stops and won't cross the picket line. Rich-American Bastard grabs her hand and attempts to pull her behind him. She fights his pull.

COLLASSA: "But Rich, they say Hawkins is an evil crook I don't want to do business with a crook. It wouldn't be right."

BASTARD: "Collassa, we can't back out now. I've already accepted their offer. We're only here to sign the papers and collect the four million pounds. Think of it Collassa, four million pounds. We could buy a ranch in the California mountains and live next to famous movie stars and hire an entire staff of underpaid minority servants and have plenty of money left over. Think of it, no more housework. Just time lounging by the jacuzzi."

COLLASSA: "What's a jacuzzi?"

BASTARD: "Don't worry about it Collassa, it's not important. What is important is that we'll be rich forever."

COLLASSA: "I don't care. It's not right. I'm not going in."

BASTARD: (waving his finger at her) "Collassa, I'm the man of the house and what I say goes. Now behave your little self and go in with me like a good wife should."

Collassa still fights Bastard's pull, but he is stronger and muscles her toward the door. The protesters grab at their clothes and swing signs at them. The struggle continues.

Act Three Scene Two
Setting: Left half-stage. Hawkins' Office.

Hawkins desk is in the left rear corner as it always has been, but there are five chairs in front of the desk.

Hawkins is seated behind his desk and Plumber is seated in the far-right chair. Jonathon enters from the left wearing the huge cross that he got in Transylvania. He is followed by Rich-American Bastard who is forcefully pulling his wife behind him.

> JONATHON: "Mr. Hawkins, these are the Bastards who are selling the house to the Count. Mr. and Mrs. Bastard this is Mr. Hawkins, the owner of our firm."
>
> HAWKINS: "Good afternoon. It's a pleasure to meet you. Please sit down. This is Mr. Houston who is here to provide security because our transaction today will involve the exchange of a large sum of cash."
>
> PLUMBER: "I'm pleased to meet you. Normally security wouldn't be needed but, as I'm sure you saw when you came in here, a number of people are gathered outside our building and pose a potential threat."
>
> BASTARD: "Yes we saw them. They tried to block us from entering your building."
>
> HAWKINS: "They've been very annoying. Early this week, they assaulted Mr. Harker. But we have contacted the police and hopefully the trespassers will be dispersed by the time you leave here."

Rilke's Dracula · 537

COLLASSA: (nervously) "Rich, that man has a gun. I don't like guns."

BASTARD: "It's just a precaution dear. Remember, there's four million in cash involved."

COLLASSA: "I still don't like it."

HAWKINS: "The Count just called, and he will be a little late. He got caught up in football game traffic."

HARKER: "What do you mean he called sir?"

HAWKINS: "Don't worry about it Harker. It's not important...Like I was saying, game-day traffic is a big problem here. Carriages back up all the way to the main highway."

BASTARD: "We understand. It's the same in San Francisco."

HAWKINS: "Plus there's not enough parking around the stadium. It seats a 101,000 people."

BASTARD: "That's big."

JONATHON: "The problem has gotten even worse since tailgating has become so popular."

BASTARD: "That's understandable."

COLLASSA: "Rich, what's tailgating."

BASTARD: "Don't worry about it, Collassa. It's not important."

Hawkins got up from his desk and walked over to Jonathon. He spoke into Jonathon's ear.

HAWKINS: (quietly to Jonathon) "Harker, why are you

wearing that stupid cross?"

JONATHON: "I got it in Transylvania and I thought that Sucker would like to see it."

HAWKINS: "Harker, you ignoramus. Don't you know that crosses scare the shit out of vampires."

JONATHON: "I've heard that sir, but Sucker is so rough and tough I doubt he's scared of anything."

HAWKINS: (standing up) "Harker, put that fucking thing under your chair."

JONATHON: "Yes sir."

Jonathon puts the cross under his chair.

Dracula enters from the left. He is pulling a train of three large toy wagons. Each wagon is full of buckets with dollar signs on them.

JONATHON: (standing up) "Count, it's so good to see you again."

SUCKER: "Call me Sucker God dammit!"

COLLASSA: (leaning over to Bastard) "Rich, that weird man has a gun too...I'm leaving!"

She starts to stand up, but Bastard stops her by putting his hand on her shoulder.

BASTARD: "Sit down Collassa. We need your signature on the contract."

HAWKINS: (offering his hand) "Hello Sucker. It's been

Rilke's Dracula · 539

a long time."

SUCKER: (refusing the handshake) "Who gives a shit?"

HAWKINS: "Please sit down and we'll get on with our business."

SUCKER: "I'll stand instead. I don't sit well with most people."

HAWKINS: "Mr. Harker. You may proceed."

Jonathon gets up from his chair.

JONATHON: "Mr. and Mrs. Bastard, as I'm sure you can see, Mr. Sucker has brought one portion of his offer for the house in those wagons. The other portion is in the next room."

He nods to Plumber. Plumber gets up and walks over to the door to his office and pokes his head in.

PLUMBER: "You can come in now Miss."

Alice Carrol walks in and stands next to Sucker and slowly turns around.

BASTARD: "Hoh...oh ly fuck!!!"

JONATHON: "Oh dribble dribble!"

SUCKER: "Deals off. I want her instead of the fuckin' house."

COLLASSA: "Rich, you two-timing pervert!!!"

Rilke's Dracula · 540

Collassa picks up Jonathon's cross and hits Bastard with it and knocks him back off his chair unconscious. Then all hell breaks loose with several things occurring simultaneously.

Alice cues the action by quickly jumping on Plumber and giving him a hip grinding lap dance while she removes his gun from his holster and tosses it off-stage.

Then a rock band begins to play the University of Michigan fight song, "Hail to The Victors," and the curtain covering the right half-stage opens revealing a backdrop painted with a crowd of football fans. Across the top of the backdrop is a sign that says, "THE HUGE HOUSE." There is a large peace sign under it.

The fight song continues to play as Lucy Hawkins leads a team of women dressed in University of Michigan football uniforms on stage from the right. Miss Partime and Alice Carrol are amongst them. They are easily identifiable by their long hair that is sticking out from beneath their helmets (red for Partime and black for Alice).

LUCY: (shouting) "Okay. Huddle up."

The players form a huddle and then clap their hands as they come out of the huddle.

PLAYERS: (with a hard exclamation) "HEY!"

The players form a shotgun formation and Lucy stands behind them as the quarterback.

Rilke's Dracula · 541

LUCY: (shouting) "39-22-36…hubba hubba."

All of the players charge forward, shouting as they go, and slam their shoulders into Hawkins, Plumber and Sucker. They drive Plumber and Hawkins hard against the left-hand wall, nearly knocking them unconscious. Sucker gets driven completely off stage to the left. Lucy grabs Jonathon by the back of his collar and kicks him repeatedly in the ass until he runs off stage to the right.

When all of the men are dispatched with, each of the women, including Collassa Bastard, take a bucket of Sucker's money from the wagon. They form a line across the stage and begin marching in place to the fight song. When the line is fully formed, they start to sing the lyrics to the fight song and split into two groups and walk off the stage into the audience.

THE WOMEN: (singing the U of M Fight song)
"Hail! to the victors valiant
Hail! to the conqu'ring heroes
Hail! Hail! to Michigan
The leaders and best!
Hail! to the victors valiant
Hail! to the conqu'ring heroes
Hail! Hail! to Michigan,
The champions of the West

The house lights come-up quickly as the women form three

Rilke's Dracula · 542

lines and walk up all three theater aisles, still singing. As they go, they repeatedly remove a handful of stage money and toss it out into the audience. When they reach the back of the theater they turn around and literally run back down the aisles and up on the stage where they are joined by the rest of the cast to take a grand theatre bow.

Hopefully a couple of people will be clapping by that time so this whole silly ending isn't a complete waste and make the audience demand its money back.

THE MAIN CURTAIN CLOSES

THE END

*Note to stage manager. If the audience starts to boo, keep the curtain closed and cue the stage pyrotechnics to create a diversion so the cast, particularly the playwright, can escape the theater.

Made in the USA
Middletown, DE
02 June 2019